HOSTILE HEIR

TOMÁS & CARINA DUET 1

HOSTILE KINGDOM: SOUZA CARTEL

AUTUMN ARCHER

Hostile Heir © copyright 2022 Autumn Archer Author Ltd

The right of Autumn Archer to be identified as author of this work has been asserted by her in accordance with section 77 and 78 of the Copyright, Designs and Patents Act 1988.

All rights reserved. No part of this publication may be reproduced, stored in a retrieval system, or transmitted in any form or by any means, electronic, mechanical, photocopying, recording, or otherwise, without the prior permission of the publishers.

Any person who commits any unauthorised act in relation to this publication may be liable to criminal prosecution and civil claims for damages.

ISBN 9798354774609

www.autumnarcher.com

AUTHOR NOTE

Hostile Kingdom is a Dark Romance world which includes the Jungle Oasis series and the Souza cartel series.

This is an extended version which includes an introduction to the deliciously addictive and wickedly passionate Souza Cartel family who were born with mafia blood and raised with cartel lawlessness.

Welcome to the dark and delicious world of Autumn Archer. Thank you so much for adding Hostile Heir to your reading list. If you haven't read my darker books before then you can expect themes that contain potential triggers.

Within in the bloodied pages of Tomás and Carina's haywire love affair, you'll find kidnapping, murder, gore, references to suicide, drugs and physical assault.

AUTHOR NOTE

Please read responsibly and know your own limits before diving in.

All that aside, keep reading if you're a sucker for tortured men of power…

*For all the misfits who find their home within a monster,
embracing your power, on your knees, as his good girl.*

1

CARINA

"Who'll die first?" The silver-haired man, with contrasting bronze skin, dabs a linen napkin to each corner of his mouth before rising from his position at the head of a long table set for a king.

The smell of freshly baked bread makes my belly gurgle, having spent too many hours without food. I swallow hard, trying my best to remain standing, even when my knees go soft. Only moments ago, I was dragged into this grand dining room with high ceilings and heavy drapes pulled open to let in the rising sun. To the side of his china plate, a tall jug of coral colored juice trickles with beads of moisture, reminding me how thirsty I am.

He straightens, the backs of his legs shoving the high back chair as he simultaneously fondles a gold necklace peeking out from an unbuttoned shirt collar.

"How about you?" He glares down his sharp nose at me, the expression cold and assessing.

I itch to cover my dehydrated lips from his scrutiny.

It's a subconscious habit I've fallen into, even after corrective surgery.

Sunshine beyond the picture window flickers. It blinds me, so I squint to watch him approach.

"Or you?" A calculated gaze of smoky quartz lands on the bearded guy beside me who's swearing under his breath.

Baggy track pants hang around his ass and a grubby t-shirt gives the impression he was tackled and fought back. The collection of gold chains draping his torso in a deep V rises and falls with every furious breath he takes.

My throat tightens, restricting a normal breathing pattern. The end of my life is at this man's whim. I find myself questioning if it would be better to finally meet death himself rather than endure my captor's torment.

"Elias, what the fuck is happening?" The second prisoner bites out, his body vibrating with a vicious temper. "I'm here on business. And *this...*" His Mexican accent grows harsher the instant his bound wrists lift. "This is a big fucking mistake."

It's just me and the Mexican, lined up before a manic guy wearing a suspicious scowl, fawn slacks, and a loose linen shirt. Armed men guard the doorway, giving him space to interrogate.

The previous henchmen who had held me captive kicked the legs out from under me and forced drugs down my throat. They stank of tobacco, were rough around the edges, and spoke as though they had to fight each other for status. Yet, he glares at us like an apex predator adorned in expensive jewelry and clothing.

After slumping on rags in the rear of a truck until the

world went hazy, I'd opened my eyes to the barrel of a gun. I can't pinpoint the passing hours or days I was trapped for. It all blurs into one unthinkable, fuzzy nightmare. Eventually, different strangers quizzed me for answers I didn't have. All I know is an evil bitch had kidnapped me and ordered her soldiers to transport me to this address as a gift for her estranged father.

Elias Souza.

Cartel kingpin and Colombian psycho.

A monster who's entirely too comfortable brandishing a semi-automatic in his grand dining hall. He projects an unforgiving aura of pompous authority with every sizing glance. The same cagey demon who thinks I'm working with this Mexican to plot his assassination. If I hadn't thought about it before, I'm sure as hell considering it now.

Elias strolls the length of the mahogany table set for breakfast, bringing the threat of his undecided aim closer. "You expect me to believe it's a coincidence how you both landed on my doorstep at the same time?"

I vaguely remember the hauling sensation. A shoulder wedged into my empty belly as I hung like a hunter's kill over an unknown man's shoulder. The lengths of my straggly dark hair danced to the movement of heavy steps. In my doped-up state, the fluidity resembled runny ink spilling from a crown I would never wear here.

Ice-cold water drenched my blurry eyes. Bitter coldness alerted the synapses in my brain to fire up adrenaline. Droplets pelted my cheeks, almost drowning me in the shock of such a rude awakening.

A travel companion was not on my radar. The last few

torturous hours were a nightmare of masculine silhouettes and lethal weapons.

"Christ, Elias. I've no clue who this *puta* is," the Mexican hisses. "I traveled alone."

Elias tips into me, his spicy cologne fading the aroma of sweat clinging to my grimy skin. He grunts low in his throat and brings silvery eyes flaring with a halo of black in line with mine. "Did you honestly think you could walk into my home and kill me?" he muses.

I inhale quickly, fear forming a rash of wasps under my skin. "I didn't choose to come here. Maria's men—"

"Elias," the Mexican interrupts. "Take this fucking cable tie off me." He swivels, jutting his hands into the air. "I came here to discuss alternative trade routes out of Mexico. Where the hell is Tomás? If I was *Sicario*, you'd be dead by now. I'd shoot you from those big fucking gates you hide behind."

Elias laughs darkly. Shadows pass behind his form as the clouds move beyond the window. They dapple the walls with splashes of white sunlight and somber shade. A sparkly glass light fixture glitters like a shoal of tropical fish in an aqua blue ocean, the joyful color contradicting his malignant aura. It catches my eye for a split second and then I'm quickly sucked back into the black vortex I've found myself in.

"Those same gates keep assholes like you out of my plantation and trap those who dare to enter uninvited." He runs ringed fingers through his groomed hair. The act isn't carefully combing, it's more anxiously plowing the peppered lengths for a sense of grounding. "You won't see the front gates again, motherfucker. I'm the ruler in this kingdom and I make up the rules as I go along." Inky pupils flare. "Do you understand me?"

I swallow hard, my eyes hunting every corner of the room for a possible escape route, which includes the open fireplace, unlit without a trace of ash or soot. But it's the high up security camera and its teeny-weeny red light that hails a new wave of panic through me.

There's a double tap on the door. It's more of a formality rather than a request to enter.

I don't see who joins us, only hear the clip of shoes striking alabaster marble floor tiles. Elias' vexed mood eases just a fraction. Pale gray eyes the color of rain-soaked clouds relax at the corners and when he blinks, they harden to vicious all over again.

"*Papá*." A masculine voice, as rough as broken glass and as seducing as sunlit shards, injects me with an odd rush of electricity. "Who the hell is Maria Rebello?"

Elias motions to the man with a crook of his fingers. "No one to concern yourself with, son. She's a dead woman after this stunt." That sentence carries the weight of my demise, said with silk coated razor blades.

My spine straightens. The devil has a son to bestow his evil ways upon.

"Why did she send a woman here?" Leisurely strides stop inches from my achy muscles. "Why is Flávio cuffed?"

"This man is a traitor, Tomás. He was ordered to kill me." Elias prods his gun in the air as he declares the Mexican guilty without a jury. "The asshole more or less said it himself." Deadly eyes pin me, considering a thousand possibilities of cruelty. "And she's his accomplice."

"Christ, Papá." I hear the whisper of a heavy sigh and sense brewing discontent at the far side of my shoulders. My eyes strain left in the hope I'd find the odd force knocking me off-kilter. "He's an ally to assist expansion. We're building relations with the Morales cartel. You know that."

"What the fuck is this, Tomás?" Flávio bites out, simultaneously twisting his wrists to free them from the inescapable plastic cord. "I come to your home in peace and this is how you treat me?" He spits down at his own dusty boots.

To my left, a divine scent of sandalwood and coffee swirls in my chaos of inner fear. Flávio continues to gripe while the man who'd lingered out of sight finally joins his father's side.

His presence commands all the air from the room, so I'm left breathless.

The two men differ in height, with Elias being the shorter. Both have tanned skin with the same shaped nose, only this new inquisitive gaze moves through me like fire chasing ice—curdling my blood and quickening the purpose of every organ.

It's both toxic and fascinating. Despite my hatred for the father and son duo, I'm intrigued by the suave prince with eyes trained on my denim shorts, bare thighs and the flimsy camisole top with filthy straps hanging off my shoulders. I'm not used to the unspoken assessment of a man as handsome as he is.

Broad shoulders eclipse the sunlight, plunging his features into a shadow of dull gray. Evenly shaded, glasslike eyes as black as the ocean at witching hour settle on my flushed face, having dawdled all the way up from my dirty bare feet to the grubby clothes I've worn for days.

I can't fathom how the depth of his intense glower swallows my returning gaze. Maybe I've hidden from society for so long that I appreciate how his darkness beckons to me.

Either way, all I can do is stare back at his emotionless expression and wonder if he's just as corrupt as his father.

"We have two situations, Papá. You've disrespected our ally." A tiny quirk flickers at the corner of his lips. "And this woman was planted in our family to either serve or kill."

Horrific flutters discharge within the bony cage, protecting my racing heart. Miniscule grenades detonate one after the other. His rich velvet cadence hunts the haywire rhythm.

It's a screwy reaction—an absolute one off. The spike of adrenaline is born from never having met a beautiful man dressed in a well-tailored suit minus the jacket. He exudes finesse like a godfather of the mafia rather than a brutal drug lord.

I raise my chin, locking his black eyes to my hazel gaze. "I'm not here to kill anyone."

A purposeful thumb swipe of his lower lip hypnotizes me in the most mystifying manner. I'm entranced by the back-and-forth movement as he thinks, like he's programming my senses to obey him.

Elias grunts with displeasure. His cynical attributes tell me he's scraped his way to the pinnacle of the narco food chain from the dregs of poverty, whereas Tomás' posture drips of unabated wealth and a degree of portentous patience. The sort of passiveness that slips into your soul and stabs every facet of your personality to make sure your entire being is well and truly dead. Only then would he take the final shot at your heart.

A man like him wouldn't offer a single, thoughtless bullet. No, he'd play the long game until you're utterly broken.

Superior diamonds glint when he subconsciously fixes a pair of encrusted 's' shaped cufflinks. Several buttons on his fitted shirt are left open at the neck where a thick curb chain hangs.

He ignores my protest, drags out a chair and positions it opposite me. When his gaze cuts back to mine, he casually pinches the knees of his precisely pressed trousers to shift the fabric covering long, lean thighs as he sits. My skin tingles all over and I hold my breath until he speaks.

"Why do you think the Rebello woman would send a teenage assassin?" he asks, looking right at me, the question directed at his father.

The sculpted edge of his cheekbones meets a dark pelt of trimmed stubble to compromise his orderly appearance with a manly edge of rebellion.

I nip the tip of my tongue to stop myself from correcting him. In a few months, I would turn twenty, leaving my hateful teens in the past.

His teenager assumption rattles my bones for some reason. Even though I technically am a teen, I've endured more than most silly girls. Maturity isn't a celebrated number, it's the path you've traveled, and the journey survived.

"What have I taught you, Tomás?" Elias tsks, his voice husky with evil intentions. "Even young girls with angel faces can slit your throat while they fuck you."

Tomás cocks his head ever so slightly, drilling his fierce eyes into mine. His neatly presented hair, so dark and thick, is shaved close to the sides and smartly textured on top.

Tiny twinkling studs subtly enhance his earlobes, so even the simplest part of him oozes fortune. He doesn't smile or offer any hint of compassion. The air thickens under his silent judgment. He makes a faint noise under his breath and rotates the thick gold band encompassing a vermilion gemstone on the middle finger of his left hand. It's a replica ring to the one his father wears on his wedding finger.

I swallow a gulp of air. The shame of my reaction to his low hum rips through me like wildfire during a blistering drought. His family deals in illegal drug trafficking, recruiting gangs, and organized street crime on a level that normalizes death for disobedience. I'm sure that's only for starters.

This nineteen-year-old may be innocent to the world, but I'm well informed on the workings of bad men. And today I'm in another snake pit where a solitary fanged bite would paralyze their enemy—me.

Yet never have I experienced such a powerful response from a singular look. A look that dares me to step out of line.

He's eyeing me up like a young doe too far from the herd. So why am I attracted to him?

What I hate most of all about this god-like man is that

his cavalier gaze hasn't left me, not for one second. The unreadable wisp of black smoke swirling in his eyes speaks to me at a volume higher than any frequency.

I shiver, exhausted from the aftermath of the mind-numbing sedatives that were forced into me and my rigidly held muscles. Worn out from the crashing wave of adrenaline coursing through my veins, constantly wondering if I'd die from one minute to the next.

It's tiring, forcing strength when I have zero control over the next few minutes. Now, the worst possible scenario of all, spirals like a cyclone of ash after a forest fire.

A sordid hook pierces my logic and connects me to this dominating man. That crazy, hairbrained thought makes my cheeks burn. I have a ridiculous fascination with his polished sophistication when I should bargain for my life.

"Do you want war, Elias?" The Mexican grits out between his teeth. One stride carries him toward his captors.

Bang!

2

CARINA

Spatters of warm scarlet blood hit me like raindrops in a freak storm. The deafening gunshot rings in my ears. I gasp so sharply the air hurts my throat. For a moment I wait in the hush, immune to the sight of blood, wondering if Flávio will move where he lays. He doesn't.

When my gaze settles on Tomás, I watch his eyes close briefly and his chest visibly rise. Then on a heavy sigh he angles into his father and removes the handgun from his tattooed hand.

"I haven't eaten yet. Now the damn walls are fucked up. Why did you do that, Papá?"

"Because I can. How about you finish off the girl?" Elias puts space between himself and the gruesome murder scene in his otherwise exquisitely designed dining room.

He fixes his hair in the glitzy framed mirror over the show stopping fireplace and gathers a fat cigar from an ornate gilded box. "I don't want any ties to that woman, Maria. She's a fucking liar who looks nothing like me. Her mother jumped into bed with anyone who offered her cocaine. She's not a Souza and never will be, especially after she put a hit out on me. Flávio would have blown a hole in my head at any chance. I can feel it in my goddamn bones, son, and the puta is in on it too."

Tomás flicks the safety and drops the gun on the table. His shirt tightens wickedly over flexed shoulders as he scratches his chin.

"I'll interrogate her. Find out who wants us dead. Otherwise, they'll keep coming." He scans his trouser legs like he's hunting for signs of blood and then pulls out his phone and types a message. "And the woman who claims to be a Souza? Is she a real threat?"

"I sent a few men to Rio to shut her up for good. We should've done it a long time ago."

White teeth peek out from a snarl. "Is she your daughter?"

Elias clicks his tongue, his expression morphs to mocking. "I've fucked plenty of women, Tomás." He shrugs like it's the proper order. "When Teresa took you and the boys away, I had my fair share of fun."

Tomás' forehead scrunches into a sexy scowl. "So, while we were under mafia protection, you stayed here to fuck hookers?"

Fire explodes in Elias' eyes, his expression tightening to sour. "I stayed here to become the biggest fucking kingpin Colombia has ever known. And don't you forget it. I've built an empire, Tomás. For you and your brothers. We're the wealthiest motherfuckers on the planet. Isn't that what Angelo wanted?"

Tomás bristles. His jaw works behind a clenched jaw.

Elias lights his cigar and stares at the twirling rise of smoke. "There were accusations and false rumors about that woman's unborn kid." He continues. "I paid her off to hide the drama from your mother's family. The last thing I needed was another visit from the Irish mafia. Whether she's really mine or not… that's up for debate." While he speaks, his eyes cut to his son's inflexible features. "Does it matter, Tomás? The bitch sent *her* to kill us, and I'm not known in this business for my forgiving nature."

Tomás' eyes skate over me, holding my uncertain gaze for a beat before he replies, "From what I can see, she's unarmed." He licks his lips slowly. "Give me time to find out why she's really here and then I'll get rid of her."

Elias glares at the gun, his fingers twitching to grab it, then sighs. "She's not welcome inside our home." His statement strikes like the first bolt of lightning. "Keep her outside with the dogs." I'm still shaking in shock when he saunters into my personal space. "I'll give her twenty-four hours." He angles to the window framing a tropical setting outside and returns to the head of the table where he sits, unfolds a napkin, and covers his lap. "Tomás. Sit with me, son."

I don't feel like I'm still breathing, let alone standing in the home of a ruthless cartel family. The stench of coppery afterlife is thick and suffocating. Blood smears the sophisticated decor with artful speckles. I fight against the urge to sit, stabbing my palms with my nails to keep me from sinking.

Bitterness burns my tongue when the spiritless body next to me is rolled up in a plastic sheet like a human *Linguiça* sausage and dragged out the door by an obedient henchman. I've witnessed unconscious men before, sliced open flesh, stitched wounds, and sterilized razor-sharp equipment.

Human plasma doesn't faze me. Bullies, on the other hand—they had tortured me from an early age, scratching holes in my confidence with pretty nails and slicing up my pride with lethal words.

Even though these men are older, they're exactly the same. Only they sit in grotesquely ostentatious thrones, and their rank is far more menacing. Tomás Souza, on the other hand––he's dangerous with the most handsome face I've ever seen in detail. It's shocking and terribly unfair.

Tomás continues to spy my discomfort from his seated vantage point. Being near this man feels like I'm grappling for my last breath, sucked into quicksand. A glimmer of stupidity makes me question if he'd offer me his hand at the last minute to heave me out.

Slimy gore smooshes beneath my fingertips when I attempt to wipe the mess off my chin. The task is made even harder with tightly bound wrists.

He rises, slots his hands into tailored trouser pockets and strolls to the linear slash of blood. I stare over at him. I can't help it. He's immaculately unblemished, towering over the crimson stain like the true ruler of this hostile kingdom.

When he subtly shakes his head from side to side, I slink back against the wall. It's a silly move. A chameleon-like wish to disappear for a foolish sense of security. It lessens the element of surprise from a brutal attack.

His lashes flick up, sensing the pitiful retreat.

Gunmetal eyes meet my elevated chin. Something paradoxical works behind the black ice facade. Trembles gather momentum, the vibration shaking me from the inside out.

In a temporary lapse of time, our gazes bind. I can't break away and something tells me he doesn't want to either. Then his mouth forms a disapproving, thin line. Although his haughty posture is standoffish, the indecipherable flicker behind his eyes suggests something else. Something seductive and unhallowed, far more dangerous than his father could ever unleash.

He's aware of the palpable tension crackling between us. Its overwhelming sizzle threatens a global blackout.

"What's your name?" He folds his arms to tighten the stretch of his shirt where carved shoulders nestle beneath.

"Carina," I reply with a dry whisper, smudging blood across my cheek and then staring at my sticky fingers.

"How old are you?"

"Nineteen."

His curiosity frosts over. Any wishful hope of this striking man becoming my savior disintegrates in one sentence. "Carina, mop this disgusting mess up." He breaks our visual deadlock, finally giving me a chance to inhale deeply. "And do it thoroughly, or I'll eliminate you ahead of schedule."

A gust of air hisses through my clenched teeth. I nod obediently, secretly declaring him as the worst sinner of all. There's no fairy tale with beautiful beasts and ball gowns. This is a bad dream in the waking state. A living nightmare where monsters prowl beneath dapper suits and wear devilish good looks as weapons.

Death had whispered to me once upon a time. Persistent despair will do that to a young girl blighted by misfortune. Nonetheless, it was my choice to roll the dice, desperately praying the suffering would end.

Since surviving against the cruel voices running riot in my brain, I had since learned to appreciate life. These days I'll do whatever it takes to live a full life. And right now, I'm staring fate square in the eyes again—in the muscular form of a suave villain.

If I have to swill blood in a bucket, then so be it. It's no big deal. My stomach is clad with steel.

"I'll need a basin with hot water, strong disinfectant and disposable wipes," I say quietly. "And a trash bag to throw away the soiled paper towels."

His spine goes rigid as he studies me for a silent second. Black holes in the form of pupils appear to breathe as they expand and contract with the fluctuation of light and shadows.

Without speaking, he removes his mobile phone from his pocket and holds it to his ear. "Bring in the clean-up kit." He listens to the guy on the other end, then replies. "The old tigers will enjoy a Mexican dinner. Put him in the truck."

When he finishes the call, he pins me to the tiles with an icy stare and a ticking jaw. The hairs on my scalp bolt upright. Intuitively, my unwashed fingertips lift to the thread thin scar on my upper lip.

A growl works through his throat. "Take your fingers away from your mouth," he snaps.

It's a natural inbred instinct. One I can't resist, not even under his command.

Darkness moves across his face. It's a cocktail of revulsion and condemnation. A glare that chills me to my very bones, quivering from exhaustion. "I said move them."

In three strides, we're face to face. Expensive leather shoes to bare toes with chipped emerald polish. Every muscle in my body braces for certain brutality. I'm pretty sure he's about to strangle me until he roughly grabs my forearms and lowers them like a lever.

The sensation of his skin electrocutes trillions of responsive cells. A ferocious scowl fixes on the hand still looping my arm. "You've got a dead man's blood on your hands. Don't put your fingers near your mouth."

A clatter in the background startles me. My head spins from his musky close proximity. Anger and humiliation trickles through my heated veins, made hotter by the dark delight I secretly harbor. The skin beneath his touch catches fire and my stomach knots.

"For fuck's sake, Tomás. Don't start this shit. Not today." Elias slams his palms on the table. "Clean the floor, girl, before my son loses his shit over the mess."

Tomás growls under his breath and steps to the side, keeping his eyes fixed on my mouth. "Once you've finished putting this room back to normal…" He angles away from me and jerks a pointed finger at the bloody mess. "You'll come with me to feed the tigers circling the plantation."

3

CARINA

I'm not sure what's worse, getting smeared in icky gore or hearing Elias enjoy his breakfast. Schizophrenic asshole.

When a willowy henchman with a short ponytail drops off the cleaning supplies, Tomás scowls at the debris like his stomach is on fire. Then he promptly disappears, his smart dress shoes clipping the tiled floor until the sound can no longer be heard.

He and his goon leave me all alone with his trigger-happy father of death.

While I maneuver on my stiff knees with wrists still secured, Elias is unaccompanied at the head of the table. He sips his morning coffee and peruses the *El Tiempo* newspaper. The beast sits in freakish silence, unperturbed by the fact a guy's brain mottles his pristinely plastered walls.

Aside from the swoosh of brown water in a basin, the atmosphere in the sunny room is otherwise serene.

My mind flits to the life I had before all this. How I went under the knife to remove a gross birth mark on my top lip when I was fourteen. Before the rare opportunity to undergo cosmetic surgery had presented itself, I was a troubled teen who hated everyone—or just the sheen of horror and pity they projected when we met.

In the early years, my mother blamed herself for the grotesque blight I was born with. Eventually, she gave up sheltering me from demons, claiming it was character building. And that it was. From the forked tongues on the playground to the internal self-loathing I drowned in.

I was the defective daughter. The ugly child. The cursed girl with zero hopes of ever finding love. My grades slipped and my bedroom became a bunker from the cruel verbal missiles, the name calling—and the beautiful world where I didn't fit in.

We couldn't afford the cost of reconstructive surgery, not until I hit rock bottom, and a ghost swooped in to save me. Friendships were a myth I wished to be real, and seclusion turned into a safe haven. Whereas boyfriends—they were something I'd never have.

Once the surgeon at the private jungle Oasis where my brother worked had cut away the growth and subtly plumped my lips with a little filler, he became an ally—an older, wiser man with no ulterior motive other than educating me.

Jackson taught me the art of sewing sutures on unconscious patients and how to prick thin veins with long needles. He trained me to help others at their most vulnerable. I liked knowing they were oblivious to my assistance, that I could be useful without scrutiny.

When I wasn't playing nurse, I helped the cleaning crew in the medical facility. I took an order and carried out the task without the need for conversation. On the odd day when there were bodily fluid spills, I rolled up my sleeves and sterilized the clinic. It was dirty work, but I enjoyed a mental escape from a life I was trying to repair. It gave me a purpose, a function, and space to consider the future.

El Fantasma, the king of his jungle hideaway and my brother's employer, gave me the precious gift of ambition. He nudged me out of the darkness and offered tactics on how to survive it.

A stabbing pain spikes through my heart, splicing it with both sadness and anger. The mournful sensation forces me to stop mopping goopy plasma. I inhale slowly and let the emotions wash over me. Nothing good would come from a meltdown in front of Elias Souza, the heartless bastard.

The older man I accidentally befriended gave me a second chance—a satisfying place in the world. And now, absorbing the fact none of them can come for me, presses heavily on my heart with the weight of a thousand sorrows.

This struggle for survival is my own. I'm trapped in a lion's den with only the filthy clothes I was stolen in.

No one is coming to save me.

El Fantasma had warned how hunters wear duplicitous masks. Unbeknown to either of us, his wise words were in preparation for this very day. No matter the hazardous attraction festering in my core, Elias and Tomás are my enemies.

I finally erase all traces of the ghastly murder. It had only taken me thirty-three minutes. I know this because the second Tomás had turned his back on his father's request to join him at the table, I spied the clock on the mantle.

My nerves are on edge waiting for him to return with those long lean legs and searching dark eyes. How can my dumb character radar be so mangled? Perhaps it's the after-effects of sedatives, the last dregs of poison distorting this harsh reality.

It doesn't matter if his masculinity makes my heart hammer. He has an agenda, to extract information from me at any cost. After that, no amount of spark can save me from this ruthless family.

"Why are you standing there, girl?" Elias glances over at me, purposefully folding the corner of his paper to see me.

I roll my stiff shoulders. "I'm finished."

He cocks a skeptical brow. "If my son finds even a drop of remnants, he'll throw you to my dear old tigers. They'd enjoy an extra femur or two."

"It's clean." I confirm, double checking my hard work with a quick glance.

The tiles might sparkle better than they did before the Mexican hit them, but my clothes are a canvas, steeped in mortality. The thought of it makes me gag.

He glowers at me like I'm the evil in the room, not him. "Well then, you'd better stand there quietly." Flicking the paper to hide his face, he adds, "Tomás has an inherent skill for extricating information from liars. You won't survive his talents. When you picked the wrong side to work for, you lost immediately."

"I'm not on anyone's side. Maria's men kidnapped me. She's your enemy, not me."

Black and white paper crumples in his fingers. "You are my enemy, girl. Don't think my eldest son will fall victim to your doe-eyed beauty, or your schoolgirl innocence. He was raised better than that. The next time you and I meet, I guarantee it won't be in the living world—and you'll be dying first—that's a promise. Once Tomás learns the truth, everyone you love will die, too." The promise of his threat slithers over my skeleton, squeezing it tighter around organs. "You come for me. I come for your whole fucking family."

The door opens. Confident footsteps announce the arrival of his son. A lump bobs in my throat from the harshness of Elias' speech.

They'd never learn how my father works in a shipyard in Manaus and earns a pittance. His pride refuses to accept the money my brother Salvador offers him every month. He's a hardworking man or simply stubborn. And I definitely wouldn't reveal how my mother spends her mornings in a Brazil nut factory and her afternoons cleaning other people's homes.

Tomás would have to stick pins under my nails before I tell him about the hidden oasis where my brother spends his days in seclusion. My heart sinks to my toes, not knowing if he's still alive. If any of them are. Maybe Salvador and el Fantasma are absolute ghosts now.

I blink in the sight of Tomás' visibly sculpted torso. He's now clad in a snug jet-black shirt encasing worked muscles and tucked into trousers that flow to designer shoes like molasses. Tight and smooth.

Those searching eyes of his are curiously hidden behind dark aviator sunglasses until he slowly slides them down the bridge of his nose to inspect my handy work.

He's the epitome of glorious evil.

"I've spoken with Morales. The Mexican cartel is pissed." He catches his father's eye, ignoring me completely.

"I don't give a fuck. They sent a guy to kill me, Tomás."

Tomás folds his sunglasses and hooks them into the opening of his shirt. "I told you, Papá, Flávio came here to talk tactics with me. I mentioned it last month after I set it up. We decided to meet here, so Blanco didn't catch wind of our business. If his men saw us with one of Morales' guys in Bogotá, he'd be all over it. Flávio arrived a day early. Now Morales will undoubtedly claim blood for blood. You've started a war."

"Send her." Elias points at me with a threatening jab to the air. "Tell them she's my whore and they can have her as a peace offering."

My blood crackles at the coldness of his suggestion. Tomás laughs, low and wicked. "They'll want a Souza. Either me, André, Gio, or Matheus."

"Is that right?" Elias ejects from his seat, slams his fist on the table, clattering dishes while a discrete maid hurries to tidy the devastation he's made. She works fast, keeping her eyes low and her mouth shut. I watch her for a second and wonder if she'll look over at me, but she doesn't. "Those fuckers want one of my sons. Who the hell do they think they are? Tell Morales I'll take out his goddamn family…"

"Papá." Tomás growls, his posture still claiming finesse.

"I'll arrange a meeting. Morales will understand who's in charge once I've spoken to him."

"I'm in fucking charge." Elias thumps his chest, resembling a barbarian with a crooked snarl. "We'll both meet him. Together."

Tomás plants his hands on his hips, flexing the curve of his back. "Morales won't come to the plantation and you won't leave in case security forces catch you."

"I'll go right now if it means blowing those motherfuckers into oblivion. Your cartel veins may run with mafia blood, Tomás, but I'm still the head of this family. I lead the Souza organization. We'll do this my way."

Tomás rounds his shoulders and stretches his neck from side to side. "Fine. I'll set up a meeting in Bogotá. Give me a few weeks to arrange it. Not surprisingly, they don't trust us now, so it will take a while."

Elias slams his palms onto the table and scowls. There's an uneasiness settling between them. A silent war of strength emanating from both men. "Find out if Morales is working with Maria Rebello. If they're in bed together, this girl..." His narrowed glare settles on my face. "Is a traitor."

"Understood." Tomás swivels in his shiny shoes and snaps his fingers, expecting me to follow. "Outside. Now."

"And Tomás..." Elias calls out. "If I see her inside, I'll shoot her in the throat."

I've already taken two steps behind, so when Tomás swivels, all musky cologne and darkness, I almost slam into him. "Please stop killing people indoors, or we'll have to employ our little conspirator as a cleaner."

Elias laughs. It's a jovial chuckle that eliminates all the

vicious comments he's made. "If you'd stop firing the cleaners, we'd have a whole team by now."

I dare to look up, catching Tomás grimace. Pretty lashes frame the corrupt unknown in the pitch of his sunless eyes. My veins thrum with life when he meets my gaze for a split second. After a beat, he flicks out his wrist to check his cufflinks are in place. "Move," he says with a low rumble.

I'm momentarily paralyzed by the rich tone of his voice, stuck to the glossy clean tiles beneath my feet.

"Back up. You're too fucking close." It takes me a heartbeat to realize I'm uncomfortably close to him. Before the insult has time to sink in, he does a one-eighty and strolls to the exit. "Keep your distance. You're not a guest or an employee. Right now, you are simply an inconvenience covered in filth."

I blink at the sight of him marching through the doorway and hear Elias shout, "I love you, son."

Tomás doesn't reply. With a glance over his shoulder, he checks I'm behaving by traipsing along behind him at a suitable measure of distance.

"Where are we going?" I trace the outline of my top lip and stare at his straight posture from behind.

"Outside," he replies matter-of-factly. "Where messes are easily cleaned with a hose."

4

CARINA

We make our way through the most impressive entrance hall I've ever seen. Pillars soar loftily to the high ceilings. A show-stopping staircase, complete with snaking gold leaf balustrade and fitted carpet treads, eventually splits both left and right from the middle.

Polished marble tiles radiate sunlight pouring in from the see-through frontage. I get the impression the sheets of glass are a precaution, doubling as a lookout to help them monitor unwanted attention on the horizon.

The entire space is bigger than my family home, times three. Echoing thuds from his shoes clip a rhythm of a somber funeral march. There's no hint of warmth in the atmosphere of this colossal home. Just a vacant silence and a crosscurrent of impure threats.

I follow him out of the main entrance, doubling my strides for every casual one of his. When I cross over the threshold, my speed rapidly decreases to navigate the stones jabbing the soles of my feet.

As I concentrate, my lower lip slips between my teeth

and I prance like an astronaut with my arms elevated on either side. He stops and angles his torso to watch. His chest puffs out and then deflates, but he doesn't offer any help. When I'm several feet closer, he turns and continues toward a collection of stone outbuildings all connected by a single archway. "Brace yourself."

My brow furrows, confused by his request. When he disappears beyond the curved entrance, I hesitate. Caught in limbo. A subtle balmy breeze with a coolness warns of a storm. Ahead of me lies a courtyard leading to a barn, and no sign of life. When I look back at the mansion, woody evergreens stretch as far as the eye can see.

I should run—steal a vehicle or hide in the bushes. Twitchy muscles buzz as the ideas churn inside me.

An ear-piercing whistle catches me off guard. I jerk to attention. "If you're considering an escape, you should know all the land you see belongs to us." Large hands slip into his pockets, his right hip dipping leisurely. "It would take a week by foot to reach the perimeter—if you even get there. The plantation workers will shoot you on sight for trespassing, and the wildlife circling the estate will attack." Tomás' impatience curls around his speech like choking vines.

An irritable brow rises, thick and curt, so his handsome face expresses nothing but infinite contempt.

I inhale deeply, aware my options to bolt are slipping through my fingers quicker than the sands of time. Putting one step in front of the other, I tentatively pad towards him.

The metallic odor of blood, clinical disinfectant, and sweat adds to my semblance of depravity. At least my hands were bathed in germ destroying chemicals. They appear clean even if the rest of me is a visual explosion of grime and limp sable locks.

The way his mouth tightens when I traverse the grit on tiptoes makes me think he's not totally malevolent. Then again, I'm his prisoner living on borrowed time.

Embers of acrimony glow in my dying pyre of faith. "You can't keep me here. It's unethical," I blurt out, anger getting the better of me.

A slight curve to his lips mocks my statement. In the movement of such a slight act, I swear a dimple dents his left cheek. It's barely detectable under the shadow of short hair, but it was there, briefly. Fire races through my veins so my cheeks flame.

"I can. I will... and I am." He speaks slowly, his refined accent dripping with disdain. "Prove to me you're not here to stick a dagger in my father, and I'll consider a merciful option."

I take a daring step into him, even though my hands are trembling uncontrollably. "What's the merciful option?"

The risk of closeness isn't missed by him. I have to hitch my chin to maintain eye contact. Rogue nipples tingle like never before. It's a flux of chemistry my body isn't used to.

His brows lift and he takes one precise step backward, like the idea of being near me is repulsive. Embarrassment scalds my insides, the sensation buzzes through me with the heat of a thousand insect stings. I wouldn't stand next to me either, given the state of my unkempt appearance.

"You assume this time together is a treaty. It's not." His words burn more caustically than acid. "To put it simply, you're a triple threat. Uniquely beautiful, unfamiliar, and have undisclosed information behind that pretty mouth of yours." My breath catches and I sway a little. "And I want to know all your dirty, dark secrets."

My pulse betrays me. The bold thrum in my neck is inescapable to his scrutiny. I bare my teeth at him as a guise. It's the only way to pretend I'm not affected by his overcast allure, or hide the fluttering emotions created by the mention of how pretty my scarred mouth is.

"I'm not a threat to you," I say with as much conviction as a girl enamored by her captor could project.

He points a finger to the gable end of a stone dwelling. "Prove it to me. Face the wall. Put your hands up and spread your legs."

My jaw drops and I shake my head repeatedly. "No… why?"

"It's not a request. It's an order." I'm completely taken aback by his harsh command. It rattles my spine like a helpless creature in the jaws of an alligator. His dark gaze, so alarming like a totem from the underworld, fixes on me without bending. "If I'm forced to get my gun to ensure obedience, I'll use it."

Outrage and despair combust in my chest. The weaving whisper of blind faith creeps around my ribs and threatens to shatter the bony shelter safeguarding my heart.

In one calculated movement, he pulls a switchblade from his trouser pocket, swoops in like he's dipping his fingers in scalding water and snips the plastic cable tie.

For a moment he stares at the self-inflicted scar tracking the inside of my right arm. His eyes narrow. And just like that, he retreats again.

"Hands up. Feet apart. No second chances."

I do as he instructs. Both of my palms rest on the rough brickwork and I hesitantly part my feet a little, but not too wide. There's a shrill squeak and then an explosion of ice-cold fluid strikes my ass, making me squeal. Natural instincts kick in and I spin around to face the enemy.

In vain, my palms try to soften the impact of fast flowing water, to lessen the high velocity whipping. He thumbs the nozzle, turning a powerful spurt into a spritz of hazy mist.

"Palms to the wall." His instruction lashes harder than any strike.

Spray catches on my lashes. I blink in the sight of his face, watching his gaze slide to my hardened nipples beneath drenched fabric. His tanned forehead creases, concentration or unwanted desire simmering behind his eyes. A pouty lower lip slips between his teeth as he douses the flame blazing from his formidable stare to mine.

"I ordered you to turn around. Clearly, you're asking for punishment."

I swallow, hurriedly sweep the hair from my cheeks, and inch into the wall backwards. "You don't have to be so cruel. I have no weapons or even a reason to be involved in your world."

He arcs the jet to create a prismatic rainbow where darkness rules. "Cruel?" he muses. "Didn't you hear my father? You're not welcome in our house. He'll shoot you in a heartbeat and pour a whiskey afterwards as if it never happened. That's cruel—if you truly are innocent. Is that what you want, sweet *little liar*?" I shake my head, scattering haphazard beads of water everywhere. "Your polluted clothes make me gag. Your sullied feet make my veins hiss and your blood smeared skin resurrects feelings inside of me that we both would rather I kept buried."

A cylindrical bottle skids to a halt at my toes. "Clothes off," he growls like his temper is tugging on a thin leash.

I fight the urge to surrender, my pulse thrumming louder than the icy fluid splashing concrete. After a quick scan of the courtyard, I note we're alone. There aren't any armed guards nearby, only a few discreetly positioned security cameras so his staff can watch my pride disintegrate at a distance. I accept there's no one here to help. It's just me and him in this open air power shower for one.

"Use the shower gel. I've sent the staff on other errands. We're alone. Now strip or I'll cut your filthy clothes off with my blade."

I've dealt with honorable men in my life—men who took care of me, protected me from evil, who offered respect. Yet never have I endured an adult devil such as Tomás Souza.

His crude order to strip naked is a step too far. A cutting demand for a reticent girl like me. There's not a single male on this planet who's seen the flesh beneath my clothes. It's deeply personal—and intimate.

A shiver of anxiety heats the absurdity of my body, not being good enough for him. Of transforming into the ugly duckling all over again.

"Turn around." He orders on a sigh. "You didn't expect to shower fully clothed, did you?" My hands fist by my thighs and I stay rooted to the twinkling puddle of water lapping at my feet.

He stares at me, unmoving and utterly in control. I hesitate, returning his stare with as much backbone as I can muster.

"If you've nothing to hide from me, then removing your clothes won't be an issue."

I swallow hard, furious and tired of this unfair situation. "I can't… It's inappropriate."

"Don't be shy," he replies with a deep mocking rumble, clearly unaware of how his monumental request teases me. "I've enjoyed the sight of many naked women. You're not the first to strip for me, and you won't be the last."

I don't want to do it out of principle. However, I'm interested to know if I'm truly any different from all the rest. "If you've seen it all before, then you won't be missing anything important. It's not as if I'm packing lies or stashing weapons under here."

An abrupt grunt escapes from his throat. I can't quite tell if it's laughter or a flippant snort. Then the corner of his mouth lifts ever so slightly. It quirks in a flash, so I doubt it ever happened in the first place. He pivots the hose ninety degrees, temporarily removing the spray.

"Strip," he orders, low and controlled.

His left hand hunts the chain circling his throat to reposition the precious metal as if it's tightening around his neck or he's thinking about choking me.

In the seconds of a reprieve, I fight for air and clear clingy strands of hair away from my face.

"Do not make me wait," he warns, clearly unamused by my stubbornness to remain dressed. "Show me you're willing to obey me."

"You're an asshole!" I snarl, each word biting out like he's choking them from me.

"I'll give you to the count of three and if you don't show obedience, I'll search every single part of your body for hidden secrets. Every. Single. Hole... One." He begins to count, completely unfazed and frustratingly expectant.

I take my time to drag the saturated top up and over my head and tentatively unclip my flimsy bra. Strands of hair flop, the dripping lengths sticking to goosebumps on my skin.

"Two." Tomás announces the word loudly, like he's playing a game of adult hide and seek. I unbutton the shorts next, bending so my small breasts hang, and lower them to my ankles. "Three," he says calmly before I step out of them.

As he claims the final number, he aims the hose behind me and sweeps his gaze over every inch of me. Those serious eyes of his burn into my flesh like he's a human x-ray hunting for malignant lies. Yet I don't detect disappointment on his face, rather something indecipherable instead.

I desperately wish for the wall to crack open and allow me to slither inside, to hide from his avid inspection. As much as it scares me to be so brazen and bare, I'm aroused by his authority and even more by his wandering curiosity. I lower my lashes to free myself from the disconcerting tingles, making parts of me wet where even the water can't reach.

When I finally pluck up the courage to meet his eyes, those perfectly symmetrical lips of his part. They don't dance to a sneering smile or creep to a smirk of antipathy.

He's an enigma of silent, hungry perusal. His strong posture, lights up under a high sun, flexes like he wants to explore, but knows the risky terrain is uncharted. "Remove your panties," he finally demands, the texture to his voice smoky and thick.

I glare at his stern expression, wondering what sort of monster demands such a thing. When he swipes his lips with his tongue, my belly flips. The synergy of such an unassuming act so unbearably rousing.

This situation shouldn't be thrilling. It's deplorable how my core clenches and how rampant chills electrify every hair on my head. Nonetheless, I continue to undress until I'm utterly naked.

As daunting as it feels to be exposed before him, it's a relief to discard the unhygienic clothing. It's freeing to let go of my inhibitions and detect something primal passing over his features. It's not a threat of death, it's a promise of something far more alarming—temptation.

"Just so we're clear, I don't want anything from you, other than the truth of how you came to be here. Nothing more."

"Good. I'll tell you the truth if it means you'll stay the hell away from me," I say in a rush of air, embarrassed by how needy I've become.

Perhaps I should cover my breasts or cup my private parts. Except when the chilling splash of water hits, I relish the opportunity to wash away the built up grime from the past few days.

A flutter of uncertainty catches in my throat when I hunker down to the gravel and collect the shower gel. His gaze burrows into every move I make, his retinas burning into my soul as he tries to read the secrets bruising my body.

It doesn't make the act of cleansing any easier. While I lather up soapy suds emanating a hedonistic manly scent, he rolls back his shoulders and dances his fingers over his belt buckle.

I coat the lengths of my hair, suddenly recognizing the familiar aroma. It's the toxic scent of sin—of him. Virile and domineering. All over me. The fragrance is heavy in my hair and musky on my clean flesh.

On that hateful thought, I lift my lashes to fuse my resentful glower with the supreme Tomás Souza's assessment. The hottest man I've ever encountered, his temperament similar to a freshly lit stick of dynamite. And the fall out of his explosion will surely cost me everything.

"Enjoying the show?" I say with a snide tone, imitating the horrid girls who used to harass me in the playground.

He doesn't answer. Instead, he shoots me a look of pure carnal seduction and aims the water at my sudsy breasts. Haphazard droplets splash in every which way. I turn on the spot, permitting a full three sixty view of my bruised abdomen, spine, and hips, all wonderfully clean and smelling of sin.

Tomás drops the garden hose and twists the faucet before gathering a canvas bag sitting idly nearby. He saunters my way, this time uncaring how perilously intimate we are, his chest merely an inch or two away from my erect nipples. In the heart racing seconds of silence that fall between us, I witness his jaw tick from either anger or something far more dangerous. "Who gave you those bruises?"

I raise my chin to return his stare. "The men who stole me and the men who dropped me off here."

Something unknown fights for supremacy behind his eyes, giving me the impression it's a rare hint of concern. "Did they rape you?"

He's too close, especially when he fixes a damp clump of hair behind my ear and my pulse stutters. The arresting glint in his eyes mixes with the kinetic energy vibrating between us, coaxing the air from my lungs, leaving me breathless.

"They punched me in the stomach until I was sick." Subconsciously, I palm my belly button, close to blackish bruises. "I was locked in a cellar with no food or water until that nasty woman ordered them to take me away. They took pleasure in overpowering me, spitting on me, kicking the wind out of me when I fought back, and they pumped my veins with drugs. But thankfully, they didn't sexually abuse me."

I'm lightheaded when I finish, dizzy from the recent events, hunger, and anger at the cruelty I've endured.

He nods curtly. "My father sent men to the Rebello residence in Rio. It's my understanding that a parked car at the front of the dwelling will explode with all of those men inside it."

Vengeance.

An eye for an eye.

He says it with such regal composure, unaffected by

the lives destroyed or the macabre arrangement of it all. This is him—organized payback and destruction.

"Does that please you?" he adds as a side note.

It does, briefly, then it hits me. My friend, el Fantasma's savior—Iris. "No!" My palms fly to my temples. "No, it doesn't."

He grabs both of my wrists, tight and unyielding, the force slamming our heaving chests together. "Why would that not please you, *little liar*? Are they your friends? Are you fucking them?"

The bash of our two bodies is powerfully sexual, more so when his chest rises with fury and his strength stirs confusing feelings within me. Despite my hatred for his dominance, I secretly love it.

"I'm not fucking anyone, you asshole. And yes, my friend Iris is in that house. She was kidnapped too. They can't bomb it with her inside. Please, don't let them do it. Not yet."

She's the only female friend I've ever had, even if we've only known each for a short time. I value the one thing she gave me—friendship without backhanded compliments or hurtful gossip to ruin me.

His grip falls away and the sweltering air sparking from him to me dissipates when he rears back. With his eyes fixated on my lips, he retrieves his phone, taps the screen, and waits.

"The Rebello residence," he says, straight to the point. "Stand down immediately. I need eyes all over the premises. Report back to me on who comes and goes. Day and night. Dispatch can wait a few days."

I hug my chest when he ends the call and pockets his

cell. He runs a hand over his hair where a crooked crown of thorns should sit. "Done. Now you're indebted to me."

Tomás Souza is a princely villain.

A blush of cherry red warms me all over. The scorching heat is molten, a flood of desire sweeping under my flesh, confusing and toxic. My fingers press the galloping pulse point in my throat, desperately seeking a way to ground myself.

"I don't have any money to repay you."

The tote bag hangs in the space separating us.

"Do I look like I need money?" he asks, his eyes hot enough to dry me all over and squeeze my pores until I sweat for him. "Get dressed, *little liar*. Inside this bag is a towel and some clothes. Do not dawdle. We have a body to dispose of."

5

CARINA

Yanking a designer hang tag off with my teeth, I shrug on a blouse made from wispy jade fabric and tuck the tails into the gaping waistband of candy pink chino shorts.

I glance at the price before letting the tag flutter to my toes. Regardless of the expense, it's not an outfit I would choose to die in. Nonetheless, it beats being naked. Thankfully, I'm covered from throat to mid-thigh.

Tomás doesn't bat an eyelid at the oversized and severely contrasting combination, only covers his intense stare with sunglasses. "My mother would never pair those together."

"Then why did you?" I mutter under my breath, staring at pale yellow espadrilles with straps coiled around my ankles. I look like a miserable popsicle.

"If I were to dress you, sweet *little liar*, you'd be naked with only diamonds cuffing your throat."

A fleeting smile dances at the corner of his beautiful mouth and for a treacherous second, it feels as though there's pure white ribbon weaving from his life to mine.

When he crosses his arms, the deep red gemstone embedded in his ring gleams in the sunlight. The color of death soaks into the invisible ribbon, ruining my wishful alliance.

"It's your task to dump the body in the reserve beyond the plantation."

"Dump the body?" I echo, pressing a palm to my growling belly.

"Dump the body," he repeats without any emotion. "It's your first challenge."

Something hideous creeps through my veins and bleeds into my heart, clogging the arteries with a syrupy shot of poison.

The skin on my spine prickles with turbulent shivers when I mull over his cruel scheme to break me. "What... sort of challenges?" I whisper, swallowing quickly.

"If I have your devoted obedience, the absolute truth will follow." His textured velvety voice cracks on the last word. He drags his ringed finger over a pouty bottom lip, slowly, thoughtfully, and then he adds, "You will obey me, Carina."

There it is, the secret swell of darkness within me that billows like a tornado of smoke. The way his well-spoken accent enunciates my name sends chills over my scalp, dries my mouth, and disperses charges of electricity to my core. Even though I have unbridled hatred for this monster, he excites me in ways I can't understand.

Anger escapes my throat in the form of a serpentine hiss. Before I can answer, a man I've never seen before strolls through the courtyard, his chin dipping and rising as if he's assessing the ill-dressed girl standing beside his boss. Both men nod at each other ceremoniously.

"Got your hands full?" the stranger quizzes, folding his arms to mimic Tomás' businesslike posture.

"You could say that. Nothing I haven't dealt with before, Shane."

"Are you sure about that? This one's a kid." The guy with an Irish twang angles his broad shoulders, so his spine twists and he can see me better. "And not bad looking either."

Tomás clenches his jaw, whips off his shades, and glares at his friend as if the suggestion is unpalatable. "Focus on the job, not the girl."

Silver rimmed aviators protect Shane's eyes from the solar rays, and his muscles verge on excessive as they strain the white shirt he wears. The top button is open and his shirt tails are loose, which makes me think he's the lifter and shifter of the two.

It's only when he turns on his heels to catch me staring that I notice a silvery scar split like a fork of lightning across one side of his face. Pencil thin scars glow within a vein-like network, contouring a clean shaven cheek and ending above his right eye.

"The truck is packed. Ready when you are," Shane says matter-of-factly while he runs his nails over hair cropped close to the scalp and stares at the blouse I'm wearing. "I grabbed those from Teresa's wardrobe. She had a shit load of unworn clothes in there, so she won't miss them. They don't look half bad on her. A bit big, but I'm guessing that's a good thing." He chuckles and drags the sunglasses midway down the bridge of his nose, offering me the palest green gaze. It's not menacing or uncomfortable, more playful. "You want her to ride in the back with me?"

I glare at them both, my pulse beating out morse code for an SOS signal. A shadow of displeasure twitches over Tomás' mouth, contorting his lips to a grimace. "You're in the back. She rides upfront with me."

"You got it, Tommy."

Tommy. It sounds so amicable and endearing, as if the two are best friends. Certainly not the nickname of a devil.

Shane repositions his shades, rotates, and saunters away. A second later, Tomás' shoes strike the ground as he covers the short distance I had to breathe in. When he nears, my spine stiffens in defense, and I fold my arms over my chest.

"Time for your next challenge, *little liar*."

I blink in the sight of my captor, how his skin is tanned beneath an Audemars Piguet watch, the golden strap and emerald green dial heavy on his thick wrist. I recognize the exclusive brand from an online advertisement, and estimate its worth as grossly luxurious.

Pure white teeth behind plush lips sparkle as he speaks with that sultry eloquent cadence.

There's nothing out of place on this man. A part of me blames his superior appearance as the trigger to my odd sexual appetite. I'm not used to seeing men in this way, except something stirs deeper within me when he touches my elbow. The skin heats instantly and a crest of prickles roll like a tsunami. From that simple contact, I learn the intrigue is far more disturbing.

"Ever met a tiger up close and personal?" His inky brow hitches.

"I've nursed a jaguar cub," I announce in a gust.

He bends closer until bountiful lashes almost touch mine. I lengthen my neck, trying not to inhale him into my soul.

Those extraordinary eyes, so rich in depth, become the only color I can see. The glossiest shade of coffee rings dilated pupils, blending blackish brown and true black. There within lies secrets of his own—memories of heinous deeds and thoughts of criminality.

In the distance, an engine purrs. Tomás splays his palm on my lower back, leaning in. "The tigers are my father's favorite pets, but they sure as hell aren't friendly cubs. Given the chance, they'll puncture your throat and eat you alive." He ushers me the way we came, towards a shiny red Ford pickup truck parked up on the gravel driveway.

Reflective chrome trims mirror the gray clouds now suffocating the sun. The immaculately presented vehicle could have rolled out of a showroom. It's that clean. Never mind the monster-sized wheels for treading over all terrain, unsoiled and spotless.

With the engine idling, Shane exits the driver's side, unlatches the tailgate, and jumps onto the flatbed at the rear

"Get in," Tomás orders, cordially opening the passenger door.

I climb inside, flinching when he slams the door shut behind me. He casually strolls in front of the hood before joining me without muttering a word.

In the enclosed space, my senses are on overload from the polished leather upholstery to him. Woody, rich undertones, delicately fragrancing my hair, and his musky, intoxicating cologne makes my belly flutter. It's too cozy.

Tomás finally slides his gaze from the rearview mirror to the ill-fitting outfit drowning my petite frame. Heat creeps up from my neck when I realize I'm wearing his mother's clothes, and by no means appealing to him while they're on me. My hair could do with a tangle teaser, and the gaunt reflection staring back at me in the glass resembles a bedraggled misfit.

His eyes linger on my bare thighs, the silent passing seconds make me squirm. I curse myself for even thinking there's a mutual attraction simmering behind his lustful contemplation. This is business for the Souzas.

I glance over my shoulder at where Shane hunkers next to the Mexican's cylindrical coffin. A jittery shiver runs through me, my heart beating so fast I could faint.

"Seatbelt on," he orders, while throwing his arm behind me to the headrest, twisting his torso so his eyes leave mine.

As the truck reverses, I clip myself in and clutch the strap over my chest for comfort.

We leave the soulless mansion in a cloud of dust, me panicking and Tomás casually tapping the steering wheel. The further we drive, the more unsettled I become.

Abundant nature frames a sky preparing for a war of thunder against lightning. A clash of rain-drenched clouds and turbulent tropical winds. Sky soaring palms sway, dancing in the newly conjured breeze. It's brewing miles away from the Souza residence, the promise of a downpour of godly proportions on the horizon.

"How did you get the scar on your forearm?" He finally breaks the amnesty of speech.

I swallow the shame, not wanting to admit the weakness a fourteen-year-old girl was driven to endure. "I did it," I whisper, the confession so weightless under the past intention.

His gaze remains pinned to the dirt track hedged by hectares of strategically sown coffee plants in far reaching rows.

"Why would you do something like that?" His tone hardens to iron, the rough edges brittle with disgust.

"None of your business," I snap in defense. "That's personal and has nothing to do with why I'm here."

Cool air blowing from the air vents curdles with my hot temper, made suffocating when he throttles the wheel as if it's my throat. Lean muscles tighten beneath the sleeves of his fitted shirt. "Fine. Don't tell me, but you *will* tell me when you're staring into the jaws of a fucking tiger." The vicious rasp to his voice immediately fills me with regret.

"Ask me something else. Anything, but that." I pivot to face his side profile, his fixed glower darker than a thunderclap in the heavens. "I promise to tell you the truth."

"What's your real name?" The words strike, making him the human form of a tempest.

"Carina Ferreira," I answer honestly. "Born and raised in Manaus."

There's an unnerving moment where his temperament

seethes. Stones pelt the chassis and my blood gushes around my skull.

A second later, he returns my stare. "Who is Maria Rebello to you? Is she your boss?"

It happens without thought. A grunt of indignation rushes down my nostrils. "Boss?" I admonish. "I'd never work for a cruel bitch like her. Maria thinks she's better than everybody else, because she's pretty and has big boobs. She's just like you, gorgeous with a mean streak. You'd like her. I think she's your type."

His lips curl before a bark of laughter rings in my ears. It takes me completely by surprise, the gruff distinctive sound so utterly carnal. "I didn't mean…" I say breathlessly, embarrassed by the thoughtless admission. "I'm tired. My words are muddled."

"Gorgeous," he repeats the word with a raspy chuckle, "And big boobs. Which means I have a big what exactly?" he teases.

"Head," I counter, feeling my naivety mount.

His smile fades, taking the humor with it. "As for being my type, you have no idea what that is, sweet *little liar*."

My glower glues to his handsome face. The idea of digging deeper into his mind is a luxury I'd love to have, if only to learn what he has planned for me.

"Let me guess," I begin, foolishly deflecting his questions. "Tall, but not taller than you, so you can dominate her. Blonde hair and blue eyes to balance your darkness. Long lean legs… absolutely flawless."

"Wrong," he grinds out between gritted teeth. "This isn't a speed date. I spared your life to find out who wants my father dead, not to share my dating profile. Do not assume you know anything about me," his voice hisses, saturated with venom, stripping any friendliness to the bone.

Fear grips my heart, squeezing it tight in a vice created by his harshness.

"Her plan for me was purely sexual. A virginal gift, I assume. A young woman to sweeten up your father in her favor. There was never any talk of killing him. I wouldn't do that, anyway. I'm not a savage like he is."

"Perhaps you are, *little liar*. And you just don't realize it."

My brows snap together. "Why would you say that?" I gasp, shocked he'd suggest such an odd thing. "I don't belong in your violent world. I'd never murder a man in cold blood."

The truck slows to a halt and Shane appears to the right of us. Through the window, I watch him unhook a metal gate, swinging it inwards before he salutes at Tomás to proceed.

"I saw that raw glimmer of fascination in your eyes when you studied Flavio's dead body. You didn't cry or throw yourself at my feet to beg for your life. There wasn't even the slightest bit of hesitation when I told you to clean up the mess. It was done efficiently, and, if I may pay you a rare compliment, it was completed to the highest standard. You understand violence more than you think."

I fall deadly silent, the truth of his fierce judgment gripping the floundering ventricles of my heart.

"We're here." The tires roll over a rattling cattle guard, allowing access through a six-foot steel fence at either side. We leave a worn track and drive to the brow of a gradual slope leading to the earthy mouth of a jungle. Tomás pulls down hard on the wheel, turning the truck three hundred and sixty degrees so the hood faces the exit. "Let's go." He pulls up the handbrake, leaving the engine running. "Do as you're told. Understood? If I'm not happy with the outcome of your challenge, this will be the last time we see each other."

"What do you mean?" I gulp, feeling icky and nauseous.

"Obedience and honesty. Those are my rules. Break them and you'll pay with your life."

I nod helplessly, my hands sweating and my head light. "Just so you know, Tomás Souza, I didn't know your family existed until earlier today. You crashed into my life as much as I unwillingly dropped into yours. I have no reason to lie to you. You've seen more of me than anyone ever has."

Tomás moves slightly, debating something. Terrible words or punishing force, both an option, yet neither occurs. Instead, I notice his wicked tongue sweeping the contour of his lips and the quiet breath he controls.

"Out here, I'm the man in charge. If there's a threat, and that danger happens to be a striking woman like you, then I still won't take any chances. My family comes first. Always. And traitors, they die… Unconditionally," he says thickly, his gorgeous face contorts to rest in an ugly, heartless expression.

My mouth goes dry like I've ironically swallowed every grain of sand on the prettiest beach and now I'm choking on it. In a thrumming heartbeat, he exits the pickup truck, marches angrily in full view of the windshield, opens my door and offers me his large hand. The beautiful beast has manners.

Both knees go soft when I slot my hand into his and land on a blanket of leaves, my lightheaded sway magnified by his solid chest right there for support.

His fingers slowly curl around my palm as he towers over me, a skyscraper of red-blooded supremacy. Before I inhale, the delicate tingle of his touch brushes the thin scar above my lip. Air rushes into my lungs at the onset of his feather light exploration.

"So many secrets, *little liar*." I look up into his eyes and find something unreal. It throws me for a second, but then it fades and he speaks again. "I'll learn every single one of them."

Shane wallops the truck's hood with two consecutive slaps, his timing perfect. "Ready when you are, Tommy," he announces.

Tomás growls low and annoyed, the disturbance zapping our haywire connection. He can damn well see it smoldering under the surface as much as I can. And what's more shameful than feeling such an illicit attraction, he senses my nerves.

He's using the power of his authority to goad me. To make the process of weeding out answers easier. Except he doesn't know me, or understand what I'm truly capable of.

I release a breath and round my shoulders, hitching my chin higher. "Some secrets are best left in the past where they belong."

Long fingers secure the hair at my nape. His wicked

mouth swoops to the side of my face, his hot breath an aphrodisiac. "We'll see about that." He tugs my head backward, only a fraction, but enough to expose the crazy vein throbbing in my throat. "I'll be the judge of what stays hidden."

For a single dark and dirty second, I think he's going to kiss me. I wrongfully pray his lips would land on mine to occupy the hollowness within me. That this man's poisonous mouth could give me a taste of the unexplored.

The therapist el Fantasma generously paid for had assured me the trauma of my past was entombed in my psyche. Apparently, I erect walls so high people can't get over them. Clearly, she didn't expect a man of this caliber to lure me out of my shell.

I pause, secretly hoping and foolishly prepared to accept what he offers.

He doesn't.

Rather than press his moist lips to my scarred mouth, he lets go, taking the air with him.

I blink furiously, blood roaring, and fingers tracing my unkissed mouth with a false look of nonchalance, masking the mindless disappointment. Out-of-this-world lips part, and a seductive tongue skates between his teeth. Rather than stare at me with disgust, he projects a hunger that burrows under my flesh and sets me on fire.

What if this man's distorted soul is the gravity to anchor me in place? If his darkness can turn mine into twilight.

I shake off the disturbing notion, certain it's purely a misfortune of female hormones. Just a forbidden fascination I'd take to my grave.

"Come on, Tommy. We've got a dead guy and a streak of tigers ready for a feed. Let's do what we came here for and get the fuck out."

Tomás scowls, fixes his cufflinks, and turns on his heels. "Go with Shane. You're needed at the back of the Raptor."

Even his pickup is named after a carnivorous bird. I take a breath in the shivery coldness of his absence, then consider it simply a reaction to starvation. It's been too many days since my last meal. A sigh shudders out of me, and I join Shane at the open tailgate. He jumps into action, climbing onboard.

"I'll take the head. You grab the feet. Don't let go until I say so," Shane orders.

With an almighty shove, he pushes the cumbersome corpse, so it nudges over the edge. Grubby work boots are visible beneath the polythene layer, something the animals wouldn't find a use for. The acrid stench of wrapped death wafts up my nose, making my stomach heave. It's an unexplainable smell that both freezes my skeleton and causes sweat to gather at my nape.

It's barbaric what these men are doing—what Tomás is making me do. Nonetheless, I have to survive, and I'll do anything to make sure it happens. So, I hold my breath, hook under stiff calves and stagger backward as the weight transfers into my arms. Shane leaps out of the Raptor, hauling the guy's shoulders into his chest and takes the lead. With me facing the jungle below us, he bears most of the deadweight as we ramble over uneven terrain jumbled with rocks of all sizes. The further down we go, the more hazardous the ground becomes with marshy puddles and slick mud close to a wooden labyrinth.

He stumbles first, and then I wobble on the inappropriate sandals he picked out for me even when he knew I'd be transporting a corpse. I lose my footing and accidently let go, hearing the distinct crack of brittle bone from under the see-through film. Shane grunts, the look of annoyance he offers speaks for him. For a split second I stare at jeans, to where the dead man's blood has leaked in drips. He lowers his lashes to the mess and sighs heavily. "Fuck, he'll make me walk me back," he bites out, shaking his head.

It takes a few attempts to manhandle my end of the body into the air again. The effort is exhausting, and my energy levels are zapped.

"Drop him here," he grimaces, finally able to drop the load. "We'll roll him out of the plastic, so the tigers can catch the scent of fresh blood."

I happily unlock my arms and shake out the burn. Feeling eyes on my every move, I glance up and pinpoint Tomás at the crest of the hill. He waits by the truck with arms folded, feet apart, and eyes shaded behind aviators—watching me like a hawk.

"What sort of challenge is this?" I ask Shane when the Mexican revolves once. The instant he's uncovered, I slam a hand over my nose and mouth as the god awful stench hits my nostrils, and the unwrapped stiff attracts buzzy insects. "That's nasty." I dry heave, my eyes watering with the struggle to suck in clean air. "What will dumping the Mexican prove to him?"

Shane inches away with the back of his hand held

under his nose. "Perhaps he'll see how utterly uncaring you are about the fact Flávio will end up torn limb from limb by wild cats." He shrugs. "Other kids would be whimpering like babies."

The Mexican's lifeless body lies before us in the dirt, now free from the blood smeared membrane, his eyes vacant. "I'm not a kid," I point out.

"My apologies." He bows mockingly. "Let's face it, though, you're a teen and we're a decade older. To us, you're just a kid."

"I'll be twenty in a couple of months." He didn't have to look at me to hear the glare in my tone. "And I don't know this man. He's already dead, so he won't feel a thing when the tigers mutilate his body."

Shane checks over his shoulder, distracted by Tomás' hand signal. "Look, if this was your real challenge, I'd give you a thumbs up and offer you a smoke." Using his boot, he kicks the plastic in half so the crimson mess is contained on the inside, then he carefully forms a large rectangle, all the while doing his best not to get more stains on his clothes. Eventually he reduces the mass to a smaller square, lifts it in the air and holds it away from his legs.

My scalp prickles. "What do you mean?"

"Your actual challenge is to wait right here with Flav's body." He nudges his boot into the Mexican. "Just you and the dead guy until the big ole cats show up."

"Wait... you're joking... h-h-he... wouldn't leave me out here?" My terrified stutter is met with a long sigh.

"I'm not sure who you think that guy up there is, but

yeah, Tommy would leave you here if he thinks you're a threat to his family."

Outrage amplifies in my chest, a surge of adrenaline shocking me into a fit of temper. "I'm coming with you," I hiss, swallowing the lump in my throat. "If he wants me to wait here, he can order it himself."

"Don't make me do this."

"Do what?"

Shane taps the gun snug to his hip. "Threaten you with my piece. If I have to, I'll blow a hole in your knee cap."

"Fuck you!" I snarl, balling my hands into fists I know won't save me from this calamity.

"Look, kid, answer his questions and don't give him any bullshit. Tommy can sniff out a lie better than the tigers sniff out stiffs. You don't come across as the usual bitches we're used to..." He shrugs, almost unhappy about his order to leave me here. "Good luck, kid."

And with that, he winks and starts to scale the gentle slope.

6

CARINA

The growl scraping my throat begins as a low snarl and finishes with my teeth gnashing.

When I dart after him, he angles his upper half and grabs the firearm from behind his belt; the aim directed below my waist. "Stay fucking put."

"No way! I'm not waiting here as tiger bait," I yell, my fierce gaze settling on Tomás.

Shane continues to reverse while Tomás asks his first question. "What's your full name?" he says with a deadly calmness like a peaceful graveyard under a sheet of bitter frost.

"I've already told you!" I throw my hands up, exasperated. "How many times do I have to repeat myself?"

Tomás drags his frames down the bridge of his nose and pockets them. "Even sweet little liars break into pretty pieces when they're under duress. A lack of consistency will help me decide if you're undercover. Now let's start over again. And don't forget, my father's tigers are used to this time sensitive game." His eyes never leave me. "What is your real name?"

"Carina Ferreira," I reply, glaring up at him as the words snap out.

Catching Shane's movements in the corner of my eye, I shoot him a hateful scowl, my fists balling with resentment as he retreats to safety.

Bastards.

Another question blasts into the humid air the second I respond. "Age?"

"Nineteen and three quarters."

The next one comes at me like rapid gunfire. "Where do you live?"

"Manaus."

"Is there a hit out on my father?"

I rub my temple, feeling woozy. My empty stomach aches and a surge of nausea has my pulse racing out of control until all I can see are black dots and blurry shapes.

"I've no idea. I'm not part of that world," I pant, my voice now small and panicky.

"Did Carlos Blanco put you up to this?"

Sweat trickles from my hairline, rolling over the furrowed lines of confusion. "Who? I've never heard of him."

"Were you sent here to kill Elias or to fuck him?"

I cross my arms over my chest, oddly aware of a drop in temperature. "Apparently, as inhumane as it is, I'm a gift." My mouth dries. "Whatever that means to you people."

"Are you a virgin?"

Sucking in sharply, my eyes bug at his audacity. That

information is completely irrelevant to his cruel interrogation. "Are you serious?" I snarl, grappling with the flimsy collar around my neck in the hope of space to breathe. "What's that got to do with this?"

I sense his dissatisfaction, noting how he takes two paces closer. "Answer the question, *senorita*." He hisses, his entire posture forcing restraint, ready to slip from his refined throne.

"Fine." I relent, praying this torture would end quicker if I play his game. "I've never been with a man before. Does that answer your damn question?"

A low grunt happens as he shakes his head scornfully. "Are you waiting for a Prince to ride in on a white steed and ask for your hand in marriage first?"

My limbs weaken, not from his snide tone, but from the surge of nausea, welcoming beads of salty sweat and unnerving lightheadedness.

"If we're comparing fairy tales, how about Hansel and Gretel? When the nasty old witch gets burned to ashes after holding the young girl hostage." I desperately try to sound plucky, my veins running hot, then cold. "Make believe witches or schoolyard bullies, they're all the same. From the pretty girls at school who poked fun at the ugly outcast, to the popular boys who used me for a lost bet. *'Tell her she's pretty. Try to kiss her without throwing up in your mouth.'*" I mock a young boy's voice. "So yeah, getting up close and personal with people isn't something I want to do." I rub my neck, heart hammering and chest heaving. "And from where I'm standing, you're just as bad as them."

A rustle from behind snares my attention. Glancing

back to never ending treetops and swaying ferns, I spy lingering yellow eyes amidst feathery leaves the size of umbrellas. Still far enough away not to pose an immediate threat, but close enough to electrify my pulse. The hoots and hollers of vigilante wildlife dulls to a murmur as the fascinated carnivore stalks through thickset vegetation. I gasp for a breath, sucking in earthy air and muggy heat. If this man doesn't believe me, I'll die a horrific death.

"Please, Tomás. I've told you everything," I plead, my cracked voice wobbly, frustrated tears welling, and my vision fuzzy with fear. "I'd rather Elias killed me with a single bullet than be mauled while I'm still alive."

I edge away from the clothed carcass, my mind buzzing with thoughts of a reckless escape. Should I risk the speed of a tiger or the crack of a bullet?

Tomás continues, unmoved by my frazzled begging, his face forged with cast iron. "Did you come to the plantation to assassinate the Souza kingpin?"

"No! I've told you already." This time I palm my forehead, my fingers gliding in the slick sheen of sweat. "I was in the wrong place at the wrong time. W-why aren't you listening to me?" I barely hear my breathy plea under the pounding of my heartbeat.

Tender shoots crack and a nasally snuffle announces the arrival of a single tiger, the biggest feline I've ever encountered. My heart bucks wildly, the pulse of it hard in my chest. Terror scorches every tense muscle until they ache.

When my gaze settles on the magnificent stalking creature, all I see is a powerful jaw crammed with razor-sharp teeth. Hefty, padded paws carry her from the leafy understory to the clearing. Vivid eyes curiously assess the scene while she lowers on her haunches, ready to pounce.

I wobble like a pendulum—knees frail and eyesight splashed with floaty blotches. My hands go numb and the earthy scented air around me gets hotter.

"Carina," Tomás growls my name, his tone impatient. "We're done. Come back to the Raptor, slowly."

His words garble behind the whoosh of dizziness ambushing me. Each step gets harder to take while I try to swallow the lump in my tight throat. Even the loose-fitting shirt clinging to my sweat laden spine makes me feel claustrophobic and trapped. Uneven ground spins beneath the sunny espadrilles and on the next staggered stride, my ankle weakens.

I crash to my knees, skinning the heels of my palms. My teeth jar on impact and an inward hiss follows, spiky slices driving into my shin.

Blood drains from my face and pumps straight to the fresh gash. While I'm hunkered on hands and knees, there's a serene calmness, a moment of stillness when the wildlife takes a collective breath and the tiger deliberates its next move.

Riding high on the wave of fear, I consider my own inevitable decision. Unable to balance, I scramble on all fours, scurrying in the opposite direction of the corpse toward my tormentor.

If I could stand, I would run. If I could sprint, I'd never look back at Tomás and seek shelter in the jungle. I'd disappear from this nightmare and from everyone in it.

However, those are the whimsical thoughts of a woman close to fainting. The constant surge of adrenaline has all but faded. My fight-or-flight reserves are well and truly depleted.

"Stop fucking around, Carina. Do as you're told." His voice casts a net of shivers, smothering me with cruel intimidation. "Get back here now."

I can't answer, desperately trying to muster the last shot of energy I have left. My stomach knots with rushed breaths, chasing my quick pulse. In my petrified state, I clutch a jaggy rock as a weapon. Helplessly prepared to defend myself.

Stones crunch beyond my whirling panic, the loud tempo beating out a rhythm of urgency. Before I gather a scream, energetic arms envelope my waist from behind. Sultry sandalwood mingles with the flurry of air cushioning me as I'm hoisted upwards. Seductive manly cleanliness tempts my senses, multiplying the chills wracking my body.

When I squirm, Tomás jerks me tighter against his chest where my dark hair clings to his crisp white shirt. Right there, cradled by him, I seek refuge in the embrace of a libertine. His powerful pace eats up the gradient until we're at the rear of the waiting truck.

"Do you believe me?" I whisper, exhaustion zapping the energy to speak.

Through blurry eyes, I study his stern grimace of displeasure as he drops me into the back of the truck and heaves himself up to join me before slamming the tailgate shut.

"Go!" he barks out louder than a roar, purposefully ignoring my question. "Get the fuck out of here, Shane."

The sensation of rapid movement churns in my stomach. Wheels spin forward, leaving the feeding frenzy massacre behind.

What should be relief warps into knotted dread. Not all predators live in the jungle, some live in expansive estates and pretend to be human. We're following the worn trail back to a snake pit where the king serpent kills by constriction.

Tomás kneels, hunched over, nostrils flaring. His serious set eyes roam the lower half of my leg, his hardened expression deeply malignant. The disconcerting shadows swallowing his features caution me of an inner war—a distressing battle of some sort.

Pitch black eyes focus solely on the wound while his lungs expand and deflate in quick succession. "Your destiny is in my hands. Not even a tiger has that authority," he spits out. "Whether I believe you or not is irrelevant." His perfect white teeth snap the words with limited control.

My eyelids flutter over the wet eyeballs rolling in my head. I'm all too aware of his kinetic vibrations knocking my equilibrium off kilter and hate how his body heat blankets my uncontrollable shivers.

"You're a monster, Tomás Souza," I say breathlessly.

Pain tingles in waves, salient and stingy. I blow out a jet of air the instant I move to prop myself up to elbows. Blinking vigilantly, I'm rewarded with snapshots of a magnificently tanned torso now bare, abdominal muscles carved in ridges from daily workouts and athletic arms moving to methodically roll his expensive shirt.

He's so close I can easily count the eyelashes framing his blackish eyes. There's no distance separating us. No barriers. No protection from the man who'd threatened certain death by feline incisors, because he doesn't trust me.

I should be horrified by his tactics, angry at his methods and furious that he made me repeat everything I'd already told him, but the reality is—I get it. I bleed distrust more than I do blood.

An indignant grunt escapes my parched throat with barely any gusto to make it worthwhile. "What are you doing?" I press my fingertips to his shoulders.

When he glances up, I finally gain focus, finding eyes so pensive they arrest me.

He doesn't answer, only continues to twist his shirt around my seeping injury. When he's done, Tomás scoots sideways, putting much needed space between us. He sits on his ass, legs bent and forearms resting on top of his knees, his bloodied hands splayed outwards.

Darkness moves over his face like a ferocious, thick smog, veiling his features with a ghastly countenance. It's a horrifying look that leaves me huddled on one side and him on the other. As if the devil has possessed his soul, he snatches the handgun from the waistband of his trousers and fires a few rounds into the sky like he's lost his mind. When his flashy gold weapon lowers, he stills again, his gaze terrifying.

I observe his muted hostility for the entire journey, wondering why he'd let me live and how he can be so oblivious to my presence now. His stare remains glazed and trancelike, unmoving like he's slipped from sovereignty and hit rock bottom.

The second the Raptor swerves left, then skids to a

halt under the grand archway, Shane exits the vehicle. He marches to meet us, eyes wide when they land on the gun Tomás is choking.

"Christ… Tommy." He hurries to help. "It's okay. You're home."

Silently, Tomás drops to the gravel. His broad shoulders are flexed, his sullied hand outstretched, aiming the barrel of his downwards, and a tightening of his jaw so rigid I'd swear his teeth would shatter.

"Get Carina a bottle of water. Lock her in a stall." That's all he says, his voice broken like a false promise of freedom.

His body is taut as if his limbs are wrought iron weapons of destruction. Behind us, the brisk crunch of his dress shoes all but crushes stones to dust.

Shane stares at my swaddled shin, the fabric steeped in crimson. His brow scrunches as he blows a jet of air through his lips. "Well, fuck me, that's a first."

Hesitantly, I drag myself out of the truck, wincing when the damaged leg takes my weight. "What? That I didn't end up as a snack like the Mexican?" I say caustically. "And now what? Will I have to spend the night locked up in a stall until he decides what other challenge I should be subjected to?"

He scratches his head. "Fuck, kid. Tommy has your blood on his hands."

When I stagger, he seizes my bicep and gives me the support I need to carry myself. I accept his help, otherwise I might end up in a crumpled heap. "Is that a metaphor? I answered his questions. I told him the truth."

Together we cross over the courtyard, toward a sliding

barn door. Large raindrops plop on us from the gray sky. One, then three, then a multitude of refreshing raindrops.

"He looked demonic," I say quietly, unsure how Shane will react to my description.

We step out of the rain, from chilly air to the waft of livestock. "I wear scars on my face like a patchwork quilt." He traces the spider web disfigurement on his cheek. "And Tommy, well, his scars are woven through his mind. Whatever happened in the back of the truck, for that shirt to be tied around your leg…" Shane murmurs, somewhat dazed. "First, Tommy would never purposefully use his clothes in that manner, ever. And second, if he gets even a pinprick of blood on his skin, he loses his fucking shit. Like off the scale, unhinged. You're lucky to be alive, kid. In fact, I'd say it's a miracle."

7

CARINA

A tropical storm batters the outside of the cavernous barn. Flashes of blinding light burst in from the cracks beneath the sliding door as it rolls to a close.

Shane ushers me into an empty stall and bolts the iron bar gate, leaving me alone in my new prison cell with no bed and stale air. I stare at my shaky palms and breathe slowly for a measure of fortitude. They're filthy and the blouse is soiled with earth.

I shiver, aware I'm in a never-ending nightmare. Taking a minute to regain balance, I stumble to the secured exit, lift to my tiptoes and peer into the extensive gloominess, unable to see anything other than a concrete walkway and a sliver of light at the far end where Shane walks towards. The second he disappears, I throw my arm over the top of the gate and feel around for a sliding bar. It's too far out of reach and the effort needed is exhausting.

The soles of my feet ache and my knees tremble in the aftermath of an unjust trauma. I sigh heavily and run my fingers through the messy, damp strands of hair mapping my chest. I'm too weak to even think about an escape yet.

Moments later, a dog yaps, alerting me to Shane's arrival. He stands in front of the gate, his solemn expression lit up with intermittent bursts of lightning as he passes through a bottle of water and a packet of cookies. Barely managing to unscrew the lid, I take a furious gulp of tepid water and feel it travel through me, gurgling in my empty stomach. I close my eyes briefly, thankful to rehydrate after such an ordeal.

I hear his boots scuff the concrete as he moves around. Before he leaves, he hesitates at the bars, penning me in and quietly tosses in a heavy blanket with straps and metal clasps. It clanks on the way in, the meeting of metal echoing to the overhead steel beams. The overpowering smell of animal sweat and damp dog hits my nostrils instantly and a cloud of short hairs sticks to my salty skin.

"You'd do best to rest up, kid." His casual shrug and light half-smile catch a flicker of white light. "Tommy has business to talk over with Elias before we leave tomorrow. Neither of them will come out here, especially during a storm."

My ribs tighten, the sensation similar to a cinched belt with no give in the tough leather. "What does that mean for me? If he's going... will he leave me here with Elias?"

Flint sparks, blazing the tip of his cigarette with an orange crackle. "I can't answer that, kid. Tommy has his father's distrust and his grandfather's patience. He's usually right down the line. If a guy fucks up, he's dead. If he's loyal, he'll receive the respect he deserves." He breathes out a smoky sigh. "After your little show of disrespect earlier, I thought you'd earned a bullet. I never expected him to save your ass or carry you back to the truck." Shane inhales deeply, then puffs smoke out of his nostrils. "You're either royally fucked, kid, or he's satisfied you'll serve them well."

"That's disgusting." I fold my arms. "I'll never let those bastards touch me."

Shane turns on his heels. "One of those *bastards* wants you dead, the other has given you time. Something tells me it's not that straightforward, kid. Sweet dreams," he calls out over his shoulder.

Without another word, he whistles to the dogs, patiently waits for the last one to scurry to his heel and shunts the barn door sideways before stepping out into a deluge of merciless rain.

The frustrated scream clawing its way out of my larynx is hidden behind a crash of rowdy thunder. I shudder, my bones stiff from burnout and my limbs heavy from a soaring dip in blood sugar levels.

I crouch low, wincing when newly crusted scabs crack under the movement of my legs. My spine straightens against the wooden partition and I nibble a cookie for sustenance.

Crumbs stick to the emotional lump forming in my throat, unyielding when I take another long sip of water.

For most people, being on their own, in solitary confinement, is punishment in itself. Me—well, I'm used to it. I'd much rather be under a smelly field blanket than in the main house with that god-awful family.

Violent storms aren't out of the ordinary in the north-western hemisphere. But what is abnormal is the cruel game Tomás had played with my life. At least his father would snap the trigger without any pretenses. Whereas Tomás had thrown me to a hungry carnivore and now, I'm trapped in a makeshift cell, uncertain of my future all over again. I understand Elias is a psychopath. He has that hallmark stamped on every glare and every evil deed. So what does that make Tomás?

A long, weary sigh blows free. What would el Fantasma tell me to do in this situation? Aside from escaping the inescapable. He fought for justice, no matter the price. In my heart, I know Shane is right. Sleep would give me the strength to run, fight, or stand my ground. Whatever horrors the morning brings, I'd be prepared.

It's been a tiresome endurance test, from the kidnapping just days ago to ending up in the belly of Hades. My body is bruised and fatigued, my mind restless. The shirt tied to my lower leg still emits the intoxicating scent of a nefarious villain.

On closer inspection, buried treasure twinkles at me—a pair of diamond cufflinks, to be precise. Slowly, I unwind the material, peeling it from the dried cut and unfasten the jeweled finery from the grubby cuffs.

For a moment, I just stare at them blankly, a surge of disgust blooming into repulsion. Yet, for some unknown reason, I'm unable to throw the sparkly trinkets away. Instead, I pocket them without a second thought and fist his shirt into a crumpled ball, using it for a makeshift pillow.

I shudder when a nearby dog howls. The rain continues to whip the building like the gods are punishing the plantation for every unhallowed sin hidden from the world.

When I squeeze my eyes shut, disturbing thoughts of Tomás plague me. A heady waft of cologne from the material close to my nose filters inside my mind and conjures all sorts of sensual sensations. It's a disgrace how an intelligent woman craves the very monster keeping her captive. But my blood runs hotter than ever.

An unsatisfied throb leaves me in a constant state of fevered arousal and my unruly nipples harden from the masculine scent haunting the muggy air. Hatred licks at the idea of this one-sided physical attraction. However, it doesn't dampen the needy urges I have when I imagine his potent hands all over me.

In my confusion, I consider how he's shown both a callous nature and an unexpected thoughtfulness. His expensive dress shirt was used to soak up my blood, even if it was his fault I fell.

I am, in the most indecipherable way, utterly captivated by him. Yet deeply adamant that I'd rather burn his whole house to cinders than let him touch me.

The quandary continues, long into the evening. I lay in situ for hours, desperately trying to ignore the niggling swell between my thighs by reliving the grim interrogation.

His rapid fire probing questions.

The urgency in his husky voice.

The order to return to him.

Sinewy arms and serious searching eyes. Did he save me? Or does he have something more heinous planned?

Despite the festering grudge I have for the man, my

body reacts to him in such an inglorious way. It's an offset reaction I'll have to endure, and I pray he never suspects a thing—ever.

My eyelashes flick up when metal rollers glide and the storm grows louder, erupting indoors. Before I have time to consider my next move, a beam of light shines into the stall, brightening the space with me in it. I squint, automatically lifting my hand to shade my eyes. The echoey clank of a sliding bolt rings in my ears like a death toll and then the flashlight lowers.

"Get up." Tomás' rich velveteen voice has a new husky edge—a sexy rasp of tiredness and acrimony.

My head swoops up, our eyes clashing as he stands there. Goosebumps run over my spine at the harshness of his order. He glowers at me from the gate, bare torso dripping and low-slung jersey shorts saturated. His golden necklace and matching bracelet are the only items next to his smooth skin. The suave businessman is underdressed, but still every bit as dominant.

I massage my heart where wild flutters bump into my struggling lungs and inch back into the shadowy corner of my holding cell so he's oblivious to my inspection of him. He doesn't need to know how my pulse reacts to the seductive scent of a freshly showered bad guy or how my insides flip from the way he oozes authority.

With the thunderstorm now overhead, his features are cloaked in intermittent streaks of lightning. Bountiful water droplets decant from the contours of solid abdominal muscles that lead all the way to an elastic waistband. A kingly posture defies fairness, feet parted and shoulders drawn back, expecting my acquiescence.

It's hard to fathom how this semi-naked version of Tomás Souza is more impressive than when he is clothed in an impeccable designer suit.

But he is. Unbearably so.

"Where are you taking me?" I sit up, returning his unfriendly expression with one of my own.

He doesn't reply.

"Is this another stupid challenge?" I hiss, throwing the blanket off, preparing to stand. "Let me guess. You're going to tie me to a tree as a human sacrifice for the devil and engineer a streak of lightning to split me in two?"

My suggestion earns a dark grunt. "I don't need to sell my soul to the devil, Carina. He's already in me," his sonorous cadence rumbles in tandem with a strike of lightning. "However, now you've suggested it, perhaps it might be the answer to your lack of fucking respect."

I bounce onto both feet, the rip of knitting flesh forcing my teeth to clench. A trickle of blood runs the length of my shin. "Excuse me? Did you actually say the word respect? I have every right to be pissed off after what you did to me."

"Perhaps I should rethink my generosity?"

"Generosity?" My voice raises a decibel higher in disbelief. "You're insane if you think any of this is generous."

"You're still alive," he points out flatly as a roll of thunder depicts his brewing mood. "Unfortunately, I don't have any mastery over Mother Nature, so electrocution isn't in the cards. However, I do have authority over *you while* you're in my domain." A smug curl to the corner of his mouth makes my heart beat faster.

I cross my arms over my breasts, wondering if he's here to taunt me with his good looks or put a bullet in my skull. Neither being acceptable. "Where are you taking me in the middle of a tropical storm?"

He cocks a brow and shakes his head, the low chuckle deep in his throat terrifying. "Something tells me I should keep an eye on you. Follow me and you'll find out."

"No..." I say breathlessly. "I won't go anywhere with you until you tell me where we're going."

In three brisk strides, his wet torso is so close that I can smell sweet alcohol on his warm breath. "You're going indoors. Into the main house." There's a hoarseness to his tone, as if he's suffered a million nights of unrest and drained too many bottles of bitterness.

I suck in a quick breath and fix my shoulders, pretending the intensity doesn't affect me. "Are you taking me to him... to your father?"

The whites of his eyes glisten with concealment, a halo of pretty opal circles reticent ebony. A low hum of thought escapes his throat as he observes me. "My father enjoyed one too many glasses of his favorite cognac. He's currently sleeping it off."

A long sigh drifts from my mouth, not from defeat, but from a rush. The second it covers his skin, I notice a flurry of goosebumps electrify his sinewy shoulders.

"If you're not taking me to him, then why bring me inside against his wishes?" I swallow in a gulp. "This is just a game to you, isn't it? And you know what I think?" His lips tighten and he stays perfectly still, harsh words held on his tongue, waiting for my unruly rant to end. "You're worse than your father, because you thrive on psychological torture."

He makes a sexy grunt noise—part annoyance, part frustration. "Stop talking." The pad of his forefinger presses over my lips. "Perhaps I should teach you manners while you belong to me." The statement hangs in the charged air around us, crackling and hissing with tension.

I try not to squirm or even blink, to stand tall in the face of a reigning prince. "Belong to you?" My jaw clenches.

If he senses even a wisp of weakness, he'd celebrate his success with even more humiliation. As if cowering before a wild animal, on the precipice of near death wasn't enough. Now he's looming over me with temptation radiating from his black aura.

"I do not belong to anyone. Least of all you."

Fire flashes in his brown-black eyes. "If you want to live, Carina Ferreira, then you'll do exactly what I tell you to do." His body crowds me. The only contact is his firmly placed finger, now tilting my chin. "Walk out of here and stay close. Do not utter a single word until I permit these lips of yours to open."

The tense vibrations from him give off wavering control. It makes me wonder if he's fighting the same unrighteous desire. If we're both drowning in a tempestuous ocean of forbidden fascination.

"If you're going to kill me, why the hell would I obey you?"

The fingers on my chin jump to my nape, where he weaves his fingers through my tangled lengths and yanks firmly. When I hiss from the sharp shock, his pupils flare, signaling a stark warning.

His spine straightens when my hands fly to his taut pectorals, both of us inhaling the same turbulent air. Static volts of adrenaline spark and catch fire.

Goosebumps race down my arms. Alcoholic vapor expels from his lungs and mingles with the oxygen feeding mine. We're close enough to promise danger, in spitting distance of my first ever interaction with a male. Not just any man—a cold-hearted villain who refuses to look anywhere other than my mouth. Crazy sparks of electricity hiss between us, shooting from my toes to my scalp.

His five o'clock shadow seems darker, his eyes molten. The slow grin quirking his lips borders on iniquitous, yet hints at hidden hunger. "Do not touch me," he growls. "Remove your hands before I remove them myself."

My cheeks sting with the slap of his request, so brusque and unkind. Embarrassment tells me I've clearly misunderstood the lust feathering his gaze. But when my hands drop, they inadvertently brush over the tented fabric at his groin. There's no mistake.

Something alarming flickers behind his eyes, darkness mixed with animosity. His features tense as he raises his head to lock his spine, vertebrae by vertebrae. Until he's taller, fiercely serious, and kingly in his stance.

My heart drops, the plummeting reaction to his distaste more intrusive than a carcinogenic allergy.

"Men have taken bullets for their lies and insubordination. Even though you passed my test earlier, my father still wants you dead. You're in his territory where intruders never get out alive."

Tingles lose control within me, the mass effect causing my body to involuntarily shake. "Come quietly or Elias Souza will kill you himself. It's your choice."

On that cold, cruel statement, he wades backwards through the foggy mist of misplaced temptation. Each step eliminating the attraction until it's nothing but a murderous promise from the devil.

With a click of his long fingers, he turns in his overpriced designer running shoes and exits the stall, fully expecting good behavior.

8

CARINA

A blanket of sinister clouds eclipses the moon, plunging the plantation into oppressive gloom. The backdrop of pitch black shows zero sign of civilization beyond the hacienda.

From behind a manicured hedge flanking the winding pathway, a drenched Alsatian circles us on the stones until Tomás mutters a sharp command and it skulks off.

There's no shelter from the downpour, not even the enormous trees offer a reprieve. They just sway back and forth like demons of the underworld, tainted by darkness. The closer we get to the substantial two-tiered mansion with pastel white walls and pillars, the more my heart races.

Rain splattered windows glow from within. It's not welcoming or majestic, more like incandescent eyes beckoning lost souls into the flames of purgatory. And tonight, that lost soul is me.

A figure lingers under a bow of twisted vines dappled with delicate windswept blooms. A cap shields watchful eyes from the storm and nods respectfully on our approach, only for the soldier to slink into the shadows when Tomás passes him.

Tomás stalks toward the house, veering left rather than moving to the front of the property. Wind whips my hair, the strands sticking to my lashes. I'm angrily trotting behind him, with no other choice than to show obedience. If that's what he wants to call it. I had weighed my options and picked him over Elias. Had Tomás truly wanted me dead, I'd already be torn to pieces by now.

Instead, I'm managing a wobbly pace in muddy sandals, heading towards a simple wooden door discreetly positioned beyond a screen of overgrown bushes. I follow him indoors, dripping wet and shivering. My chest heaves with every pant, our hurried pace taking its toll on me. He waves his hand into the night air as if signaling to someone and then closes the door with a gentle click, his muscles tight and mouth even tighter.

"I'll lock up, sir." A rough-looking guy sporting a plaited goatee and wearing a Hawaiian shirt saunters along the hallway, his steely eyes trained to the doorway as he speaks in a hushed rumble. "The surveillance cameras will be up and running again in a minute."

Tomás nods, his dusky eyes pinning me to the slate gray slabs of an austere hallway, which I assume by its bland appearance is the staff entrance. I refuse to fall into the disorientating expanse of his stare all over again, purposefully tearing my gaze away from his face.

Soft light catches the waterfall of droplets covering his sculpted chest. The very setting where my eyes land. My cheeks feel flush, the thrum of my pulse charging through me. Without thought, I dab my top lip, cautiously hiding the disturbance in my unruly libido.

He lifts his finger to his mouth and signals for silence, then nods his head, beckoning for me to continue following behind.

In tandem, we climb a set of stairs and walk along a corridor leading to the rear of the building. Tomás opens another door, pauses as he checks the opposite side, and then saunters through.

We immediately step into luxury I'd expect from such a wealthy family, where priceless artwork lines high walls and a plush carpet soften every step. The steady tick of a grandfather clock slows time. An intermittent metronome counting down the seconds to my incarceration.

Beyond a set of twin doors, Tomás' lair awaits. I hesitate by the entrance, uncertainty scratching its way through my gut with pointed talons and no way of escape. Even my emotions are trapped, my racing mind is just as confused as my senses.

He stops in the middle of the large suite, slowly doing a one-eighty until we face each other in a silent standoff. I freeze, stuck in his far reaching shadow sprawling over a stone colored rug.

I watch his finger lift and leisurely crook to summon me inside the room that screams of unadulterated masculinity. The lump in my throat bobs uncomfortably when I gulp.

His dark persona glows beneath a crown of lamplight, and a few remaining raindrops glisten on tanned skin giving his solid torso a jeweled complexion. But a flicker of the unknown edges his features, something I've never seen in a man's eyes before. Something terribly wicked.

"In. Now. And shut the doors," he demands, his tone tipped with frost.

A central black bed frame with pointed corner posts is softened by alabaster sheets, precisely tucked under the mattress, and a sprawling downy duvet resembles a layer of untouched snow. At the foot of it, two oblong bolster cushions sit at opposite ends of an upholstered bench as if their positions were equally measured. At a quick count, six silky pillows line the padded headboard with the seventh resting proud of place, the letter 's' stitched into its ebony material.

My gaze travels around the almost black walls, darting from one strategically hung piece of artwork to the next. The images are unusual, somehow illustrating various degrees of chaos. He doesn't need to turn on the lights as amber bulbs without shades already alter the mood to offer a sensual haze.

I bite my lip, the rush of nerves fluttering in my throat. Does he expect me to spend the night in that bed with him?

The second I pivot to draw the doors together; he strolls up from behind me to reach around my waist and easily locks us in together with a twist of a key.

His mouth dips to the side of my face. The only thing touching me is liquored, warm breath. "Leave your clothes by the door."

The order scurries over my scalp with equal measures of trepidation and desire. A heatwave prickles my spine, quickly cooling as he leisurely backs away and prowls through the symmetrically arranged room.

I rotate on the spot, reluctant to move. The gravity of this situation ripples over me in waves, each one cresting higher than the one before. I'm afraid, having entered his private domain as the enemy. A woman to use as he pleases, without regret or remorse.

The comforting habit of tracing my top lip fails to appease the anxiety as edgy anticipation fizzes through my veins. My stomach churns with dread. I slip out of the damp shorts, unbutton the now see-through blouse, and fold them both into a neat pile on the floor. Next, I carefully lower to unwind the straps twisting my sore ankles, letting my bare feet flatten on the softest rug when the espadrilles are finally removed. After revealing my all to him earlier, I'm no longer concerned for my appearance. It gives me a boldness I'm certain he's not expecting.

"Can I have something else to wear?" I say in a whisper, unsure if I'm allowed to speak at this point.

Earthy black eyes study me for the longest moment. Then he begins to drag his own shorts down his powerful thighs. The intensity of his stare never wavering. My neck stretches high in defiance of his strip tease, eyes fixed to his face to prevent my hungry gaze chasing the material.

I've wasted lustful thoughts wondering how magnificent his naked physique would be, and now that he's before me, confident and divine, I like what I'm pretending not to see.

His mouth curls at the side like he's aware I'm refusing to stare at the thick cock hitting his navel. Intimidation is his cruel game of choice this evening.

I have no doubt women drop at his feet, doing whatever he demands in a bid to obey him. He has high expectations woven through his naturally dominant demeanor.

While I struggle to act detached, he lowers to his haunches, collects his shorts, and rises. Then, without a word, he saunters further into the room and disappears around a corner.

In the space he's given me, I realign my impure instincts. He's a murderer and a professional lie detector, apparently. I've nothing to hide, except for the fact he turns me on—even if I detest his intentions.

That alone makes me hate him even more. I was sent here to serve Elias, and now an unhealthy part of me wants to do those very things with his son.

"Carina," his voice calls to me with a firmness I know I shouldn't ignore.

I pad in the same direction as the sound of running water, passing a comfy sitting area by vast windows and finding him in a floor to ceiling granite bathroom, his face impassive.

He's washing his hands under a waterfall faucet, the lever so clean it shines like liquid silver. Behind him, a pair of rain shower heads sprinkle water within a wide open cubicle, meticulously covered in glassy black mosaic tiles. Fluffy white towels are presented on floating shelves beside the deepest freestanding bathtub I've ever seen. Under the babel of rushing water, a far-off melody catches my attention. I glance over my shoulder to the inset flat screen with touch buttons for song selections. The ambience is nothing short of high living.

I stand before him, bare, yet warm from the notable

heat under foot. Watching him quietly watch me, sets me on fire. His chest is silky and solid. Those powerful thighs of his, so thick and muscular. And his substantial cock is a stony masterpiece. Together, they all form one hell of a package that regrettably creates a villain. A man I shouldn't crave like I am.

I despise him for conjuring such a wet heat between my thighs and for testing my self-control. I've never felt anything like this before, so terribly wrong but so very exhilarating. And even if I had of, I wouldn't admit to it.

Without a word, he strolls to me, cuffs my wrist, and leads me to the modern vanity. I catch my reflection in a large mirror built into the wall.

Our reflection.

His flawless appearance and my purplish bruises. My petite stature next to his imperial form. Quite the unmatched pair.

He spins me around, my ass hitting a stone basin. I'd understood torture was his method of extracting the truth. Yet I never dreamed it would be like this, forbidden desires and wild inhibitions. Just the two of us, baring all. My biggest challenge is being vulnerable to his dark temptation.

Tomás reaches for a steel box on the counter, flips the catch and retrieves a pair of latex gloves. I go rigid, my spine locking in a jolt.

"No way… you're not serious. You wouldn't. You can't… I won't let you… this is fucked up… you're fucked up," I say in a rush, throwing my hands up as a barrier.

I'm so tense, even my eyelids fix open. He continues to

squeeze his large hands into the stretchy gloves, linking his covered fingers and rolling his wrists.

"You're a pervert!" I hiss when he slots his hands under my armpits and effortlessly heaves me onto the charcoal countertop.

His thighs brush between mine—skin to skin. The simple touch like an inferno, exploding through my veins with raging heat. The unusual combination of lust and hostility plays havoc with my sensibilities.

I'm hooked on the tingles vibrating inside me. For the first time in my life, I'm finally alive in my own skin. Like the beast that lives inside of him is calling to me, awakening urges I've only dreamed about.

Unfortunately, I appear to exist within his darkened abyss rather than the glorious sunshine.

"Don't touch me." I scowl at him, puffing out my chest and crossing my arms.

Inky eyebrows drift high. "Those goosebumps tell me you love my hands on your skin." He nods to the obvious prickles on my arms, caused only by his sonorous hoarse voice and that body of his presented before me like the god of seduction.

"I don't," I lie with a dismissive grunt. "I'm just cold. Whatever warped challenge you have in mind, forget it."

"What do you think I'm going to do?"

Heat flames my cheeks. "Violate me with those horrible gloves on."

"Violate you?" He muses. "I don't need to violate any woman. They always want what I give them. And I'm starting to think you'll have to beg me." The half-smile he offers flips my belly.

My mouth waters, my core clenches, and I shift from buttock to buttock. "Never."

He cocks his head, running his tongue over his lower lip. "So I can't do this…" His hand slides under my knee, scoops the injured leg higher and sets my foot on his tensed abdomen. The gentle movement reveals my private parts. Such subtle exposure, done so slowly that I could be fooled into thinking he's not abominable. Rather than taking a look, his expression remains blank, drawn to the cuts lining my shin bone.

He leans sideways, grabs a square packet from the container and rips it open with his teeth. Extracting a clinically scented wet wipe, he dabs the crusty wound. I quake. Not from the biting sting, but from the benign manner to which he carries out the task.

This version of my stark-naked captor is utterly perplexing. I've never truly lusted after a man. Not like this. Not in such a way that my dignity is torn to tatters and my sanity questionable.

Yet, at this moment, I'm speechless. Devastated by his tender act of pressing gauze over the cleaned cut and gently securing it to my skin with tape.

The mishmash of this new found benevolence, his rocklike cock proudly on display, and such a haughty disposition, bends my mind.

Once he's done, he lets my foot drop, simultaneously diminishing all contact. He systematically peels off the gloves, turns them inside out, and drops the balled up mess in the trash.

"Thank you," I whisper, unsure if it's appropriate to thank the man holding me prisoner in his bedroom.

Long ebony lashes lift, bringing earthy eyes in line with mine. "Don't thank me." He tidies the area, closes the box, and studies his handiwork in the disconcerting silence. "Tonight, you're in my bed," he says like it's in order. "I don't want my sheets covered in your blood."

9

CARINA

My mind scrambles for words, for a vicious retort. He actually expects me to share a bed with him. While I collect a breath, he doesn't wait to hear what I need to say. He casually strolls to the shower and drenches his head under the jets.

I'm left on the counter, frozen and confused. Bitterly angry and naively offended. He'd given me the night sky, painted it with a trillion stars and then stole them all away.

The voice inside my head warns me of danger. It whispers ideas of sneaking from his room while he's uninterested in my whereabouts. Could I run the risk of bumping into Elias and his trigger-happy tendencies? Or do I spend the night with a man I can't piece together?

I look around the suite, searching for an answer to my dilemma, looking anywhere that isn't the water pouring over manly broad shoulders. His body is magnificent. Unlike anything I've ever seen in the flesh.

Staring at his drenched torso, my hate turns inwards.

My indignation coils with need. "I won't share a bed with you. Take me back to the barn." I drop off the counter and place my feet wide to secure my bold stance.

With a controlled swipe, he drags both hands over his face, flips the lever to cut off the water and prowls from the cubicle. The unrighteousness of this unruly yearning plaits into a noose and slips around my neck. I'm drawn to his every move, spying his tight buttocks as he turns his back to me to fetch a towel. He shakes it out and circles his hips, ignoring me completely.

"I've never even kissed a guy before, so the idea of a psycho like you taking what's not yours is…"

It happens in a blur, a sputter of time. From zero to sixty in a split second. That sublime body of his launches at me, ushering me backward until his palm slams to the tiles and my ass presses against the grout. Our touching skin burns with deadly lust.

"Firstly. Call me a psycho once more and it will be the last word you ever say." I inhale, and so does he. "Secondly, in basic terms, you were given to my father. As you've so adamantly pointed out, you were sent here to fuck him. For your body to serve him. And guess what? He'd rather you were buried under a row of coffee plants." His free hand swathes my throat, raising my chin a notch higher, connecting our gazes. "So from where I'm standing, Carina Ferreira, your life belongs to me, as does this…" His knee nudges into my groin, hard and unyielding. I say nothing, completely dumbstruck. "And for the record, I'm not your Prince Charming, or anyone's, for that matter. If you stare at the sun long enough, you'll go blind." His mouth lingers before mine, teasing and unethical. "I *will* shoot you if I have to. No questions. No regret."

My mouth snaps shut after his admission and my hand flies up to his wrist, wrestling for freedom. I want to slap him, to rip his hands away, and smother the tinder of lust cremating my soul to embers. Solemn dark eyes study me for a fraction of time. His harsh statement murdering my pride like cyanide.

"Now who's the liar?" I strain my neck and thrust my hips, suddenly aware of his steely arousal. "If you were going to kill me, you would have done it already."

I've never had expectations of how I'd eventually fuck a man, or be fucked. I'm not a romantic fool with fanciful notions or a wish for tender loving care. Yet, I didn't expect the call of this man's sadism to resonate so deeply with me.

So when he trails the tip of his tongue over the seam of my upper lip, deliberately tracing the old scar, a dark thread tugs at my core. It snakes around the code of conduct any normal girl would have and chokes it with lust. My skin blazes. His unreadable, wild eyes trap me in place.

"I don't like complications." He hollows my cheeks with the tips of his fingers.

"Are you serious?" I spit, a raging temper barreling from my chest to my voice. "You're the one keeping me here against my will."

Featherlight fingertips trace my collar bone, causing me to tremble. "That's interesting." His solid erection jabs my belly. "I know what you really want," he says close to my lips. "I can sense your lust crawling out of every exquisite cell in your skin. You need me to fuck you, hard and unforgiving. To fill your untouched little pussy with my cum and feel it ooze out as I lick it from you. You crave it, fear it, and can't understand it." His eyes darken, like the depths of a never-ending starless cavern. "But most of all, you think it will bond us. It won't." He licks his lips and I literally feel moisture bloom between my thighs. "Sex is simply chemistry and endorphins. Nothing more, nothing less."

I hate him.

"I don't want anything from you." I swallow the lie in a flustered gulp. "If you want a fight, I'll give you one." My brave snarl is matched with my most hateful glare.

His low hum sizzles over my cheek as a dirty whisper. "Fight me?" He muses, a subtle dent dimpling his cheek. "That will only add to the fun. We both know you'll obey me like your life depends on it."

"Is that so?" I tip into him and reenact the very performance he used to steal my sanity. I lick his pouty bottom lip until he retreats like a strike of lightning—quick and fierce.

I smirk up at him, curiously fascinated, noting his pupils dilate with a thick swirl of smoke.

An unabated growl rumbles in his chest, stimulating the hairs on my scalp. "Ready for your next challenge?"

My muscles tense. He removes his hand from my neck, skates his wicked fingertips over the contour of my breasts, nipples, and belly until they locate the apex of my thighs. A terrible shiver of seduction runs through me, hedonistic and intense with longing. My spine tingles when his mouth opens and he taps the slickness I've no way to hide from.

"I don't need to steal women to enjoy fucking." His chin dips as his fingers glide between my folds. "But the reality of having a sexy little thing like you all to myself for the night, with no complications and no consequences, it's painfully tempting." His mouth moves to the shell of my ear. "Your cheeks are perfectly flushed, because this is turning you on. Isn't it?"

"No…" I whisper, almost inaudibly, my buzzing senses a traitor to my mind.

"You sure about that?" he taunts, fingers roaming through the slickness I'm both thankful for and disgusted with myself for producing. "You're lying. Were you lying to me all this time?

"I've never lied to you." I rush my denial; aware he could snap my neck easily if he thought I'm a traitor.

"Perhaps you really are a devious siren with a fuckable body worth dying inside of." He laughs darkly and my stomach clenches. "It would take an exceptional woman to impress me enough to risk everything. But they don't exist."

Every natural born instinct for survival gets pushed to the side under the weight of the excruciating sexual snare he's caught me in. Nonetheless, I swallow it back and force myself to pretend I'm not a freak lusting for his touch.

"Like you said, there's nothing special about me or my vagina. Let's save us both the embarrassment and call it quits." My voice sounds alien to me, the breathless tone betraying me. "Send me home."

The thrilling sensation of pressure circling my super sensitive nub is pure corruption. I gasp, the back of my head butting the tiles. Urges I never knew existed sprout horns and grow gnashing teeth. Depraved stimulation hurtles my soul towards flames of perpetual insanity. It's exhilarating, unlike anything I've experienced.

"I'll decide if it's good enough for me." He grins, the negligible wink a cruel weapon to slay me with.

"It won't be." I dig my fingernails into my palms to stop a moan from escaping.

"You're not putting up much of a fight, Carina." As he continues to explore, I shudder, strengthening his valid point. "There's nothing about this you don't like. You want me to take control. To force you so you have someone to blame when you come all over my hand."

"I hate you," I spit, instantly sucking in a ragged breath the second he inserts a finger deep inside of me. "Oh my God." My involuntary groan is met with a quiet hiss of his own.

I've never felt anything quite like this before. A girly noise breaks free from my throat, simultaneously matching the thick grunt he offers. I'm moving with the slow rhythm, riding his hand as he closely observes my reaction. I don't want to enjoy the out-of-body experience this man's touch has given me but I can't help myself.

Tomás looms over me, his forehead close to mine. The tips of our noses brush, but our lips stay apart. Alcohol still laces his breath. His eyes, those flinty eyes of his, turn to liquid pools of deadly desire, as if he's loving the dirty interaction as much as me.

He angles his wrist and harshly adds a second finger,

immediately turning me into a mass of mushy flesh with no way of ever escaping this divine torture. My heartbeat takes off when he speaks into my ear with a sinister, yet erotic growl. "Your cunt is so fucking tight. My dick will demolish that purity and stuff it full. I'll enjoy watching my cum spill from your holes and then I'll take my time to feast from each of them."

Unable to avoid the mis-mash of chaotic sensations awakening every nerve ending in my body, my hips involuntarily buck, begging for more, urging him to take me to the supreme heights so I can experience it all. I swat away the nagging voice whispering through my brain, the subconscious thought that reminds me of this man's savage capabilities and his father's homicidal impulses. But I'm too far gone. Drowning in the building frenzy, so much hungrier than a simple need, it's an overpowering compulsion for Tomás Souza.

These are the addictive sensations people lie for—and lie to themselves about. How they crave a stranger's touch and seek the all-consuming kick of adrenaline. Need crackles and spits under my naked flesh. The impatience for a starved release coming at me from within like a thunderbolt. Butterflies crash inside my chest with the sole purpose of taking the climax to another level.

His eyes glow with bane while something carnal simmers beneath the surface. "I could keep going until I hit the right spot. But the question is, do you deserve pleasure or was it your flimsy plan to seduce me all along?" His voice is hoarse, like a tornado of sand sucking me in just to spit me out. "Are you working for Carlos Blanco?"

My swollen insides demand his fingers to move inside me, sucking around them tightly in the hope he'll continue. "I've never heard that name before. I don't work for anyone," I pant, my vision blurring.

He grits his teeth, gradually removing his fingers like the very act pains him. For a moment, I think I'll combust from the unsatisfied emptiness until he makes an odd noise. From my vulnerable position, I witness his entire persona shadow in an aura of smoky black horror. He stills before me, muscles absolutely rigid and fingers splayed.

My brows snap together when he staggers backward, staring at feminine essence marbled with blood.

He hesitates as if his lungs have decompressed. His avid scrutiny is so focused on the slight red staining that I'm unsure how to react.

I had warned him of my sexual innocence. It's not a crime for the first encounter to be messy. But his eyes, his posture, his silence—it has my nerves on edge and my heart in my mouth.

There's a palpable hush in which Tomás glares at his fingers as if he's slipping into a disturbed version of himself. A version unlike the suave god I'm used to. In a millisecond, lust is wiped from his eyes and he transforms into a glowering beast, any shred of decorum gone.

"Fuck!" His nostrils flare, and the main vein in his corded throat pulsates like a leash tugging at his fraying humanity.

His hands shake and clench into fists, the muscles in his arms working hard to stay tight. Veins pump under his golden skin and his chest lifts as he sucks in through his teeth.

I remember Shane's comment, how the man before me loses his shit if he gets covered in blood.

He's dangerous.

Rather than feed the flames of desire, he's preparing to detonate contempt from within. He's going to blow us both to smithereens with a grenade of rage.

I sway, ready to flee, yet unsure of where to go. A flicker of a thought dances into my frozen mind. Distract him from the blood.

So I do the only thing I can think of. I sink to my knees, loosen the towel from his angular hips, and face his imperial cock. The instant my fingers skim the satiny skin, it switches from hard to stone. Angry crimson flesh oozes pearly pre-cum, the liquid glistening under twinkly recessed downlights. The shiny crown looks inviting, the girth intimidating. Flutters in my stomach fight for a way out, just as enamored by it as I am.

Kneeling before him, I lift my gaze to search his, to anchor him in place before me. He senses the hunt. His narrowed eyes, vicious and tyrannical, immediately cut to mine, leading him from the void he's lost in.

Something familiar feathers around the awareness of us. An inexplicable feeling that winds around one girl's affliction and this man's unspoken tribulation. I get the impression we're both damaged and astray in darkness. Perhaps that's why I'm so drawn to him. Our connection transcends the normal, with both of us wholly unbalanced.

My hands tremble at the recklessness of my snap decision. I'm somehow demented with lust, my pulse hammering fast.

Without direction, I do what comes naturally, flicking my tongue over the bulging tip. The second my salvia connects, his sturdy legs brace. A monster in the hands of an untainted woman. A woman who's feeding off her desires.

I savor the salty fluid, hearing his sharp intake of air. That secret gasp alone ignites a greedier arousal within me and gives me the incentive to continue. He growls low and foreboding, entranced by my experiment.

As soon as I wedge the entire thing in my throat, his regal crown slips into the gutter. Ruthless hands dive into my messy hair, fisting the lengths to force himself in that little bit further.

I gag around the overstuffed intrusion, spittle leaking from the corners of my stretched mouth. When I pull back, he restrains my head, locking me in place. Long legs cage me against the wall with his cock so deep, tears stream from my eyes. His hips begin to piston, the art of fucking my face his crude savior.

"That's it… take it all. Choke on my dick, *little liar*." His low baritone rumbles from his mouth in a breath, as if he says the words against his will.

His order drives me wild. Heedful of how much this sinner is seeking refuge in my innocent mouth. I moan with a packed gullet, sending vibrations from me to him. He clutches tighter. Such a sharp grip around my roots gives way to more heady chills. The more I moan, the harder he fucks until my jaw is covered in saliva and I'm blinking tears.

On my knees, I willingly surrender to his manic plunder, getting off on the thrill. Though desperately seeking a friction of my own. The urgency for my release makes me wetter than ever, swollen, and voracious in my pursuit to suck him off.

His mouth contorts to a snarl, his thrusts merciless. As his cock plunges in hard and fast, he fixes me with the sexiest look. Pure white teeth capture his lower lip in the dirtiest way and the filthiest grunt works its way through his throat.

"Get yourself off," he growls, the order hissing out behind his teeth. "Be a good girl and put your hand between your legs. Touch yourself. I'm going to cum in your throat any second and you won't waste a single drop."

The bold woman I've become is no longer self-conscious or riddled with shame. She's empowered and drunk on the idea of sex. I'm swept up in the heat of it all, in the intensity of our fused gaze. His dark eyes drill into mine on a collision course for an explosion.

"Do it," he barks with a fierceness bordering on a howl.

I obey without delay, fondling myself like I've done so many times alone. I'm drenched, my body parts sensitive to the touch, and my jaw aching. Rubbing my clit has me craving the brutality of his thickness. I crave more of him. The forbidden taste of his cum and his power. Blindly banishing rights and wrongs. Surrendering to the high. This is so wrong.

It doesn't take long for Tomás to detonate. The savage growl crumbling his self-discipline turns his eyes feral.

When he lets go, warm cum erupts in spurts almost choking me. I gag and writhe on my knees, exhaling a guttural hum when my own orgasm hits with force. My thighs go rigid with the powerful energy bursting inside my core.

When I'm all spent, he pulls his cock free and fists the length to expel the final dregs one my lips. A salty bead proudly remains on the glossy crown until I lap it up.

We both breathe hard, staring at each other in the aftermath. My fingertips reach for my lip in comfort, unsure of what will happen next. He mutters under his breath and takes a notable step towards the vanity.

A part of me wants to be ravaged right here on the floor. The other part hopes he'll simply kiss me. My horny state revs at a million seconds per minute. I know it's a foolish wish. A mishmash of toxic confusion where intimacy doesn't lead to an affinity, or a promise of freedom. I'm just a girl who's found satisfaction in the wrong man.

He turns on his heels and storms to the sink, methodically foaming his hands with liquid soap. Over and over.

I sit on my haunches, subconsciously tracing my Cupid's bow, watching Tomás wash his face and blot it dry. Glancing back over his shoulder, he stares at me for a heartbeat and then tosses the towel. "Clean yourself up." His head rotates, and he glares at his handsome reflection in the mirror. "Thoroughly," he adds, his voice clipped and to the point.

My limbs go weak from his detached demeanor and seemingly unaffected stroll through the bathroom. Before he exits, he says quietly, "And don't get the dressing wet."

I could scream at my captor, beg him to fuck me, and

chase his cock for fulfillment, but I'd never reduce myself to those levels. He expects groveling and obedience, so I'll bite my tongue. I caution myself on how immoral this journey actually is and wait for the opportunity to escape.

My hormones are to blame. They'd taken control of my senses. The female frenzy came alive when his turbulent disposition spoke to me. Now I'm all alone on the bathroom floor, cold, used, and emotionally confused.

Anxiety flips my stomach. How the hell would I get through the night with this impenetrable man?

10

CARINA

Steamy showers used to relax me. Until I was hosed down like a filthy slave in broad daylight.

An hour later, I'm under a hot waterfall balancing on one leg with my injured shin hanging out of the flow. I'm both hiding from my recent indiscretion and celebrating it.

Dirty memories whirl with the mist--my actions unfabled. I had inhaled a glorious cock before experiencing a meaningful kiss. The irony isn't missed. Why would my damaged lip require tenderness when all it's known is suffering?

My nerves won't settle, and my fingers have wrinkled from staying under the steady stream for too long.

Tomás may well be waiting for his unsullied prisoner to join him in the bedroom, but I'm not ready to face him. Not yet. I'm unsure how long I've taken solace in his bathroom, with creamy suds and the door shut. Me on the inside, trapped and edgy, and him on the other side, prowling like a beautiful beast.

The cold-hearted gangster had taken what I offered, then brushed it off as insignificant. That's how he rolls. How men who possess everything treat women who have nothing—with a callous, cruel temperament, ownership, and orders.

If I'm to survive this journey, the sooner I understand his intentions, the better. He's not the master of my life—he's the anti-hero I should run from. Those boundaries are clear. Scraped into the dirt with sharp stakes and sealed with my blood.

We are enemies. Not lovers.

Stepping out of the shower, shivery, clean, and free of lust, I swaddle up in a soft towel and stare at the young woman in the mirror. I'm washed out, drained of color. Disheveled sable lengths undulate over my covered breasts and my pouty lips are bruised red. I still look the same on the outside, even if desire had overshadowed me earlier.

I'm so tired and nauseous; deprived of a decent meal and a safe bed to sleep in. The latter being one I no longer wish for. I doubt he expects me to rest in that king-size bed with virginal sheets.

My cheeks blush a shade darker than rose. The prospect of Tomás fucking me isn't quite as daunting as it should be. I swallow down a lump of guilt stuck in my throat. This isn't a situation to get comfortable in, even if my armor has turned wafer thin.

Unable to ignore my overspent energy any longer, I rough dry my hair and comb the damp strands with my fingers. Then I stare at the closed door and debate opening it. I step closer, fingering the handle only to retreat, skirting the wall until I'm wedged into a corner.

In another world, this shower room would be sexy with its dark edges and heated floor. The grim reality is there's only one exit which leads me to the devil.

Exhaustion plays with gravity, dragging me downward. I tuck my thighs close and rest my chin on my knees. All the events leading up to this point crash over me in ice cold waves. Fretful tears spill from my eyes and muted sobs shake my shoulders. Have I really lost everything? My brother. My mentor. My life.

There, huddled on the floor, I wish for somewhere to lay my head that isn't in Tomás Souza's noose. Then I pass out.

The first thing I feel is weightlessness. Floating. Body heat. The smoothest skin. After a sleepy sigh, I'm bouncing on a mattress.

I jackknife to sit, my eyelashes simultaneously springing open. My sedate heart rate jerks to manic when I see him. All my muscles brace as I lock eyes with my antagonist.

Tomás Souza wears silky boxer shorts the color of the night sky and an unimpressed scowl.

I freeze, refusing to say a word. A towel still covers my bruises and keeps his eyes primed on my face. The grogginess from my nap switches to hyper aware and my throat stings from his deep throat thrusting. I'm pretty sure if I speak, my voice will be rougher than broken glass.

He looms over me, every bit the regal criminal I suspect him to be. Exhaustion clots my anger. If I had the ability to set him on fire with my glare, he'd be a heap of ashes. I shimmy backward and slide my ankles under my buttocks so I'm upright.

Just because I'm partially naked, on a four-poster bed where rich cotton sheets beneath me feel like heaven, doesn't mean this setting resembles a bridal suite, or anything even close. His masculine room within this immense house is simply a showy prison cell. The walls are lined with drug money and the foundations built upon lost lives in cartel gang wars.

As he stares at me with his earthy black eyes, I'm overwhelmed by the distinct feeling he's about to devour me. Neither of us break the uncomfortable silence. A deadly hush heightens the sound of my pulse hitting its maximum tempo.

Adrenaline courses through my poor veins, pumping harder and faster to keep me both alert and focused on Tomás' every move. I'm aware how each breath expands his lungs and how his ribcage lifts ever so slightly. So when he folds his arms and moves a hand to his mouth, I witness every curved muscle work under his unyielding authority.

I squirm while watching how he casually thumbs his bottom lip, his unprincipled mind running wild. He moves closer to the bed, the front of his legs butting the frame and his entire body stiff like he's fighting control. The tenseness of his physique has me petrified.

He could kill me—and no one would know. No one in this house would shed a tear or fight for my redemption. It could be that simple. That quick and heartless.

I wonder what he's endured in life to choose the path of a villain rather than a prince. How the sight of blood doesn't bother him in the slightest, but its presence on his skin flips a switch. I wish I had the answers to understand my nemesis better, or to remove him from under my skin.

Either way, his taunting gaze has me blushing from my toes to my throat. His eyes glint under the lamplight like a secret treasure unearthed in a shipwreck on the seabed of a turbulent ocean. The shadowy pigment catches specks of gold, each one swirling in the depths like a part of him seeks salvation.

Inwardly, I chant unkind words to train my mind into thinking he's vile. Except descriptions of demonic, disgusting, and loathsome—they're all lies. Diabolical untruths I can't stand behind with vigor.

Regretfully, the outer shell of Tomás Souza leaves me speechless. The athletic package is every girl's fantasy. Until you dig deeper into his cavernous chest where his dead heart hangs. That coal textured muscle belongs in a predator to match the flash of fire behind his eyes.

Slowly, he lowers his hand and wets his lips with his tongue. "You'll be glad those boys didn't waste your time with childish kisses." He sounds tired and tortured, as if he's spent too many nights searching for a high that doesn't exist. A euphoric thrill that surpasses narcotics, alcohol, and sex.

Perhaps he's finally found it in the control he has over me. "You deserve a man. A man who will teach you obedience and match your fight. A man who will fuck you properly."

"And you're that man?" I say indignantly, scampering off the bed and glancing at the locked door.

A grunt bursts from the back of his throat, almost in a laugh without giving it the light of day. "Going somewhere?"

"Getting off on your new perversion?" I retort, crossing my arms over by breasts.

His bare feet slap the tiles as a furious storm of musk and flesh lunges at me.

I dart sideways.

He easily catches me.

My heart leaps into my mouth when he grips my throat and reverses me into the wall. His solid form pins me in place and in a fleeting second, I witness his shoulders prickle with goosebumps.

I smother his wrist with my palm and dig short nails into his skin, helplessly trying to free the hold. His unforgiving grip makes it difficult to swallow until I stop struggling.

The second I surrender; the harsh pressure weakens and the lump in my throat freely bobs against his palm.

"I hate you," I hiss with venom.

He stays perfectly still. Our bodies pressed together, my chin elevated, and our eyes locked on each other's.

"You think I'm the bad guy, right?" His mouth dips to the side of my face. "So, why do you look at me the way you do?" His husky voice catapults tingles over my scalp. "Why did you inhale my dick like it was your last fucking meal if you hate me so much?"

I try to break our fiery connection by looking away. "It's called survival."

He nudges my jaw, realigning my gaze with his, and cocks an eyebrow. "Do you think kneeling before me with your fuckable mouth and sexy golden eyes would spare your life, or worse, that I'd choose to keep you in my bed?" His mouth closes in on my ear. Warm breath welcomes a deceiving shudder, and my skin visibly prickles.

I bare my teeth. "I'd rather stitch my mouth shut than let you do that to me again. The only reason I sucked you off was that familiar look in your eyes. You were wrangling demons and couldn't find a way out of your head. In hindsight, it was a stupid move." Our gazes clash, rich molasses to spirited amber. "I regret every second of it," I lie.

We stare at each other without speaking. Only our chests collide as we inhale and exhale in tandem. My pulse jumps when his head tilts a fraction. A slow, featherlight finger traces my sternum, becoming idle at the seam of the towel shielding gooseflesh.

"Is that so?"

"Strap me up to a lie detector test." My left eyebrow hitches. "Oh wait, that's not your style. You'd rather use wild animals."

I return his cryptic glare, my hateful glower shooting trillions of frozen arrows that only melt in the tempting heat his body radiates. We both hesitate in a defiant standoff—me unwilling to show my freakish emotions, and him quietly calm except for the solid arousal stabbing my hip. Sparks ignite from skin to skin.

Before I can question his silent assessment, he strips the towel from me in one firm, abrupt act. I hear it swoosh and land beside us. I'm on fire. The insanity of his magnetism sizzles under my skin. It's uncontrollable—a vapor of intrigue, so toxic and hedonistic.

"I'll put a million dollars wager on your tight little cunt being perfectly wet all over again." A ghost of a smile plays out before me, then vanishes. "Your body delivers a different message than your mouth. Those hard nipples and sexy as fuck moans were all signs of how turned on you were. Isn't that right, Carina Ferreira from Manaus?"

When I narrow my eyes at him, his own turn feral. "That doesn't mean I like you. I'm not crazy."

"Perhaps you're not crazy, but I am."

Then, for the first time in my life, violent lips descend. They crash on top of mine. A bullish tongue drives inside so our saliva becomes a hybrid of corruption and seduction. He tastes of sweet alcohol and ruined decadence.

My limbs are fluid. No longer owning the power to fight against this man. The pathetic heart hammering in my chest levitates in a coffin of danger. Yet it doesn't wilt, it oscillates with passion.

I want his lips. I want all of him.

I'm a melting pot of hormones, adrenaline, and anger. His urgency nearly chokes me with a divine tongue. I whimper, loving and despising it all at once.

He releases a hungry groan into my mouth, firing up all sorts of unwanted impulses. When I shunt my hips into him, he presses his weight into me and deepens the kiss. On one side, a large palm skates to my cheek. On the other, ruthless fingers weave into my hair, adjusting the position of my head to fully control me.

His lips hijack my mind.

His influence becomes my drug.

His sinful flavor monopolizes my senses.

As if it's a dream, the heat of our kiss evaporates. His fingers still hold straggly strands of my hair, but the slight space allows me a second to suck in a gulp of oxygen. Pitch black pupils become a firestorm as if havoc reigns within his twisted mind.

Beyond the intensity of my stunned silence, a phone is ringing. The intrusive melody bursts through the fog of harrowing lust, rotating around us like a tornado.

"Hold that thought." Tomás drags the pad of his middle finger over my thin scar. "Get into bed," he orders, his husky timbre so potent that my belly flips.

When he steps away, I'm still pinned to the wall with failing stamina. Shock debilitates my entire body. He owns too many of my firsts—my first kiss, my first unbalanced attraction, and my first ever eruption of intense flutters. And those are just for starters.

Tomás strolls across the room, with his silky covered ass to me and his broad shoulders rolled back with confidence.

"André, perfect timing, as usual." He glances over his shoulder, soldering me in place with a fiery scowl that quickly cuts to the bed in a non-verbal instruction. "You're supposed to be in Miami, Dré." He continues to talk while opening a vast see-through door. "What the fuck are you doing in Vegas?" There's a playfulness to his voice, almost jovial. Is it possible the devil understands how to forge relationships? "I can't fly out," he continues. "Not after Papá took out one of Morales' guys in the fucking dining room. He's started a war with the Mexicans." He's quiet for a beat. "I won't let Blanco move in on the Mexicans. It's crucial we keep the smuggling tunnel from Tijuana into the US."

That's the last thing I hear before he puts double glazed glass, space, and time between us. I follow the straight lines of the wall with my spine pressed to the plaster. When I reach the only exit, my hand hesitates at the brass handle. Freedom isn't behind the door—it's a shot in the dark—a maze of corridors and acres of land.

It would only take one call from Tomás to order my assassination. One bullet in my brain to finish this. Or one deranged drug lord to catch me creeping through his home like the spy he thinks I am.

Not that I have the choice to debate an escape—Tomás has already removed the key from the keyhole.

I really am his prisoner.

My forehead nudges ridges of wood when I tip into the door for support. Lack of food has diminished my energy levels and my overworked brain is cloudy.

His baritone carries from the terrace like far off thunder, the words indecipherable. In my exhausted state, the master bed, with its trickery of sumptuous pillows for a peaceful rest, calls to me.

Accepting the unusual circumstances, I cover the soft rug underfoot, roll back the Egyptian cotton bed linen and climb onto the royal mattress. Warmth caresses my bare skin like a much needed hug. A hug I wish came from my mother's arms--or my brother's. On that woeful thought, my ribs tighten and a wave of nausea reminds me of this hazardous reality. There's no love to be found within these walls.

I angle my pelvis in the direction of the terrace, locking my eyes on the silhouette prowling back and forth outside. Something tells me it's going to be a long night.

There's no doubt Tomás is sexually experienced. It's a cruel twist for such natural beauty to bestow a man with zero principles and temptation as a wicked skill. The awareness of his indecent past rattles through me.

Comforted by the fact I'm occupying a bed and not a chilly stable, I sigh in a gust and wonder why he's gone against his father's wishes by escorting me indoors to his private sanctuary. Perhaps he gets off on rebellion. Charlatan butterflies assemble in my chest, inciting a flit of fascination.

Maybe fucking him is a risk I'm prepared to enjoy. I groan inwardly and punch the downy pillow to appease my temper. This man is a brutal gang member. He's a murderer, for goodness' sake.

Those conflicting thoughts fight for leadership, each of them chasing the other. Short minutes burn into ashes. Time flurries in a muddle of mixed emotions. The false cocoon of snugness tugs my eyelashes so they drift closed.

Once again, I fall asleep.

11

CARINA

A ghastly night terror of fierce flames and never-ending darkness becomes unbearable. I jerk awake like the devil stabbed me with a pitchfork.

My lungs scream for oxygen, thankful when I inhale deeply. I blink quickly and gaze up at the ceiling, tainted with a salmon blush streaming in from the windows. The early rise of a glorious sunrise brightens the spacious bed I've woken up in.

Curled up on my side, I freeze, the memories of my encounter with Tomás swarming over me in a tingly rash. I tentatively stretch out my leg, cautiously moving it across the mattress. Rather than finding him, my daring search continues until I'm certain the opposite side is empty.

He's not in this bed—we didn't have sex—he didn't wake me.

The mattress beneath me holds secrets of a night I'd slept through. Did Tomás lay beside me at all? I sit upright and hear only the thump of my pulse.

The morning light is cheerful. A welcome to the oppressive shadows I've spent too long in lately. To my right, the expanse where I'd expected him to be is neat and the pillow undented.

My body tenses, ready to shatter like a brittle statue. Something isn't right. The fogginess of my sleepy mind is busy mulling over why he didn't pursue me—why he didn't screw my brains out. Whereas my achy, bruised limbs are gradually moving, waiting for danger to pounce.

When the soles of my feet hit the floor, the quick rise of my chest isn't a hitch of breath. It couldn't be from disappointment after a night of safety rather than hours of sexual exploitation, so it must be out of relief. That's what I tell myself when I pat the scar on my lip, wrap a sheet around me and pad to the bathroom on my tiptoes.

The door is wide open, showing the space is unoccupied. I rest a shoulder on the doorframe and consider my next move. If he's not here, then maybe he left the door unlocked.

I gather the Egyptian cotton train trailing behind me and hurry to the exit, too foolish and hopeful. There's no key, yet that doesn't stop me from yanking the handle and rattling the secured doors in the hope they'd magically part.

Bastard.

The clothes I'd left in a pile have gone, as if I haven't been here. Swallowing my nerves, I begin a quest to find another way out. Doing a one-eighty, I make a beeline for the window separating me from the sprawling wilderness and press my fingertips to the glass. The pretty view fogs from the adrenaline puffing down my nostrils.

There's no sign of him on the balcony, so I push the weighty panel sideways and step into a tangerine sunrise, scented with an earthy waft of vegetation.

Delicately fragranced roses teeming with dainty orchids, grow in huge terracotta pots. To my right, sky blue water twinkles in a jacuzzi and a duo of sun loungers look out toward the misty mountains.

He's disappeared.

A chalky wall slashes the impressive view of the Souza estate in half. Alpine evergreens blanket far-off hills. The daunting expanse leaves little opportunity for an immediate getaway without packing supplies for a week-long trek. A chorus of early morning birdsong harmonizes with the rhythm of my panicky heartbeat.

I peer over the balcony to assess the drop. Only a deranged person would try to scale a trellis woven with blood red petals and thorns. Or someone whose life depends on it.

Trimmed shrubs in full bloom and tropical trees border a pebbled path snaking a palatial garden like a winding river. It's ironic how such elegance is appreciated by brutal men, or perhaps it's the feminine influence of Tomás' mother. Another perplexing character I've yet to meet. Something tells me I'm better off never coming face to face with her.

I trace my Cupid's bow out of habit and squeeze my eyes shut to appreciate the familiar aroma of the jungle. Tomás may well have awoken the sexual woman inside of me, but I don't need a man to spin a web of temptation and think it's his right to trap me. It's not. None of this is right. Whether I'm captivated by his mystery or not.

It's my decision whether I lay with a sinner or saint. And right now, I'd rather get the hell out of here and return to the Oasis to search for my brother.

I'm almost certain, if I surrender my virginity to Tomás, it would be the best experience of my life. However, I'm also positive it would be my biggest regret for the short span of time he'd keep me alive thereafter.

He's not my hero.

Besides, I'm not his virgin to do with as he pleases.

Psyched with a buzz of survival, I move inside on the hunt for clothes. That's when I find his real lair. A walk-in closet, five times bigger than a working-class person's home.

LED lights under towering cabinets automatically turn on the instant I pull open the door. Rows of suits hang with irritating precision and racks of unworn designer shoes reach to the ceiling. A central island with a glass top houses designer watches. After an awestruck mental count, I tally fifteen and a tray of jeweled cufflinks sparkling under their own spotlight.

I finger the luxurious suit fabrics, designer sportswear and baseball caps that don't quite fit his business-like persona. It's clear to me there's more to the one-dimensional man I've met. The sexy masculine scent of his cologne hangs in the air, along with the vision of absolute wealth. Tomás has it all—looks, lifestyle and luxury.

Stopping at a custom made chest of drawers, I peer inside where layers of black t-shirts are professionally folded as if new. Unraveling the king-size sheet I'd slept in, I let it puddle to the floor. The t-shirt I've picked is silky soft against my skin when it slips over my head, the size far too big. It's like an obsidian nightdress of seductive nightmares, manly and forbidden all at once.

After a hurried scavenge, I step into his track pants and choose a pair of *his* socks. Everything in this walk-in is him. All of him.

Dressed in his clothes, my gaze reverts back to the display of designer items lit up like treasure. It's only then, from this angle, that I see car keys. Three sets of fobs with logos on each.

Ferrari.

Maserati.

Bentley.

All of them are methods of liberation.

The exhilaration I feel in this moment is wrongly shadowed by another emotion—a sinking calamity, an embittered regret. I stupidly wish Tomás Souza had finished what he had threatened. My thoughts aimlessly wander to the darkest part of my mind, to forbidden climaxes and wicked stolen kisses.

I quickly suck in a steadying breath and snap myself out of the silly daydream. A sigh escapes me and I round my shoulders. My head shakes at my ignorance as I flip up the see-through lid.

It doesn't matter which fob I steal, or which car I select for my getaway. A man with money to burn would buy a replacement before I've eaten my next meal.

The facts are, if I don't get out of here, I'm a dead woman. My natural instincts to survive are stronger than any fleeting fascination. So what if he let me sleep in his bed all night? There's clearly a calculated method to his unnerving plan. And I'm not prepared to hang around to find out what challenge comes next.

I take one last look at the opulent suite before meeting the wall on the terrace and checking for any sign of life below. Certain his armed guards aren't close by, I climb up onto the ledge and squint as the blinding ball of golden fire kisses the high level mist.

Rotating my body, I gradually lower to my belly so my legs dangle and my toes feel out a foothold in the flimsy frame of climbing roses. My heart is beating so fast, making me lightheaded. Sweaty palms make the descent more precarious. The weight of the fob in my pocket reminds me of the half thought out plan I've put into motion. To leave the Souza behind in a cloud of dust raked up from the spinning wheels of a Maserati—if I have enough time to find the car garage and creep under the radar of the surveillance cameras.

My teeth bite down as I concentrate. One wrong step and I'd likely break a bone, putting an end to any chance of an eager getaway. The second my foot rests on the gravel, my pulse picks up speed. I crouch low to hide from the windows beneath the terrace. At this angle, I don't see any outside security cameras, nor do I hear any movement.

After tucking strands of unkempt hair behind my ears, I stare at my shaky hands. It's all or nothing. Now or never.

I take a moment to breathe and scan the manicured garden for a glimpse of human life. Once I'm certain there's no one around to see me escape, I scramble on hands and knees under the windowsills. There has to be a garage where cars are parked out of sight.

Rounding the side of the mansion, I recognize the stone archway leading to the barn I was held in, but it's in the distance. And I'm out in the open. A badly dressed stranger who'll be visible to any of the working staff or eagle-eyed henchmen if I continue.

Nonetheless, I gulp down jaggy fear and run. I dart across the gravel, feeling gritty stones burrow into the soles of my already achy feet. If I make it to the barn, I can hide in a stable, catch my breath, and think of a winning plan.

"DON'T FUCKING MOVE." A masculine voice riddled with bitter authority booms through the stillness. "Take one more step and it'll be your last. Put your hands where I can see them."

The second I obey, Elias storms into view dressed in casual creamy slacks and a baby pink linen shirt. "Where do you think you're going, huh?" His accusing tone slithers over me in a shiver. He reaches behind his back and produces a handgun. "I knew I should've killed you yesterday. My gut is *never* wrong. And here you are. A rogue motherfucking *puta* in my territory who thinks she can get the better of the Souzas."

His silvery gaze roams from unbrushed tendrils to the sports socks on my sore feet. The silent assessment swallowing the baggy clothes belonging to his son. "Why are you out here?" On that last word, he aims the barrel of his gun at my chest. "Never mind. Tomás was going to kill you after breakfast. I'll save him the hassle and finish you now."

"Papá!" The crunch of determined footsteps carries in the pause between life and death.

Tomás appears from under the archway, every determined step spitting up tiny stones in his wake. One step behind him, Shane whips off his reflective aviators and pockets them in an untucked tribal print shirt, his eyes narrowed and unreadable. The second I see them, my ribs tighten.

Tomás' stubble appears darker. The diamonds in his earlobes catch the sunlight, a contrast to his pitch-black stare. He's dressed casually, wearing a baseball cap that shades his eyes, and low slung jersey shorts sitting below bare washboard abs.

For a fleeting beat of time, fear feathers with desire. Yet his stern expression doesn't falter, doesn't soften, nor does it offer me any hint of compassion.

Without saying another word, he stands by his father's side. "What's going on?"

Elias laughs darkly. "Just in time, son. This angel faced traitor was spying on us. She's even wearing your clothes."

Tomás rolls his neck and scratches his jaw. "I brought her inside last night, Papá." He glances over at me, then seizes the gun from his father's hand. "She was in my bed last night."

"You fucked her?" Elias narrows his eyes.

Rather than deny it, Tomás simply shrugs. I swallow hard, my veins scorching and my mind spinning. I'm so confused.

Fury contorts Elias' mouth as he makes a blood curdling growl. "Christ, Tomás. I thought André was the whore hungry Souza. Why the hell did you fuck her in my house?"

"I was bored. Anyway, I can fuck whoever the hell I want. You taught me well, Papá." Tomás repositions the cap on his head and shoves the gun in the waistband of his shorts. "And now I'm getting rid of her like you asked."

"You should have slit her throat last night. Fuck knows who's she contacted. Don't forget who runs the show around here. You…" Elias stabs the air with his finger. "You do what I fucking tell you to do. Give me the gun, Tomás. I'll end this bullshit once and for all."

Taloned fingers of anxiety squeeze my ribs, puncturing my lungs, and robbing me of breath. I stagger backward, gauging my chance to run. My gaze darts from Tomás to Shane, and returns to the devil demanding my death.

Tomás nudges his father's elbow and guides him a few paces away from me. "I'll deal with her. It's under control, Papá," he says through gritted teeth, his spine poker straight.

Elias shirks his arm free. "I gave you twenty-four hours to find out if she's working for Blanco and you fucked the bitch instead. You let your dick jeopardize everything."

"Look…" Tomás' persona changes from amicable, a veil of darkness creeping over his features. "Maria Rebello sent the girl here because your dick screwed her mother. This one is an innocent. She knows fuck all about Blanco or anything else we do."

"She's a liar," Elias hisses, with an angry vein popping at his temple. "You screwed the enemy."

"No, Papá. I fucked around with the enemy, so she'd trust me, and now you're messing up my plans." His admission rattles me. I clutch my stomach as he continues to speak. "Go back inside and get washed up for breakfast. I'll join you when I'm done."

Elias angles into his son's personal space and juts out his hand. "Give me the gun. That's an order."

"I said I'd deal with it," Tomás growls low and foreboding, his fists clenching.

"Gun. Now!" Elias snarls, his face turning crimson with anger.

I immediately scan the area, adrenaline pumping in my veins. In a blur of panting breaths and racing heartbeats, Tomás snaps the weapon from his waistband and points it right at me.

We've finally reached a deadly impasse. The rebellious Prince is ready to prove himself worthy.

I shudder when our eyes lock. My knees go weak when I notice the slight squeeze of his chest and the subtle flare of his nostrils. I shake my head from side to side, desperately wishing a stranger would pick my life over his own flesh and blood. There's a tremble to his hand that quickly rectifies itself, and then he pulls the trigger.

Searing pain splinters through me like scorching lava erupting from a sleepy volcano. A loud breath expels my lungs in a gust of shock. The force of a speeding bullet clipping my shoulder knocks me off balance.

My vision blurs and my knees give way. The floaty sensation of falling brutally meets a million stabbing stones. All of them burrowing into my heavy torso.

The high sun eclipses behind a broad silhouette. Rather than pinpoint the man who shot me, my terrified gaze settles on Shane who's with me in a second. Cigarette smoke billows around him and ash twirls in the breeze.

I freeze in utter fear, feeling the weight of a large palm press down on my sternum after he crouches beside me. I'm immobilized by the searing pain rocketing through my biceps and the pressure of his large hand.

He whips his sunglasses from his eyes, lowers his face. "Stay down," he says quietly, the breath releasing a cloud of thick smoke. My eyeballs widen like glassy marbles as I quietly hold his stare. Warm fingers move across my throat. "Good shot, Tommy," he shouts, drilling his green eyes into mine like he's sending me a subliminal message. "She's a goner. I'll dispose of the body before I drive to Bogotá. Save me some breakfast for the road."

I hear clapping as if the final curtain has fallen, and the show is over. A single tear escapes the corner of my eye. I remain where I am, perfectly still, with blood oozing and a tangle of emotions twisted around my heart like choking vines.

"Well done, son. You always fall in line, eventually. Next time, don't fucking hesitate or I'll shoot you instead. Now, tell me about your mother. Have you seen her this week?"

I close my eyes and try to control my breathing. Nausea roils in my stomach. A wash of sweat drenches my brow as I bravely pretend to be dead.

Shane rises, his weight on me vanishes. Yet, I still don't move. I feel numb beneath the hum of confusion festering under my skin. Anesthetized by the actions of a man who had tried to steal my life—and failed. He shot me. Tomás was going to kill me all along.

"Don't move, kid." Shane flicks his cigarette butt away. "As soon as they're out of sight, we'll hit the road. I'll drop you off in the city if you promise to behave."

I whimper, choking on a hiccupping sob. I've no right to feel betrayed. He didn't claim me as his. Hell, he didn't even want to fuck me after all of his threats. Nonetheless, I'm left bereft of a dumb fantasy with a beast toying with me for intel. Once he'd realized I didn't hold the secrets he wanted, his interest waned.

Tomás Souza is a callous bastard.

12

CARINA

After a clump of gauze is roughly stuck to my shoulder with tape, Shane manhandles me into the passenger seat of a glossy SUV. He turns on the radio and controls the volume from the steering wheel, making sure it is high enough to drown out the possibility of any conversation.

I don't mind. I'm not in the mood to talk, anyway. For the first couple of hours, I drift in and out of consciousness. In the moments I'm awake, I watch the world whizz past the window like a blurry television screen, and when sleep takes over, I wrongly relive the sexual snare Tomás trapped me with.

Asshole.

Even if I meet him thousands of years from now, it would still be too soon.

We stop off at a gas station to refuel. From the passenger seat of the SUV, I study Shane through the tinted glass, wondering why he'd saved me. It doesn't add up. He'd lied to Tomás and Elias—for me. A girl he doesn't know.

I thought about running while he paid for the fuel, but my gut told me to stay seated and get answers.

When he jumps into the driver's seat, he tosses a bottle of water at me and a massive bag of potato chips. It isn't exactly nourishment, but the saltiness helps to perk me up a bit.

The rest of the ride is accompanied by the sultry voice of Chris Stapleton and the not so harmonious tone of Shane's backup vocals. We've been on the road for hours now. I subconsciously feel the car slow to a halt and reluctantly bring my awareness back to my stark reality, city lights, and the sign for Bogotá.

Seething fury still ripples in an undercurrent of unanswered questions. "Why are you doing this?" I finally ask. "Why did you pretend I was dead?"

Shane keeps his green gaze fixed on the windshield and his hands on the wheel. "If I ever find out you really *were* a threat to my family, I'll kill you myself. Understood?"

"Family?" My forehead scrunches. "You're Irish."

"Tommy, your hero for whatever reason, is my cousin."

"Hero?" I scoff. "Are we talking about the same gangster who shot me?"

He shakes his head and chuckles. "Shot you. Christ, that's only a scratch, kid. Next to his brother Gio, Tommy has sniper precision. He never misses or wastes a slug."

"I don't understand." My face pales, shell-shocked by Shane's testimony.

"All you need to know is that you're alive." He sighs. "Because of Tommy."

Shane reaches across my thighs and pops open the

glove compartment. Inside there's a gun, a plastic pouch, a packet of smokes and a clear bag of grass. "Take that. It's yours." He points to the fat pouch.

I wince into the movement and retrieve it using my good arm. It's not sealed, making it easy to see crisp, unused notes tucked neatly inside.

"What's this for?" I wave it at him.

Shane shrugs as he taps out a cigarette and lights it. "Money to get home. Money to spend on clothes. Money for food. Money for whatever the fuck you need."

"Eh, there's too much in here." I cast my eyes to the stack and back to Shane, unsure if I should take it. "I'm grateful, but…"

"It's not from me, kid." Smoke fills the front of the SUV when he speaks. "As per Tommy's request, before Elias caught you sneaking around, I had to transport you to Bogotá and give you the cash. All of it."

I swallow the tight lump stuck in my throat. "Why didn't he kill me?"

Shane sucks hard on the tip and inhales. "I've no idea. You're a phenomenon from where I'm sitting. Uninvited strangers never leave the plantation. No one has ever been in your shoes. Now hurry the fuck up and get out. I need to get home."

"You live in Bogotá?"

He smirks. "We live everywhere. The Souza's run this city--they rule Colombia."

Once my seatbelt is unclipped and I open the door into the bustling city street, Shane seizes my wrist to stop me from exiting the vehicle.

"I'd like to think Tommy wasn't played by his archenemy. You seem sweet and genuine, a lot like my sister. But even pretty, young things can lie." His fingers fall away. "He's got photos of you in his bed, which, in simple terms, means you're associated with Tomás Souza. You've become the enemy of his enemy, and every other cartel rival out there. Stay out of trouble or the next bullet won't miss. Nor will the bullets fired at your parents. That's not my threat, kid. It's his."

I nod curtly, fist the cash, and climb out of the SUV to the sidewalk.

You're associated with Tomás Souza.

He took photos of me in his bed. It was a calculated plan all along. I muster the strength to turn around and meet Shane's lopsided smile. "I hope we never meet again —for your sake. Whatever the hell happened between you and Tommy is over, kid. It's a level playing field. If you know what's good for you, you'll go back home to your family and forget all about us."

Shane winks. A cigarette dangles from his lips as he motions for me to close the door. I don't realize my hands are shaking until I press my palm to the cold exterior.

The vehicle pulls away from the side of the curb, leaving me all alone with a gunshot wound, enough Colombian Pesos to charter a private jet to Manaus and a lingering emptiness.

Guilt makes my stomach ache. I should hate the man for everything he's done to me. Except, I don't. It's like I'm losing my mind and Tomás has taken up residency in every single confounded thought.

Maybe there's a slither of goodness in him. A warped decency that set me free, because he saw the same ghosts in my soul that haunt his own. Perhaps he'd felt the sparks of our touch too.

The undeniable attraction.

The voiceless connection.

The inescapable delirium.

I'm shaking, flustered and adrift in the middle of a city I've never visited until now. Yet, it's not fear spiking my adrenaline. That's a notably absent emotion, like I'm numb to the future. I guess being shot by a gorgeous gangster does that to a girl. Even if the bullet had only skimmed the top layer of flesh on its way past.

With freedom and cold hard cash in my hand, I'm ready to start a new life somewhere different—in Tomás Souza's territory.

13

TOMÁS

Twenty-four years ago

"Good day in prison, Tommy?" Uncle Angelo sparks the end of a Marlboro cigarette and inhales a lungful of smoke.

Thrilled he's the one collecting me from school today, I chuck my backpack in first and sink into the custom red leather bucket seat of his convertible Maserati GranCabrio. I grin as we speed off. There's nothing subtle about the Souzas. We aren't your typical Colombian family.

"Sure was." I wiggle my eyebrows. "One kid brought a massive bag of candy into class. The teacher told him to put it away or she'd confiscate it. So, I bought the whole bag from him for dirt cheap and sold them individually."

The high sun glints on the shiny onyx hood and a cool wind carries the scent of Angelo's fresh coffee in a takeaway cup. "So yeah, today was a pretty good day. I made a killing. *Papá* will be proud of me."

The cigarette clings to Angelo's lips as a chuckle rumbles from his throat. "Never mind your Papá. I'm proud of you, kid."

It's a tricky swell of adoration that grows within me. He's my father's elder brother—powerful, sharp, and a nonconformist.

Even the tattoos decorating his hands sketch out war and authority. We have an unspoken connection. Both of us being the eldest of younger siblings. I go to my father if I want to buy the latest Xbox console and Angelo to learn about the family business.

"You've taught me well." I snicker. "And that girl I like, she tried to kiss me."

When he glances over at me, I meet my boyish face and eyes the color of soot in his mirrored sunglasses.

"Did you let her?"

I laugh. "Of course not. She can wait, like you taught me." My knowing wink makes his roar of approval louder than the wind rushing over the windshield.

The car changes lanes, pulls up at the side of the pavement, and rolls to a stop. Angelo pinches the cigarette butt between his finger and thumb. Smoke swirls down his nostrils like a dragon. "Hand over your profit, Tommy."

I know better than to disobey him, so I drag every last coin from my pocket and drop them into his waiting palm. A small, civilized smile twitches the coarse hairs edging his mouth. "Good boy."

It takes him all of two seconds to count the change. The rush of coinage pelting the inside of the cup holder skitters like a spray of bullets. I had worked my ass off on the playground and walked away with a buzz in my veins.

"It's not much…" He drags his sunglasses down the bridge of his nose and stares at me, his expression impassive. "For all the effort you went to. What you need to learn now is how to make the little guys do all the hard work for you. One day you'll head our organization, like I did after Nico was gunned down in the club."

"Do you think I have what it takes?"

Angelo's amber eyes narrow at the question. He replaces his shades, throws his arm over the back of my seat, and inhales more smoke. "A week after I took over, your father was engaged to a mafia princess. The Irish saw it as a strategic business move. A way to control the most powerful cartel organization in Colombia. But I knew their firstborn would be the heir to the Souza family business. That you'd be more powerful than anyone." He cocks his brow and chuckles low in his throat. "If I wasn't already married, I would have happily taken your mother as my bride."

"Gross." I pull a face at him.

"With your superior bloodline and my good looks." He winks. "You'll be legendary when the time comes. You'll teach them all a lesson on how to rule. I can't wait to see the day you turn into a fucking hybrid king." His brow creases, lost in thought.

Angelo's ringed fingers slip inside his leather jacket. "This is what you're entitled to, Tommy. Get used to it." He whips out a stack of paper money all cinched together in the middle with a rubber band. "Here. Take it. You did well. Set your sights higher and learn from me."

A wad of crisp notes lands in my lap with a thud, the

weight telling me there's more than enough to buy a million bags of candy.

I've spent the last few months trying to prove my worth to my uncle. To let him know I'm all in. The fact Angelo and I are close works in my father's favor, being one less child he has to protect. Rival gangs wait in the flanks with greed dripping from their veins. Danger walks beside power.

A wake of honking horns follows the custom Maserati after Angelo slams his foot on the gas and cuts across the lanes. He flicks his cigarette into the oncoming traffic and extends his finger, flipping off the line of angry drivers behind us.

The dark red stone wedged into a thick gold band dazzles in the sunlight as his hand gesture defies the laws of road users. Angelo doesn't give a fuck about rules. But family is everything.

Where Angelo is the monster under your bed waiting for the right time to strike, Papá is the unhinged demon who shoots first and then decides if you are guilty. They're both cut from the same cloth, except Elias Souza wasn't quick enough to stake his claim as the newly crowned leader. These days, he does Angelo's bidding and bites his tongue out of respect and honor.

"Where are we going?" I hold the brick of paper money close to my pumping heart and haul my backpack onto my lap.

It's my first official salary. My family has an impressive portfolio of homes all over the world. We own churches, hotels, gyms, and even jet planes. Financially, I'm set for life. Yet, nothing beats earning your place at the table or garnering respect from this man.

"The *Halcones* have an update." He parks on the chaotic street and exits the car. "They're the eyes and ears of the streets, Tommy. That information is worth more than the cash you're stashing in your backpack."

I pull the zipper closed and swing the straps over my shoulders. "Is Papá coming?"

We cross the busy road, him strolling ahead and me trotting behind to keep up with his long strides. Sunlight glints on the custom gold-plated handgun tucked near his hip. I fucking love that gun. One day I'll have my own. Just like his.

"Nah. Carlos should be here already. My men are waiting for us outside the bar, and a few guys from across town are coming to hear the news." His voice booms over the cacophony of city life and engines. "I'll speak with your Papá when I drop you home later. Apparently, your baby brother has a fever."

"Babies." I roll my eyes and reach for his hand when I catch up to him.

Matheus is the newest addition to the Souza family. That makes four sons. Three of which would have to die before Matheus ever has the opportunity of ruling. He most likely never will.

"Yeah, I ain't got time for things that can't answer my questions."

Angelo squeezes my fingers and glances down at me. The sardonic grin stretching his goatee isn't missed. I'm probably the only person alive who sees the softer side to the kingpin of Colombia's Souza cartel.

"This afternoon, your job is to listen. I want to know if you think they're bullshitting me or if what they say is true. Use your gut, Tommy. If something doesn't feel right, I'll kill the fuckers, and we'll go for a milkshake."

I nod, unsure if my instincts would work like he wants them to. I'm only eight years old. "What if my gut lies to me?"

He lets go of my hand to open the glass door of a swanky bar. "The last person who will ever lie to you is yourself. In this business, instincts are gold."

Angelo looks back over his shoulder and acknowledges the trio of men who join us. I instantly recognize his right-hand guy and two burly bodyguards. Together we enter the unusually quiet establishment. It's not unheard of for meeting venues to be vacated ahead of time. It's a safety measure and keeps uninvited guests out of the loop.

The barman nods to a metal staircase as we approach. "Go on up," he adds, drying a pint glass with a tiny towel.

Angelo takes the lead as usual and I fall in behind him. The higher we climb, the odder I feel. It's not dizziness or nausea, more of a queasy uncertainty. I've never met the lowest ranks of our cartel before, and after today, they'll put a face to Angelo's protégé.

"Where the fuck is Carlos?" Angelo strolls through the cramped mezzanine. His shaded stare hunts for Carlos Blanco, my father's best friend, and the second man who had wanted Nico's throne. "He said he'd be here."

Rowdy chatter dwindles. All eyes land on the six-foot tower of authority dressed in ripped jeans and radiating a volatile mood. From the pensive hush, a bearded guy by the window speaks up. "He's running late." He tips his glass in a greeting.

I sense my uncle's aura shift from wise mentor to quick-tempered drug baron. "I don't have all fucking afternoon. We'll start without him."

Instinctively, I stay close to his hip, my short steps double his assertive pace. When he weaves around the lacquered tables, cutting through a haze of cigarette smoke and sits among the men, I do the same. When he flicks his ankle to the opposite knee, I mimic him. Some kids my age look up to role models like cops or Marvel superheroes, whereas I idolize the most savage man in Colombia.

"Who's the kid?" A hollow-cheeked guy with a mustache, twisted at either end like Ape Hanger handlebars, scoots his chair adjacent to our table. Close enough to speak with us, but far enough away to show respect for my uncle's invisible boundaries.

Angelo taps out a cigarette from a half-empty pack and bites the butt between his front teeth. Flint sparks and the tobacco catches fire. Slowly, in his own time, he inhales. Before answering, he mouths out a series of smoke rings. "He's the baddest motherfucker in this city," he mutters on the last of a smoky exhale, his face deadpan.

Mustache smirks. "Oh yeah? I thought that title belonged to you."

Angelo rakes his fingers through choppy hair, throws his foot onto a neighboring chair, and pulls a compact knife with a glossy bone handle from his boot. I recognize the weapon—the very one he had handcrafted after his first kill. To some it would seem barbaric to save such a trinket of death, but to Angelo it's a small reminder that our enemies walk beside us.

When he straightens, he calmly sets the pocketknife on the table and flicks the polished handle so it spins.

"It's the quiet ones you have to watch out for." Angelo laughs, low and husky. "He'll cut out your heart when you're sleeping and serve it to your family for breakfast while it's still pumping."

I draw in my lips to stifle a smile. He knows I've only ever fought my twin brothers, André and Giovanni. Even then, I had to hold an ice pack on André's mouth after I accidentally busted his lip open.

"That's if you are a threat. Which you aren't, right?" Angelo slides his frames up and over his forehead, so they rest on top of his mussed-up hair.

Mustache pauses, his wide eyes jumping from the blade to my boyish face. Nothing feels as good as being a Souza, or a Souza with an uncle who'd quite literally murder a whole room of bad guys if they looked at me the wrong way.

"No threat here, Angelo. I'm not the one you need to worry about."

I bristle at the statement. Danger is never too far away in this business, and the longer a drug lord rules his kingdom, the more assholes gather in the shadows.

"I'm glad we're on the same page. I like you, Davi." Angelo declares, staring him down. "So let's cut to the chase. What fucker thinks he can take on the Souzas and survive?"

Beyond the window, wispy clouds drift across the sky,

so the sun rays burst through the gaps like lasers. The hidden ball of light brings about a sinister shadow that creeps indoors and covers the seated men before us. A temporary change in atmosphere prickles my spine, the sensation unnerving like spiders crawling over me.

I'm not sure why my belly is in knots or why the temperature cools, making my nerves skitter.

"We don't know exactly who the order is coming from, but I know a guy who might help me find out… for the right price." One man speaks up.

"The threat is real. We know that for sure." Another joins the conversation.

The chaos of a bustling city street seems to freeze like the hands of a clock having melted with no more time to tell.

"What's your guy's name?" Angelo sets an elbow on the edge of the table and leans in.

I turn to him and stare up at his stormy expression. There's an unusual wave of calmness outside. Perhaps the Earth has stopped turning and gravity sucked up all the pedestrians. Or fate has pressed a giant pause button for a moment of concentration. Nonetheless, my pulse gallops at the rarity of stillness. Something isn't right.

"Uncle."

Immediately, eyes of flaming amber settle on mine. His head cocks, fully aware that I know my place and it's not in this conversation.

I swallow, scared my amateur instincts are wired to the moon. "You said to tell you…" I whisper behind my hand, "if my gut could sense…"

Instantly, he cuts me off with a curt nod. "Brandon."

Angelo waves to his second, a skinny guy wearing a bandanna. "Take photos of every face in this room and record all their names. Davi, I need that name right now."

When my uncle rises, he cuffs my wrist, so my knees unlock and we're side by side, standing tall.

Davi opens his mouth to speak. At first, for a millisecond, I imagine the pale clouds have carried a riotous thunderstorm when a flash distorts my vision and an ear-splitting boom shakes the building.

An almighty force throws my small body backward, helplessly disoriented in a mortal blast. Darkness blinds me and the weight of an ox bears down on me from above.

Seconds speed by as the rhythm of beating hearts weakens. The ringing in my ears is louder than any other sound I've ever experienced. I'm temporarily deaf.

My lashes bat rapidly, my eyes straining to see through the suffocating pressure pinning me to the floorboards.

I gag, my throat fighting against the coppery slime in my mouth, denying its passage into my stomach. Perhaps I was knocked out, or simply dazed by the explosion. The unaccounted moments spent lying in a heap are inconsequential until the synapses in my brain fire up.

Angelo.

Car alarms wail, sounding far off. The mind-numbing repetition competes with a tinny, high-pitched noise in my aching skull. It's all I hear, that and my racing pulse. Adrenaline kicks in, and I push up to sit.

The warm mass trapping me rolls sideways. I scrub my eyes and watch ashy debris settle like snowflakes. The tips of my fingers are wet, the skin on my face coated in stickiness.

"Angelo?" My mind swims in confusion, my tongue blanketed in a foul-tasting cocktail.

Tremors attack my hands, quickly turning volatile when I hold them outwards. Crimson stains varnish my sun kissed skin. There's no cuts or gashes on my limbs to warrant a hemorrhage of this magnitude.

I spit out a salty goop, realizing it's not saliva. My belly heaves at the vile taste I can't get rid of. The clean clothes I'd worn to school are steeped in crimson and dust.

"Uncle!" I yell, finding the power in my lungs.

"Tomás." His usual authoritative tone is unsteady. "Here." A breathless hiss is close by.

Fire rages and crackles outside the demolished gable wall. Thick black smoke rises into the sky, announcing an explosion of catastrophic proportions.

"You okay, Tommy?" The husky rasp to Angelo's voice licks my spine with fear.

As I try to rise amidst busted bricks, my hand lands on a tattooed arm. A singular body part, unattached to the torso of its owner.

"Fuck!" I cry out, mindlessly checking my own limbs in a panic to make sure it's not mine.

Tears sting my eyes at the sight of it and fright electrifies my muscles with spiky barbs. I slam my hands over my ears to block out the excruciating chorus of groaning death and deafening sirens.

Still dazed by the event, I take a brief moment to locate Angelo in the carnage spread out before me.

Dismembered corpses litter the rubble. Live wires

hang from an eroded ceiling where sparks flit like fireflies and the neighboring building across the road seems much closer now with the front of the bar demolished.

I move and heave simultaneously. Filth clings to the blood on my hands and the liquid terror spilling from my eyes. Turning clockwise, I find my uncle's eyes. Those energetic amber irises once burning with flames of domination. Only staring back at me now, missing the fire that commands supremacy.

"Let me see you, kid." He grits out.

I kneel by his side, biting my wobbly lower lip. He's in bad shape. Nothing a surgeon could remedy. I'm sure of it. His right leg is missing, the other is bent behind him, and blood pours from a vicious head wound.

"You... hurt?" He grits out.

My heart is broken. "No." I shake my head and wipe my runny nose with the back of my grubby hand.

"Thank... fuck." His breath rattles.

It's only now when it hits me. How he had shielded me from danger. How he had put himself between me and the blast. And now he's suffering because of it.

"You saved me, Uncle," I choke out. He's my real life superhero. The coppery taste polluting my mouth is his blood. Every claret speck painting my skin is his. I'm wearing his bravery all over me.

He tries to prop himself up only to sink like a stone.

"Don't get up. Help is coming." I grab his hand. His ruby signet ring bites into my flesh when I link my fingers tightly with his. "Papá will make sure you get the best medical treatment."

Angelo gnashes his teeth, snarling untamed like a

starved wolf. "Listen to me. Elias is... next in line. Then... you." His lashes flutter. "He must... step up... immediately." As he tries to reach for me, he grimaces and hisses. "You're the only one... who knows I'm... dead."

I swallow the lump in my throat, my eyes welling up with liquid fear. "You're not dead." I struggle to speak with the courage he'd taught me. "The surgeons will fix..." My lashes lower as I dare to peek at the hemorrhaging artery in his groin. Vomit rises, the acid burning my tight throat. It looks brutal––fatal. My pulse slams in my tight throat, forcing out a whimper.

Creases slash the corners of his opaque eyes, the life slipping from his mutilated body. "No one can fix..." He wheezes. "... this."

My stomach churns at the gruesome state he's in. "We'll fly in the best doctors and surgeons money can buy," I say in a gust of hope and reassurance. "I promise. I'll stay with you in the hospital. You'll be okay... this will be okay."

Angelo seizes my arm, groans with pain, and yanks me into his rattling chest. "I—I love you... Tommy." He gasps for air. A hard ball of fear bobs in my throat when I witness the sincerity pooling in his eyes. "Remember what I said. You'll be... legendary, kid. And to be that man one day... you have to save me... from this." He pins me with horrifying intensity. "Shoot me now. End this fucking mess." My heart rate goes off the charts. He fumbles with the gold pistol close to his hip. "Take it... use it... keep it." His hand drops from the weight of the gun in his palm.

I suck in a harrowing breath and finger the engraved lettering on the barrel. Chills scurry over me, the horrifying sensation resembling a bombshell of lacerating debris. The shudder with his order almost breaks my courage.

"I'm dying anyway, kid." He coughs up bloody spittle. "Give me a quick... honorable death."

"I can't... n-no." I rear back, only to feel his ruthless grip cinch my elbow.

"*Never* hesitate." He gulps, struggling to continue. "... always trust your instincts. No matter... what anyone tells you."

In that moment, my heart screams with anguish, but my queasy gut—it tells me to obey.

"Do it." He winces in mortal agony. "That's an... order." The command pelts my racing young soul with sharp splinters of cracked ice. "Send me to my grave... with love... and pride in my heart, Tomás Souza." He coughs up a bloody clot, his face now whiter than a glacier with the faint coloring of wintry blue.

I choke on a tattered sob. The ache in my stomach hurts like never before. My conscience begs me to hold on to the man I adore until medics arrive at the scene. They'll save his life, albeit maimed and dysfunctional.

"Love is death, Tommy. If you love me... do it."

And that I do. I love him with every fiber of my existence.

I take possession of Angelo's favorite pistol. My hand shakes and sweat mingles with the slimy blood smearing my cheeks. "I love you, Uncle Angelo."

Bang.

14

TOMÁS

Present Day

My hands twitch with the desire to feel the cold comfort of my revolver. The one I've carried and used until I know it better than my own body, and every woman I've ever had in my bed. It's tucked in my waistband, ready for any threat this city throws at me.

A distant wail of sirens has my pulse on high alert. I hate Bogotá during the daytime and always will. The memory of that horrific afternoon permanently lives in my head rent free. That's why we're meeting the Mexicans after midnight in a back street bar. Our ally, Morales, is now a pending enemy. His next move hinges on the outcome of this conversation.

"I hope these motherfuckers don't waste my time." My father stubs out a fat cigar in an empty glass as we pass through the noisy bar packed with twenty-somethings looking for a good time.

As we move deeper inside, the drinkers move out of

our way like a changing tide. Every single one of them backs away. They all sense the ripples of power we exude.

A pretty woman with a nice set of tits slides closer, her red lips wrapping around a fat straw as she sucks. Hooded lids offer a snare of temptation and her curvy ass sways as she tries to tease.

She catches Papá's eye, but it's me she's staring at. Unfortunately for her, I'm not in the mood to play. Tonight, I'm untouchable. This is a business trip and I have zero tolerance for distractions.

"You killed their top guy, Papá." He's a law unto himself and a liability. With power comes madness, and that madness has manifested into a permanent state of paranoia. Everyone's a threat to him these days.

"The cocky cunt was in our home." He bares his teeth at me, anger flaring the pupils in his steely gray eyes. It's more his home than mine. I had never really warmed up to the place.

I fix my cufflinks and rotate the signet ring on my finger. "He was a guest." I repeat for the millionth time in the past few weeks. "And now they've lost faith in us. We could lose the smuggling routes and start an unnecessary war. The last thing we need is Blanco taking advantage of the situation. I'm sure he's heard about the shitshow by now."

"All war is necessary. You'll eventually learn that." He shrugs. "I'll blow their hairy assholes into the sky. That'll teach the cunts not to mess with me. If Blanco wants to come for me again, I'll hack his ugly head off."

"No one came for you this time, Papá."

He ignores me. "At least you finished off that angel-faced *puta*." Ringed fingers dive through my father's waxed hair to ensure the salt and pepper strands stay swept back. "Who knows what havoc she would have caused? I sent a few men to Rio to sort it out."

Carina.

The gilded Pandora's box.

My instincts had told me she was innocent. A misfortunate archangel thrown into the underworld without an escape route. Over the years, I've mastered intuitiveness. It's my one true skill and curse.

What my father will never find out is how I spared her life. The weapon I pointed at her womanly physique had unleashed a killer bullet. Except my typical aim hits the bullseye every single time. Lucky for her, the slug only grazed her flesh rather than sinking into muscle and bone.

The truth is, Carina Ferreira temporarily fought off my demons with her pretty mouth and amber eyes. For that perplexing act alone, I owed her a debt. She'd offered me peace in the mayhem of harrowing flashbacks. And I saved her from dying young.

Now we're even.

Colliding ships in a stormy ocean, never to cross paths again.

"Yeah," I agree with a half-hearted shrug. "Let me talk this through with Morales. Okay?"

Papá stares at me for a split second. "Fine. Angelo wouldn't take this shit, and he certainly wouldn't tolerate a traitor. Don't fuck it up."

The hairs on my nape rise like hackles. "Angelo wouldn't shoot before he understood the facts," I bite out, enraged by his lack of faith in my ability and the fact I had known Angelo better than him.

I had promised my uncle I'd be the best. Every day following his death, I've paved the way for unlimited success and studied the business inside out. Made important allies and garnered respect. To hear my father's doubt is like a flesh-eating disease gradually thinning my efforts. In his eyes, I'd never be as good as him.

"Yeah, yeah." Papá waves his hand in a dismissive gesture. "My brother would have hacked his head off for being a snake. He wouldn't hesitate."

And there it is. The big, fat, fucking white elephant in the room that haunts me. My entrenched trigger—paralyzed seconds where my mind betrays me. When it slithers into unavoidable darkness.

My one true flaw, the uncontrollable delay before an ultimate deadly rage strips my senses. It's a lapse of time where I'm vulnerable—frozen. That short-lived glitch makes me weak.

"The trouble is, you think everyone is a snake, Papá." I deflect his backhanded criticism of my proficiency.

I haven't lost my mind. It simply sucks me into a maelstrom and tosses me out, ready for war. At least I'm not like him. Papá would slaughter anyone who gave him a reason to doubt their loyalty—including his own bloodline.

We're granted entry beyond a velvet curtain lined with chain mail. The weighty screen shields us from the regular drinkers. This is where business deals of all types take place.

"Gentlemen." Morales crooks his fingers. The smile he

offers in welcome is a lie. We all know it. He beckons us to join him at the oval table. "Take a seat, Tomás. Elias."

On quick inspection, I note four of his men standing in each dark corner and one guarding the door. I prowl across the room, unaffected by his bodyguards, and drag out a chair. Papá circles the table before selecting a seat next to Morales.

We have a team of armed men in the alleyway and a few more discreetly positioned in the bar. Across the road, there's an SUV filled to the brim with explosives, should I need to wipe out the building with these fuckers in it.

I had learned the hard way. I never enter a building or step into a meeting without taking appropriate precautions beforehand.

These guys have witnessed the backlash of my father's psychotic temperament. He's old school—ruthless. On the flip side, they've only ever experienced the diplomatic side of my character. The refined and cultured half that understands business. I'm more calculated and controlled —more mafia than cartel—until I'm triggered. They think they know me, but they don't.

No one really does.

Those who meet the ruthless version of me never survive. Luckily, I'm stone-cold tonight. Numb.

The Mexican cartel is here to barter with us over crossed wires. Granted, it was a fatal mishap, but if they think we'll bow to demands, they're wrong. One shady move and I'd shower the room with lead. They won't get the chance to threaten my family. If that's the path they choose, I'll take every motherfucker in this place out.

A full bottle of Grand Old Parr separates us. "Scotch?" I lean back into the velvet padded chair and unbutton my jacket. "Good choice."

Morales' chunky gold bracelet noisily skims the table's wooden surface as he grabs the liquor and pours. He systematically fills three glasses halfway. The overweight asshole isn't stupid. In this scenario, he has a slight advantage of justice and control over transit hubs in the Mexican ports and crucial smuggling tunnels. Valuable assets I'd rather not lose. I'm not afraid of war. Though losing established trafficking points is a headache, I'd rather not endure.

"So..." His lashes point in the direction of my father like daggers. "You invited Flávio to your home and murdered him?"

Papá reaches across the table and swipes a drink. "I did," he answers, void of emotion. At least, he's keeping himself in check. "As it turns out, it was a simple case of mistaken identity."

Morales' brown eyes widen with displeasure. His vicious snarl hides behind a raised crystal cut tumbler.

"Didn't he explain why he was there? You invited him, Tomás." Morales glares at me, surprise etched on his swarthy face. "Surely you wouldn't start a war with us, would you? Is blood for blood the only way?"

My instincts tell me this guy wants something, and it's not a feud. The Souzas have unlimited resources, government officials eating out of our hands, and most of the police department on our payroll. We make the law, and he knows it. A war with us wouldn't be pretty and they'd be the ones burying loved ones.

Over the years, I've progressively legitimized a hefty percentage of our businesses. Yet, we still hold the monopoly on cocaine production and distribution. So, having these guys in our corner only strengthens our position and ensures the smaller cartels don't get too greedy.

The Souzas stay on top.

"Morales, we've been peaceful allies for a long time. Tell me, what sort of compensation will clean up this misunderstanding?"

Morales sits straighter in his chair. His gaze cuts to my father and then back to me. "I don't trust the Souzas like I used to."

Papá silently swills Scotch and proceeds to knock it back like a shot. I sense his impatience unravel when he sighs.

"I can't say how long it will take to establish that trust again." Morales continues.

"A week?" Papá mocks, then clears his throat as if he's about to say more.

I swiftly interject before he pulls out his gun and fires a bullet into Morales' eyeball. "What does that mean, exactly?"

The dark-haired Mexican with a scraggly ponytail retrieves a packet of cigarettes from his shirt pocket. Morales' quick movement has my fingers twitching in a subconscious reflex. He lights one, sets the zippo on top of the box and sucks in loudly.

"It means I've put a hold on all trade routes for the foreseeable future." The acrid tobacco odor reminds me of my uncle. Same brand. Same smoky swirls. It's both pleasant and painful. "Unless you'd be open to rekindling a show of faith with something far more binding than your word?"

"Spit it out, Morales, before we all die of boredom." Papá drains another scotch, his attention slipping.

A smirk stretches Morales' thin lips. "Either I cut off your access through Mexico and put a bounty on each of the Souza brothers' heads or you, Tomás, marry my niece, Bianca. Rather than spill blood, our families will blend and forge a stronger bond."

Well, fuck, tonight just got a lot more interesting. This guy has big balls. War or marriage. One I was born to orchestrate, the other I have zero desire to participate in.

Papá's rumble of laughter takes Morales by surprise. When he claps in tandem, it's clear to me my father is dangling from a filament of decorum. He'll lose his mind over this.

"You want a Souza to marry your *niece?*" my father guffaws. The fact he focuses on the marriage proposal makes me smirk. We both know we'd easily annihilate the Mexicans—if we wanted an inconvenience. Nonetheless, I don't take kindly to threats made against my family.

"That's the proposal," Morales replies, his expression deadpan. "I'm sure we'd all appreciate a day of celebration rather than months of mourning."

"A Souza and a Morales?" Papá chuckles.

"Till death do they part." The second Morales' eyes lock with mine, his eyebrows drift skyward. "Well?"

"It's never gonna happen, motherfucker," Papá announces, his scathing tone so acidic it could strip paint from the walls. His chair skids backward as he bounces up to stand. "Never."

Both hands settle on his hips, barely restrained, yet waiting for me to rise with him.

What's the worst that could happen—I'd marry a woman I have no desire to fuck? Big deal. I'd get it elsewhere.

Who needs a wife to better their life? Certainly not me. I would rather stay as a bachelor and wallow in untethered loneliness for the rest of my days.

But an arranged relationship, with no expectation of love. Well, it would stop my mother searching for the perfect unwanted bride and possibly present an opportunity to carry on the Souza name for another generation—if I'm up for consummating the marriage. Currently, that's up for debate. Me and kids aren't a thing. I've no desire to speak to them or create them.

A simple contract with mutual benefits. I'd garner a firmer hold on the transport corridors and make sure my product isn't cut with fentanyl to lessen demand.

I don't seek emotional attachments, nor do I crave them. Outside of my family circle, I'm emotionally unavailable.

Papá's eyes drill into my quiet contemplation. It's not that he wants me to marry a nice girl of my choosing and settle down. No, he wants to build an empire on his terms. And he's blinded by paranoia.

"Tomás. Let's go. This is bullshit. These fuckers can rot in the shallow graves our men dig for them."

His obvious disapproval makes this decision easier by the second. Lately, I've found it refreshing to push the boundaries of his authority. He makes disastrous, off-the-cuff decisions that negatively impact the organization, and that puts him at risk of being shoved from his throne. Our men are restless, and I'm growing tired of cleaning up his messes.

I wish he'd retire and see out his days on a super yacht in Belize where he can tame his growing neurosis. Years of being our leader have made him hungrier. He's even more determined to expand further than his predecessors.

My father is a twisted son of a bitch. Always has been. Despite that fact, his blood runs wild in my veins. I've withstood his mean temperament and still continue to prove I'm worthy of praise more than constant criticism. His harsh and ruthless ways have carved me into the man I am today.

Eventually his reign would come to an end and the old man would have to congratulate his first born as his successor. Though at this rate I'd be fucking gray by the time he hands over the crown.

Until then, I'll stand by my father as I've always done. Loyal to the core, but I'll also enjoy a little head fucking. I'm capable of doing things my way too, and he'll get a taste of it now.

"What age is Bianca Morales?" My fingers drum the table while I think.

"Twenty-two, and a real beauty, let me add. This isn't a disadvantage, Tomás. You'll be a happy man with my sweet Bianca in your bed."

Instantly my mind blips out. The face of a woman I recently watched sleep in my bed pops into my head.

Those fierce eyes and that imperfect thread thin scar on her pouty lip. So, delicately fine, it was almost invisible, but I saw it. That and the slash marks on her arms. There was something about her courageous spirit that caught my attention and bred curious intrigue.

She reminded me of myself.

Tortured.

Detached.

My dick swells below the table. *Fuck... focus, cabrón.* It's not normally so active during important meetings. Angelo had taught me to ignore irrelevant shit and keep my wits about me. So it's a mild annoyance how I'm aroused by thoughts of a sexy young thing that I'd never see again.

"I need an answer, Tomás." Morales' chair squeaks as he leans back, a blank expression masking his uncertainty.

"How about no?" Papá speaks on my behalf, his reply a blunt snap. "Not. Going. To. Happen."

I'm an unapologetically rebellious man at times. It's the inbred waywardness of my Uncle Angelo. He's to blame and to thank.

"Perhaps," I say with an air of nonchalance. "I'll think about it."

Papá's scowl darkens before his expression turns into a wolfish glower. "Tomás," he warns.

"Will you reopen the smuggling tunnels immediately and continue distribution of our product? Then, pledge your allegiance to us?" I could blow this fucker off the face of the earth. Except my goal isn't fucking up the business, it's containing his loyalty. Not to mention securing my family's safety and ensuring Carlos fucking Blanco stays beneath us in the pecking order.

That alone is worth marrying the niece of an ally.

"Will you bring more product our way?" Morales swills his liquor, deep in thought.

I shrug casually. "Of course. How much can you handle?"

Morales nods solemnly. "As much as you can supply."

"Show me the dollar bills and we'll increase the orders."

"Then you'll have our allegiance, as long as you hold up your end of the deal. Marry Bianca—with one rule."

I quirk a brow at him. He's pushing his luck and my patience. "Divorce is off the table. Till death you part and all that shit. This isn't a stunt to get my forgiveness. It's forever."

My lips quirk to a detached smile. "Fine. We have a deal. I'll marry Bianca Morales."

15

CARINA

What a night.

I've been on my feet for five hours straight. The regular jazz band packed up an hour ago and the final stragglers have dwindled, slightly afraid of Layla's no nonsense last call. It's just the two of us left to close.

I look over at her while I clean a sticky tabletop, in awe of her style, sassy attitude, purple braid, and facial piercings. Zero fucks given.

Behind the bar, Layla counts tonight's tips and mutters about the sleazy creep who left a folded fifty pesos note under his pint glass.

"Cheap ass punk. I'll break his neck the next time he touches my ass," she mutters under her breath.

I squeeze the paper towel saturated in antibacterial spray and walk the length of the quiet room, doing a final check. My feet are throbbing, but I'd never admit it to her.

Although she's not like the girls from school. They had gotten off on sneers and false gossip, taking any opportunity to rip holes in my soul. Whereas Layla tells it like it is.

You're either friend or foe, and nothing in between. I love that about her. Luckily, she seems to like me, which is a whole new experience. Then again, she didn't meet the ugly kid from my past.

These days I get to be a modified version of myself. More beauty than beast. Well, easier on the eyes, at least. I certainly wouldn't tally up points to be princess pageant worthy. However, I am more resilient than before. A stronger character built from adversity. Besides, Layla accepts me, scars and all.

I catch her eye. "I'm done, unless there's anything else you need help with?"

When I first moved here a few weeks ago, I walked the streets and knocked on many doors. Layla was the only person willing to take a chance on an inexperienced teenager. Since then, I've been a human sponge. Learning the ropes and cleaning the velvet pintucked booths after the last drunken customer falls out the door.

"Be a doll and take the trash on your way out." She slides a stack of notes across the bar. "That's your cut... with a little extra." She winks.

I squeeze between two red leather bar stools and pocket the cash. "Thanks, Layla. Every bit counts."

"Don't go saving all of it. You need to have fun too." Her lips curl into a naughty grin.

"Yeah... fun." I laugh lightly. She has no idea; this girl doesn't know how to have fun. I've never had a best friend to lead me astray. The only *fun* I've ever had was reading on the roof of my parents' house under the moon. And then recently it was something very, very bad. Like licking cartel dick and wanting to bounce on top of it.

Christ. My sex drive is out-of-control. I guess that's what happens when a nineteen-year-old virgin finally inhales a penis.

Aside from experiencing what could lie ahead in my non-existent sex life, it's a cool feeling to earn a wage. To earn something for myself. To *live*.

I don't use my salary for rent, because my big brother Salvador bought me a modest one-bedroom apartment on the north side of the city, not far from here. It's located in the safest district in Bogotá. Nothing short of a well-planned move on his part. He's my knight in shining armor, which makes me even more determined to repay the debt I owe him.

Every time I bring up a payment plan, he changes the subject. The guy makes a shit ton of money that he doesn't really need right now. So in his big brown eyes, it's an investment.

It's only fair if I show him the same sibling love by saving most of what I earn during my gap year. After a few calculations, I'd figured out it would take an unthinkable number of working hours-days-years to match the price he had purchased my compact apartment for. Yet, handing him a fraction of the cost would give me a sense of independence and show him my gratitude. I owe that wonderfully stubborn guy my life. Literally.

Bonus tips pay for food and the snazzy patent leather Doc Martens that were a rare find in a neighborhood thrift store. I spend my money wisely. We were raised in a hard-working family with very little money to spare. I don't want much in life other than happiness and acceptance.

This new adventure of mine, in a city where no one knows my name and where strangers aren't armed with knowledge of my tragic past, is priceless.

"Sure thing. I'll dump it now." There's no air or grace about me. Everyone makes trash and someone has to get rid of it.

Layla rolls up the remaining notes and tucks them into her padded bra. "It's best if you leave through the side door. There's a fleet of SUVs parked out front. Either someone's gonna get hanged from the bridge, or the Souza cartel is here in person." She sighs. "I would not want to cross paths with Elias Souza. He is one psycho motherfucker. His eldest son Tomás... Jeez, he's Satan in a tailored suit. An incredibly sexy task master who'd choke you for answers while he's fucking you like a jackhammer. If they weren't evil fucks, I'd happily let all four brothers take their turn." Layla blows out a jet of air and fans her face. "But I don't have a death wish. No one gets inside their circle and if they do... they disappear. Poof!" She expands her fingers wide to signify an airy explosion.

A shiver runs through me.

Tomás Souza.

Is he in one of the SUV's?

Even the name holds so much power in these streets. It didn't matter what screwy connection we shared a few weeks ago, or how he saved me from his deranged father and set me free—he's dangerous with a capital letter D.

He's the hero I want to forget and the sinner I'm stupidly fascinated by. I still blush when I think about how I'd gagged on his salty tasting dick. Those noises I made were all slurpy and undignified—I loved it. Even now my clit swells to the point it's painful. Who knew sucking a guy off would be such a turn on? Maybe it was his wild eyes or his thick, dirty grunts that made the thrill so intense.

I wander to the front window, making sure I'm half hidden by the wall and peer through a smattering of raindrops, ignoring how my pulse gallops in warning.

Directly outside are three Cadillac Escalades with blacked-out windows, each one darker than the night sky. My forehead thuds the glass as I tip forward, looking for more.

"People get killed for being nosey, girl." Layla warns, wagging a finger in my direction. "I'm serious. You do not want to land on their radar."

My veins warm beneath my skin. The same charge of adrenaline pulses within me every time I remember his soft lips. I know I shouldn't fantasize over a ruthless criminal, but the memory of him festers within me like a rampant disease.

In reality, if I'm unlucky enough to ever bump into him again, I'd run as fast as I could in the opposite direction. Men like him have unrepentant minds. Their wealth is in another league and every vein in their magnificent bodies carries lethal poison.

Layla twists the top of the trash bag into a knot and sets it at the end of the bar. "Here. Go home and I'll see you on Saturday."

"Do they come here often?" I ask, careful not to sound too interested.

She shrugs. "Not the head guys. They hide out in their fancy mountain compounds while the street gangs keep order. It's been a long time since I've seen a convoy like that. The Souza cartel are like royalty around here. If you ask me, they're just ruthless jerks with pretty faces and too much power."

New chills prickle my spine. I turn to the bar wearing a tight smile. She doesn't know the horror I've endured and how I somehow managed to cheat death twice. The first time was a gift from an angel. The second was a token from the prince of darkness.

A few weeks ago, Elias Souza wanted me dead. Abusive henchmen dropped me at the gates of hell in the middle of nowhere, drugged and beaten. My body, a gift for the merciless drug lord, sent by the woman who stole me—his illegitimate daughter. I found out after his godlike son fired at me that his aim was purposefully askew.

If it weren't for that particular bad guy, I'd be a rotting carcass for his father's pet tigers to feast on. Whatever his motive, Tomás had saved me.

I finger the bullet graze beneath my sleeve. The wound almost healed. Maybe I'd get a funky tattoo over the scar. Something to signify my narrow escape or to remind me of how I dirty danced with a devil and survived.

"You okay?" Layla bobs her face lower. She's a head taller than me, even without her utility boots. "Want a cheeky shot for the road?"

My lips curl into a grin. "Sure. Why not?"

While she pours the syrupy liquor reeking of aniseed, I grab my purse out from under the bar and check my phone. I'd told Sal to stop pestering me. He's worse than our worrying mother. The twice daily phone calls were a nice touch in the beginning when I was finding my feet in

Bogotá. Since then, I persuaded him to cut it to a weekly chat.

Thankfully, there's only a simple text message waiting—a heart emoji and a smiley face. I tap out a quick reply, picking a peace sign and a pink flower.

"*Salud*!" Layla raises her glass and waits for me to do the same.

"Salud!" The side of my shot glass clinks with hers and we throw back the Sambuca in tandem. "Sheesh… that's interesting stuff." I cough when it burns my larynx. "It tastes like medicine."

Layla laughs. "It's medicine alright. See you on Saturday." She sets the liquor bottle on the glass shelf behind the bar and wanders over to the cash register to close.

I slip the purse strap over my head and gather the bag of trash. "Have a good night, Layla," I call out as I leave and slip into the dim corridor, which takes me to the fire exit at the side of the building.

The clunky metal door slams shut behind me, locking me outside. Drizzle gathers in my lashes and settles in my loose waves like tiny water bombs. There aren't any streetlights in the narrow alley, only sinister shadows under pale moonlight.

Colorful spray-painted walls are dulled by darkness, and broken glass decorates uneven cobblestones like tiny jewels. Lattice grills of metal cover the windows to keep thieves out and thick electrical wires stretch the length of the sky above.

Goosebumps race over my bare arms as I shiver at the drop in temperature. Since the afternoon shift started, the air has cooled below comfortable. Perhaps I should have worn a denim jacket with my cute floral dress, but I didn't.

I curse my bad planning and swing the plastic bag into the air, taking a beat to watch it hurtle like a grenade and land on top of a busted wood pallet. It disturbs a nesting rat from beneath folded cardboard boxes. The scurrying rodent draws my gaze to a metal fire escape almost touching the building opposite.

In the dim light, I notice movement further ahead. Silhouettes dressed all in black, holding monster machine guns, their backs flanking graffiti murals. A dog barks in the distance. Its repeated yap is muffled by a sudden loud crack of iron walloping plaster.

The neighboring door flings outward and a ruthless tornado explodes from within, busting the hinges in its wake. A manly figure storms free, arms long by his side, and hands balled.

He dodges a puddle. "Fuck!" the man snarls, his tone so harsh it could singe skin with flames. "I'll fucking kill that boy one of these days."

I freeze, caught out in the open with nowhere to hide other than a shallow doorway. I'm just about to hightail it away from the stranger preparing for a war I want no part in when an ear-splitting crack stops him in his tracks. His body soars backward, the force of gunfire hitting him like a raging bull. He lands on the ground with an almighty thud.

I press my spine into the wall, blinking, swallowing, and disoriented by the sight of his convulsing body. He's been shot right in front of me.

The sound of retaliating gunfire from the street echoes

like fireworks. The men who guarded the doorway are now on the ground, either dead or injured. I'm alone with the angry man who's grappling with his throat.

It's unknown to me why I still possess empathy, how it wasn't completely obliterated by bullies. Nevertheless, I'm drawn to him. It's in my psyche to help the weak and injured. Having been there before myself, I feel it's my moral obligation.

I land with a crash by his side, my bare knees splashing in a shallow puddle. Hot blood spews like a burst dam from his neck, the flowing fluid draining beneath him. Under the silvery sheen of moonlight, I meet a rain-soaked face and the whites of eyes belonging to a man I had prayed I'd never meet again.

Elias Souza.

Murderer.

Father of my single-minded obsession.

It's chaos behind us. Men are firing in every direction with innocent people screaming amidst a street siege. The ticking hands of time speed up as Elias' blood drains.

The hostility fades as I study the Colombian drug lord, a simple man... not a god, vulnerable and dying in a grim alleyway—and I should let him. I should run away and keep going until I reach Manaus.

Confused by my rash decision, I quickly press down on the leaking artery and apply pressure. He's Tomás' father, after all. Even if helping him sends a sickly shiver of fear down my spine at the thought of what he had wanted to do to me, I owe Tomás.

The hairs on my scalp prickle when a bloodthirsty roar steals my attention away from the fragile life slipping through my fingers. I look up to the silvery sheen washing the wet cobbles and witness another man pounding stone with designer shoes. His son. My nemesis, Tomás Souza.

His ebony suit jacket flaps open as he runs, midnight satin catching the moonlight. The crisp white shirt close to his torso is almost opaque from lashing rain, the downpour now heavier as warfare unfolds.

"Papá!" he yells, his deep voice menacing like the god of the war, ready to extinguish the city. "Get the fuck away from him."

I suck in sharply, lost in the swell of horror his violent storm exudes. Without hesitation, I scurry into the adjacent doorway, my hands covered in Elias' blood. When he slams to his knees and bows over his father, I almost cry out. My heart hammers against my lungs, so they burn with every quick breath.

A horde of daring droplets caress his cheeks and roll from his pointed nose. They plunge into the bloody horror where his hands smother the bullet hole. For a second, his fierce expression morphs to childlike. Searching fingers slip and slide until the movement turns slow, almost frozen. Powerful shoulders rise and fall with every lungful of air he sucks in through clenched teeth.

"Papá... Christ." He arches over his father, listening to the rattle of a man choking on his own life source. They both know Elias will meet his maker tonight. "You should have stayed at home, Papá." His voice strains, the hoarse tone hinting a sorrow so bleak it could shatter any second.

Elias retches and convulses—powerless to communicate, his suffering gravely ugly. As if the moon decides to hide, a sinister veil blankets the narrow alley. There's a hiccup of stillness where Tomás freezes. It's a heart-stopping beat of paralysis. His thick lashes are set like daggers and his limbs are cast in concrete. The untamed hunter has been snared in his own trap.

I huddle on my haunches and watch a sudden insurgence of oxygen fill his lungs. Barely visible tremors in his gory hands eerily cease. He slams the heel of his palm into his temple and growls low in his throat. The predatory sound is so evil it makes my skin ice over, ready to shatter under the weight of vengeance. His stillness of mind erodes, leaving only glacial control.

Methodically, he wipes his hands down his thighs, then removes the ruby red ring on Elias' finger. Tomás unfurls from his kneeling position, straightens, rolls out his shoulders, and pulls a golden revolver from under his jacket. In silence, he aims at his father's forehead.

Fear makes me quake. He looks demonic, like every scrap of humanity has drowned in a slick oily pool, covering his character with an evil residue.

"Love is death, Papá. Tell Angelo I miss him." And then, without hesitation, he snaps the trigger.

I crumble within, thoughtlessly padding my lip and holding a breath to catch the terrified scream I'd be foolish to let escape. Machine gunfire from the street beyond is constant. The galloping pulse inside my skull thunders like the hooves of the four apocalyptic horsemen are nearby. I squeeze my eyes shut and wish for the pandemonium to fade. For the darkness surrounding us to swallow me whole, so I'm hidden from him.

My inner chant prays the fatal calmness of his next move would blur my presence.

I'm a mess. Disheveled, wet tendrils are stuck to my face. The stain of death pastes my trembling hands, blending with tears when I wipe at my eyes.

It's too much.

For the past few weeks, I foolishly forgot about the evil tainting his aura. In my mind, I had placed him on a pedestal in the clouds—my secret hero. A man completely different from his merciless father. And now, he's shown himself to me. The real beast I should fear more than anyone else.

"Get down!" Shane rushes up from behind and launches himself at Tomás, bringing them both to the ground in a tangle of limbs. "You need to get the fuck out of here, Tommy."

Elias' signet ring tumbles and bounces, stopping shy of my boots. While Tomás coughs, the wind knocked from his lungs, I reach out and grab it. Heavy gold burns my skin, the ring a trinket of justice, and a souvenir of karma's work. I stuff it into the tiny pocket of my dress and then regret it.

The thought of Elias' death, how it unfolded—it terrifies me. Tomás had switched from a loving son to The Reaper in a single heartbeat.

The death-soaked atmosphere splits with persistent shooting. "Kill them all!" Tomás bellows, his thunderous tone dripping with wrath. "Kill every fucker in sight."

Rolling to his side, Tomás fires bullets at incoming henchmen, kneecapping them with a round. When they crumple, he scrambles onto all fours and athletically jumps to his feet. As he rises, his entire posture flexes, showing zero fear. "Bomb the fucking Mexicans and their entire family tree."

"Wait," Shane pants, his white motif t-shirt almost transparent from the downpour and showcasing his muscular physique. "They're fighting with us. It's not them." Silvery light catches the web of thread-like scars exploding over one side of his face as he checks for more ammunition.

Tomás' lungs expand in bursts. He's brandishing two guns now, firing round after round into the street where a few armed men shoot back at him.

He's indescribable. Saturated by a deluge of rain and tarnished in so much blood that his smart suit is forever ruined. Terrifyingly brutal in his retaliation. Unnerved by the mortal danger he appears to be in. And most importantly, oblivious to my identity.

A sleek SUV reverses at speed and skids to a halt, quickly followed by another. Doors open. Men jump out. Twisting his neck around, his rage fueled gaze settles on me.

"Her." He jabs his gun into the air sideways, pointing it at me. "Grab the bitch. She's in on this." Tomás doesn't wait, he storms toward the farthest vehicle with a murderous cloud swirling in his wake.

I'm abruptly hauled to my feet and yanked by the hair.

"Cover her head," One man orders while the others heave Elias' corpse into the closest waiting Escalade.

"Shane!" I finally find my voice. "Please… it's me… Carina…"

Shane glances over his shoulder as I'm manhandled

and dragged. His unfriendly glower chills me to the bone. "You?"

"Please... this is a mistake."

"You're in it up to your fucking eyeballs, kid. He doesn't give second chances. You're all outta luck."

16

TOMÁS

I'm one breath away from detonating.

Papá's blood is everywhere. The suit I'm wearing is swamped in the one thing I despise more than deceit–helplessness. He was dying and there wasn't a single thing I could do to change it.

His time was up, so I did the only humane thing a son could offer his dying father. A quick shove into the arms of death. Not before I blanked out for a beat. As he would undoubtedly predict, I hesitated—the very thing he tried to beat out of me.

I shirk out of the seven-thousand-dollar jacket ruined by blood like it's scalding my torso. Blind panic tightens my ribs, making me mentally unsteady. I repeatedly punch the headrest in front of me. My filthy fist leaves an ugly streak of gore on the leather.

Knots wrangle in my stomach, the uncomfortable ache creating waves of nausea. But it's the sharp pain in my heart, the very thing I swore would remain forever impenetrable, that shatters under the weight of memories.

Flashbacks that are too similar to the shitshow in the street behind our convoy.

It's a waste of time loving a soul when death is inevitable—it's the only absolute promise in this life. The emotion is a hex. A curse from the gods to weaken us with its complexities.

Maybe if I shed a tear, the hell galloping free inside me could escape, but I'm void of tears. I slip into the mental coma I've lived in since my uncle was mutilated by war. Since the boy with stars in his eyes had ended his life in an act of *love*.

Lost in anarchy, I don't see the city lights fade or feel peace as the vehicle eats up the slopes to my isolated mountain refuge. From up here, amidst abundant greenery and swaying palms, I'm able to survey the domain we rule over.

A chill spikes my pulse. Papá's dead. And now—now it's my turn to rule.

"Tommy." The driver twists in his seat to see me. It's only then I realize we're parked outside my home. "You want us to come in?"

I stare him in the eye and cock my head. This madness whirring through me is a motion picture of past and present. It's misting my usual level-headedness and quickly flipping me to psychotic.

"Gather everyone by the pool. There's an assassin in one of the vehicles." An ache spreads across my brow. "She'll tell me everything she knows and then I'll cut her throat."

"Understood." He nods without hesitation. We both

know this is proper protocol for treachery. "I'll do it, Tommy. Let me sort this out for you. For Elias."

I swallow hard, my fingers curling around the gun by my hip. I'm perfectly capable of an interrogation and a termination. Tonight, these men will learn how my reign will begin—with zero tolerance.

"No." I hear my tone, harsh and thick, like I've lost a year's worth of sleep in one night. "I'll look her in the eye before I pull the trigger. No one fucks with us and survives the fall out. No one."

The door opens into the chilly night air, but I don't feel a thing. Shane peers inside. "Tommy," he greets me with a faint wisp of wariness.

He's witnessed my episodes before, and tonight, my father's assassination has pulled the pin from inside my brain. I'll erupt at any second.

The lights have gone out within me. Any final scraps of humanity were macerated. Demons run wild and I've no inclination to tame them.

Not anymore.

His eyes rest on the mucky shirt tarnished with death. "We need to talk." He clears his throat and gives me space when my grimy shoes hit home soil.

I swallow hard, fumbling with the buttons. Quickly losing my temper, I rip the filthy shirt from my torso, fist it into a ball and shove it into his chest. "I've nothing to say until I've spoken to the woman. Burn the shirt."

He lowers the garment and cautiously tosses it to the guy standing beside him. "That's what I want to talk about."

I hold my hand up to silence him. "Unless she's a fucking queen, she'll die."

Shane blows out a breath and drags a hand down his face. "Tommy, look at me." He angles into my feathered line of vision, my fury clouding his visible scars. "We need to tell Teresa and your brothers before the word gets out. They need to hear it from you. You're the head of the family now—and the Souza cartel."

His firm hand grips my bicep, the fingers squeezing affectionately. In an instant reflex, I shirk away from him. He's my closest friend and the only man I trust outside of my brothers. But tonight, I'm mentally untouchable. I'm too far gone in grief and vengeance to appreciate sense.

"Once I've dealt with the prisoner, I'll call them." My feet move with ghostly strides. Tonight's events are all too surreal. "I need you to arrange transportation for my father's body to the plantation."

The buzz of security gates closing behind us fills the natural peacefulness. I follow the paved path fringing the villa. An orchid zephyr does nothing to appease my unhallowed mood, nor does the Bogotá skyline with far reaching lights glittering like lost souls.

When I round the two-story building, men congregate in a circle on the terrace, their shock from my father's death thick in the damp air. Drizzle settles on my chest and catches in my lashes. I blink at the scene, fully understanding what I have to do next.

My pulse skyrockets. Every step eats up the distance between me and the bitch who had her hands on my father's neck. She either killed him or she knows who did. And now her fate belongs to me.

"Tommy." A guy bows his head in reverence on my approach. The rest follow suit, each one thumping their hearts in comradery.

I step into the manmade ring and glare down at the shaking form of a woman wearing a red plastic bag over her head and a slash mark where her mouth is. Panicky breaths lift her breasts high, partially visible under the neckline of a soaked dress.

At the end of lean thighs are tattered knees, scraped and bleeding. Any normal man would feel compassion for her raw scratches, but I feel nothing.

I'm dead inside.

"Take the bag off her head," I bark out the order, my tone harsh like a splintered mirror with a jinx of eternal bad luck.

Shane appears to my right. He gives me an odd look, a stare I can't quite decipher, and then steps into the captive to remove the bag. The second it leaves her face; she sucks in a gust of air and touches her stained mouth with shaky red fingertips.

Sable tendrils hang limply, mapping her cheeks like a delicate net, but it's those huge watery amber eyes pinpointing me that stab my chest.

I inhale a sharp breath of my own and swallow. "You?" I try so damn hard to stop myself from blacking out with rage. The beauty I'd set free has done a U-turn back into my life again. "You came back to finish the job to assassinate my father?"

Straggly lengths whip side to side as she shakes her head wildly. "No!"

I lunge at her and sink the tips of my fingers into her

teary cheeks, squeezing them so her pretty lips pucker to an oval shape.

"Liar!" I yell into her face and sense her insides recoil. Liquid horror streams from the corners of her fiery eyes, still bold and feisty, like I remember.

Only this time, I see my reflection in her flames and feel my skin blaze from the touch of her.

"Why the fuck were you on your own in an alleyway at night?" I grit out through clenched teeth. "Tell me the truth before I kill you, like my father ordered."

I hear a collective murmur from the ranks. It's unheard of for a man to disobey a direct order from the cartel king, never mind let a potential threat to our kingdom walk free.

Lessening my vice like grip, I give her the chance to answer my questions.

"I was trying to stop the bleeding," she chokes out on a sob. "Someone shot him. I was leaving the jazz bar after my shift. He dropped at my feet."

"Bullshit! You expect me to believe you'd help the man who wanted you dead?" The laugh bubbling from my throat is both deranged disbelief and searing pain.

A horrifying weight of deceit. My instincts told me she was far too innocent. Once before, I stared into those beautiful wide eyes of hers and felt my dead heart jostle when all I found was her inner turmoil. I got off on the lust she tried and failed to suppress.

Something about her naivety spoke to me in a way I'd never expected. She felt like sunlight after war--a life-saving lungful of oxygen with a sharp kick of heroin.

Deep down in my gut, I knew she was the most addictive drug I could ever survive.

So rather than heed an instruction, I had duped my father into thinking I'd killed her all because she fascinated me in a way that was unnatural and unacceptable. Carina was a seductive siren in the madness of my mind, coaxing me to her sandy shores where I found a filament of peace for a brief moment in time. And then I let her go.

"It's the truth." Her chin wobbles beneath my palm, dragging me out of the vivid memory that reminds me of what she did with that sinful mouth of hers. "I don't have any weapons. And how the hell would I know he'd be in that alleyway, in that part of town?"

I hollow her cheeks once more, irritated at how being this close to her makes me relent a fraction. It's a plausible answer, as much as it kills me to admit it to myself. "Then why the fuck would you help him?" I hiss with a sardonic grimace, the words burning my throat.

"Because he's your father." Her lashes lower and she swallows. "I was helping him for you. For what *you* did to save me."

The tremor in my hand starts as mild. I shove her face away from mine, taking a deep breath while she just sits there on her knees with bloodied hands trembling by filthy thighs. But when she raises two fingers and subconsciously pads the scar I know exists on her lip, my patience snaps.

An uncontrollable urge to both fuck her, mark her, and make her mine mixes with the desire to kill her. It twists within me like a fiery serpent. I lift the gun to the sky and shoot. Carina tries to scurry away, but I'm too fast, too fucking pumped with adrenaline and poison.

My own blood-stained hands seize the fragile bones in her wrists. Big tears tumble when her hot little body slams into mine. A deeply magnetic gaze paralyzes me. I'm dying to bury myself inside her and forget about trauma for the next few hours.

Our connection, although violent and cataclysmic, is undeniable.

"There's one more thing I should have done before I gave you freedom." I jab the barrel of my gun into her navel and gaze at the thin circle of fire bordering her enlarged pupils.

"Do it!" spits a guy on my right—from the men I'd forgotten were watching. "Slaughter the bitch. Do it for Elias."

Diego bustles in beside me, brandishing his handgun, pointing it at Carina. *No...* my fucking prisoner. I spin on my heels, unwilling to release her and warring within myself for a speck of decorum, so this doesn't end up as a massacre.

"Are you telling me what to do?" I snarl, balancing on rationality.

"She has his blood on her hands, Tommy," he growls back at me, slightly tamer than before. "He's dead, because of that lying *puta*. You said it yourself."

Diego jostles his gun too close to me, the ultimatum of rebellion vibrating from his form to mine. But what angers me the most is the audacity of his actions—his obvious disrespect toward me.

I lean into him, teeth bared. "You think I'm weak,

Diego? Incapable of justice? Softer than my father? Or maybe you think I shouldn't be in charge. Is that it, huh?"

The whites of his eyes gleam with provocation. "Show us you're the rightful leader and shoot the traitor. Elias wouldn't hold back."

I laugh coldly. "I'm my father's son—*not* him. I've nothing to prove to you."

My guard dogs howl from indoors, ready to be unleashed on my order. He shuffles from foot to foot and in a thoughtless second cocks his gun and points it at Carina's face.

I'm fire and ice. Choking flames and an avalanche of snow.

Without delay, I step between her and the threat of death. I want an excuse to terrorize someone and it's going to be this motherfucker—because it can't be her. Not yet.

"Loyal men don't point a gun at their king, Diego."

Shane appears tight to my side in solidarity and points his rifle at my new enemy. "Lower your weapon," he says calmly. "Or I'll blow your brains out."

Diego offers it to him slowly, his face contorted with bitterness. "Elias knew how to control insurgents. She's the enemy here, not me."

I throttle the grip of my own gun. "I don't take orders from anyone."

Even though I'm riddled with a bloodthirsty need, my tone belies the slip of control. I see double Diegos and my heart rate has elevated higher than the screening palms.

"I'm in charge of the whole motherfucking show now —*me*." Carina sways into me, her own dizziness making her weak. The heat of her body next to mine does something unheard of. It grounds me like an anchor amidst the mental fracas.

I suck in a gust and simultaneously squeeze her wrist until I'm certain it's just hysteria getting the better of me.

Then I exhale slowly before continuing. "I'll stake my claim as head of the Souza cartel. And after this evening's war, I demand answers. This woman has those answers, you dumb fuck."

Diego tries to speak, but it's too late. He wanted a show of strength and that's what he gets.

Bang.

His heavy corpse drops, and my adrenaline flies off the charts. Carina flinches, her muscles tense, following my erratic gesture. But it wasn't really a thoughtless act. Diego was my father's special tasks lieutenant, which meant he had no boundaries or moral code. A warped bastard who had taunted the mute little boy left in shock after his uncle's death. I swore I'd kill the fucker when the time was right, and that time is now.

Papá was suspicious of everyone, because Diego Ramirez systematically poisoned his mind. When I suggested getting rid of him, my father stuck a knife to my throat and asked what I was hiding from him. From that day on, I made it my mission to do my own thing while respecting his authority. But the hate for the man now lying on the ground never went away.

My glare scours the rest of the men idly standing by in position to either support me or try to take me down.

"Anyone else want to challenge my authority?" I don't have to yell to be heard. Each of them witnesses my chest heave as quick breaths flare my nostrils. They know better than to question me and face death without hesitation.

"Good. I'm in charge of the operation now, like I said. Arrange for our men to guard the house tonight. Shane…" I turn into him. "We'll talk later. Right now, I have unfinished business to take care of. Let the dogs out."

17

TOMÁS

With one ruthless yank, Carina falls into line behind me.

Together, we pass each of the men vying for justice. She stumbles in a half bowed position, unable to free herself from my clutches.

Brutus and Sniper, my fiendish German Shepherds, bolt free of the property. They brush past my legs on the hunt for fresh blood, sniffing the dried plasma both Carina and I share.

My father's blood.

She doesn't make a sound as Sniper runs his inquisitive wet nose over her bare legs. When he flicks out his tongue to taste her salty skin, my chest implodes. Even my dog is captivated by her.

Shane whistles and the curious duo dart off into the shadows. In the half-light crossing over the threshold, I catch my reflection in the glare of the bi-fold doors. I'm surrounded by judging eyes and the city lights of a kingdom I now control.

I'm a man unhinged by sorrow, raised in warfare, and

brainwashed into believing violence is the only answer. The pitiful woman trailing in the wake of my storm is an unfortunate slave snared on a merciless hook.

I barely recognize myself anymore, if I ever really knew who the man inside me should be. I've lived in the shadow of fate for too long. Hiding in the darkness of a gruesome deed carried out by a young boy. And now, history repeated itself twenty-four years later.

Beyond the need for bloodshed lives a new infestation. A surge of lust so powerful that it's choking me with every glance at the little liar.

She's in my home now.

Under my control.

Mine.

"Please..." she hiccups, and I almost buckle with an odd sensation of empathy. "I had nothing to do with it."

I ignore her pleas. Simply because I'm not in the mood to debate her involvement or talk about what will happen next.

She falls silent when her explanation receives a cold shoulder, and we climb the spiral staircase to my suite. This isn't the plan. Then again, shooting my father in the forehead wasn't on my agenda for the evening either.

My stomach physically heaves at the thought of him. I'm retching and simultaneously twisting away to hide my inner struggle. I'm driven to wreak havoc and she's back for more. Whatever happens in the coming hours can only distract me from what will happen tomorrow.

With her soft hair tangled in my fingers, I usher her into my bedroom and kick the door shut. We continue to the adjoining ensuite, freshly redecorated in obsidian marble to match my soul.

"Take your filthy boots off." I force myself to release her and glare at the elegant shape of her grazed shins, letting my eyes glide upward to bare thighs. My dick jerks. She swallows a gulp, all the while keeping her gaze locked with mine, clashing like killer knives. "Do it." I snarl.

Slowly she lowers, sits on her ass and tugs at the laces to untie the sweet little bows. Once she's kicked off the Doc Martens, I lunge at her again and force her to stand upright with a merciless grip on her bicep. The beat of my pulse is off the charts, making my abdomen clench. I can't decide if it's a thirst for bloodshed or a hunger to fuck.

Nonetheless, I roughly shove her into the open shower and flick the lever, inviting a rush of water to rain down on her filthy state. We're both plastered in brownish scum. It's disgusting and fucking stomach churning.

She cowers under the jets, but her eyes are glowing amber irises, blazing with injustice. I set my gun on the countertop and stare at my hands. The hands of a god, or the weapons of a devil. Both titles are unable to show mercy.

Carina stays still, her skin draining of Papá's blood as I kick off my shoes and drag my pants past my hips. My boxers are next to join the grimy fabric on the heated tiles underfoot.

Doing what I always do, I lower to my haunches and scoop the filthy garments in a bundle to incinerate them later. The second my hands are full; she bolts from the shower to snatch the gun. Kamikaze splashes shoot in every which way as she finds the perfect stance to take aim.

"Don't move," she hisses. "Put your hands up."

Droplets plummet from the tips of her soaked hair, and the blossomy dress clinging to her curves is wickedly transparent. A hedonistic shiver prickles my spine as intrigue clashes with my cruel intentions. Her belief of control has my dick painfully throbbing. I admire her boldness—her insane bravery. That shred of craziness is closely matched with mine.

Most men shy away from confronting a guy like me. They know the consequences. They understand respect. Those who cross me die.

When I drop the clothes and give her an eyeful of my solid dick, she takes a quick sip of steamy air as her pretty cheeks blush to a fuckable shade of pink. Her eyes dart from my hard-on to the wall tiles. It's that reaction that fires up my feral cylinders and reminds me that I can claim her virginity as mine.

In fact, knowing I'll be the only man to take it turns me on beyond crazy. I'll earn two titles on this fucked up day. Leader of my kingdom and master of her virtue.

"You think you can take me on?" I step into her, bringing the bite of cold steel to my naked pec.

"I'm the one holding the gun, Tomás." She actually fucking smirks and a wisp of something warm whispers around my icy heart.

Instead of grabbing the weapon, I widen my stance and fold my arms. I'll play her foolish game on my own terms.

"You won't shoot me." I sneer, the desire for bloodshed completely erased. I need something far more rewarding.

"Try me." Her mouth contorts to an evil snarl, but the bloodied hand holding my gun trembles enough for us both to see it. "You think I won't protect myself? That I'll let you torture me for whatever perversion you need satisfied." Her eyebrow hitches as my dick pulses. "I'll shoot you alright, Tomás Souza. I'm not scared of you."

I laugh darkly. "Then do it. Shoot me. I fucking dare you to pull the trigger. It's easy. Just count to three and squeeze." She swallows a gulp, but keeps her arm raised. "Before you kill me and meet your own certain death outside this room, why don't you honor me with one last request?"

"Oh yeah?" She scoffs. "And what's that? Suck your dick again?"

My pulse quickens. It takes all of my training to stay grounded and not slam her elegant body into the wall.

Her game. My rules. One winner.

"Confess," I growl. "Tell me who wanted my father dead and where you stashed the weapon."

She scowls. "Do you *still* think I tried to kill him?"

"I do."

"Christ…" Her delicate shoulders fall and she shakes her head gently. "The only interaction I had with Elias was pressing my hand over his neck… to stop the bleeding. Then you arrived seconds later." I'd forgotten how charming that sweet voice of hers was, and how it made my scalp tingle. "I should have run away and left him there, but all I could think about was how he was your father."

I take a confident step so her elbow bends and the gun prods in deeper. "And that's your final admission before you shoot me. You were trying to save the man who wanted you dead for a debt you owed me?"

Her face pales and she scrunches up her forehead as if thinking of the truth a bit harder. "Not a debt…"

"Then what?"

She stamps her foot and growls. "Does it matter?"

"I guess not. Go ahead. Pull the trigger." I goad, my patience thinner than a sheet of ice marbled in cracks.

Her hand trembles, and I know I've got her, even if her bravado doesn't match the visible panic fluttering in her pulse. "Couldn't you let me go instead?"

"Not gonna happen." Apprehension flashes behind her eyes, masking her fear of me. "Either shoot me or get your ass back in the shower."

As she contemplates her decision, my hand flies out to cuff her wrist. She strains against the grip and locks her elbow so the gun points to the ceiling. I shove her rigid arm sideways at the very second she pulls the trigger.

It clicks, already emptied of bullets. My temper instantly flips to nuclear. Whether she meant to do it or not, she had actually fired the gun. I knew there weren't any bullets left.

But she didn't.

I snatch it from her shaky hand and chuck it against the wall. Then hunch over and unsheathe a small bone knife I wear strapped to my shin.

"Tomás," she pants. "I… I… didn't mean to…"

As I stalk forward, she reverses into the shower. Water sluices over the swell of her breasts. Power courses through my veins. All the fucked up events of the evening run riot in my mind. I'm on the verge of losing myself and doing something eternally damning.

She slams a hand to my chest in a pathetic attempt to halt my temper from breaking. Too late. The touch of her dainty hand on my skin sets alight every toxic cell in my body. Her kindling warmth sucks me into a vortex.

Out of control splashes dive to our feet, so they aren't a witness to my fraying control. I hook the blade under the top button of her dress, next to her braless breasts. Indecent chills almost cripple me.

My dick throbs for this woman, so painfully solid. Perhaps fate had thrown us together for the greater good —for a reason far beyond death and destruction. I cut the threads in vertical succession. Buttons ping and the fabric splays open to reveal prickled flesh and plump tits.

Fuck!

In a flash, I wrench the sopping dress from her shoulders and let it fall. I catch a glimpse of the healed gunshot snick on her bicep, the one I had given her. The war wound that saved her life. An emotion similar to regret squeezes my motives to fuck her. This isn't one-sided and I'm too far gone to stop.

The next to come off are the feminine panties protecting her innocence. A snip of lace at either side of her angular hips and they plop to our feet in a dirty puddle.

My gaze slides from her parted lips to the swirl of Papá's blood flowing into the drain. Nausea creeps up from my stomach, forcing my palm to the glossy tiles at my side for support.

I cup her chin and force her wide gaze to meet mine. "I shot the last bullet into the sky as a precaution." My voice is thick with the mania she's injected me with. "Want to know what that precaution was?"

She returns my stare, naked and hellishly beautiful. "Yes," she whispers so softly I could have easily missed it had I not surveyed her mouth closely.

"To stop me from using it on you. After tonight, there's nothing left of my soul, *little liar*. I'm numb inside except for the sick urge to sink my dick inside something pure. To spoil your untouched pussy and to know I'm the man who owns that title." Her nipples poke out and her skin bristles. "Had it been anyone else, they'd be floating face down in my pool by now... but you... you're something else. You're bad fucking news and I'm this close to..." I squeeze her jaw, my eyes narrowing on the lip she dents with her teeth. "It can't be a coincidence you were in that alleyway. I'll figure it out. That's the only reason you're still alive."

As I lie to her face, she pants in feathery puffs that tingle over my skin. I stand firm, getting off on her nakedness. Her knees quake and she see-saws into me, as if fighting a hot-blooded reaction to our close proximity. Clean fingers curl tightly to stop herself from touching my fiendishly hot skin.

She's alive, because I'm going to finish what she started at the plantation a few months ago. Tonight I need to use her body as my salvation. It's either that, or my kingdom would fall to shit around my breakdown. Rather than fail during my first night stepping up from my father, I'll pour my all into the little liar I have as my captive.

After an age of staring at her, I drop all contact and dip out from under the warm waterfall. My retreat receives an audible sigh—a sexy gasp that could be misconstrued as disappointment.

I glance back and witness her naughty tongue peek free as searching eyes linger on my ass. It sweeps the contour of glistening pink lips. That simple act invites a welcome memory to return. How she had willingly stuffed her throat full of my dick. Instantly, my heavy dick twitches. I'm alive inside, my veins buzzing with a hunger I never knew existed.

If the men downstairs could see how this woman is affecting me, they'd certainly doubt my ability to rule as a cutthroat leader. Over the years, I've earned a reputation as an emotionally detached businessman and now that I have an important role to fulfill, it's even more crucial I maintain that persona. Yet Carina's presence both calms my inner turmoil and incites confusion.

I move to the vanity where my stash of condoms is kept and toss the carton to the floor for her to see. A dainty hand presses to the wall tiles. Rather than move further away, she waits in the shower with proud nipples and a provocative stance. Her hip dips and an expression of intrigue draws her gaze the length of my bare chest. For all my threats, she's showing zero resistance, which makes this all the more fun.

In the seconds we're apart, I curse myself for allowing the distraction. Uncle Angelo's voice speaks to me, his warning loud and clear. *Don't give them what they want, give them what you need. On your terms. Make them wait.*

The memory of him floods my mind, made worse when I see myself in the mirror. Papá's blood streaks my left cheekbone. Shadows dance over pale features, and the stubble coating my jaw seems darker than before. I look haunted. Horrific. Unkempt. Nothing like I should.

Following habit, I rinse my hands under the faucet with scalding water to cleanse away my sins. They follow me everywhere, because that's who I am.

The dark angel of death.

"Tomás?" A feminine voice infiltrates the inner whirlwind, grinding my bones to ashes.

I glance sideways to witness the gap close from her body to mine. Her forehead creases as she stops before me and takes a quick breath. What she does next has me riddled with sadism and left breathless from an unhealthy fascination.

Her small hand reaches for my wayward dick. Like she did during our last encounter in a bathroom suite. Even this time, it still catches me off guard.

Sparks catapult through my chest when she finds the courage to speak. "If you really thought I was capable of murder, you would have killed me in front of your men. That's a fact. Instead, I'm in this bathroom with you, naked and surrounded by steam."

I bare my teeth at her. No one calls me out. In a tornado movement, I seize her long throat. "Understand this, *little liar*. I need a woman to fuck for the night, and you're the only woman here. I will happily shoot you dead if I find out you were involved in my father's assassination. *Comprende?*" I spit out, leaning into her face so the tips of our noses brush.

Truth is, having tasted my share of females, I've never met anyone with the ability to soothe the corruption spreading through my veins like hot tar. Until her. And the night she dragged me out of the black mist with her voodoo, witchy spell, using her pretty little mouth and hungry groans.

I lost control—and she took it.

Her fingertips skate to my balls, ticklish pressure forces my abdomen to clench.

"I was in the wrong place at the wrong time. Get the security footage from the bar. You'll see for yourself. It wasn't me."

With her hand still on my dick and mine cinching her throat, we stand in silence. I contemplate her honesty and she pushes back her shoulders to correct her posture.

"You still a sweet little virgin?" I growl, aware of her daring fingertips coaxing my troubled mind to a safer place. While fondling my shaft, she nods her head ever so slightly. "If you continue to touch me like that, you won't be for much longer."

Those eyes of fire drill into mine, the challenge set as she whispers, "Is that a threat?" Her voice is smoky and provocative, like she's feeding off my moonless state of mind.

I walk her backward into the shower, pressing my weight into her slippery body. Her breasts tease my chest.

My mouth drops to the shell of her ear. "No threat, *little liar*. It's a fucking promise."

18

CARINA

"Get on your knees. Tonight, *little liar*, I am your king."

I inhale sharply at his command, my heart racing. Remarkable pitch-black eyes glitter under pinprick recessed lights, making them off-the-charts magical. Firm hands apply pressure to my shoulders, the weight forcing me to kneel before him on my scratched knees.

I ignore the shudder of fear shaking me from within and accept he's a full-fledged maniac. With his vicious demands comes an indescribable look, where the cruel beast is barely contained––for either his sake or mine.

He's not a misunderstood eldest child searching for redemption. Tomás Souza is a wicked sinner who wants to set my world on fire. With me in it. And what's even more alarming is that I want him to join me.

I don't know why or how, but the fascination kindling like embers in my core is obvious by the unbearable ache in my sex. How my mouth waters at the thickness of his solid dick now tracing my mouth as he steers it from corner to corner.

"Like what you see?" His breath catches as if he's struggling to breathe.

Salty fluid coats my lips as I hum in agreement. I flick my tongue out to taste him and wonder if it's normal to crave a man's cum as much as I do.

The threatening grunt from the back of his throat gives away his hunger, even though he's fighting to stay unfazed. Something tells me he doesn't let go very often and I'll enjoy the privilege of witnessing it.

For the life of me, I don't understand why I'm not sinking my teeth into the angry crown of satiny skin that strikes one of my cheeks and then the other. But my hands glide over his strong, wet thighs, feeling his hip dips and flexed buttocks.

I've never truly understood the concept of worshiping. Yet right now, on my knees before a man with a physique like his, that's exactly what I'm doing—adoring him.

"Open your mouth." The order cracks like a long-tailed whip, lashing me with shivery tingles. "I want to feel your pretty mouth all over me again." He gathers my hair into a messy ponytail and traps the lengths in his fist. His firm hold burns my scalp where his fingers clamp shut. "Want to know why I want my dick in your mouth?" he murmurs.

I meet his coal-colored eyes and nod, struggling with the illicit desire he's tarnished my innocence with. "I haven't stopped thinking about it since you sank to your knees and sucked me off… when I should've obeyed my father." His voice switches to infuriated and callous. "It was the best fucking blow job I've ever had." He spits the compliment into the swirling steam and catches it with snarling teeth, before drowning his praise in the pool of hot water lapping my shins. "Now take it all again... every last inch of me."

He yanks my head back and watches the tiny droplets catch on my lashes. I take a gulp of air and relax my jaw a little to let him slide in halfway. The weight of him sits heavy on my flattened tongue. He stills. We both do. Me obediently bowing before the new sovereign and him silently finding his way through the darkness he lives in.

Tomás releases my sopping strands and stretches his arms out at either side of his glorious golden torso, his defined abdomen as tight as a drum and leg muscles tensed. His masculine sway infects me with a disease that will ultimately destroy me.

It's a powerful and unexplained urge to obey. The sight of this man vibrating with raw need––with a dark and smoky desire for me––obliterates the warning signs and showers me with feverish chills. He *wants* me. And in this moment, I want him too.

"Eyes up. You already know how I like it." Our gazes clash like swords freshly sharpened on a whetstone.

It's electrifying to meet the eyes of a killer who hunts pleasure with the woman he's branded as the enemy. But he doesn't stare at me with the evil gaze of a man who'd slice up my throat. He sinks his teeth into his bottom lip and sucks in a tattered breath when the length of him fills my mouth completely. I gag when the tip rams my epiglottis, my stomach convulsing.

Rather than retract, he blows out a breath and simultaneously lowers his chin so black eyes pin mine in position again. "Give me your all," he growls, diving long fingers into the hair at my nape and locking me onto his dick. "Suck my dick, *little liar.*"

My reflexes produce even more saliva. It pools around the substantial girth and escapes in clingy streams from the edges of my stretched mouth.

He pushes in and holds my head in place, so the length of him waits in my throat. I'm breathing through my nose in bursts and blinking up at the eyes glued to mine. Hypersensitive nipples ache to be touched and I'm uncomfortably swollen between my thighs. It's a sensation that would drive me insane if he decides to walk away.

But he won't. Not by the wild expression on his gorgeous face. He's searching for temporary amnesia, and I'm the vessel to take him there. When I dig my nails into his ass, he starts to move again. He doesn't go easy on me. If anything, he turns feral, going harder to fuck my convulsing throat without holding back.

He's in control and by his throaty grunts, he's turned on. Which only adds to my own freaky arousal.

"Fuck!" he growls and pauses, so I'm practically swallowing him. "Your pussy will feel a thousand times better than this."

Suddenly, he pulls out and a gust of air fills my starved lungs. He slots his hands under my armpits and hoists me into the air. My ass slams into the wall. A hand lands at the side of my head, so he's arching over me. He's panting now and palming his dick.

Under hooded eyes, he makes me wait. He teases me with anticipation. My heart rate elevates with every passing second and I start to feel scared. I pat my lip for comfort and drag a palm over my belly. It would be easier to fly away than fully satisfy a man like Tomás. If only he would set me free again and save me from the mistake I'm about to enjoy.

The hand stroking his dick jumps to my jaw and he dips into my face. We're closer than ever. Water crashes on the top of his head and glides through his ebony hair, sailing over his tight features.

I'm on fire. Hungry for the one thing I shouldn't crave. Temptation hits me like a forbidden bite from the juiciest red apple. Tingles crest in waves. The delightful wickedness is a thrill more enslaving than anything I've ever known.

Nose to nose, he hollows my cheeks and growls an order, "Turn around."

In the silent second it takes me to debate my actions, he grips my pelvis and forces me clockwise. My palms hit the misted tiles and I blink at the darkness before me.

His jaw rests on the crown of my head while he grinds his hard-on into the base of my spine. I could fabricate a flimsy lie and tell myself this surrender is survival. But it's something far more unforgivable than that. Something I'll never recover from. It's a sickness smearing my soul without a known cure.

The unique scent of this man's pheromones is a secret weapon to make me involuntarily wet. I'm forever damned. His simple cocktail of musk and sweat lowers my defenses.

After tonight, Tomás will mean more to me than the devil he is. For some unknown reason, I don't fear him like I should. Not the man himself. It's his fleeting inner madness that truly petrifies me.

I almost cry at the hypocrisy of it—how he thinks I have the resourcefulness to butcher his father and how he loathes me for being part of it. Except, I'm certain his instincts know I'm not the true villain, otherwise I'd be dead.

Yet here we are, getting off on this chaotic attraction. When teeth graze my shoulder, my pussy throbs and hungry hormones burst in my core.

He grabs a clump of saturated strands and manhandles my head, so his mouth brushes my ear. "I'll enjoy knowing every cell in your sexy body has surrendered to me. That I've left a mark on your skin and your mind." His edgy voice rumbles in his chest, growling within me.

The sexy pitch drives my senses wild. My heart pounds with acceptance—my first time will undoubtedly be rough, and stretched beyond comfortable. Secretly, I'm hoping it will be exactly that, yet I'm fearful it will be too much to handle. It's pathetic and immoral to crave his wickedness like I do, but I'm not in a position to pass judgment on my warped desires. Not when our unspoken bond has saved my life twice.

"It's going to hurt, *sweet little liar*, but it'll be worth the pain when your tight pussy is riding my dick all the way to an orgasm," he mutters into my ear, the deep tone of his voice inciting an uprising of delicious tingles.

I'm not sure if his foresight is reassurance or the gateway to a Hell I'll never leave, nonetheless, it pushes me over the edge with greed.

My flesh catches fire under savage groping hands in

ways I never imagined possible, even if my pride is begging me to fight against him.

His forearm scoops my pelvis while his other hand pushes between my shoulder blades, so I'm bent over at a right angle and fully at his mercy.

"Spread your legs," Tomás orders and then slaps my ass.

I flinch, letting the sting wash over me, then obediently do as he commanded.

He sinks to his haunches and spreads my buttocks. Suddenly his mouth is on me—his tongue inside of me. Then it's replaced by a probing finger that's quickly followed by a second. The erotic sensation of slippery sweeps exploring my private parts and scissor-like penetration has me trembling, lick by lick.

What was once untouched is now claimed—by my captor. I feel him move. Stubble scratches and fingers glide. My legs quake, making me rock into his face, urging him to take me.

I cry out when he slaps my ass for the second time and pulls away from me. I'm left empty and soaking, but not for long. He quickly replaces his fingers with the tip of his dick. It nudges my entrance, but I swear it will never fit.

"You'll feel every single bit of me." His lean legs spread mine farther apart. "I'll own every part of you." I whimper when unforgiving teeth graze my shoulder. "And you'll *never* forget it."

His free hand slides around my front, squeezes my breast, and then he pushes in so deep, so forceful that I scream. A second of fear licks my lust with tingles of the unknown. He'll surely split me in two at this rate.

"That's it, *little liar*. Be a good girl and take it all." He freezes for a fraction of time to allow my inner walls to relax, adjust, and receive him.

I trap a lungful of air, dizzy under his scandalous spell —stretched wide and finally filled by him. The sharp sting of tight flesh compressing his overwhelming size makes me wince. It's like no other sensitivity I've ever felt. Gluttony and discomfort unite to create a nirvana where this man's gargoyles guard the gates, ready to attack at any moment if I go against him.

Hot lips trail the curve of my neck to help me relax. Without warning, he ruthlessly yanks my head back, angles his hips so the fullness wanes and then slams inside again.

"Fuck, yeah," he hisses.

The harshness forces me to yelp, so insanely consumed by his control. The searing burn inside of me ebbs and with the next thrust, it switches to bliss. This time he doesn't hesitate, he fucks me with so much stamina that my hearing goes wonky. Piece by piece I come undone. Warmth rushes over me like the rays of the summer sun. I feel him underneath my skin and buried within me.

My senses become three dimensional, bouncing off walls, charging my muscles, and energizing the water vaporizing on my skin.

"Oh… my… God…" I gasp, supporting the upper half of my body with both hands while he controls the lower half.

"I'm no god, *little liar*," he grits out close to my ear.

"And I'm no fucking saint either. But I will be the master of your body."

A surge of endorphins rally inside me, collectively building to a sensation so intense it surpasses the heights of a tsunami. It starts off as trillions of tingles and builds to a rogue wave of ecstasy.

I lose the part of myself I've kept hidden—the tormented girl who only dreamed of a man's touch and never believed it would happen. With every brutal thrust, I completely let go.

As I move with him and pant for more, the realization that he's the most lethal drug to be found drowns me.

All the hatred I've stored within my heart, body, and soul over the years morphs into a guilty beast. I shouldn't feel so free, so enlightened. But those shadows don't terrorize me when I'm this close to Heaven.

His toxic sex enslaves me. And I'm charged with an unquenchable thirst. For the first time in my life, I'm in the powerful arms of a man and thriving on danger.

Beyond the pleasure I'm drowning in, I hear a sexy grunt and sense his ruts turning crazed. The savage snarl ripping from his throat warns me he's about to cum. Instinctively, my pelvic muscles squeeze around him.

"Fuck!" he snarls, slapping my ass with an eager crack.

The offending hand quickly swathes my throat from behind and jerks my spine into his solid chest so I'm trapped between sinewy muscle and hard tiles. With one last upward thrust, he goes absolutely rigid except for the hot breath against my cheek.

In the aftermath, I'm like molten jelly. Both of us pant for oxygen and stay silent in a moment of vulnerability.

His hands fall away first. I start to shake when he reverses, and his semi-solid dick slips out. Exhaustion paralyzes me, my legs weak and wobbly.

Tomás moves away, so we're no longer touching. There's a bountiful waterfall separating us and a sinister truth—that's earth-shattering.

I use the wall for support and straighten my spine, keeping my chin high so he doesn't see how much he shook my world.

He exits the shower, rips off the filled condom, wraps a towel around his hips, and strolls toward the door. "Use the bandages in the vanity for your knees. Get into bed. I have business to take care of." His confident countenance returns and a veil of ice frosts his tone. "Congratulations, *little liar*," he says over his shoulder. "You've offered your soul to a Souza, and I've taken the first bite. There's no going back for you now."

And just like that, he saunters out of sight like nothing life altering had happened to either of us.

Bastard.

I stay in the large shower and hold a hand over my out-of-control heart. It takes a while for my daze to vaporize amidst the steam. All those teenage years of wondering how the touch of a man would change me, and now I'm shivering in the aftermath of the most convoluted experience of my life.

Somehow, what happened to me as a young teen has manifested into the worst possible affliction. Leaving me truly damaged from within, I crave the wrong kind of touch. It's not gentleness and tender kisses that fire up my desire—it's his dark side.

There is no way to know if that disturbed savagery is normal for a woman to lose herself in. Perhaps this is all I deserve. Eternal sadism and a hallucination of attachment.

Under the powerful jets, I let the water sluice over my aching body and relish the odd sensation between my thighs. It's a burn of satisfaction, not regret.

I'm oblivious to the time spent nursing my sick mind after his kingly dick completely demolished me. But no one came to get me and I'm thankful for the respite solace offers.

Chills scurry over me when I turn off the shower and mummify myself in an oversized, fluffy towel. In the silence of the room, I hear my conscience telling me it was a bad idea to offer myself up as a sacrifice. Except, my gut tells me Tomás enjoyed it more than he expected, too.

I pick up my ruined dress and check the tiny pocket where Elias Souza's ring is hidden. It's still there, the stone as deep in color as his blood I wore. In a weird ripple of an aftershock, I panic. If he finds this in my possession, he'll undoubtedly think I took it as a souvenir of my handy work—that I murdered his father. I open the vanity and wedge it behind a few unopened bottles of shower gel.

Tomás might think I belong to him, but he's wrong. What we did in the shower has toughened my wings with an armor of forged steel. I'm a phoenix rising from the ashes of a tormented past. He can't break what's already broken.

I hold my hands up and admit how I had *wanted* him.

His violence set like the rays of the western sun, and I loved every disturbed second of it.

And as much as I surrendered to him, Tomás conceded to me. The only question I need to answer is whether it's only him—or would another man offer me the same escape?

Regardless of what we just shared; I know it won't last. Tomorrow I could be on the firing line again. I'm living on borrowed time, which means I should run away at any opportunity.

19

TOMÁS

My teeth ache from clenching them so fucking hard. Walking away from her had felt like the tug of stitches hacked out of a deep knife wound—excruciating.

It was necessary. Brutal. And the way it will always be with me.

Sniper sniffs my ankles and sits on the floor by my dripping legs, his proud head high, expecting his master's touch. I'm stretched out on the sofa, hair wet, a towel slung low, and my mood contemplative. Far off lights beyond the vast floor to ceiling windows glimmer as if the earth is truly breathing. I prefer to keep the lights off and spy on the world while I'm cloaked in a comfortable darkness.

Shadows move on the terrace as armed soldiers roam the compound, dutifully doing the night watch. They don't make a sound, but every now and again I see the orange glow of a cigarette. It's not uncommon to have guards patrolling my territory. However, after tonight's massacre, I've tripled the men.

Hung on the wall near the liquor cabinet is the one and only photograph I have of my uncle and me. As the years passed, the colors have faded. I had a local artist duplicate the image of my hero wrapping his arm around my neck, his usual stern expression relaxed with a rare smile. A smile he only offered me.

I guess that was the last time I felt true happiness. Even though the portrait had turned out like a carbon copy, I still prefer the original, time tarnished snapshot.

In need of a hard drink, I swig a large measure of scotch and let my head fall back onto supple leather, taking a moment to settle in the quiet aftermath. My mobile phone sits on the coffee table beside the newly opened bottle of liquor. I need a few drinks before I call Mamá and offload the bad news. It still hasn't sunk in.

"What a night." Shane wanders through the open plan lounge, his face shaded in shadows. "Do you need anything?"

"I'm fine." I keep my gaze fixed on the amber liquid.

If only he knew I'd just had a hit far superior to drugs or alcohol, something that's reconfigured my manic thirst for bloodshed and given me a degree of control. It shouldn't be such a buzz to know I'm the only guy who's had Carina's tight little pussy, but that feeling is mind-blowing. I could have let her fuck me to death.

Right there, in the shower, I self-divided, splitting torment with pleasure. She fascinates me in a way that scares me. With the life I've led, nothing fucking scares me anymore. Not even the afterlife.

And still doesn't now my father and uncle are waiting on their fiery thrones in Hell, saving a seat for me when my time is up. Which could be anytime in this business. That's the risk we take. The rules we play by. The life we lead.

I shiver, exhausted by the night's macabre events. Every slow sip composes the tremors of an aftershock. My adrenaline levels are well and truly spent. All my limbs ache and although my wrathful thoughts have somewhat eroded, they're still distorted.

My father is dead.

I can't find his ring.

And the little liar upstairs in my bed gave me freedom from myself.

I cock my head on Shane's approach and raise my glass. "Someone wanted Papá dead. I won't rest until I find out who ordered the hit. And when I do, I'll teach the motherfucker a lesson that Colombia won't forget. What have you got for me?"

"Tommy." Shane grabs the bottle and unscrews the cap. "I'm sorry the guys failed to protect him." He pours himself a double, straight up, no ice. "But I swear to you, we'll find the bastard who did this. Our men are working on it as we speak... shaking a few trees to see who falls out."

My eyes settle on him, devoid of warmth. "Start with that traitor Morales. He had every reason to seek revenge. Flavio was his best lieutenant."

Shane sits at the far end of the couch, sips the amber liquid, and closes his eyes briefly, obviously needing it as much as I do. "It wasn't him."

"How can you be so certain?"

"He lost a lot of men tonight. They were slaughtered in

the street alongside our guys. If you need more proof, he was shot. Whoever took out Elias went for him too."

Brutus covers the marble flooring; his nails tap with leisurely strides until he reaches us. He doesn't settle next to me, which isn't a surprise. His nose sniffs the length of my shin and, rather than curl up by my feet, he saunters to the window and points his nose toward the view.

The rescued German Shepherd is a true soldier, insanely faithful and terrifyingly hostile when required. A year ago, I found him by the side of the road, grossly emaciated and mutilated with no tail. The poor guy was beyond abused—broken.

Thankfully, he didn't have the strength to argue when I scooped him up and brought him here. After six months of rehabilitation, he took to training like he was born to protect. Now, he's a lithe beast with a shiny coat, bright white teeth, and a home to guard.

There's a familiar glaze to his chestnut eyes. A stern glower I can't figure out, like he's hurting inside or lost in the same mayhem as I am.

I like space and so does he. We have an understanding. Brutus might be thoughtful, but he'd rip out the throat of any fucker who entered the compound uninvited. It's savage loyalty that reminds me of Uncle Angelo. The sort of insane dependability I treasure.

Knocking the scotch back, I savor the burn as it travels into my stomach. "Is he alive?" I ask, uncaring if the Mexican survived or not.

"Yeah." He nods, slouching forward and dragging a hand over his disfigured face. "He's gone underground for surgery."

I eye him as he takes another sip. "Then we have a big fucking problem, Shane. We met with him in secret, which means someone close to us planned this."

He holds my stare, the whites of his eyes sparkling in the dim light. "Where's the girl?"

"Upstairs." Sniper rests his chin on my knee. When I pat the empty space beside me, he immediately accepts the invitation, jumps up, curls into a ball, and sighs with contentment.

Shane swills the scotch, coating the inside of his glass. I know what he's thinking. We've always been on the same page and a woman won't change that.

He's the closest thing I'll ever have to a best friend, even though I'm his leader and he's my second. We've done some shady shit together since we first met in Boston.

I was a traumatized kid under the care of my strict grandfather, and Shane was my cousin. My mother's Irish bloodline runs in his veins, the son of her eldest brother. We bonded over competitive target practice and a love for traditional homemade potato bread. I trust the guy with my life and I'd take a bullet to protect his.

It's an unsaid meeting of minds between two men raised in a deadly world where emotions lead to vulnerability.

"Look into her exact movements since you dropped her in Bogotá after she left my father's plantation. Find out where she lives and get intel on everyone she's been in contact with. Get me security footage from every establishment in that area. I need her bank accounts too. And the last place she ate. Map out every single step she's taken." Shane falters a beat, a question sitting heavily on his tongue. I give him a tired glare. "Go on, spit it out."

His shoulders bounce. "It's unusual for you to be so…" He raises his eyebrows. "Lenient."

I can see where this is going. "I know." I admit. "Papá said she was a traitor. My gut told me she wasn't. And now I've seen her again, I can't help thinking she's here to serve another purpose. She wasn't sent to execute Papá."

"Serve another purpose?" he muses. "And by that, you mean be your fuck toy?" The asshole laughs into his glass. "You're a horny son of a bitch, Tommy. We've had hundreds of women, so what makes this one any different?"

She takes my breath away every time I look at her. "Fuck if I should know. Angelo taught me to listen to my instincts, not interrupt them."

Shane blows out slowly, his eyes heavy with tiredness. "It's okay to like someone, Tommy. You have a habit of collecting broken things. But you gotta look at the full picture."

"She's not broken…" I take a gulp of my drink. "It's something else…the way she…"

His brows pop up. "What—sucks you off?"

I shake my head and chuckle, pretending his comment is absurd when really that's it in a nutshell, with one other thing. "I've never met anyone who could settle the chaos within me like she can. It's either a gift or a curse."

Shane eyes me with caution before he speaks. "Then what's gonna happen if she really did shoot Elias?"

I let his question settle before I reach for the bottle and refill his glass, then my own. "I guess you'll have to follow me into Hell. If I can't trust my instincts anymore, then everyone's a threat. I'll end up as paranoid as Papá was."

Shane lowers his lashes with compassion. "Will you finish her if she's a threat?"

He tips the glass to his lips and drains the contents. I swallow hard, get up, and pace the wall of windows. "Show me the CCTV footage the second it lands."

"Tommy... you're not alone, mate. You know that, right? Whatever you need from me—I'll do it."

I look over at him to find his shoulders pushed back and his spine rigid in a business-like posture. He'd kill her for me except, he's sorely mistaken. I know what he's thinking, that she's the one to tame me. The guy should know better.

The bullets I had gifted Angelo and Elias were out of love. Family bonds are the only threads that keep me grounded and look at what I did to the two most powerful men in my life. If that's what I'm capable of, then there's no need to question what I'd do to a sexy teenager with the body of a goddess.

"In the grand scheme of things, she's simply another woman who keeps popping up. She might interest me now, but we both know that'll wear off soon enough. If I have to get rid of her, I'll do it. No hesitation."

I return my gaze to the midnight blue sky, aware of Brutus' wet nose nudging my curled fist. He sits at my bare feet, the two of us staring at the heavens in silence.

"Okay," Shane replies with an exhausted sigh. "Aside from beating the guts out of the tight lipped Halcones, there's one more matter to clear up." I hear his boots hit the coffee table as he slouches into the sofa. "Apparently, there's a fancy-ass wedding to plan. When the fuck were you going to tell me you're engaged to Bianca Morales? Not only is she young, she's fucking gorgeous. You lucky son of a bitch."

Sniper stirs beside me on the sofa.

Instinctively, I check for my piece, finding it on the coffee table where I'd left it. He lifts his nose, sniffs, and then rests his chin on my thigh. Even though he's settled again, the hairs on my neck lift in warning. I rotate my wrist to check the time. It's early morning, minutes before sunrise.

The glass in my hand is empty, drained only an hour ago before I dozed off. Shane dragged his ass to the spare room after our fifth drink together, giving me alone time to call my family with the news. I'd held off as long as I could. No one should have to tell their brothers their father was gunned down in an alleyway. The discrete detail of the final bullet will be my secret to carry to my own grave.

One after the other, I repeated the same phrase. *Papá was assassinated in Bogotá this evening. I lost his ring in the street, but I've got men searching for it. I'll find the fuckers who did this and kill everyone they've ever known.*

And it's true. Whoever targeted us would regret the decision to start a war with the Souzas.

Footsteps lower from step to step, descending the staircase. I know it's not Shane's usual stomp, because he's heavy footed. My housekeeper wouldn't be here for another few hours. These steps are elegant, graceful... Carina.

Unlike the first time I stashed her in my bedroom at the plantation so my father didn't find out she was indoors, I hadn't felt the need to lock her in my master suite on this occasion, given there's no way she can escape the compound without being noticed.

The second she goes for a door; my dogs would bark and quite possibly maul her to death if I give the command. For some reason, that thought jostles my deficient conscience.

I stay still, intrigued by her diligently careful movements. Carina assesses her new surroundings, glides behind me, flanking the wall, and disappears into the kitchen. After a few minutes, a shiver, like someone's walking over my shallow grave, sprinkles me with goosebumps. She quietly rounds the sofa and stops for a beat, catching sight of my false slumber.

I'm vulnerable and in an unparalleled position for a bullet to the heart, should she decide that's the route to take.

Instead of reaching for the handgun beside the empty liquor bottle, she sighs softly. That secret little exhale tells me she's reflecting. Either debating or remembering. And I need to know exactly what's running through that confusing mind of hers. I want to find out every little thing there is to know about her.

With my eyes still shut, I hear an odd noise, like munching. It rolls through the morning stillness and lessens when she moseys to the glass doors. Aware her back is turned, I squint, secretly lifting my lashes a fraction to spy on my curious captive.

And there she is, with one of my pressed shirts buttoned once in the middle and the tails teasing her mid-thigh. Rich white material veils her smooth skin, complementing long wavy strands and showcasing eternal fiery eyes. The same sable hair I want to wrap around my fist spills over narrow shoulders, the strands so dark they could be woven from sin itself.

She stuffs a small hand into a jumbo cereal box of frosted flakes and stops next to Brutus. He shifts to sit and raises his somber gaze to meet her quiet intrigue.

I quietly scoot upright to watch their interaction, knowing he's a grumpy fucker most of the time. One wrong move and he'd go straight for her jugular. One command from me and he'd sit obediently without hurting her.

"Hey…" she whispers. "Are you trapped indoors, too?" Then she slowly offers him a sugar-coated cornflake. "Don't tell anyone we're having breakfast together." I hold my breath for the second it takes him to gently accept the treat. "Good boy. Let's get out of here."

What the fuck?

Carina sets the cereal carton on the ground, heaves the hefty glass door aside, scoops the box under her arm and rubs his muzzle. "Come on, big guy," she whispers.

To my shock and annoyance, Brutus obediently follows her out onto the stone terrace and calmly stares up at her while she takes in my secured paradise. The men have moved to the front of the property in preparation for the day ahead. However, the electric gates at either side won't open without a key fob and beyond the screening trees at the edge of the flourishing garden there's a deadly drop.

With a long sigh, she accepts there's no escape, unties her laces and kicks off the clunky boots. My chest nearly implodes when Brutus strolls by her heels and happily plonks himself beside her as she lowers to the edge of the pool and slips her bare feet into the otherwise undisturbed water.

Slashes of pomegranate pink burst from the horizon, illuminating the skyline behind them. The view is fucking stunning with her in it and just like every other time she's been in my company, the traitorous rhythm of my heart skips a beat.

My untrusting dog and exquisite prisoner share crunchy cornflakes on my sunny terrace like the world is simple. Low rising rays catch in clusters of verdant ferns, dappling the precisely paved pool area where she sits. It had cost a small fortune for a high-end landscape team to create a sophisticated sanctuary where I could relax, but nothing they designed looks as inviting as that woman on the pool edge. Her ease of presence in my domain unsettles my mood.

I stay on the couch and survey the unmatched pair together. Then I wonder if they aren't that dissimilar and all three of us are fucked up beyond repair.

He's somewhat content, and she appears momentarily angelic under the rising sun. It both angers and breeds jealousy within me. I jump up and grab my piece, confused by the swell in my chest. What she's doing is criminal.

In a few long strides, I'm outdoors. As if sensing my approach, she stops talking to Brutus and turns, her gaze pinpointing me like a dart.

"Oh... you're up." She pops a cornflake into her lush mouth and crunches with purposeful intent. "I didn't mean to wake you. Want some frosted flakes?"

Carina waggles the box at me, doing her best to look all sweet and innocent. After last night, we both know she's far from incorruptible.

"I don't eat that shit. Those are Shane's." I fold my arms over my bare chest, the gun in my hand pointed away from her.

"He has good taste." She adds. "I'll be sure to tell him."

She grabs a handful and holds them in her palm, so Brutus can have more. And he does. The dog who wouldn't take a treat from my own hand for six months cautiously has his fill.

"Don't feed my dog that crap." My sharp tone makes his ears prick. He stops eating and cocks his head. "He's on a strict raw food diet." I suddenly feel the need to defend my outburst.

Carina dusts her palms together and looks away. "When can I leave?"

A laugh rumbles in my chest, her request absurd. "Leave?"

"Yeah, leave," she repeats, her amber eyes narrowed. Her face contorts, anger mixing with frustration. "I thought you were the big guy around here, haven't you got the security footage from the jazz bar yet?"

I don't entertain her efforts to rile me. "You can leave

when I give you permission to do so. And that's not today."

She bounces to her feet like a jack-in-the-box and stomps toward me until there's only a flimsy blue box separating us. The carnage of a fiery sun kisses her loose hair and a reckless storm brewing behind her glare.

"You got what you wanted, didn't you?"

My brows tug together and I stare at her, focusing on the thin scar on her plump upper lip. "What did I want, *little liar*?"

"To fuck me," she snarls. "That's what this is about, isn't it? Your rotten fantasy to claim credit for fucking the virgin. We both know I didn't kill your father. So I can only assume I'm here for your entertainment?"

I laugh darkly. "I think *you* were entertained when I fucked your tight little cunt."

Her jaw clamps shut, and she hisses behind clenched teeth. "You're pathetic."

My hand is on her neck like a bullet, steering her to the edge of the pool. "Don't ever call me that again." She fights against me, clawing at my chest with her nails. The scrapes only make me feel alive. I roll my shoulders and tip her backward. "You saw what happened to Diego when he stood up to me. That bastard liked to call me pathetic when I was a kid. Don't think for one second I'll offer you mercy the next time you say it."

She whimpers when my nostrils flare and I tighten my grip, pressing against the cartilage in her throat. From behind, a low growl catches in the light breeze. I glance over my shoulder to find Brutus hunched on all fours, head low, warning me. Something uncomfortable squeezes my insides—it's guilt.

I let go and wait for her to straighten. She rubs her neck and swallows, her gaze locking with mine. "Are you telling me I'm a prisoner again?"

That's exactly what she is. A slave on my tight leash until I'm finished with her. "You can leave at any time." I lie.

Her brow creases and her sugary lips pout. "What's the catch?"

"I'll easily track your movements, kill anyone who tries to help you, and then I'll punish your disobedience." A smug smile dances at the corners of my mouth. I love watching her pupils flare. There's a hot thrill to it. "When I'm done with you, and only then, will you be permitted to walk free."

"I hate you!" In the second it takes her to scream at me, she darts sideways and catches me completely off guard.

Tiny hands butt into my ass and I'm propelled forward. As I fall, I quickly encircle her wrist and drag her into the pool with me.

I come up first and spit out the mouthful of chlorine flavored pool water I inhaled on the way in. Beneath the choppy surface, she thrashes wildly before suddenly bursting into the morning air like a sexy mermaid and sucking in a deep breath. She sweeps inky strands away from her serious face and blinks rapidly.

We face each other in a silent impasse. My dick is like stone, the towel is nowhere near me to cover it. Not that I would. I'm not ashamed of being a red-blooded male.

See-through cotton showcases her pebbled nipples.

The devil doesn't wear a dress, she wears my own damn shirt. Her chest rises, not out of fright or anger, but something much more toxic.

A desire to fuck.

She takes a deep breath. My eyes are all over her. I observe every visible prickle and slight shiver. She's aroused. I know by the flush to her cheeks and mindless tap of her lip.

After a heated second, she swivels away and paddles to the mosaic steps. The quick retreat wrenches my senses back to where they belong. I'm in control, not my *little liar*.

I plunge under the water and swim toward her as a starved predator. When she clambers onto the bottom step, I set my feet down, grab her hips, and yank her into my chest. Her shocked gasp makes me feel bad to my bones. Despite that, it's a fucking buzz.

"If you leave the compound, I *will* find you. My men are everywhere," I growl into her ear from behind, loving how she fights against me.

When her ass bangs into my throbbing dick, it gets her full attention. She freezes. Goosebumps rain over her arms and her head falls back to my shoulder. Together we breathe—deep, heavy breaths.

We stay in that position for too many racing heartbeats, and then she digs her nails into my arms.

"Get off me," she hisses. "You used me last night, and you know what? I used you too. That's all it was. Two people fucking their way out of the shadows. Don't ever touch me again."

Second by second, what was once mine, is stolen away. Her permission.

"You're right, *little liar*. You served your purpose. And until I figure out why you're back in my life again, you'll stay here. You'll stop denying me, eventually. We both know what gets you off and how hard you like it."

"Fuck you." She squirms.

"Leave if you must. But I guarantee it won't take long until your ass is dragged back to this villa, so you can feed my dog frosted flakes." I unarm her body and pull myself away, the urge to claim her more powerful than the madness I'd eventually die from.

Carina scrambles away from me, her long legs working quickly to carry her out of the pool. I follow in hot pursuit, loving how her ass moves under the expensive cotton.

One ruthless order is all it would take for her to obey me, to suck my painfully hard dick the way I like it, deep and messy. But I'll let her play out this charade and see who wins.

Her forced restraint vibrates off every inch of wet skin. She's fighting a magnetic pull. We both are.

I watch her squeeze water from her hair and pad over to Brutus before slipping into the villa. I'm lightheaded from the surge of lust. Charged with volts of lightning, ready to strike at any second. I laugh to myself and shake my head when Brutus trots after her.

She'll beg for it.

20

CARINA

I grabbed my boots, stormed back up the snaking staircase, stripped off his soaking shirt and threw myself onto the super king-sized bed I'd barely slept in overnight.

For the hours I'd spent alone in a stranger's bed, I hardly closed my eyes. It's times like that when I crave my personal little sanctuary. My safety zone, tucked away in the corner of my parents' modest house.

I'd hide in my bedroom for days with a binge-worthy book series or a gripping movie. The last film I lost myself in was Top Gun, Maverick. It had all the parts of a roller coaster—highs, lows, anticipation, thrills. And a happy freaking ending.

It's hard for me to see where this journey with Tomás is taking me. Would I get a happy ending when this death-defying ride screeches to a halt?

I had drifted off once or twice, only to wake in a sweat when Elias called to me from far away. He might be terrorizing the afterlife now, but he's still haunting this world. A part of him lives and breathes in Tomás, making all of this a tragic nightmare.

There's no rational reason for being in awe of a killer or a newly crowned drug kingpin. He might call himself a king, but I can see his position for what it really is. He's a monster. Just like all the other ruthless drug traffickers out there.

Even with that admission, he's still the most ruthless, hottest asshole I've ever met. Despite his hard dick and incredibly good looks, I won't hang around here at his beck and call. Rolling onto my ass, I stare up at the ceiling and fist the sheet. I'm so turned on.

Every time he looks at me with those coal-colored eyes, there's a rebellious cord of desire yanking us closer. It's uncontrollable, like a throbbing vein or a silk leash attached to a leather collar. I both loathe and seek it at the same time.

I lay here in a huff, naked, for an hour at least, and my skin is still on fire. To the point I'll combust into a poof of ashes if he comes near me again with that dimpled smirk of his. Nevertheless, I've made myself a promise to dodge his advances and ignore the satiny soft tip of his splendid dick. Even if it would offer me a few rounds of hardcore dirty sex—the sort of thrilling intensity I'm now hungry for. It's like he's popped open a carton of Pringles and I can't stop thinking about the salty snacks.

Somehow, the guy effortlessly winds me up like a clockwork toy. He's so certain I'll give in to him. It's his self-assured cockiness that makes me despise our misplaced fascination with one another even more.

I don't want to feel this way about him and I don't

want to be locked up in the mountains with a psycho either. My hand skates to my belly where flutters swoop and dive. I sit upright and run a hand over my face. The skin feels tight after the splash in chlorinated water.

The dress I wore yesterday is a tattered mess. Without my own clothes to wear, I'm reduced to wearing his. Before I pick out another shirt from his regimented color arranged racks, I wander into the black ensuite.

Massive marble tiles are warm underfoot and twinkly lights scattered in the ceiling highlight my rosy cheeks and air-drying hair. I feel different inside, even if the reflection staring back at me is the same nineteen-year-old girl. Between my thighs is notably sensitive—in a naughty and nice way.

I grip the washbasin and let a delightful shiver race through me. This feeling is unnatural. Then again, when have my emotions ever been normal?

I search his cabinets, use a spray deodorant, and add a bit of hair product to tame my frizzy tips.

In that moment, when my thighs clench at the scent of such a man, I decide to take fate into my hands and get the hell out of his lair. Today. Now.

There's a commotion behind the bedroom door. A hive of activity sounds from the ground floor. Cell phones ring. Dogs bark. Men call out in loud conversation. Boots stomp. And then it all goes quiet.

I quickly pick out a black shirt from his collection, cinch my waist with a silk necktie and roll on a pair of socks before sliding into my boots. Taking a deep breath, I venture out of the master suite and onto the gallery landing. It's nothing like the plantation hidden in the wilderness where I was trapped the first time Tomás and I met. I pause at the top step, set my hand on the glass railing and listen. The voices are muffled, contained in another room downstairs.

They'll be too busy plotting destruction to notice me slip out into the daylight. The stairs sweep downwards in a wide corkscrew, passing under an artsy, obsidian crystal light fixture.

Two story windows frame hefty transparent doors that lead to a majestic infinity pool. Light gleams over the Spanish marble floor, flooding in from outside. Such a contrast to his sunless countenance.

On the right, housed between two potted palms and a thick border of glass, is the front door—the escape route.

"Can I help you with something?" A female voice startles my reconnaissance. "Tomás told me you've already eaten. Perhaps a coffee?"

I twirl around to meet the softest shade of brown eyes belonging to a slim sixty-something-year-old lady. Her quaint accent tells me she's not from here. It's more of a Mexican twang than the familiar melody I hear in Colombia.

A tight braid of thin gray hair snakes her shoulder with wisps framing aged features. She smiles with motherly wholesomeness.

"Uh... no thank you." I brush a fingertip over my lip in thought. "I was hoping to go for a walk."

She wanders toward the kitchen, looking back over her shoulder at me. "There's only open roads and no shops for miles. It's dangerous out there, *niña*."

I can't help wondering if she knows Tomás threatened

me and understands he'll ruin my life if I disappear. That's if he could find me, and today, it's a risk I'm willing to take.

"I'll be in the kitchen if you need anything. Anything at all."

She smooths the black material at either side of her hips. One hand works at full capacity, while the other is almost rigid with arthritic nodules on the joints.

"He'll be busy for the next few hours. The veranda is a beautiful spot to relax if you'd like a morning coffee. You only have to ask."

With a tight smile, she disappears into the connecting kitchen. I blow out a breath and decide not to follow her. To the left there's a corridor with gleaming floor tiles. I'm almost certain it leads to Tomás and his crew. I can hear hushed murmurs travel through the quietness and decide to follow the sound. With every step, I do my best to tread carefully, sneaking past several doors that are all closed, except for one at the very end of the long, wide hallway.

When I finally reach the last door, I press my palm to the white lacquered wood and listen. My chest tightens, instinctively recognizing his voice. That profoundly husky tone and authoritative bass makes my skin flame without effort.

"No one slaughters my father in the street without epic repercussions. Get into the heads of every motherfucker in Colombia. Rattle cages. Poke the snake pits. Kill anyone who fights back or shows signs of turning on us." I shiver at the cruelty he projects. "We have unlimited resources to rip the heads off any cunt who thinks that move was a checkmate. This is war, men."

"I heard there was a woman in the alleyway." One man speaks up. "What have you done with her?"

There's a moment of silence and then Tomás speaks again. "I have that situation under control. Don't worry about her."

"Is she here, Tommy? The last thing we need is a tight-assed assassin taking out another leader."

Tomás laughs, but his sharp response snaps every syllable. "Trust me. I'm all over it."

Collective chuckles spark my anger. "All over her, more like it."

There's a loud thump as if someone hits the deck like a bag of shit and then Tomás commands the room with a controlled bark.

"Have I got your attention, Tony? You're here to talk over tactics for the most important mission of your career. I need a team running the day-to-day business and a second team to remind the smaller cartels exactly who's at the top of the food chain. You're my best guys, so don't fucking disappointment me. There are zero distractions for all of us. Understood."

I reverse away from the door, almost tripping over my own feet to hurry back along the hallway. That's my cue to leave. The housekeeper doesn't reappear, and the two dogs are nowhere in sight. My heart pounds, caught in fight or flight. While everyone in the house is distracted, this is my only opportunity to run.

By the tropical plants manning the front door, a glass bowl the color of the ocean sits on a glass console table. Inside are three sets of car fobs. It couldn't be that easy, could it?

I peer over my shoulder to the kitchen and catch a glimpse of the old woman loading the dishwasher, one plate at a time. It's now or never. I take the door handle and twist, but it won't budge. From the corner of my eye, I spot a black button on the wall and decide to push it. A mechanical click sounds and I try again, opening the door and stepping out into the break of day.

A nomadic breeze reminds me we're at a higher altitude than the city. I clutch the fob and its keyring in my sweaty palm and check out the emblem—Audi.

Following the flagstone pathway hedged by a network of bushy foliage, I jog to the front of the property and meet a collection of swanky vehicles. I'm guessing a few belong to the guests indoors, and one of them must belong to Tomás. I press the fob and hear locks click near the high steel gate. A graphite black A8 with a sleek hood, just like its owner, is parked facing the exit.

I weave around the other cars, quickly open the door, and dare a peek behind me to check I'm in the clear. Brutus stands by the path, nose to the air, and eyes fixed on my speedy getaway.

In the silence of a mountain hideaway, I sink into sporty leather upholstery and notice a rolled-up wad of paper money in the cup holder. The interior smells as if it had arrived straight from the manufacturer, so incredibly fresh that I'd argue it's never been driven.

I push the start button and panic when the engine growls to life. At that exact moment, Brutus howls. His repetitive bark competes with the sexy purr of the Audi.

Thankfully, it's an automatic, so I put it into drive and let the tires roll forward. The gates automatically slide open as the sensors detect motion. I check the rearview mirror and blow out a jet of air when Brutus' eyes are the only pair to see me leave.

It doesn't take long for the car to pick up speed along the quiet descending roads lined by thick rock and abundant weeds. The sun hides behind a layer of clouds, making the sky gray and the risk I've taken a bit more ominous. I repeatedly check the mirrors, praying I'm not being followed. I feel like a pilot from Top Gun, finally finding my wings. The closer I get to the city, the more my adrenaline hits an all-time high. I love every heart pounding beat of it.

After a short drive, I'm in the city without a plan. I can't show up at my cute apartment, because that would be too obvious and schoolgirl stupid. So, I abandon the stolen car on the outskirts of the city, certain a man like Tomás could easily track it, and start to walk without direction.

A light breeze tussles my hair. It feels like freedom, if that's what this is called. More like being on the run. The day-to-day chatter of the city has me second guessing everyone. I constantly check over my shoulder and look away from every stranger who eyeballs me. Tomás has connections everywhere. I bet the street rats even know his name.

A haze of drizzle soon turns to heavy rain and I'm forced to take shelter in a busy backstreet café that stinks of hot, greasy food. Before I left the car in a parking lot, I had thumbed through the stack of cash and tucked a few notes into the front pocket of the large shirt I'm wearing. I didn't need to take it all. I'm not a thief. But I do need food and a place to stay for the night until I figure out what to do next.

I drag out a tall metal stool, perch at the slim wall mounted bar, and stare at a cladding of aged photographs where diners from this small establishment smile for the camera. The interior hasn't changed much, except for a wash of cream paint on the internal brickwork, and the wooden chairs set around tables are painted different shades of blue.

A waitress, not much older than me, wearing massive hoop earrings and red lipstick, takes my order and hands it to the stocky chef with grease stains on his striped apron. The tamale and drink I ordered will give me more time indoors without getting thrown out for loitering.

I'm not hungry in the slightest, since my stomach is in knots. Though when the waitress thuds the hot chocolate down next to me, I don't hesitate to swipe the creamy topping with my finger. I'm a little disappointed. It doesn't taste as yummy as it should.

Perhaps nothing would ever taste as good as the dick of a macho cartel leader who's fucking your throat. *Ugh! Not even cream satisfies me anymore.*

"Is there a decent motel nearby?" I ask her, watching as she unties her apron and slings it over her arm. "Or a hostel?"

She shrugs. "There are a few hostels dotted about. I don't know much about them. Ask him." Clearly unenthused by the conversation, she nods to the guy in the kitchen, hangs up her apron and disappears into the back. Apparently, her shift is over.

While I wait for the food, my thoughts drift to my

brother, and I debate phoning him. However, even if I hadn't left my bag behind in the alleyway, I couldn't pull him into this, or el Fantasma. After the trauma they'd suffered, the last thing they would need is the Colombian cartel firing more bullets and issuing death threats.

Instead, I'll lie low for a few days. Tomás will give up hunting for me and eventually forget I exist. Then I'll put my apartment up for sale and tell Sal I'm moving on to somewhere else. He'd be happy enough if he knows I'm safe and feeding my wanderlust.

"Here you go." The smell of the freshly prepared tamale makes my belly flip flop with queasiness.

"Thanks." I push the plate away just a fraction and lean back when the chef plonks cutlery next to it. "Are there any hostels on this side of the city?"

"One or two. My wife would know more about them than I would. What she doesn't know isn't worth knowing." His chubby cheeks apple as he chuckles. "I'll get a name for you. *Comer niña.*" He instructs me to eat and wanders off, scratching his head.

I reach for an abandoned newspaper and mouth out the headline. *Businessman and notorious narco ringleader assassinated.* The next line reads: *Will his successor and firstborn son rule the city with a bloodied iron fist?*

My eyes eat up the short article, which doesn't actually give any information about the Souzas. It's all speculation and guess work—nothing solid. Nevertheless, I did the right thing to bolt. Nothing good would come from a toxic captive scenario. Even if he sets off all sorts of curious fireworks and naughty impulses within me.

It's the first time a man has shown any real interest in

my body. Other than strip searching me and assessing my figure for potential value after I was stolen by a woman claiming Elias was her father. Depending on how I look at it, in the grand scheme of bad scenarios, I was lucky the bitch had decided to send me to the Souza palatial plantation in the Colombian countryside rather than sell me off for a life of slavery. Small mercies.

Despite hating Tomás and at the same time wanting him to ravage me, I'm thankful he was with his father that day. He kept me alive against terrible odds. Despite the glimmer of clemency, I'm not naive to think he'd spare me with no ulterior motive. Men in power do heinous things when they know they can get away with it.

Bogotá is such a big city. It would take him a day to figure out where I am now and even then, by the time he pulls up in another flashy car, I'd be dust in the wind.

A door chime tinkles, but I'm too engrossed in the newspaper to look up. The bustle of life in the cafe stills as if the earth was obliterated by a meteorite and all the fragments sucked into a whirlpool. The hairs on my scalp prickle, my gut tingling with unease. My lashes lift upward bringing my gaze to the entrance.

Tomás.

Shane.

Both of them stare right at me. Only it's Tomás' glare, that dark shadow of anger and smug smirk of confidence, that both freezes me and sets my world on fire. He's dressed all in black, fitting for the grieving son attending to business in public.

I swallow back the jitters in my throat when he covers the short distance like a predator, leaving Shane to close off my only escape. The smart tailored jacket he wears is left open and a pressed onyx shirt has his signature diamond cufflinks peeking out from the sleeves. Rather than wear a tie, the top button is undone to show glorious golden skin.

When he reaches me, he sets his handgun beside the uneaten tamale and drags a stool closer. He sits in front of me, so my knee is positioned between his thighs.

"If you wanted a tamale that badly, Marta would have made enough for all of us. We could've had breakfast together."

My grunt makes his eyebrow hitch. "Are you talking about the elderly woman who cleans up after you?" I stare at him, not faltering from his hot gaze even if it wilts me like a flower in the midday sun. "You're a grown-ass man capable of tidying up after yourself, aren't you? Or do you enjoy having women work for you?"

Tomás nods. "I can tidy. It's not a problem." He admits. "But then Marta wouldn't have a job, which means she wouldn't have money or a roof over her head. She'd likely be homeless. It has nothing to do with her being female and everything to do with giving her a place in the world." His shoulders bounce lightly and I can't tell if it's a calculated chess move to get cheap labor. "Besides, she enjoys working for me. Ask her yourself when you get home."

"Home?" I scoff. "I don't live with you."

"Okay." He shrugs. "Let's call it your temporary accommodation, where you will stay until further notice. A bit wordy though, don't you think?"

I roll my eyes at him. "You're killing my appetite."

Discrete stares watch our interaction. Breaths pause,

waiting for trouble. Perhaps they're in awe of his rogue authority as much as I am. How he carries himself with a certain imposing grace that makes him untouchable. I can't tell whether they're fascinated or terrified. Or if I'm angry he found me or wishful he'd kiss me.

My gaze flicks to his weapon and when I look back at him, he's smirking.

"Did you really think you could run from me, little liar?" The tone he uses doesn't warrant a response, it's more of an egotistical statement. "That you could hide in my city and not be found. Not everyone who enjoys your company is your friend."

Featherlight fingertips skate across my knee. The sensation causes my nipples to harden like he knows the exact buttons to press to get a reaction out of me. The teasing pressure turns up the heat within me to sizzling. "My dog is loyal to me. And the second he barked; my surveillance cameras caught you stealing my new Audi."

"I didn't steal it," I say on a breath, doing my best to contain my soaring libido as he touches me in public.

His hand moves under the shirt tails and when it stops at the apex of my thighs, his pupils expand and his nostrils flare as he inhales a slow, controlled breath. "You're living up to your name, *little liar*. From what I can tell, you've stolen my boxer shorts." He fingers the fabric of his designer underwear close to the uncontrollable wetness forming beneath them. "My shirt." Dark eyes trail my torso, temporarily pausing at the makeshift belt cinching my waist. "My tie—*and* one of my cars." One of his cars. Of course, he has more than one. "Should I add thief as a double-barreled extra?"

My core clenches. "I borrowed your car." The obvious hush around us makes me painfully aware of the spectators. "It's safely parked. I'll make sure your clothes are dry cleaned before I send them back to you." My voice lowers, my shoulders almost tipping into him, an involuntary reaction to the chills he's giving me.

A ghost of a smile plays at the corners of his mouth. I visibly stiffen when he takes his hand away from my inner thigh, shrugs out of the expensive jacket, and drapes it over my legs. A luxurious inner lining scented with smoky sandalwood conceals his intentions. With his eyes locked on mine, he angles his torso in a way that shields me from the other diners.

He dips into the shell of my ear. "You say that as if you'd be somewhere other than in my bed?" His accent switches on the last word ever so slightly. I assume he's spent too many hours with the Irish sidekick guarding the exit.

My heart rate picks up pace, unable to escape his touch without making a scene. "You can't seriously expect me to willingly walk out of here with you? I'll scream."

"No one will bat an eye."

"Someone will."

"Maybe… and if they do, I'll shoot them in the face for getting involved in cartel business."

"I'm not… cartel business," I growl indignantly.

He smirks. "As of last night, you are very much the Souza cartel's business."

"I'll run away again." My fists tighten.

"You didn't run very far on the first and final attempt, so I'm guessing this…" Confident fingers slide under his borrowed boxer briefs, this time hunting the slickness he'd created. I flinch, hating myself for the neediness unfurling in my core. "This part of you didn't want to leave." I squirm, my cheeks flaming. "Fight against me and I'll fuck you over the breakfast bar before your next breath."

"You wouldn't..." I hiss through gritted teeth, then rashly snatch the gun to jab it into the muscle over his heart. "I'm not a threat to you. Let me go."

Slowly, his brow creases and long lashes framing starless eyes lower to the loaded weapon. With his free hand, he snares my throat quicker than a viper attack.

"Do you have a death wish?" He stretches my neck, so my chin hitches higher. His hand moves upward and cups my chin, the pad of his thumb dragging over my lower lip.

I manage to shake my head. "No," I reply honestly, the tip of my tongue meeting his short thumbnail. "I don't wish for death anymore. But I'm not scared of it either."

When his head cocks to the side, the diamonds adorning his ears sparkle. "So what does scare you?"

"I'm scared of not living. And never finding where I belong."

He takes a slow, steady breath, glances at the gun, and then leisurely slides his gaze all the way up to my mouth.

"I promise you this, *little liar*..." Between my thighs, he flattens his palm, cups my pussy, and angles a finger inside of me. I bite my bottom lip to stop a whimper. "If you shoot me, everyone in here will die, including you. My men would retaliate immediately. Without question."

My hand trembles, the weight of deadly steel a pointless curse. "Don't do this."

I suck in a ragged gasp when he drops his forehead to mine and growls. "I'm not doing anything your body doesn't want." He puts a sliver of distance between us and unhands my jaw. "This is your punishment for stealing my car. Keep quiet, so it's a dirty secret between the two of us or I'll show everyone behind me how much your darkness craves something far filthier."

"I hate you," I whisper as my pelvis lifts to welcome the cruel intrusion.

He chuckles, low and dirty. "But you love this, don't you?"

Tomás sets his large hand over mine and nudges the threat away from his vital organ I know to be frozen. I keep my chin poised high in defiance, while doing my best to pretend his roaming fingers don't feel amazing inside me.

"You don't have to do this. Just let me go," I whisper, panting into the side of his face, hungry for his torture and ashamed of how I'd shrivel if he stopped.

"You smell like me." He bites my earlobe. I grab his forearm to steady myself. "It's sexy as fuck." Coarse hairs scratch my cheek as his throaty cadence scatters shivers over my scalp. "I haven't given you permission to walk free. I have unanswered questions. Your reappearance doesn't add up. Until I find out what's going on, you'll voluntarily come outside with me like the good girl you say you are." His wrist angles. "You're caught up in my world now. This is my city. My rules."

My forehead bows as my body deceives me. I'm regrettably close to a physical surrender. Right here in this cafe before all of these people who are fueling up for the morning. I can't help my spiral, not being used to this sort of strained secrecy—this illicit behavior or level of naughtiness.

He senses how my insides contract around him. In that moment of recognition, his jaw twitches and he pulls his hand out from between my thighs. I shudder at the loss, only to have his coated finger slip into my mouth.

"Suck it." He commands, his expression impassive.

And I do. I'd be lying if I said I don't want him. Our confused gazes fuse. That second of an unspoken bond highlights his wide pupils and grimace. While my thighs remain parted, I circle my lips and pin him with fluttery lashes.

The ball in his throat bobs and his head cocks ever so slightly. And then, as if danger is closing in, he jerks away.

From my left, the chef wanders out of the kitchen, oblivious to the henchmen with guns and my uninvited breakfast date. He's happily muttering to himself and scrawling on a piece of paper with a stubby pencil, his gaze focused on the information he's noting.

"Okay. I've spoken to my wife." He stops beside me. "There are a few hostels in the area. Here's the name of one she recommended." As he looks up, he's greeted by Tomás' unmoving expression. His cloudy eyes immediately dart to the exit where Shane is standing.

"Hostel?" Tomás glares at me. "You'd rather stay in a flea infested, stinking bunk bed with a drunk cunt pissing in the closet because they think it's a toilet?" The look he dishes out could be misinterpreted as hurt, but the twist to his lips tells me it's likely disgust.

"Thank you." I take the torn page. "I really appreciate your help."

The second I glance at the penned name, Tomás snatches it quicker than a snake bite, crumples it up, and tosses it to the floor. His muscles go rigid and he rises with the threat of a volcano spitting out liquid fire in a warning.

"Shane." He barks over his shoulder. "Get everyone out." My chest tightens at the sharpness of his command. "I need a few minutes alone with her."

"Wait... it's coming up to lunch time. I..." The owner's jaw drops, his fretful eyes filled with horror as he blindly shoves the notepad into his apron pocket.

Behind him, Shane flings open the door and orders the customers to leave, waving his gun to indicate the seriousness of his instruction. My insides wither, unsure of what to expect when we're alone.

Tomás sets his hand on the man's shoulder. "What's your name?" he asks calmly.

A glimmer of sweat mists the man's forehead and he rubs his palms across the grimy material covering his round belly. "Juan Pablo," the nervous man replies, his eyes flicking from me to the infamous towering predator before him.

"Okay, Juan Pablo." Tomás gathers his expensive jacket and pulls out a wad of notes from the silky inside pocket. "You know who I am, right?" Juan Pablo nods slowly. "So you know what I *could* do to this place... if I wanted to?" Tomás continues in the dumbstruck silence. "This cash is a token. No strings. Think of it as compensation for giving me half an hour of undisturbed privacy with this beautiful young lady. She was in a bad state when I picked her up in an alleyway late last night. I brought her into my home, gave her a steamy, hot shower, fed her frosted flakes this morning, and let her play with my big..." he smirks. He actually fucking smirks. "Play with my big dog."

"Your dog was certainly more welcoming than you were," I mutter.

His mouth quirks. "I didn't hear much of a complaint when we swam in my outdoor pool earlier. It's a bit like that movie, Pretty Woman. Except she's not a hooker and I'm filthy fucking rich. The only difference is I'm not a nice guy." He almost chuckles, the tone to his voice deep and dangerous—a toe-curling turn on. "You and I know this city is unsafe unless we know the right people. And this lucky *senorita* bumped into me." Tomás winks at me, the corner of his mouth dimpling his cheek. My skin flushes from my clit to my face. If eyeballs could blush, mine would be on fire. "I'm offering you more money than this cafe earns in a whole year. My advice would be to take the money and finish up early for once." Tomás' voice is commanding, as always.

But when I shift in my seat and unintentionally brush my hand over his, I notice a sudden urgency in his breath. No one else in here would detect it and had I not witnessed him unravel, I wouldn't recognize his mood falter, either.

"Go home and show your old lady the time of her life. Buy her a bottle of Dom and a new dress. And... Juan Pablo..." His lips curl into a cruel smirk. Devilish ebony lashes dagger the man holding drug money in his hand.

"Go straight home and forget who you've seen here today. Mention it to anyone and I'll come for your whole family. That's a promise."

Juan Pablo glances at my side profile, his shocked expression turns ghostly pale. He knows what's happening here. The guy has unwanted hero status written all over him. Which makes any secret signals for help pointless.

Tomás slides his arm around my shoulders and cuddles me against him like a macho boyfriend. Even though it's purely for show, I find his absurd show of affection really arousing. It's then when I notice he's taken possession of his golden revolver again, draping it over my chest with the aim directed at the checkered linoleum.

"So what will it be, big guy? That's a life changing sum. Bet when you woke up this morning you didn't think a Souza would stroll in for breakfast. You can thank her." He squeezes me. "She's a hot little rebel with a mouth to die for."

I swallow hard. What a sexy as fuck jerk. I can't decide if I want to slap his face or sit on his lap. Despite his crude praise, the three of us know Juan Pablo's life is on the line if he does anything stupid.

I've seen what Tomás can do and how his temper rules. Instinctively, I know the guy will pick the cold hard cash over risking his life for a stranger. Who wouldn't? So, I keep my mouth shut and peer at Tomás. He meets my stare, his own smoky with lust and amplified by a hint of impatience.

Juan Pablo's hesitation lasts for a heart stopping beat.

His decision is obvious when he nods curtly and obediently hurries out behind the last person to leave.

"Thirty minutes, Tommy. We don't need any more trouble." Shane nods, leaves, and stands directly outside the closed door.

Tomás releases me, shoves his stool away in a quick temper, seizes my jaw, and puckers my lips with his long fingers. "Run away from me again and I won't offer pleasure as a punishment when I catch you. And believe me when I tell you that I *will* catch you. I run this city. There's no one here I can't pay off. Everyone is willing to accept a healthy bribe. Got it?" His spine arches and his mouth covers mine, hard and hungry.

A kaleidoscope of colors burst behind my eyes when I squeeze them shut. He steals my breath with a vicious, heart pounding kiss, the prickly roughness of his trimmed hairs showering me with feverish tingles. When he grunts into my mouth, I can feel the reverberation of darkness dancing on his hungry lips. It vibrates through my soul, daring me to play with him.

Just as I turn into melting bones and burning flesh, he rips his mouth away. My eyelids ping open.

"Do you understand?" he clips.

Foolishly, I nod against his palm, unable to disguise the swell of desire crippling my decisions from within. This is a mutual sexual attraction. Once he accepts I'm a victim of bad timing, he'll open the door himself and watch me leave. In the meantime, I can play his game and seek the fucked up buzz his dark soul offers.

He releases me like he's scalded his fingertips on my fiery flesh. Spinning in his immaculate designer shoes, he swipes an arm across the neighboring table. Salt and pepper packets scatter like broken promises.

A cylindrical drink menu glides through the air and a single red carnation furnishing a miniature jar crashes to the floor. I stare at the smashed pieces of glass for a split second, finding the shattered shards and scarlet petals a hodgepodge of pretty destruction.

Shivering, I look up to find him quietly watching me. His face is impassive, except for the subtle flicker of something enigmatic. We stare at each other for a fluttery heartbeat. Silence crackles with charged energy. I intuitively pat my lip to settle the wild thrum taking over my pulse.

He eyes my every move as I study his and how his breathing deepens so his chest lifts. An unshakable tension flames my cheeks. I shouldn't want him like I do. Nor should I find comfort in the corruption that exists behind his black eyes.

He slides a hand into his pants' pocket and nods to the clearing. "Get on the table."

The brusque command snaps me out of the realm of fantasy and I freeze. "Do I have a choice?"

"Not today. Your actions have consequences. You have nowhere to go, except for that table. On your back. Legs parted." His glare turns wolf-like.

"Tomás."

"Now."

He loses patience, snares my wrists, and swings me against the edge of the wobbly table in full view of the front window. Without waiting for me to obey, he presses his palm between my breasts and shoves me backward.

My hair spills off the opposite edge and the soles of my boots land at either corner. I twist my head to the exit and find a line of men with their backs to us guarding the front like a human shield.

His eyes drill into mine as he roughly drags the boxer briefs to my ankles and unhooks them. Just as I think he'll unbutton his trousers and fuck me; he sinks to his haunches to spread me wide and drops his face.

My feelings are tied up. I can't escape his torture—and I don't want to. From our time together so far, he's pacified the hurt within me and the ability to torch my barriers with his wicked tongue. He's dangerous and sinful. A toxic combination that only serves to turn me on.

His fingers work and his tongue teases. Not with brutality like before. This time it's hungry like he's lost in the taste of me.

He's right, this is punishment. The sweetest form of cruelty that exists. My insides go from simmering heat to a scorching inferno in zero to sixty villainous sweeps of his tongue. The sensation I struggle with next is understanding how my usually polar world is in flames, and how he's the sole source of this comforting heat.

As I teeter at the boundary of euphoria, he meets my gaze, his fiery eyes locked to mine. The searing connection from his skin to my own ignites in my core like a bomb explosion. He doesn't take his eyes off me, not for one second. Instead, he watches as I detonate before him like a sacrificial animal.

From the heights of a hedonistic orgasm, I barely hear the clatter of glass. Tomás rears back, brutally stripping me of all contact. He seizes my wrist and hauls me into his chest. I barely stand on shaky legs, held by him as gunfire explodes in the street outside. Shane strikes the door with his fist and signals to Tomás to leave through the back exit.

"Do exactly what I say." Long lashes lower as he roughly forces my arm into the sleeve of his oversized suit jacket and wraps it around me. "When I say run, you fucking run."

21

CARINA

Tomás rams his shoulder into the side door. It's locked, and the only way out is through the main entrance. Straight into the line of fire.

"Fuck!" he snarls, squeezing the bones in my wrist so hard they almost shatter. He pulls me after him. When he reaches the front of the cafe, he glances down at me.

"Keep low. Understood?" I hear the sound of intermittent shots fired and witness the purest form of fury unfold behind his eyes. A veil of black smog cloaks his aura, and I doubt he can actually see me. "Stay close to me."

I nod and wait for him to make the next move. Once he cracks the door open, he starts to run in the direction of a nearby SUV. We both do. He doesn't take his burning touch off me, firing a few rounds at the guys shooting at us. We keep going even though the incoming bullets are relentless.

"Get down." He uses his weight to bundle me onto the pavement, my lungs deflating in a sharp exhale when he lands on top of me. Flat on my back, he straddles my pelvis to shield me and continues to shoot into the street.

The scene above me unfolds in slow motion. If I should die here today, I'll know this dangerous man had tried to protect me. He didn't abandon his runaway captive to save his own ass or use my body as a human shield.

From down here, his eyes are so venomous and his expression vacant. Every bullet he unleashes doesn't faze him. Not one bit. There are no visible signs of fear in his features. Until he glances down at me and I get the strangest feeling he's anxious.

With his muscular body as my only cover, he hurriedly frees me from under him.

"Move." He barks out the order. "Get to the SUV. I'll cover you."

I rise to my haunches, my heart thumping in all the madness. More bullets speed through the air, one of them too close. "Fucking run, Carina." His voice booms.

I scramble forward and start to move, my feet carrying me away from him. The closer I get to the vehicle, the more I panic. Looking over my shoulder, I witness the first bullet soar through the air to find its mark. His body jars and he crashes to his knees. Blood blooms from his bicep and his gun skids across the sidewalk, out of reach.

In that fearful second, he catches my eye, his face contorted with so much anger that he's barely recognizable. The next bullet slows in the precious seconds of time, missing him by a whisper.

A shout sounds from behind me, followed by a gunshot. I freeze and more shots are fired and men yell.

And then I run, not to the glossy black SUV, but to Tomás. He rises amidst the fracas, his shirt decorated in crimson and his gaze locked with mine. Maybe this is the dumbest thing I've ever done, but I couldn't leave him. I have to help. It's in my nature.

He ducks to grab his gun and I latch onto his good arm.

"Come on!" I pant, pulling at him.

Together we run, him beside me, both of us dodging a spray of machine gun ammunition. Whizzing slugs shatter shop windows and superficially burrow into the bullet proof vehicle we're now hiding behind. The back passenger door swings open and Tomás pushes me in first, his hand on the crown of my head to keep me low.

When the door slams shut behind him, wheels screech, and the gunfire fades. The further away we get, the deeper I breathe. I'm huddled on one side and he's on the other. His hands are upturned and fresh blood oozes from the wound under his shirt. He just sits there, motionless, eyes glazed, and his horror-struck attention focused on whatever hell exists in his mind.

I shiver, unsure of how to approach him. This isn't any normal car journey. He's bleeding and on the verge of a crisis that might not work in my favor. And I'm a prisoner to the tortured man who can set my world on fire.

"Tomás," I say his name softly.

"What the fuck is going on, Tommy?" The henchman driving the SUV says to him while staring at our reflection in the rearview mirror. Turning his head to catch a glimpse of the blood, the whites of his eyes gleam with fury. "Fuck, the bastards shot you... I'll call the doc." He taps the screen on the console and the audio speaker connects to a gruff voice. "Tommy's been hit. Bring Luciano to the compound. We'll be there in thirty."

The driver swears and thumps the steering wheel. His gaze returns to the busy road where he recklessly weaves the blacked-out vehicle through busy traffic.

I shrug out of the expensive suit jacket that holds the muskiness of Tomás' cologne and slowly unbutton the shirt I'd borrowed. It's a crazy thing to do, but these days I'm more than a few degrees off balance. One decision away from insanity, and this damaged man, is the catalyst.

When I'm naked, I hang the jacket over my shoulders again and scoot across the leather upholstery, reaching his rigid physique. The familiar coppery waft of blood doesn't bother me at all. Not in the same way it affects this man. Turning into him, the side of my knee rests on the slippery seat, now covered in a dark red slick.

Long lashes lower to hide his coal-colored eyes and he inhales steadily, as if taming the feral beast hurtling through his grisly thoughts.

Certain the bullet missed a main artery, I twist the shirt to form a long snake shape, then cautiously slide it underneath his arms and tie it tightly over the wound. He doesn't flinch at the pressure, but when I go to move away, his head snaps around like I've woken a viper.

My belly flips, immobilized under his dangerous glare. Neither of us speaks. We just stay still, both of us breathing in the same quick rhythm. He swallows and licks his lips with dark intent. I sense exactly what he needs from the animalistic flare of his enlarged pupils.

He needs an anchor.

Tracks of blood cover his hand like broken veins. He holds it before his nose and stares at the mess as if the shock of it all is finally hitting. Rather than lose himself to the pain, he lowers the injured arm and narrowed eyes settle on me again.

"You didn't run when I told you to." The strained tone he uses doesn't invite a response. "Which means you disobeyed me."

"Would you rather I'd left you on the pavement?" I sigh loudly, frustrated by his interpretation of my helpful deed. "I'm just as annoyed as you are about it. My good nature seems to get me in trouble with bad people."

In a flash, his clean hand seizes my neck and he winces at the sudden movement. I suck in sharply, my own hand flying up to his.

"You were told to keep running." His voice is thicker, full of grit and authority. "Getting yourself killed is not helping me. Do you understand what I'm saying to you?"

By the demonic expression on his handsome face, I'm not sure I do. He's manic, almost deranged, and no longer in control.

"Yes." I swallow against his palm.

"Then prove it." He bares his teeth.

Oh, no.

"How?"

"Obey me, *little liar*." The grip on my neck weakens. "Sit on my dick." His nostrils flare and he dips closer. "I don't need help from anyone. What I need is a mindless fuck with the cunt I've claimed."

"What if I say no?" I choke his wrist with my hand, pointlessly trying to pry it off.

The chuckle rumbling from the back of his throat mocks me. "I suggest you give in to me or it won't end well for either of us." He half-smiles and I wonder if he really has it in him to take from me without consent. "You don't have a choice. And what's worse than a woman without a choice?" His head cocks, eyeing my hapless struggle. "A woman who lies to herself. Your silky skin is flushed with frustration, your nipples are hard. You're ready to be fucked. I can sense your arousal like a sledgehammer to the chest."

He's right. This cruel king knows my body is under his spell. I'm incensed by the crawling lust heating my skin and the addictive rush of adrenaline pumping through my veins. I'm beyond aroused, with no rational reason for it.

He's intoxicating, and I've never known this whirling mania within me before. It's uncontrollable like the talons of a vulture ripping apart its prey in a frenzy. I don't stand a chance against these urges my body feeds off.

"Turn up the volume, Marco," his growl could crush diamonds to dust. The driver does what he's told. "Louder."

Energetic beats thump in my haywire brain. Tomás releases my throat and yanks me into him. "If you're not wet, I'll stop the car and let you go," he growls close to my ear.

Bastard.

He knows that's an empty offer. My insides clench at the texture of his urgent baritone, making it impossible to think of anything else other than sexual gratification. The shameful desire within me is unstoppable.

In any normal situation, I would scratch out his eyes

or launch a fist into his jaw. But this syrupy greed spreading within me is worse than a devastating forest fire or an avalanche wipeout.

All I feel is unsatisfied hunger. Swept up in the fight-or-flight reaction to warfare and filthy requests. I'm drunk on how his eyes make me feel weightless, how I'm the one he protected with his own body when bullets were coming at us in all directions.

Truth be told, I'm in awe of him. And I love knowing he needs this, maybe more than me.

I blink quickly when he unbuckles the Italian leather belt at his waist, then carefully unzips his trousers. Tomás grabs his cock from under his black boxer-briefs, all the while glaring at me with those impenetrable eyes of his. Shiny skin erupts with a glossy bead of pre-cum, the pulsing vein angry like his tyrannical mood.

Rather than invite me again, he strokes himself and lets his head fall back. My belly flips at the exquisite, slow suggestion of something untouchable. I mindlessly trace my lip, unsure if I want to give in so easily this time.

"Do it," he snarls, jack-knifing upright as if he needs to take cover from a bomb blast. "Fuck my cock. Do it, because you want it. Do it for me, *little liar*."

A husky male singer sings in the background, his lyrics warning me that the blazing fire within this man would one day turn blue. Yet, Tomás still waits for me to carry out his order. The screening of sound makes it feel secretive and dirty, especially with the driver so close.

Without second guessing the mistake I'm about to make, I obey him because there's a universe of desire scorching my veins and only a solitary flame of hatred.

The lust siphoning through me is hotter than the burning sun, blistering and all consuming.

If at all possible, he grows harder when I carefully position my shins at either side of his thighs, making sure not to kick him with my Doc's. An unused seatbelt clip digs into my grazed knee, but I'm too far gone in the urgency for satisfaction to care.

The color coordinated soft fabric of the interior overhead forces me to hunch over his torso, obediently hovering in place. His palms glide under the suit jacket drowning my frame. Firm fingertips dig into my left hip as I lower onto him and shudder when his pelvis lifts to spear me.

He blows out a gush of air when I'm completely filled, eyes drilling into my parted lips. The broad intrusion is too intense. I'm still tender from the first time he'd fucked me.

I cry out when he bites my nipple, the relieved moan muffled behind a chorus. My spine arches, spilling disheveled strands over his shoulders. I throw my arms around his neck and drop my forehead to his shoulder.

Tomás gives me the illusion of my control. He permits the seductive pace I offer him, the chance to breathe in this unorthodox affair. Even if I'd tried to pretend I didn't need his cock inside of me, the surge of tingles prickling my spine would reveal the lie.

There's no point playing coy or fighting against his command, because I'm not like any normal girl. I crave adventure—and he's the man to lead the way. I'm way over my head in a nightmare where my tormentor knows how to welcome me to the dark side, and possibly leave me there.

"This isn't what you really like, is it?" His gritty voice is a tornado of pelting shingles, hard and fast. I pant, sinking down on his solid shaft again. He grabs a fistful of hair at my nape, slowly pulls my face before his and licks my scar. "We don't do gentle."

22

TOMÁS

I can't shut it down.

The angel on my dick is killing every wisp of warped mania within my head. The touch of her is a priceless drug more coveted than narcotics and more valuable than world class psychiatrists.

Hatred still blisters my senses and melts the humanity from my evil bones. Except, the violence I normally vented without control is contained. A toxic antidote to my curse claims my dick as hers.

Blood. Sex. Violence. *Carina*.

Everything that shouldn't forge together has. The mishmash of chaotic urges makes me feel invincible. It sickens me to the pit of my stomach. This courageous young woman, spoiled of her innocence, has the unearthly power to incite impulses within me that run deeper than the sea. And right now, I'm adrift in that immeasurable ocean, losing myself inside her.

She grinds deeper when I yank her messy hair kissed with the scent of my sandalwood soap and acidic blood. I hiss through clenched teeth, the gunshot wound burning as I try to capture her neck. It continues to ooze under the makeshift bandage she'd thoughtfully wrapped around it.

What girl would willingly treat the man who tracked, hunted, and snatched away her freedom? She's a perplexing anomaly. And that fact alone makes her the most powerful woman I've ever met.

From the minute I first saw her at the plantation, intrigue haunted me. The beauty with exquisite firestorm eyes and delicate scars gave me a buzz. Her imperfections seized my attention and became the very things that saved her life. She'd already ventured to Hell, just like me.

I had chosen recklessness. I went against my father's decree, because the shadow of her soul rested on mine.

The enchanting teen wasn't a meek, unfortunate soul cast into my kingdom as fodder for the wildcats. My attuned instincts told me she was so much more. A virginal goddess with an unquestionable thirst for the darker side seeping out of me.

For the monster born of duty and violence, soldered together with ice, blood, and unease, would be the death of me—and quite possibly her.

Yet, my goal is simply sex, to master control over the crippling flashbacks. When blood stains my skin, I'm swept into a pit of pain. The sight of it pouring doesn't bother me in the slightest. In fact, causing a human spillage is common practice in my world.

However, that slippery sensation on my skin, the coppery aroma, the acidic taste—it all takes me back to that time and place, where my eight-year-old self forever relives in a loop.

Carina offers the distraction to snap my glitch in two. Her body is the education to discipline my inner demons. And once I've learned how to monopolize the trauma, she'll be gone. Far away from me.

I attack her with an anarchic thrust, so she's well and truly impaled on my dick. Her eyes blaze and she hunts for my mouth with hers. I jerk my face away and refuse the connection. She can fly without wings. We both can.

There's nothing merciful about this fusion of feverish skin, slick blood, and salty sweat. Red stains coat her hands and streak her soft belly. Rather than repulse me, I'm consumed with how I've claimed her on so many levels. Her skin is a canvas, my blood the artwork. Her pussy is nirvana and I'm the creeping twilight.

"This is the second time I've fucked you," I hiss into the side of her face. "You're not quite the good little girl you like to think you are. I see you…all of you." She swallows hard, her skin a mess of goosebumps. "You're a bad girl. Isn't that right? *My* bad girl, my *little liar*."

Feral eyes fuse with mine. We both breathe hard, our exhales quick and dizzying. The touch of her hand makes my pulse react, knocking the rhythm out of sync.

"I may as well take what you're offering to spare my life." She speaks with confidence into my ear.

"That's a lie," I growl, scooting down the seat a little to give me a better position to piston my hips. "If I stopped now, you'd beg me to keep going." Plump breasts hang before me, perfectly still as I deny her the satisfaction of moving. "Isn't that right?"

The truth is, if I pulled out, I'd likely snap. Stopping is not something I could do, even if she begged me. Her tongue skates across her lips as she balances over my new placement. I'm hypnotized by the wetness coating the landscape of her damaged mouth.

The paltry flaw is only visible to anyone who's this close to her. This near—within kissing distance. And I'm the one who's claimed that enviable spot.

It would be so easy to kiss her again. Too fucking easy, but I won't welcome that hedonistic fuel. It only crosses wires that have no place in this arrangement. Right now, I don't need to kiss––I need to fuck––her.

She writhes, her tight pussy clamping down on my dick, hunting the savage movement she craves so much. Whether she can tell or not, I have the same chronic thirst. If there's enough space to spin her onto all fours, she'd be screaming by now.

However, my right arm is slowly becoming unusable, and she's primed for a hard ride. I grab her wrist and slam our chests together. Her flushed cheek lands next to mine, her chin in the crook of my neck. And then I start to fuck.

I can't remember a day in my life when I'd been so turned on by something so indecent. I'm violently jack hammering my painfully swollen dick into a virginal prisoner. It doesn't matter that I've already battered her tight inner walls, because the grip of untouched flesh is still vice-like and beyond snug. We work together in the restrictive back seat, me grinding and her bouncing into the motion.

Those fine-tuned instincts I live by willfully argue with the damaged muscle in my bicep. They command me to strip the jacket from her dainty shoulders, throw her on the seat and violently take her from behind. I would if my driver didn't have a front row view of her body. She's my little liar to screw as I please.

An untamed snarl of ownership mangles with my intentions to use her and leaves me bitter. Hating the need, but I crave it at the same time.

Lightning strikes from within my ribs, the sharp bolts casting fucked up sunbeams onto the turbulent shadows choking me. I could be mistaken to think her body is paradise, but it's like taking a precise aim blindfolded. Impossible.

Silky strands tickle the skin on my shoulders, the black lengths wild and unbrushed. The featherlight strokes offer softness against rough thrusts. I focus on my destructive pounding, noticing her tight nipples and the sharpness of her nails diving into my hair. It takes everything within me to halt the natural impulse to ejaculate.

Her forehead lifts, butting with mine. Before I inhale the intoxicating scent of sex, her hot mouth crashes over mine. Lips smash with brutal hunger. Tongues joust at war. Then she bites my lip, not enough to break the skin, but enough to initiate the first wave of an orgasm. The skin on my balls tightens.

Euphoria hits like a grenade with only seconds before detonation. It starts off as a zealous ripple and quickly rockets through me with an annihilating explosion. Somehow, it's far more intense than the mind-blowing shower fuck.

She gasps on the precipice of her own eruption, then grinds one last time before letting go completely.

My dick pulses inside her, unprotected and expelling cum. I might be clawing my way out from under the weight of discipline, but I'm not that delirious. Not foolish enough to impregnate her.

That's the vital piece of information I already know about her. After she plummeted into my life for the second time, I opened a dossier on Carina Ferreira.

While she slept in my bed, I bribed a high up medical professional to give me access to her files. It didn't matter that it was three o'clock in the morning when the call connected with the asshole. He owed me a favor and I was cashing in. Everything I needed to know was sent within minutes.

What I learned is that she was born with a defect on her lip. And was hospitalized for a short period of time as a teen.

Recently, she had an implantable contraception put in her arm. Bonus. She's never had another sexual partner and I always use condoms. Which means I can fuck my naughty virgin until her inner walls are well and truly raw, and my cum spills out of her cunt.

And most importantly, she was telling the truth all along. My instincts were spot on. Security footage shows her leaving the bar with a trash bag and my father hitting the deck from a bullet. She didn't kill him—technically, I did.

She responds to my throaty growl with a full body shudder. Her thighs shake and her core convulses.

"Holy shit," she pants, then pats her upper lip like she always does.

I notice every single time she does it without thought. It's an act of either self-doubt or a grounding gesture. Either way, the subconscious tap gives her a vulnerable edge, even when I know the woman has prevailing strength. My teeth almost shatter with the measly self-restraint I muster, denying the currents of compassion tempting me to draw her into a hug.

The fact her fingers are decorated in blood should crank my temper to volatile. However, in this moment of peace together, with my semi-solid dick still buried inside her, my pulse thrumming, and the knowledge that the blood is mine—well, it fucking gets me off.

I'm a mess.

Sin incarnate, in every sense of the term.

It's an unholy melody sung by a choir of ugly gargoyles who contain my demons.

Such a warped arousal shouldn't exist, yet it fuels my veins with a charge of mindless urges to fuck her all over again. When she fingers the buttons on my jacket, an angry erection fully fills her again.

"We're here." The driver parks behind the automatic gates, leaves the radio blaring, and exits without looking back at us. Marco knows better than to interrupt me. He's seen my temper scorch the earth when blood covers my skin.

I could demolish her in the rear of this SUV for a second time. Grant myself the permission to seek gratification until I can't breathe, but not today. We were under attack in the streets of Bogotá. The very city the Souza cartel rules with an iron fist.

News of my father's assassination has ruptured the pecking order. My family is under fire and I will restore order. Rather than continue to indulge in the rebellious distraction sitting on my lap, I have to roll my sleeves up, stop at nothing to figure out who we can trust and who we will slaughter.

But most importantly, the main priority is to warn my brothers that insurgents are closing in. Danger is close by.

With painstaking control, I push her away with my good arm. Her hips elevate a fraction to allow my rock-hard cock to escape. It slaps onto my messy shirt tails, the tip glistening with a cocktail of cum and feminine essence. When she shuffles to the empty space beside me, her hand glides to the creamy goop clinging to the inside of her thigh.

Fuck!

If I continue to sit next to her, my willpower would split down the middle and my family would be at a higher risk of danger.

"Get out." I force my painful erection into my trousers and zip it away. It's the hardest thing I've ever done. "You're not allowed to set one foot past the gates of this property."

In that second of separation, something flashes behind her searing amber eyes. A toxic mixture of seething anger or molten hatred. She knows I'm the one calling the shots and that doesn't sit well with her.

Quickly, without any hesitation, she snatches the edges of my jacket, cloaking her torso and drags the material over her chest. She doesn't look at me before exiting the vehicle with the spirit of an energetic merengue dancer.

I take a steadying breath and drag a hand over my face. She's both cursed and saved me at the same time. I'm no longer a slave to the nefarious memories when my *little liar* is riding my dick.

I groan loudly and burst into the late afternoon sun, barely controlling the urge to throw up or pass out from the pain of the gunshot wound in my arm. She stands by the trunk, hair disheveled, arms hugging her belly, and her chin pointed to the skyline.

It hits me like a rolling ocean wave. The need to take everything from her. To own her. To feed off the chemistry we've created and become the best version of myself ever. I'd become the legend Angelo claimed me to be.

She'd become my secret weapon. The tool I'd use to fuck when my mind starts to fail me and the war within me threatens defeat.

Shane rushes over to my side, his eyes scanning my blood-soaked shirt and the make-shift tourniquet. "Christ, Tommy. It looks bad. The Doc will be here any minute." His eyes flick to Carina, knowing she's the only one who could have tied the shirt around my arm, and then his serious green gaze jumps back to me just as quickly. I'm numb all over, except for the throbbing erection trapped behind my zipper. "Here... let me help you." He adds without touching me.

He expects my world to implode with violence as it would have before. But now—now all I can think of is cold-blooded revenge and fucking Carina Ferreira until she can't breathe anymore.

"It's my own blood, Shane. It's fine. Meet me inside."

His jaw slackens, and he narrows his eyes at me. "You gonna take a shower first?" he quizzes, trying to figure out my altered persona. "And let Luciano check you over?"

"Of course." I nod, then stalk past him.

I hear his sigh and biting order to the men around us to get indoors.

Carina's lashes flick up on my approach, our gazes locked tight.

"I have a job for you." I muster the strength to gently tuck a strand of hair behind her ear without smashing her lips with mine.

Those beautiful amber eyes flash with fire, but her head involuntarily tips to the sensation of my touch. "I have a job already."

I ignore her sassy tone, because this needs to be said. "I'll only make this offer once. Employment, under me... and only me. As soon as the terms are honored, you'll never see me again. You will be free."

"I don't understand. What could you possibly want from me?"

23

TOMÁS

I capture her chin and dig my bloody fingers into her skin. "I want four days. And your body to do with as I please. Whenever I want, however I want... And at the end, you will leave as a wealthy woman."

She doesn't answer straight away. Her expression turns stone cold. Ebony lashes blink to block any chance of tears. I note the trickery of light in her amber eyes, how embers of misplaced lust twirl with unfaltering abhorrence.

"I'll give you time to think it over."

Her brows snap together. "I don't need to think about it." She scowls up at me, shoulders drawn back in defiance. "It's a no. A big fat no. I'm not your whore. We fucked because I wanted to do it. Purely out of curiosity and my own reasons. Not for payment, and certainly not for your personal gratification. I'm not an object you can buy and sell. Find another woman willing to suck your dick and let you fuck them like you own them. It won't be me."

It's baffling how I let her talk to me like this. Truth be told, it's both a miracle and frustrating. Somehow, she thinks I won't hurt her—or kill her.

Would I?

I'm mulling over the question when her eyes settle on the blood still seeping from my bicep. There's a subtle shimmer of concern behind her stony contemplation. This woman challenges me to roll the dice, and every time they land, she wins.

"I'm offering a truce between us, a simple arrangement with a termination date and a substantial payout on completion." I let those words hang for a second. "After I'm done with you, you'll have your freedom again, and enough money to live off for the rest of your life. However, if you'd rather, I'll make it happen without any benefits."

"Get over yourself," she spits, clutching the jacket tighter. I watch her transcend from the ill-fated *little liar* to a staunch queen who isn't afraid to lose her head in this war she finds herself in. "I don't need your dirty money. And you're crazy if you think I'd actually choose to be your sex slave…" She inhales quickly. "I'm worth more than that."

My lips curl into a smile before I can stop them. "But you would do it if I didn't pay you?"

Her stormy gaze cuts to the men traipsing onto the property behind us. "What happened in that vehicle will *never* happen again. *Never.* It was a mistake to think there might be a scrap of compassion lurking inside that cold heart of yours."

A throbbing ache spreads across my brow. I'm lightheaded and sweating under this grimy shirt I desperately need to burn. This argument isn't going anywhere and it's not worth using the last reserves of my energy to debate it. Besides, she's not leaving the property until I let her go.

"We'll talk later. I have a bullet wound that needs attention. Get inside and clean yourself up."

I reach for her arm and flinch as the tendons in mine scream. Excruciating pain darts through shredded muscle like a missile.

My arm drops, the fingers tingling from loss of blood. I drag the opposite hand through my hair, fully aware my bulletproof crown is slipping and there's nothing I can do to stop it. The fine cracks in my composure have fractured and she's treading on the destructive surface.

"We don't need to talk. I'm not interested in your proposition." Her hostile countenance is beautifully sincere.

"Inside. Now." I command on a hiss. I roll out my shoulders and take a tranquilizing breath. "Jackal…" The forced texture of my speech is harsher than a tornado spitting out sand and rubble when I bark my guard's name. "Take the Escalade to the other side of the city and blow it to fucking pieces."

The interior would never be the same now I've bled all over the upholstery.

Carina catches a few strands of flyaway hair dancing before her lashes and sweeps them behind her ear. Her gaze settles on the cityscape, purposely choosing not to meet my angry stare. But she doesn't move an inch.

Her obvious resistance twists like a knife. "Should I

throw you over my shoulder and carry you indoors?" I threaten.

I watch a subtle sigh escape her lungs, how it deflates her ribcage. Yet her self-assured posture doesn't alter. She pivots without looking at me, clips my good arm on her way past, and weaves around the parked vehicles. Rather than explode, I say nothing. Wild rage hisses inside me, the threat of it winning becoming very hard to suppress.

I fist my hands to stop myself from dragging her into my chest by the hair. It would only take a single order to have her forced on her knees to the gravel before me, to punish that brazen attitude with my dick. Use this as an opportunity to destroy the blistering connection we have with perverted, depraved deeds. Give her a lesson in respect and obedience, but that would be too easy. And nothing about this predicament is easy. She's unlike any other woman I've ever encountered.

When she agrees to my terms, I'll own her heart, soul, breath, pain, and pleasure... at least for a few days. Her everything will be mine. And the second our time together is up; our paths will be separated by a cast iron partition. Four days will allow me to get my shit together, kill a few motherfuckers, bury my father, and pave the way to an arranged marriage.

She storms ahead like a cyclone chewing up a rainbow, speeding past the guy holding the door open for me. The instant her dazzling aura bursts into the airy entrance, Brutus and Sniper race across the polished tiles in our direction. My ear-piercing whistle makes her jump. I smirk, knowing my German Shepherds are well-trained, and respond only to me.

Sniper hurries to greet me like he always does. He circles my legs, sniffs the blood, and positions himself at my heel. What happens next both mystifies me and pisses me the fuck off. The dog I had rescued from the brink of death takes me by surprise. Brutus trots around me, sniffs my hand to check I'm safe, then prances to Carina in the lounge and sits by *her* feet.

I'll have to rename him Judas.

Her hand settles on his head and her tight expression falters. His serious chestnut eyes drink in her effortless beauty as she leans into his muzzle and kisses the tip of his wet nose. For some reason, a crackle of jealousy sparks through my veins. Christ, even my emotions are betraying me.

When she bends, the hem of the jacket creeps higher to reveal lean thighs and faint bruises. Bold red fingerprints show the violence she'd accepted, and the passion she craved.

I should hate myself for inflicting those oxygen-rich smudges on a woman, but I don't feel remorseful at all. No pity. No regret. No thorny twist of anxiety. Truth be told, I fucking love seeing them on her flesh, knowing it was me who put them there and marked her.

My balls cramp with an agonizing arousal. It's getting harder to maintain the level-headedness I require to conduct business. It doesn't help that my throat is dry and my feet are heavy like I'm wearing concrete boots.

The men caught up in the shootout mingle around us, each of them spitting out bloodthirsty threats for what's to come. "Shane." I call out, knowing he'd be in close range. "You know what needs to be done after that shit show. Make it happen."

He steps up from behind me. "Who the fuck would chance a bloodbath in the middle of the day?"

I grunt as Carina wanders further inside and my so-called lethal guard dog prances beside her. "The Mexicans are lying low." I point out, forcing myself to walk. "Apparently, they're on our side. Petty street wars aren't Blanco's style. He'd rather blow shit up. Did we lose any men?"

"Not this time." Shane confirms. "Leave it to me. Whoever is responsible will get the message."

"It needs to be sorted out before we head north to my father's plantation."

"So do you, Tommy. For fuck's sake. How are you still standing... and not psychotic?"

I shake my head and hide a slight smile. Fucking Carina in the back of an SUV has changed the dynamics of my usual lethal outbursts. I'm learning to channel the deviant side of my personality into something pure.

Her.

He follows my gaze to the woman now perched on the edge of the couch. I can't let my men see how much she's getting to me. They'll think I'm too preoccupied to rule—or worse, they'll use her against me. On that fleeting thought, my stomach roils and I stifle the sudden rush of nausea with a cough.

"Christ," he mutters. "Tommy."

"I need to wash this shit off." I interrupt him. "Do your job, Shane, and give me space. I need fucking space to think."

I leave Shane to take charge of the men calling for

enemy blood while I take a breather from it all and make my way out to the terrace through the sliding doors. With every labored step, I feel her eyes all over me.

She's probably wondering if I'd die from blood loss so she could sprint back to her shitty shoebox apartment. Except if I dropped dead, my men wouldn't value her like I do. They'd shoot her in the face and roll her off a cliff. My ribs tighten as if they're protecting my heart from caring too much about her safety.

The infinity pool glitters under the Colombian sun. Orchid scented air grounds me to the ascending heights of my mountain home and the soft breeze prickles my scalp. I kick off my shoes, tug at the saturated compress until it drops, and then gingerly strip.

I toe the soiled garments into a bundle, ready for incineration. In a hurry for cleanliness, I stagger over the flagstones, crossing onto the slate base of an open air shower at the far end of the pool and flick on the icy water jets.

Needles of water spear my salty flesh. They pummel my forehead when I raise it toward the cerulean cloudless sky. Bamboo leaves rustle in the breeze and the stench of acrid copper flips my stomach.

Energy drains from my overused limbs. The loss of blood and expenditure of sexual tension has left me depleted. I'm growing weaker by the minute, which only serves to make me vulnerable, even in my own home.

Shane appears with a towel and worried creases around his earnest eyes when he witnesses red water flowing down my arm.

"Luciano's inside now." He watches me fumble with a

bar of soap. "One of the guys recognized a shooter. A small-time cartel from the coast thought they'd seize the opportunity to catch us off guard. They'll be dead by midnight." He sighs. "Tommy…"

"Don't fucking say it." I know he's about to tell me we shouldn't have gone into the city on a mindless whim, chasing after a woman of no consequence.

Rich red blood splashes around the onyx tiles underfoot, almost camouflaged, my uncovered gunshot wound still bleeding. I stifle a retch and suck in air through gritted teeth.

It's my blood. Not Angelo's. Not Papá's. Mine.

"You know she didn't do it. So, why did you bring her back with you?"

I shrug, my heart rate slowing. "Why not?"

When I glare at him over my shoulder, his features blur temporarily. I press my hand to the wall to support my wobble.

Don't show weakness.

Angelo's imprinted sermon springs to the forefront of my mind. Shane understands my struggle, but the rest of the men in here don't have a clue. And I won't give them an opening to assume I'm a sitting duck.

"Does she know about Bianca?" he asks.

I almost laugh. "She doesn't need to know about my fiancé. I'm fucking the girl, not working on a relationship." My reply burns his suggestion to ashes with the callous tone I hit him with. "It's a Russian Roulette situation. And I know when the next bullet is coming. She'll be gone after the funeral," I tell him, turning to face the pool.

He hands me a towel after the shower stops. I bury my

face in Egyptian cotton, then press it over the seeping hole rather than hide my cock. It's not like he hasn't seen it before.

"You've lost a shit load of blood, mate. Are you feeling okay?" He eyes me closely. "You look half-dead."

"I feel fucking dead. Nothing a bottle of Jack and a few stitches won't sort out."

My head rings with retribution and when I walk, it feels like I'm floating. Sometimes I wish I could turn my back on it all and leave the violence and bloodbaths behind. The pressure is overwhelming at times. Especially now I'm heading the entire operation. But this is what I do. It's all I've ever known and now I have to live up to my uncle's high expectations—to become legendary.

"Where's the girl now?" I ask, making a beeline for the liquor cabinet.

"She went upstairs." Shane joins me. Without being asked, he unscrews the Scotch and fills two tumblers. He hands me one. "You'll be out of action tonight, Tommy. I dunno if those motherfuckers know they shot you. I'm not taking any chances. I've arranged for a crew to man the compound tonight. And I'll crash here again." I nod, my head woozy. "You need to stop bleeding everywhere."

I make it to the couch without my knees giving way, and sink like a rock. The breath leaves my lungs in a triumphant sigh, yet my body is tense and stressed.

Luciano appears out of nowhere. He slides round frames further up the bridge of his crooked nose and sets a leather medical bag on the coffee table. I gulp down the Scotch when he arches over me, eyes squinting. His bald head shines and aged fingers carefully assess the wound.

"The bullet is still in there, Tomás. I'll have to fish it out. Do you need something stronger than booze?"

"No," I hiss when he stops poking my screaming muscle. "Just get the fucker out and stop it bleeding all over the furniture. I'll have to torch the couch at this rate."

It all happens in a cloudy haze of stabbing pain and alcohol. Shane refills my glass. Luciano pulls on a pair of latex gloves and peels open a pair of sterile scissor-like tweezers. I drain the whiskey and let my head fall back when metal touches bone.

My fingers go numb. It's a challenge to keep my eyelids open. I fight against the promise of sleep long enough to see the bullet leave from the same hole it entered.

"Get some rest." Luciano pings off his bloodied gloves. "You're not the first Souza I've patched up. And you won't be the last. This is only the beginning, Tomás."

24

CARINA

I hover on the landing long enough to watch an old man extract fragments of lethal steel from Tomás' arm with a pair of surgical pincers.

It's nothing I haven't seen before. Except, those patients I'd observed were medicated to the eyeballs. In Tomás' sober state, he barely flinched. Zero response. No yells or pleading for the pain to stop. No ragged breathing. He just sat there sipping whiskey and then waited patiently for Shane to fill the glass again.

His muted reaction isn't a show of strength, or a shield of power that he's trained to use. It's all him. Constrained. Expressionless. A true sovereign.

Somehow he had stayed hidden behind the mask he wears and easily traveled into the darkness he exists in. I am both impressed by his dauntless reaction and petrified by the cold display of fortitude––how utterly numb he must be inside.

There's no way to win against a man like him.

I left the doctor to stitch him up and took the opportunity to shower alone with the ensuite door locked from the inside. A safety measure on my part, but pointless as no one came to find me.

Later that evening, a knock on the bedroom door is followed by a sing-song feminine voice. The housekeeper, maid, or whatever Marta's role may be, left a tray on the floor outside, announcing a bowl of chicken soup that had to be eaten on Tomás' order.

Out of spite, I considered leaving it uneaten, just to prove he couldn't dictate my every move, but hunger got the better of me. It tasted amazing, even if my belly gurgled after every mouthful.

There's something ironic about enjoying a bowlful of warm soup while wrapped in a cashmere soft blanket and huddled on the plush gray rug of a master suite owned by a powerful man.

His out of nowhere proposal was a hard slap to the face. A soulless proposition with a termination date and currency. He expects me to spend four days of my life with him, to accept his temporary ownership of me, and succumb to his wicked appetite. The devil asking me to sell my soul.

I should be appalled by such an immoral suggestion. Freaked out by the idea of spending more time with a lawless criminal. Enraged by his audacity. However, in a distant part of my brain, I've unearthed all the hurt I suffered. I remember being the outcast who wished her life away and dreamed of childish fantasies.

Whether I want to confess it or not, there's a connection sizzling between Tomás and I. Something absurdly profound. For the first time in my life, a man wants me in his bed. He overlooks my imperfections without pity or disgust. It's not that I'm grateful for his attention, or mindlessly taken by his sexual abilities. I'm simply intrigued and very attracted to him.

Anxious threads snake their way around each rib so the bones create an impassable cage for my troubled heart until I eventually fall asleep on his bed. Damp hair dried naturally, and a large t-shirt hides the bruises on my thighs.

My body jerks awake. I blink in the muted glow of a bedside lamp. Through the heavy glazed windows, I see the velvety sky of nightfall. I'm curled up in a massive bed with a thin sheet covering my legs. He didn't join me.

I press my palm to my racing heart, the reason for my sudden awakening. Panic pumps through my arteries, the sensation hammering in my chest.

My family.

Sal will go out of his mind if I don't reply to his messages. I have to find a phone or a laptop and contact him. But what I need most of all is to escape this confusing nightmare—a perilous game, worse than fated death.

My destruction's written all over it in blood and tears. I'm stuck in the belly of a beast who thrills me with his beautiful danger. And that realization spikes my survival instincts. I haven't fought away the dark days to end up defenseless.

I hate myself with a despicable passion for wondering about him if he's recovering somewhere in this glass house. It's not normal for a woman to let compassion cloud her judgment of an insensitive man. But after our time together in the back seat of a chauffeur driven Escalade—with every hair follicle electrified, skin cell on fire, and piece of flesh reacting to his feral touch, I find my thoughts consumed by him.

I was finally living.

Moving on top of him, both of us vulnerable, was like dancing in a rainstorm on a thunderous afternoon––revivifying.

Yet the erratic pulse in my throat won't let me settle in a life where I'm paid for sex at the mercy of a man who can so easily snuff out a heartbeat. That's not how my future would play out or what my conscience deserves to juggle with for years after.

I rake shaky fingers through my thick, wavy hair and untangle the air-dried strands. Dropping off the bed, I pad to the doorway and sneak onto the landing, holding my breath to help me hear better.

There's a ghostly stillness. An unnerving calmness blanketing high ceilings and sturdy hallway furniture that was designed to fit the space where they sit exactly. Several closed doors are dotted clockwise, and a few lanterns fixed to the freshly painted walls offer a subtle warm radiance.

I silently drop down onto each step of the coiled staircase, snaking lower. On my descent, I notice the couch is gone and Tomás is nowhere in sight.

Shadows move in the moonlight as I creep along the corridor to where I suspect his office is, at the very end, where I'd heard him once before. When I place my fingers on the handle, I blow out in annoyance as it depresses, and the door stays shut. Of course, he'd lock it. I bet there's a trip wire attached to the handle or lasers ready to slice off an intruder's head—my head.

Not planning to give up, I backtrack and hurry to the sliding glass doors. Sliding one open with a sliver of space to squeeze through, I slip outside.

Cool air tingles over my thighs and goosebumps scurry the length of my spine. The high moon reflects on the glassy pool, appearing to drop off the hillside in an illusion of never-ending flow. If I didn't know better, I'd think his luxury bachelor pad's a little piece of paradise.

But I've kneeled beside the fire pit on this grand terrace, bound and hooded, ready for his temper to ignite. It's more like a beautifully disguised waiting room for Hell.

I shiver and hug my belly for comfort. He's had plenty of opportunities to kill me. And yet, here I am—still alive, fighting, and trying to get away from the eye of a storm.

Flanking the brickwork, I keep low and lean into the towering wall. If I'm right, the office is on this side of the house. I'm getting desperate. The buzz charging my veins lets me know my covert sneaking is risky. But it's worth it to reach out to my brother.

At the corner of the property, I cross over from flagstones to a stony pathway fringed with dense flower beds and tropical palm trees, and take a beat to steady my breathing. If he catches me out here and suspects I'm looking for an escape route, he'd lock me up and throw away the key. I cast my eyes along the gable's end wall and check the windows. In that split second of contemplation, I'm interrupted.

"What the fuck are you doing?" The sinister hiss of the question crawls over me like a thousand millipedes.

I straighten to face a guy whose small eyes are sunken into his skull below a tight navy bandana that hides his forehead. His slow skulk makes me uneasy, especially when his reptilian slitted eyes dawdle on my chest as he scrubs an unkempt goatee with nicotine-stained fingers.

"Stretching my legs." My reply is less than friendly with my guard up, even though there's only air and cotton protecting me.

"Like fuck you are." His eyes slither over my skimpy attire and exposed flesh. Then he glances over his shoulder as if checking no one else is around.

"Where's Tomás?" I ask, taking a quick scope of the manicured gardens in case I need to run.

His lips curl. "None of your business, *puta*." Patting the gun snug to his hip, he advances toward me. "You think you can sneak about, and no one will catch you?"

"I'm not sneaking." I spit out, standing my ground. "In case you haven't noticed, I'm not wearing any cuffs. Tomás has allowed me to walk about."

"Is that so?" Bushy brows hitch to the stars and he thumbs his lips with a contemplative swipe.

Disgust prickles my scalp. I can see what he's thinking by that one glance. That lewd glaze crackling with wrongful intentions.

"Seems to me like you're looking for trouble. And guess what?" I swallow hard and stay quiet, refusing to give him what he wants. Fear. "You found a whole heap of trouble tonight. You're a nobody. When Tomás is finished with you, he'll bag your corpse and pack it in the walls of his next construction project. Do you really think you could survive the Souzas?"

"You're not a Souza," I bite back. "You're a hired goon, paid to do what *they* tell you. The only difference between you and me, is that you choose to take orders, because you've got no future of your own. I'm here against my will."

It happens like a lightning bolt, sharp and instant. The crack connecting with my head knocks me sideways. Pain spreads through my skull and my teeth jar. Heat blooms in a trickle, exiting the wound he'd created from a chunky silver ring.

Blood trails out of my hairline like he's split my face in half with a bold marker. My lungs expand and contract in bursts, the anger becoming untamed within me. How fucking dare he. In mindless retaliation, I slap his clean-shaven cheek with so much force that he staggers.

"You fucking bitch." He stretches out his jaw and glares at me. "You'll pay for that." Adrenaline spears my lungs, so they heave.

My vision blurs and my heart rate soars in preparation for flight. He snares my wrist, shoves me hard, and crowds me against the wall of the house. I try to duck low, only to feel a choking grip on my throat.

Anger vibrates from his muscles, his smoky breath close to my face. I struggle to gasp for air, to scream, and claw at his vice like grip.

I'm pinned to the wall, fighting a battle I'm powerless to win. Boots kick my ankles to part my legs. His free hand dives under the t-shirt and gropes my breasts.

"Stop," I wheeze out.

"Remember what I said?" He lifts the fabric higher to reveal my body to him. "You're nobody."

My stomach churns when his mouth hunts out my nipple and his teeth snare it. This isn't the violence I crave. This is unwanted, repulsive, and wrong. It's nothing like the wicked torture Tomás introduced me to. So far removed from his touch that I only wish I could scream at myself for being aware of the difference.

The more I thrash, the harder he bites. My head slams into the sandstone and my fists fly. I somehow muster enough strength to punch his temple. Rather than stop him, his menacing laugh cackles in the dead of night.

He releases my nipple, unhands my throat, grabs a fistful of t-shirt, and ruthlessly yanks the material. I hear it rip like he's stripping the flesh from my bones.

But he underestimates me. He thinks I'm weak, a cheap whore for his amusement. Filling my lungs, I project the air outwards in a blood-curdling scream and dart sideways. A bulky arm blocks my retreat and a hand covers my mouth to muffle the ear-piercing shriek.

We wrestle until he skillfully cuts my legs out from under me. I hit the stones with force, landing awkwardly. He pins my wrists above my head and climbs onto my pelvis.

"One more scream and I'll ram my cock so deep into your throat you'll choke on it." His arching form suffocates the serene glow of the all-seeing moon, casting me into darkness. The whites of his eyes glow as he fumbles with his zipper.

"Get off me." I buck my hips and yell again, only to watch his hand glide through the air and feel a harsh slap against my cheek. My eyes roll on impact and tears finally fall.

As he burns my ability to fight to cinders, I curse the day I moved to Bogotá for an adventure.

"I caught you spying on us. You're a lying puta who's planning to assassinate Tommy. No one will care what I do to you. This pussy is all…" As he reaches between my legs and cups me with a grotesque grunt, I hear a whirlwind of stones and feel his body lurch.

Soft fur skims my legs. Without delay, razor-sharp teeth clamp onto his left shin and Brutus snarls like the savage protector he was taught to be. The man throws his other foot at the crazed dog, doing his best to shake off the savage jaws yanking him off me.

I take the opportunity to reach for his revolver, still wedged in his belt. Once it's in my possession, I clamber to my feet and take a distorted aim. My hands tremble with cold blooded anger and the desire for justice. But the second he punches Brutus in the ribs, I snap the trigger.

"Bastard!" I yell, watching the speeding bullet hurtle through the air and clip his earlobe. "I won't miss the next time."

"Carina." My brain engages with the sound of a baritone voice, so chilling, so like home, that it pulls me from the frenzy of payback. I peer up from the satisfying mauling and pinpoint Tomás surrounded by the twinkly skyline.

In the soft skyglow, he appears dangerously handsome. Deadly dark eyes trail all over me with quick searching sweeps. His brow furrows and the scruff on his jaw seems so much darker.

Tomás' face holds an expression I've never seen on him before. A look that's impossible to interpret. It whispers through me with an unthinkable warmth.

On the periphery, Shane lingers by his hip, prepared to carry out any order.

Tomás lets out a high-pitched whistle. It breaks through the pained yells of Brutus' captive. Immediately, the guard dog obeys, unlocks his fiendish jaw and trots toward his owner.

The slimy fucker who had his hands all over me is no longer detained. He attempts to sit, dragging the tattered ends of his trousers higher to assess the carnage.

A rage like no other rips through me. I take my eyes off Tomás and widen my feet to give me a stronger position before I shoot. The buzz of retribution makes me nauseous. I'm almost loving the power I'm holding in my hands. Could I really kill this man?

"Lower your weapon," Tomás commands.

I shake my head and swipe my brow with the back of my hand. "No…"

25

TOMÁS

I've never felt this way before.

My heart is on fire and my dick resembles a stone column holding up the weight of the universe.

Her body trembles in the pale moonlight. The t-shirt hanging on her dainty shoulders is torn. A single line of blood streaks her teary face like war paint. Yet her posture is solid, her loose hair wild, and her wrath weighted shoulders fiery with embers.

She's absolutely captivating. Her integrity is feathered with a resolute need for vindication. I won't allow her to do it—to take a man's life and suffocate under that decision for eternity.

I close the distance, quickly assessing Bruno's wretched state. His cheeks are scratched, his shin is chewed to the muscle, and thankfully, his dick is still stashed behind his boxer briefs.

Filthy asshole. Every grain of my existence turns murderous. My hands ball into tight fists that could punch through the flaming iron gates of Purgatory.

"What are you doing, Tommy?" Bruno's face drains of color, his fretful eyes drilling into my golden gun. "It was her. The fucking spy. I caught her snooping. I bet she's planning to kill you the same way she murdered Elias. Finish the *puta*, she's nobody."

My lungs burn. Carina shakes her head back and forth. "I needed fresh air, that's all. I couldn't sleep."

Her lashes flutter as if she's doing her best to stand without fainting. She's not a fragile petal wilting under the monstrous deed of an aggressor. She's a warrior marred from battle, and bravely holding her ground. I admire her willful spirit.

My dogs don't attack for no reason.

"You're mistaken, Bruno." The thrumming pulse in my skull whooshes louder than his snivels. "She's nobody to you, but for now, she's somebody to me." Bruno's mouth quirks into a grimace. "And you tried to take what's mine. Which means you've crossed a big fucking line. I won't tolerate disrespect."

Bang.

The instant I unleash a bullet into his abdomen, Carina's gasp follows. Her watery gaze darts to my side profile. Bruno swears in Spanish, doubles over and spits at her feet. A crippling rage crests within me, the rush so intense my hand shakes.

Not enough for her to notice, but enough of a quake to warrant the death of this motherfucker. With a snap of the trigger, I discharge the final killing bullet.

The dogs prowl, both of them sensing a volatile medley of her anxiety and my uncontrolled temper.

Slowly, her torso twists and the weapon in her small hands turns on me.

"Stay away from me. Get back or I'll shoot." She hiccups, salty and terrified. "I've had enough of this shit."

Shane immediately moves an inch ahead of me in defense, his gun aimed at her heaving chest. "Lower the weapon, kid," he says softly, not speaking in his usual ornery tone.

The soles of her slender bare feet make no noise when she shuffles behind the trimmed topiary's and keeps her aim high. "No chance."

"Don't make me shoot you, kid." Shane warns. "You know I can't let you point a gun at the boss."

Brutus circles the scene, head lowered and hackles raised. His decision on who to protect now is a challenge. Sniper growls by my calves, obediently guarding his one true master. I stare at her scrunched-up face colored in a tide of fresh blood and feel myself slip from the throne I sit on with pride.

There's no pleasure to be found in watching my sweet little liar suffer. We all know she was plotting an escape. The enchanting woman is a survivor, an angel who had slayed her own demons. Realization explodes inside me, the maddening concept of admiration so raw and revealing. It's her personal experience, her knowledge of an all-consuming darkness with its vicious thorns and venomous vines that snare me.

She's traveled the same path and survived. Her deep understanding is the scribe for my unspoken affliction. The interpreter of a language so undefined that it was impossible to translate—until she appeared. And now, I'll use every inch of her body and soul until my affliction is no longer an issue.

A tornado gathers momentum inside my chest. It begs to cover the high moon on a quest to camouflage the crimson stain creeping closer to her scarred mouth. Those sexy lips that can do no wrong.

My spine stiffens, braced for conflict of the worst kind. I need her alive. "Stand down, Shane," I bark, low and cagey.

"Tommy…" he argues. "You know I can't do that. Tell her to put the gun down first."

"Both of you… fuck off…" Carina yells, jabbing the gentle floral breeze with unfriendly, cold steel.

Brutus hovers close to her long, lean legs, his threatening glare glued to Shane.

"Throw the gun away, Carina," I say firmly. "You're making things worse."

Sniper yaps, his ears pricking up at my fractured tone. Her throat bobs as she swallows, unsure of what her next move should be. She swipes her brow with the back of her hand again and smears the leaking trail of blood.

Our eyes meet, hers riddled with confusion and valiant strength, mine cautious.

"She won't pull the trigger, Shane," I say confidently, letting her see my own weapon pointed at the gravel under my feet. "Carina. Don't test my patience. This won't end well if you shoot. For your own safety, do not defy me."

In the moments of rippling unease, my dogs sense the gravity of my command. Brutus howls and Sniper lunges.

The two animals go head to head. One defending Carina, the other protecting me.

The chaos distracts her. I lunge forward and seize the gun from her curled fingers while she screams at the snarling duo to stop brawling. Finally taking control of the firearm, I raise it to the starry sky, fire a warning shot and whistle.

Both dogs separate on my command, lower to their bellies and pant hard in the aftermath of war. They've never fought before. Not once.

"Check them over. Call the vet if you need to," I snarl at Shane, all the while glaring at Carina.

Her face is ashen beneath streams of tears, cheeks glistening. As she tries to stifle a sob, her throat jerks. A tiny hand glides to her stomach and stays there as she stares up at me in silence. She glances over her shoulder, wary and uncertain. The ballsy woman thinks I'll punish her. Perhaps I will.

My jaw tightens, determined to keep my cool and not toss her over my shoulder to carry her indoors for a lesson in obedience.

I hold out my hand in the space separating us and wait for her to take it with strained patience. She mindlessly fingers her mouth, takes a deep breath, and ignores my offering.

The instant she darts left to dodge my show of peace, I snare her bicep, roughly halting her getaway. I ignore the spasm of pain rocketing up my shoulder, disturbing the perforated muscle healing under a clean dressing.

"Take my hand, Carina. That's an order." My stern request clips her unruliness.

Her bottom lip wobbles. Immediately, she captures it between her teeth. In her own time, she sets her small hand on top of my palm and returns my glower with watery, wide eyes, still dignified in our momentary truce.

Knots curl and twist around my gut, thick and corded in their pursuit to hamper me. I stare at the fragility of her untrusting expression. How the glazed sheen coating her seductive amber eyes begs for a grain of clemency.

Unspoken wishes shadow her elegant features. And the realization I would steal a fistful of stars from the heavens to help her shine again hits me hard and awakens a new concern.

This woman is more to me than just a somebody.

She's mine.

The hairs on my nape stand tall, like soldiers of war assembling for battle. I don't need emotional ties of any sort. They only serve to distract from the end goal of my destiny—to prove Uncle Angelo was right—to become legendary.

I'm no longer an apprentice standing beside the throne. I'm seated on top of Colombia, wearing my rightful crown.

My time has finally come.

Carina doesn't belong in this lawless world. It's too malignant for an innocent like her. That's why my temporary arrangement would work well for the both of us. Four days together and then all this emotional deception would be a distant memory.

Interlinking our fingers, I lead her along the pathway, through the gap in the glass door and up the stairs to my suite. Neither of us speaks. She trembles from shock and

I'm lost in thought, mulling over all the painful ways I could have slaughtered that bastard for hurting my woman.

As my bare feet hit the floor sized rug in my room, I let go of her hand and lock the door behind us. The resounding click echoes through the room.

Unwilling to look at me, her tear clumped lashes stay closed. Her eyes are fixed to her toes and her forearms rest beneath her ribs in a self-hug. The ripped neck hole of the t-shirt she took from my closet reveals just enough flesh to offer a glimpse of cleavage. Every scrap of pride she once projected is hidden behind vulnerability.

She hurries to the adjoining bathroom and slams the door shut. It would be sensible of me to leave her alone for a while. Unfortunately for Carina, after what just happened, I can't do that.

I march to the door and throw it open. She's standing by the vanity with her back to me. My eyes settle on her reflection, watching as she carefully dabs the cut at her hairline.

"Stop." I instruct, coming up behind her, painfully aware of the bloodied toilet paper scrunched up on the countertop.

She freezes. Her lashes bat wildly when she pinpoints my gaze in the mirror. I drop to my haunches and search inside the low level cupboard for medical supplies. It's not unusual for me to have surgical tape and sutures close at hand. Sometimes I encounter scrapes, braised knuckles, or worse after a night of dirty dealings.

Unpacking a pair of latex gloves, I cover my hands and

straighten. When I press an antiseptic wipe to her wound, I expect her to flinch. She doesn't.

"Why were you outside in the middle of the night?" I ask, following a slow sigh. She doesn't move an inch, except for her pupils. They rapidly expand as I lean closer to inspect the damage. "Tell me what you were really doing."

I watch her take a steady, deep breath before she answers, "I was looking for a phone, or a way to contact my brother. Your office was locked. I went outside to climb through the window if it was open." Her voice holds a sexy rasp of tiredness. "He messages me to check in." Her eyes search mine. There's absolutely no doubt in my mind that she's being honest. "If he doesn't get a reply, he'll worry. I put him through enough when I was kidnapped..." Her sentence trails off, both of us knowing how that ended.

When I'm certain the bleeding has eased, I toss everything in the trash, followed by the gloves. My hands are free of blood and my mind is clear from flashbacks.

I gather her hand in mine and usher her out of the bathroom. Nearing the bed, I whirl her around to face me, seize the hem of the t-shirt and drag it up and over her head.

She holds my gaze, her nipples hard and provoking. Yet her skin doesn't run cold, it blazes with warmth. Behind her reticence, I sense red-hot flames. Not disgust or fear. Only crackling lust.

Suspicion glitters in her eyes. "What are you going to do with me?"

My mind spins. In different circumstances, I would

chuck her on the bed and spread her legs wide. I'd bury my face in her exotic essence and make her eat my dick until she gags. However, tonight I'm war-torn and she's as delicate as an icicle in the midday sun.

"Nothing." A slight smile creeps over my face. "Get into bed," I murmur, putting streaming moonlight between us when I walk away, round the frame, pull back the fresh bed linen, and climb in.

Her brow creases as she hesitates, taken aback by my hands off approach. After a heartbeat of silent consideration, she concedes by slipping under the sheets and lying perfectly still.

The heat of her body next to mine proves hard to resist. Luckily for her, my willpower is as solid as the agreement I'll forge with her. Our little understanding will ensure her life is simple after we part ways. The financial reward is a parting gift. Absolution. Payment to highlight this entanglement isn't anything more than a business transaction.

Until we've cut a deal, I won't muddy the terms, even if it feels wrong to crave more of our anarchic connection.

"You're not going to punish me?" she asks incredulously, turning her head to look at me.

"Do you want me to?"

"No."

"Liar." I chuckle with an odd hint of disappointment. "When you've agreed to stay, then I'll fuck you so hard you'll forget what freedom ever felt like."

She rolls her eyes. "Why do you need me to agree? It didn't stop you fucking me in the shower."

My hand is around her neck before I exhale. Not stealing a kiss from her glistening, parted lips tests my theory of this being temporary. I want to devour the glistening landscape of her pink flesh and stick my tongue down her goddamn throat.

"It's a clean-cut formality. I like my instructions to be clearly understood. For my expectations to be met. Once you leave my employment, I'll need an assurance that you won't run your mouth off. If the wrong people figure out you've got Souza intel, even about the size of my dick, they'll pull out all of your teeth, one by one, until they get what they want.

Snitches are disposable after they bleed information. If my enemies don't finish the job, my men will." She narrows her eyes at me, almost daring me to hurt her. "And then they'll go after your family. Starting with your parents in Manaus."

She easily swallows against my palm, her breathing unrestricted. "What if I refuse to be your whore?"

I rub my thumb over her soft lips. "You're a good girl begging to be bad. That doesn't make you a whore." My dick jerks awake. "If I wanted a *puta*, I'd have three at a time, all lined up, begging for my dick to destroy them. Instead, I choose you." I witness her quick intake of air. "You'll agree to it."

"How can you be so sure?"

Because I sense her arousal mount and feel her pulse under my palm like a major earthquake. "I have your cell phone." I skim her jaw with the pads of my fingers and witness the uncontrollable shiver it brings. "Agree to it and you can send your brother Salvador a message. Don't agree to it, and you'll put everyone you love in danger. This is the only way I can trust you. Give me what I want and your family will remain under Souza protection."

"You won't hurt them," she hisses.

I can hear Papá's voice warning me this senseless plan would bring trouble. Trust should be earned and never freely given, especially to a woman. It's too late for that. Trouble is already in my bed with big amber eyes and a mouth so sinful it gives me chills. "I wouldn't. But my men are paid to obey without hesitation."

Warm air blasts from her nostrils as she huffs. A sexy little scowl creases her forehead, deep in thought. "Why are you doing this?"

"Because I can."

"Four days?"

"I'm burying my father and heading up the family business. The next few days will be a challenge. You'll be my outlet to ease the tension. It's a win-win situation."

She studies me, quiet in her inspection. "You're the only one winning." Her voice is soft and sleepy.

"Really? What about your parents?" I point out. "As of tomorrow, your father will be offered a promotion. He'd be foolish not to accept it. Your mother could give up her cleaning job if she wants. Plus... their lives will be protected."

"Are you joking? You're actually meddling with my family's lives?" Her lips pull back to a snarl, but she doesn't dare move. "How's that winning?" She ignores my gracious consideration for her parents' future. "Pfff!" Her tiny nostrils flare with rage, making my wayward dick harder. "You're bribing me to get what you want, and think I'll respect you for it. What exactly will I get out of this trade?"

I lick my lips, only to hear an exasperated sexy whimper behind her clenched teeth. "I'll fuck you exactly the way you like it." I muse, pretending she's not affecting me. "No strings. No consequences. No commitment. Just my dick slipping in and out of your wicked little holes, whenever and wherever I want. We both know how much you enjoy it."

"Four days and it's over? Then you'll let me walk away, and you won't hurt my family." She blinks. "I find that hard to believe."

"Four days. That's it. I promise." I slowly breathe her into my lungs. "However, now that I think about it, you'll likely crawl away rather than walk. I guarantee your pussy will be fucked hard and your body truly exhausted."

Carina growls at me. It's a hot, snarky rumble. Completely forgivable under the circumstances. She knows I could make her orgasm until she faints, but won't dare admit it.

"How can I trust you'll let me go? That this isn't some lame-assed plan that ends in tragedy?"

When I chuckle, I'm oddly aware of how her light shines over me. I roll onto my back, scrubbing my face, exhaustion sucking me into the mattress. "I'll personally see you out the door. Once we arrive back in Bogotá, I won't have any need for you."

"So, in basic terms, I'm a convenient fuck." She tugs the sheet higher. "It doesn't matter how you try to disguise it, Tomás. I'd be a glorified whore, without a voice."

It happens before I can think. Heat flames in my veins.

I lunge across the bed and smother her hot, naked body with mine.

"Let's get one thing straight, *little liar*. I can have you whenever I want. Agreement or no agreement." Her soft breasts squish into my muscular chest. "You're not a whore. And I'm not a saint. As for your voice, I'll only silence it if you disrespect me. I'm looking forward to hearing you scream."

I unintentionally thumb her chin and then unscramble my mind. Being this close to her is playing havoc with my pulse.

"You crashed head first into my life. I could throw you out in the city tonight, but where's the fun in that?" My face is directly before hers, both of us fighting to inhale the same oxygen. "Or…" I whisper, knowing what I'm about to suggest next is a lie. "I could kill you now and save myself all of this hassle."

In a thoughtless moment of insanity, I drag my tongue along the faded scar on her upper lip. She whimpers beneath me. Not out of bubbling hatred, rather from simmering desire.

"You'll be well compensated for your time." I add.

I see a flicker of hurt in her big eyes. Regret knocks me off balance, long enough for her to launch a wad of spittle at my chin.

"I'm not a destitute teenager whose only option is to sell herself for a few bucks. You're throwing money around like confetti and expecting me to celebrate. Well, I've got news for you. I don't need your big payoff or your big dick. I'm a girl with dreams. And you, Tomás Souza, are a heartless bastard."

Before I know it, my fingers hollow her cheeks, so her sassy mouth opens. Leaning over her, I spit into her mouth. It makes the skin on my balls tighten when the halo of amber circling her pupils catches fire. Instantly, I slam my mouth over hers—hard, forceful, angry. I expect her to protest and ward off my advances. Instead, she accepts my brutal tongue and her fingers dive into my hair without retaliation.

Just as she parts her thighs to invite me in, I pull away. It takes every stitch of self-discipline to peel myself off her tempting curves. Her hair catches in my fingers, silky loops pulling me back to her again.

"Agree to my terms. Then I'll give you my dick." There's a thick rasp to my voice that warns us both of my threadbare compassion.

"Fuck you." She pants, dabbing her lip.

I smirk, push away from her, and settle flat on my back. "You'd like that," I mutter.

"So would you." She smiles over at me, her lips curling with satisfaction. "Wrap it up in dollar bills with a fat ribbon tied around and pretend it's an agreement. But you're only paying for my company, because you think having all that money gives you limitless power."

"It does." My eyelids are heavy, and the gunshot wound throbs under a clean dressing.

If not for my slamming pulse and solid dick tenting the sheets, I'd easily fall asleep straight away. Though something tells me it won't be that easy. As I lie beside this frustrating woman, it'll be the biggest challenge of my life not to punish her for making me feel off kilter. As much as her presence holds the weight of an anchor, it confuses the fuck out of me.

I sigh loudly for show. "I'm tired. I have a busy day scheduled for tomorrow." I ignore her glare. "And you're coming with me."

"Where to?" She fists the sheet, practically mummifying herself in cotton so there's no naked skin on display.

"We're going back to where it all started. To the plantation where my father waits in a gilded coffin."

26

CARINA

I wake up naked in a bed fit for a king.

My sticky eyelashes peel open, encrusted with salty distress from the harrowing events a number of hours ago. An achy cut on my head has dried to a gross scab and my lungs are as tight as a drum.

The empty space beside me is where Tomás fell asleep. I listen carefully to detect a telltale sound, to hear water jets in the gargantuan shower or splashes from the faucet. There's only the quick thrum of my pulse and a low groan as I throw back the high thread count sheet to sit up.

I'm still in shock from how he had killed one of his henchmen without questioning why I was really outside. He just fired, once, then a second time. It shames me to admit the flutters in my chest are born from the words he chose. *She's somebody to me.*

The ruthless king had shot one of his own in a monstrous act. He murdered him because of me. For justice—or an important reminder of the pecking order. I shouldn't be so compelled by his reasons for doing it, but I am.

I want to understand why he didn't accuse me of spying himself. Why am I safely tucked up in his bed, untouched, and a slave to his mystery?

It's not the first time he's spared my life. Since he cut me loose from the plantation, to caging me on the pavement while an influx of bullets soared straight at us—he's kept me safe. I'm balancing on a tightrope, wearing a false harness of trust when the truth is, he could snip the rope at any moment.

He could have beaten, abused, or tortured me in the hours that followed. But he didn't. For a man so caught up in wrong doings and evil, he revealed a softer side. Humanity shone from those serious eyes of his, those shadowed, ever assessing irises that quietly study my every move.

Threatening expectations spat from his mouth, yet soft full lips teased as if he struggled to keep them off mine. Quick reactions didn't choke or hurt, they only warned me of his capabilities. Whether that was desire for a kiss would remain his secret.

The battle within me clashes like sharpened daggers. How can I agree to his crazy sex pact? He refers to it as an agreement, but that would mean I'd already agreed. I haven't. Why would I consent to a perverted contract written by a gangster? Can I trust him... even when he's saved my life more times than he's fucked me?

If I don't agree, he'll do unspeakable things. My family wouldn't stand a chance against his arsenal of weapons and loyal goons who stalk the country without consciences.

I swing my legs over the edge of the bed and settle the soles of my feet on the deep plush rug. Daybreak streams in through the windows, spilling pale sunshine on the robust masculine furniture. It's a reminder that not all things reject the light, that maybe Tomás has another side to him. A duplexity to his personality that I've somehow uncovered. Or perhaps it's my own wishful thinking.

Hollow and bruised, I pick another of his folded t-shirts from the walk-in closet and dress. The never worn before fabric holds no scent of him, just a muted cotton aroma of newness and wealth. Hurrying to the ensuite, I squeeze out a blob of toothpaste onto my forefinger, run it over my teeth, then rinse, and spit.

When I stuff my fingers into my tangles to tease them out, I realize I'm trying to look half decent for him. I hit my fist on the counter and hiss when it hurts more than I expected.

Fuck him.

In a bad mood, I stomp through the bedroom and find the door unlocked. I'm still free to roam through his home, even after the accusations thrown at me. My light-footed steps descend the serpentine staircase encased by a glass handrail.

Rather than obey the growl coming from my empty stomach, I aim for his office door at the end of the long hall past the living room. The closer I get, the faster my heart races.

From beyond the closed door, I overhear his silky voice scored with a thousand unforgiving blades to harshen its texture. I freeze, subconsciously tapping my lip. All the valid reasons not to enter his realm of business are nailed into my mind one by one, with arrows of doubt. I'm nervous—not scared.

My spine straightens, vertebrae after vertebrae, in preparation to meet my nemesis. I suck in a lightning breath, lightly bang the door twice, and trap the air in my lungs. He stops talking and the hush that follows whirls me into a vortex of apprehension. When the door swings inwards, I blink in the breathtaking sight of him ignoring everything else.

My mouth goes dry and I wilt a little under his brooding silence. He's bare-chested, his sun exposed muscles flexing and gleaming under the first light of a new day. Diamond studs in his earlobes catch my eye, the tiny jewels glinting like beams from a lighthouse, warning travelers of the peril ahead.

A twenty-four-carat chain the color of a Brazilian sunset sits above his collar bones, enviously snug to his skin.

Orderly ebony hair holds a glossy sheen, still wet from an early morning shower and the dusting of stubble on his strong jaw is trimmed to a shadow. Loose black gym shorts sit comfortably on angular hip bones, low enough to reveal a scattered collection of shorn pubic hairs, regretfully trailing out of sight.

He clears his throat. The rumble of that one throaty reverberation instantly loops my gaze and whips it upward. I swallow swiftly to drown the annoying flutters in my chest, using what little saliva I have left.

Furious he's so insanely sexy. Out of defiance, I fold

my arms and look away, focusing on the massive black television housed in a towering wooden cabinet.

"Sleep well?" Tomás moves back further into his home office, making no sound as his bare feet cover a woven rug.

He skirts a matching pair of ebony leather couches and sits in the high back leather office chair behind his uncluttered mahogany desk, blocking the warm haze of dawn trying to kiss his bare skin and rests his elbows on the surface.

I nod in response, having fallen asleep beside him without feeling afraid.

"Do you want a couple of tablets to ease the pain from that cut on your head?"

"It doesn't hurt. I've had worse." My gaze drifts to the unusual artwork hung on the grainy gray wallpaper behind his head.

An obscure canvas, riotous and spine-chilling—like every nightmare I've suffered and every unspeakable thought I've sealed in a box within my mind. The cataclysmic image taps into my psyche and projects a visual destination.

It somehow connects me to the grisly emotions I thought I had suppressed all those years ago—when I mindlessly concluded life wasn't worth living. Before my younger self eventually chose to keep fighting in a world where cruelty reigns.

Frenzied streaks in the evilest pigment of red collide with endless slashes of deathly black to create a massacre of brush strokes and art. I cock my head, hypnotized by the artist's chaos. By his depiction of mental hell.

"You painted this, didn't you?" Eyes glued to the artwork, I unstick my feet and glide toward it, entranced by the stirring bond it somehow offers me. "This is where you go, isn't it?" He doesn't reply. "I'm not scared of your darkness, Tomás." My voice haunts the silence. "I recognize it."

"Well then, you'll understand how it swallows people whole." He warns.

Thoughtlessly, I brush my fingertips over the ridges of dried paint, unintentionally shifting the canvas' position ever so slightly. His chair swivels and he stands, our arms lightly brushing. Tomás reaches up and fixes the offset artwork back in place.

"Have you eaten?" He changes the subject, his tone dismissive, like I've shone a flashlight into his soul and pinpointed a terminal disease.

"Not yet." I stare up at him and swallow when his gaze merges with mine.

His perfectly black eyes aren't callous or malignant. They project an unreadable depth leading to his tarnished soul. A force of nature so compelling it draws you in until the world you once knew is left in dancing dust.

He pivots to the desk, collects an envelope from the top drawer, and taps it on his open palm, deep in thought. "This is for you. It's non-negotiable. If I suspect collusion of any sort, I'll take matters into my own hands." Tomás offers it to me and lifts his brows expectantly. "Read it while you have breakfast."

I frown, unsure if this is the moment I make the biggest mistake of my life or welcome the most profound adventure. "Will I need a legal team to review it?" I ask sarcastically, plucking it from his fingers.

The corners of his mouth curl as he grunts from the back of his throat like a rare rumble of laughter. "I imagine your *legal* team would advise you not to accept."

That sexy sound, so enticing and yet very criminal, has my heart rate at full throttle. "Then perhaps I won't."

Tomás pauses, his eyes fix to mine as those large hands of his shelf on his hips. "Opportunities like this don't exist in the Souza cartel very often, if at all. You'd be wise to strongly consider your next move." He stretches out his hand in the palpable space separating us and swipes a thumb over my scarred mouth. "I believe you'll make the right choice. Follow me. You need to eat."

He stares at me as if he's using an invisible power to manipulate my mind with seductive persuasiveness. Then he takes my hand, interlocks our fingers, and guides me out of his office.

"You know this is immoral," I admonish. "Imprisoning a woman and threatening her family, so you can screw her whenever you want."

Tomás doesn't even try to hide the smirk ghosting his handsome features. "You're right. Nothing about this is morally just—for you. However, for me, it's simply another business deal." He shrugs. "On the bright side, I guarantee you'll enjoy it."

"A business deal?" I admonish. "You mean you've done this before?" My voice raises a decibel higher, oddly annoyed that I'm just a number. "With other innocent women?"

He glances down to meet my stern glare blistering his

handsome face. "No, Carina. No other women. Just you. You're the first, and the last." A shadow washes over his features. "And you're far from innocent."

"What's that supposed to mean?" I bluster, wrangling with his hand to wriggle free.

He frowns. "Are you telling me you didn't instigate any of this? That you didn't willingly kneel before me and take my dick in that dangerous mouth of yours all those weeks ago? That you didn't enjoy having your tight little cunt broken in by me?" The growl breaking from his throat terrifies me. "You're not innocent anymore, my *little liar.*"

I stumble in shock, only to be swung into his naked torso like a wayward magnet and secured there. My veins work faster than ever before, catching fire from his irresistible warmth. The flirtatious grin he offers is playful. It baits me to an exquisite shore of temptation where I'll either inhale a lungful of water or tread sun-soaked sand.

My heart pounds with fear and attraction, oddly mimicking the pulse in his corded neck. Dark eyes flit from the wilted crown of innocence I once wore to my gaping mouth. For a second he stills. I pray he'll kiss me. He doesn't.

Fingertips trace a shivery path along the curve of my neck, gliding across my jaw until they push past my teeth. Without thought, my lips circle his fingers and his pupils magnify. I moan softly as he swiftly removes them and licks the moist tips to taste me.

"Minty." His sonorous voice ruptures the airless atmosphere like a blazing comet.

I blink up at him, unsure of what the hell is happening to me. Between my legs, a treacherous wetness forms and my chest heaves as I try not to give in to the scorching arousal. I'm off balance by the threat of his physical dominance, his impressively sculpted abdomen, and the unknown look he's silently dishing out.

Is it so wrong for me to want this man? To be curious about what his terms are, and consider them no matter how irreverent they may be? What if he's the key to unlock the life I've always wanted, and unearth the peace within me I've only ever dreamed about? The sort of peace I only get when I orgasm at his mercy.

I shake my head and almost scoff at my greenness. Four days of sex does not equate to a lifetime of happiness, nor does it mean anything more than a woman bought for indecent services.

A sigh escapes me. Tomás steps away, a tiny smile twitching his lips. He continues to walk, strolling ahead while I shudder from the loss of heat his body injected me with.

"Chop-chop." He clicks his fingers and turns away. "You'll need a bowl of frosted flakes before we get down to business." I glance at the ivory paper rectangle quivering in my hand and consider opening it in private. When I don't follow, he halts and peers over his shoulder at me. "Food, Carina. This way."

I swallow and obey, somehow mustering the strength to act nonchalant as I amble to his side. Together we leave the sun-drenched open living space and wander into the ritzy kitchen I had visited once before.

Opposite walls of silken gunmetal cabinets frame an elongated island finished with a streamlined marble countertop. Herringbone tiles, the color of roasted coffee beans, sprawl the length of the room to meet glazed French doors at the far end. Copper tube ceiling fixtures hang over the freestanding island in a cluster of three, oozing a dreamy radiance when Tomás flicks the light switch on.

"Take a seat." He pulls out a padded stool and lightly places his palm on the curve of my spine to guide me. "Marta is unavailable this morning. You like that sugary cereal shit, don't you?" he smirks, cocking a brow with disdain. "Or are you in the mood for something else?"

Conflict jabs my heart with a needle thin dagger as I settle. He's not a good man. This temporary truce of suspicion is simply the calm before our war. I must be out of my mind to even consider the outrageous small print contained within the envelope.

He's fucked me, antagonized me, threatened my life, and the lives of those I love. Yet somehow, beyond all the evil warping his words, there's a ghost of something so undivided that it rattles my bones.

"Sugary shit will do," I reply lightly, my shoulders bouncing. "It's cheap and cheerful."

He stays quiet and opens the cupboards one by one as if he's not sure where to look for the frosted flakes. I take a moment to watch him hunt and quickly understand that this isn't somewhere he spends his time. Whatever Tomás Souza needs, he's given. People worship him. They serve him.

I place the envelope on the white and gray counter before slipping off the stool to my tip toes. Saying nothing, I walk past him to the larder and select one of the unopened boxes from inside. There weren't very many the last time—just a half-empty box—and now there are four.

"It's good to see you know your way about," he muses.

"A kitchen?" I retort with a sulky huff.

"*My* kitchen," he adds with a sexy as fuck smirk. "You fit in well."

Every hair on my nape stands to attention when I see the unique wink of a dimple in a half smile that seems so scarce it must be priceless. It activates something inside me, so my temperature soars and my belly flips. I drop my eyes to the cardboard box and start to peel it open for something normal to do, rather than be loath to admit I fancy him.

"You'll need a bowl for those." He folds his arms across his chiseled chest and narrows his eyes at me. "And a spoon."

I shudder in the carnage of my out-of-control arousal and spin away from his scrutiny to catch a breath. In the awkward silence, I march back to my seat, wondering if he knows how shamelessly turned on I am.

Once I'm perched on the stool again, I rip open the plastic packet inside and pop a flake into my mouth to antagonize him. I can eat my breakfast whatever way I choose.

I don't hear him come up behind me, too lost in the adrenaline of defiance pumping through me. He rests a hand on my shoulder and dips into the side of my face. Instantly, I suck in and almost choke on the mush I haven't swallowed yet.

Hot breath warms my cheek and his gravelly voice destroys any shred of rebellion I think I'm capable of.

"Never disobey me. Perhaps you should review the terms now… before I feel the need to punish you."

I cough into my fist and wish for a glass of water. "Okay," I say on a raspy half bark.

His grip on me tightens before it vanishes without a trace. Tomás silently moves behind me and when I dare to look over my shoulder at him, he's facing the open fridge and unscrewing a bottle of water. In a heartbeat, he's by my side again.

"Drink." The firmness of his tone tells me it's not a suggestion.

When I press the bottle to my lips, he strolls away again, giving me space to breathe and gather myself. I don't speak, but gladly sip plenty. A tinkle of cutlery is followed by a clatter of bone china.

"Do you like coffee?" he asks, completely out of the blue, calm and, dare I think it, ordinarily conversational.

I clear my throat, slowly bringing my gaze to his muscular form. "Yes."

"That makes two of us." He carries two mugs toward my seated position and sets them both down on matching coasters. "This is made from our very own coffee beans. They're grown on a plantation further west. It's my favorite."

Content they're neatly presented, he moves around the island, collects a few items, and returns. Tomás methodically sets a bowl before me and aligns a bronze spoon next to it. He's gone from potential punisher to conscientious host in the flap of a butterfly's wings. I like this domesticated side to his otherwise entitled persona.

Before sitting, he carries over a pouch of milk, one-handedly tips a flurry of sugar-coated flakes into the waiting bowl, and pours in a dash of milk.

"Enjoy." He taps the envelope. "Go on, read it."

Tomás prowls around the edge of the island, takes a stool and sits across from me, watching me with a thoughtful look. A breathtaking pause of suspense for my decision of his terms.

This could be the moment when I lay down my own rules and offer some sort of bargaining into the mix. Except under his avid assessment, I have nothing coherent to say and that angers me to the point of detonation. The king has the upper hand and I'm merely a pawn in his fucked up game.

"I'll review it when I'm ready." I glance over at him with a saccharin sweet smile. "I'm hungry and you did tell me to eat, didn't you?"

Tomás reaches for his coffee and takes a sip. "You're only delaying the inevitable."

I raise the spoon to my lips and slowly open my mouth. Milky drips plop in an irregular tempo in the hush. My belly rumbles in preparation for nourishment.

He carefully positions his mug back in its rightful place on a coaster, leans back, and folds his arms with slow control. "Go on then, let me watch that dick hungry mouth of yours work."

Bastard.

My skin blazes from my toes to my throat. "Can I please eat alone?" I say through gritted teeth.

"Nope." He shakes his head, making his diamond studs sparkle. "You'll have some time to yourself this morning while I'm out. After that, I intend to make good use of our time together." The left side of his mouth curls ever so slightly. "*Very* good use... of you." He repeats.

"Maybe I like being alone."

"Maybe we both do."

I drop the spoon into the bowl and snatch the envelope. "Fine. I'll read it."

Unfolding the thick paper, I scan the handwritten terms neatly set out in black ink.

27

CARINA

My heartbeat thunders in the silence as I read.

Terms of arrangement,

Never speak of the Souza Cartel to anyone or pay the price of disloyalty with your life.

Obey me without question.

Pledge your allegiance to me, unfaltering with every breath you take.

Employment will commence on the date our agreement is discussed and will terminate ninety-six hours thereafter. The sum of one million US dollars will be paid in cash for each day of service.

-T.S

The temperature rises and prickles careen over my scalp. I look up from the falsely oversimplified arrangement to find his unnerving, expressionless face. "There's nothing in here about afterward."

He shrugs and takes a sip of black coffee. "You'll leave and keep that fuckable mouth of yours shut."

Although utterly crude, his comment skewers my Achilles heel—the inner narrative of my tragic past. He thinks the suffering that almost killed me is appealing. I practically recoil at the pitiful emotions barreling through the soul of a young woman aching for this man's attention.

It disgusts me how much I desire his mastery—and his malformed affection. Right or wrong, I want to roll the dice and see where it falls.

"Tell me the real reason you're doing this... no bullshit. The truth," I demand, folding the paper in half, so the words disappear.

He calmly positions his coffee mug and scrubs his chin with manicured nails. Everything about him is meticulously presented—from contoured abs to the clean rows of teeth, straight and dazzlingly white.

"What do you want to hear?" Broad shoulders bounce once. "That when I'm with you, the darkness inside of me fades and all I see is you. Or maybe Carina Ferreira has an unfathomable way of governing the glitch I've endured since I was a boy." His mouth quirks, making it hard to know if he's lying to me.

Unfurling his arms, he pushes out from under the counter, strolls to my side, and places his large palms on my shoulders. "Or maybe the real truth is I get a kick out of knowing my dick is the only one you've ever had." His face dips lower. "That I'll always be your first." Pitch black eyes swallow my glower. "Your best. The only man who's claimed these untouched lips of yours."

Tomás licks his thumb and glides the pad over the silvery scar I'll always own. The thread like imperfection will forever remind me of the dark days I've left behind. And he sees it, just like I had recognized the meaning of every tortured brush stroke on his painting. I inhale a thimble full of air, enough to keep my lungs active.

"I'm also the first to claim your remarkably tight cunt." An unbearable arousal sabotages the anger in my veins.

The cocktail of his words and delicate touch are like a layer of gasoline on a stormy ocean, sending a tide of flames through my core.

"And your life…" He continues, pinching a lock of my hair and carefully tucking it behind my ear. "You want to know what happens after I set you free?" The hoarseness clinging to his decadent accent belies the restraint he's trying to portray. I sense it. He feels it. "When you leave, you'll compare every man in your bed to the king who retains ownership of your virginity."

A shudder runs over me. I raise my chin, fix my shoulders, and boldly meet his subtle smile. "Or perhaps, in the future, I'll find out your sex isn't that fantastic given I've nothing to compare it to right now."

Tomás blinks at me, his mouth tightening to a grimace as my audacious suggestion settles between us. I witness his spine stiffen and his lungs shift with slipping discipline.

While he stands there considering his next move, the muscles in his neck twitch so the chunky chain moves ever so slightly. Quiet observation slithers across my shoulders as if I've struck a match, tossed it into the shadows and awakened a pit full of poisonous serpents.

"We'll see about that." The texture of his perfectly controlled voice, so deep and dangerous, wraps me in a spell I'm not sure I want to be released from.

I clear my throat, dropping my gaze to the bowl of cereal. "Don't worry..." I gather the spoon, shovel up milk-soaked flakes and shove the mush into my mouth. "You'll never know when you slip from top position," I say around the mouthful. "So you can continue to pretend that you're the god you think yourself to be."

He lifts one inky brow at me and simultaneously lowers his mouth to the shell of my ear. "There's no pretense here. I will remain unbeaten, Carina." His imposing bass rumble forces me to swallow. "I'll be the best fuck you've ever had." The warmth of his breath disturbs my hair. His tone cracked as if I'd stirred something primitive inside of him. "Do you promise to honor the terms and pledge your allegiance to me?"

"What does my allegiance entail exactly?" I whisper, almost tipping into the musky scent of his freshly washed skin, so close I could lick it.

"It means you'll remain protected by the Souza cartel for as long as you stay faithful to us... to me." His mouth quirks into a triumphant smirk.

I growl from the back of my throat, frustrated when the attempt to appear rock steady sounds more like a purr. "So, I'll never truly get away from your world?"

He laughs, a low, threatening chuckle that electrifies my blood so it pelts my veins. "Not really. That was determined the moment you tried to save my father."

"And you? Will I ever see you again?" I manage to cover the regret in my voice with annoyance, refusing to let him maintain control over me a second longer. "Not that I enjoy being in your company. I'll be relieved when this charade is over. I deserve to know what I'm facing afterward... what my future holds."

Tomás straightens, his expression tight as if my comments are wilting his fantasies. He calmly lifts the agreement from the countertop. The vermilion gemstone wedged in his signet ring, glints under the light, reminding me of his father's damned soul. How his family is grossly polluted by power, wealth, executions, and deception.

"I have an organization to expand and control. While I'm out of sight, I'm never really gone. If you stay out of trouble, there won't be any reason for us to meet again." Tomás waves the folded page. "What will it be?"

"I suppose you want it sealed with my blood?" I scowl at him.

Haloed irises darken to deadly, so the whites of his eyes glow with a supernatural intensity. The noticeable change to his countenance makes me regret the very word I know to be his weakness. Firm fingers snare my throat, locking me in place before his bared teeth. My pulse slams, the pounding vein visible over the scream I suppress.

"Your word alone is binding, Carina. And your blood..." His breathing hitches. The sunless depths of his pupils gleam with an inferno of copper—my own gaze reflects back at me. "Every drop of your blood is precious. Don't offer it so easily." Searching fingers trace the silvery ridges lining the inside of my forearm. The ticklish sensation showers me with corrupt tingles. "Understand?"

I nod into the vice-like grip on my neck, unsteady and breathless. "I'll ask you one last time. Do you agree?" My head tilts to acknowledge approval. "Words," he hisses. "Your words need to match your actions."

"Answer one last question..." I say in a rushed breath.

An inky brow quirks. "Go ahead."

"You didn't kill me the first time we met. Why did you let me go?"

White teeth bare at me, his eyes flashing with bane. "I'm not my father's puppet. I make my own decisions based on my instincts. I didn't think you were capable of murder. Now what will it be?"

"You think I'm weak?"

"The fact you're sitting here in my compound having breakfast with me means you're far from weak. You're dangerous, but definitely not an assassin."

"Fine. For the sake of my family. Nothing else." My crazed heartbeat chases the danger of acceptance.

"Liar." He chuckles, hellishly close, the richness to his tone velvety like the darkness that covers the many hours of nightfall. "You want this..." Wet lips hover a breath away from mine, threatening a fire of desire so fierce it will destroy me. "Say it... agree to this... to us."

"I agree... ninety-six hours and not a second longer."

Tomás moves a little, his exhale controlled, and his expression indecipherable. The hand around my throat releases.

"Good girl," his voice breaches the space darker than swirling smoke.

To my shock, he kisses my forehead rather than my mouth. It's gentle and quick, and had I blinked, I would have thought it never happened. But it did. He offered me softness instead of brutality. When the hand on my skin retreats, I unwittingly pat the residual warmth left from his rough touch.

Taking the agreement with him, he strolls to the gas cooktop and sparks up the burner. What was once neatly presented evidence of an unheard of arrangement, goes up in flames. He casually drops the burning document into the stainless steel sink and watches the ink perish. Once he's content, every trace is obliterated, he washes away the debris.

It's done.

I must obey him.

The unknown wedges into my chest until it suppresses my appetite. Casually strolling past my seated position, he glances at his designer watch, glittering with gold and a pavé of tiny diamonds. It's ridiculous how maddeningly handsome he is. How every move is dangerously sexual—how it appeals to me on a cellular level.

He catches my eye. "I have an important message to deliver this morning."

Then he stalls by the doorway and thumbs his bottom lip. The intensity of that one stare doesn't weaken my bones with terror. Instead, it melts my uncertainty and spikes it with flames of desire. Our gazes fuse in a temporary moment of recognition or risk. The hunger he projects is breathtakingly sexual and spine-tinglingly erotic.

"Don't get used to wearing my t-shirts." He winks and continues to walk away.

It's too late now.

I've sold my soul to the cartel, or more accurately, to the devil king I'm captivated by. He strolls away with the swagger of a sinner who always gets what he wants, by whatever means necessary. I bite my tongue to resist the seething rage begging to escape. Knowing better, I dig my nails into my palms to stop myself from throwing the cereal bowl at his sexy, self-assured gait.

The tanned skin on his sinewy shoulders is flawless, leading to a narrow waist and solid ass cheeks beneath loose fitting shorts. Even the reverse of this man is a sight to behold. I notice a sterile dressing on his bicep, so fresh and unsullied it must have been changed recently.

He's a hallucination of godliness. Fake perfection spoiled with rotten capabilities.

I hurriedly eat the pulpy flakes drowned in milk. My belly flips in protest, queasy and jittery from the monumental decision I just made. What else could I do? Refuse him and risk my family's lives in a war they wouldn't see coming?

I half expected him to take me over the island the second I agreed, not peck my forehead with the gentlest kiss I've ever experienced.

He has a way about him. A manipulative method of unsettling the ground beneath me, so I'm unable to anticipate his next move. No doubt it's a tactic to always keep me guessing. One thing is certain, no matter what happens in the coming days, there will never be anything between us other than animosity.

He has my permission and that's all. My hopes, dreams, and future—they belong to me. My soul isn't for hire.

I drop down from the high stool and scrub my face. I'm dressed in his expensive clothes, eating his food, wandering freely through his hillside mansion, and for some reason I'm not uncomfortable in these surroundings.

Shane's boots scuff the tiles as he enters the airy living room when I'm on the bottom step of the staircase, ready to go upstairs. His damaged features are shaded with a baseball cap and a black handgun is holstered close to his waist, cinching a khaki colored t-shirt.

"You okay, kid?" He strolls into my space and sets his hand on the frameless glass handrail.

I know this man is loyal to a fault. One threat toward his king and he'd eliminate the danger without a second thought. Yet the way he looks at me doesn't make me uncomfortable, far from it. His usual gruffness is mollified, as if he's communicating with a little girl. That's how he sees me—a kid.

"I'm fine," I reply with a tight smile, not willing to reveal a sliver of ire.

"Good." He nods once and checks the time. "I hear you're hanging around for a few days?"

I shrug. "Seems that way."

His head dips sideways, allowing a sunbeam from behind his head to temporarily blind me. "If it turns out you're a rat, I'll cut out your lying tongue and personally deliver it to your parents' house in a cardboard box." The calm timbre he uses doesn't threaten me as it should given the ultimatum. It's controlled and honest, like a charming fable with an unexpected sinister ending.

"That's a bit dramatic, don't you think?" I goad him.

"Plus, a courier service would save you a heap of time. Manaus is a bit out of your way. I'm sure they have special rates for refrigerated packages."

"A smart ass and a looker. You've got it all, kid." He glares at me. "I'd hate to be the one who has to bury your fine body."

"Don't worry, big guy." I pat his shoulder. "When your time's up, it's up. I've nothing to hide. However, if you're the one digging a hole for me, make sure you say a few nice words."

His mouth twitches to hide a smile. "Behave yourself and I won't have to."

"I've agreed to be his sex slave, or whatever it is he needs from me." I scowl at him, aware of his brawn and lethal prowess, yet completely at ease beside him. "I'd hardly go running my mouth off about something like that. Would I? I'm not in a hurry to tell the world I've jumped into a never-ending nightmare."

He chuckles lightly. "It's better to jump than to be pushed. Don't you think? You've positioned yourself in his direct line of sight with a big fucking halo on your head. If you do what he asks, kid, he'll be the light at the end of that tunnel and not the suffocating darkness." He winks and simultaneously lowers the peak of his cap a fraction in a respectful gesture. "One word of friendly advice…" Shane pivots on his boots.

"Are we friends now?" I fold my arms over my chest, popping my brows high with fake surprise.

He shakes his head and sighs. "Don't make yourself too comfortable by his side. You'll never be his Queen. It's impossible."

28

TOMÁS

I check my phone, three unread messages.

The most recent is from my mother about funeral arrangements. Before hers, my youngest brother Matheus is flying home and wants to know when I'll be at the plantation, and the other message is from Shane.

One of our pharmacies was hit during the night. A few years ago, we'd invested millions into legitimate businesses to provide a smokescreen for the chemicals we need to refine the coca-paste. As usual, Shane acted fast and he's given me the names of the motherfuckers who had the confidence to do it.

I don't usually roll up my sleeves and take part in lower-level warfare. It's not my style, nor is it necessary when I have *sicarios* on standby to deliver the message of death. But stepping up and taking over for a psycho kingpin like my father has left high expectations—and my reputation is on the line.

I'll adopt his ruthlessness when appropriate, while adhering to my grandfather's lessons in savvy scheming and diplomacy. Mickey Hennessy, otherwise known as Mad Mick, is a notorious Irish mafia don, who taught me there's a place for cunning strategy and a time for brutality.

It's those principles my brothers and I were raised by, those and the erratic, troubled rants of a drug lord.

War isn't coming on the horizon.

It's arrived already.

And I'm leading the army.

I stroll to the walk-in wardrobe and pick an outfit fitting for a son in mourning. It's only right I respect Papá's death by wearing a pressed midnight navy shirt, fitted black jeans and brand-new shoes. I leave the top button open and secure my signature cuff links in place.

Checking my reflection in the wall-length mirror beside my watch cabinet, I make sure my hair is sitting as it should and my shirt tails are tucked in. I've no idea why the act of buckling my belt makes me think of Carina—lately she's the first and last thing on my mind.

And this belt could teach her a lesson or two. Not that I want to whip the spirit out of her. I enjoy her gutsiness. Her desire for sexual corruption and the horny buzz I get when I think about her plump tits brushing against every t-shirt of mine she wears.

Christ, I'm hard again. For the umpteenth time this morning. And she's solely to blame. I should punish her for making me want to fuck her so damn much.

Just as I reposition my swollen dick, the hairs on the back of my neck lift. She's right behind me, arms folded. The hem of the claimed t-shirt skims her lean thighs. Disheveled sable tendrils spill over narrow shoulders, sexy and wild like the fuckable siren she is. Her fiery eyes drill into my reflection.

"We had a deal." She pads closer. "I'd like my phone now, please." Her hand juts out in the space separating us. Expectant and unafraid of me. Adrenaline turbocharges my veins, so I'm alive with the urge to ravage the dainty beauty.

I turn into her and stare down at those big amber eyes that remind me of an exquisite sunrise. Carina pushes her shoulders back in rebellion of my silent inspection and elevates her chin. Her chest expands in the movement, drawing my sole attention to her plump tits.

She traps her bottom lip between brilliant white teeth and dents the soft flesh. I imagine her glistening pink lips encircled around my impossible hard-on.

Reaching out, I pluck the shirt's hem grazing her thigh and slowly hitch the material higher. Her skin visibly prickles and her waiting hand flops to her side. With the cotton still hiding her tits, I lift it a little higher to reveal two half-moons of pillowy flesh.

Fuck! I swear my dick just wept a bead of pre-cum. Her eyes widen when a thick grunt escapes my throat. I force myself to let go and check my cufflinks again in an act of self-preservation. It's not wise to let her see how she affects me.

"I'm going out." I don't want to leave her unsupervised, but business is the highest priority. She won't be alone. Marta and the service staff will keep her out of mischief. "Once I get back, we'll talk about your phone."

"How long will you be away?" She crosses her arms over her belly and scowls up at me.

"Why—will you miss me?" I muse, offering her a wolfish smirk.

"Every second you make me wait is another second my brother will worry."

"He's a grown man, Carina. He can wait a few hours." Content I'm respectably dressed, I grab my gun, then tuck it in the back of my waistband before strolling out of the closet with the stunning dick tease hot on my heels.

"Why can't I have it now?" She whirls up from behind like a tornado contained in a glass jar and confronts me head on. "You promised."

"Earn my trust." She unintentionally licks her lips and my mind goes blank. After a beat, I finally exhale and shake off the mania she incites within me. "Prove to me you can do as you're told. And I'll reward you for being a good girl when I return."

Carina blinks. Her nose scrunches as she takes a courageous step into my personal space. For one uninterrupted moment, we stand face to face, locked in a temporary spell of mutual fascination, and then her angelic voice tempers the steel bars my heart is caged in.

"I'm not a little girl, Tomás. I'm a woman." Featherlight fingertips fiddle with the opening of my shirt and trail lower, stopping shy of the belt buckle. Her eyes sparkle. "You don't really want a good little girl, do you?"

She's fucking with me. This is payback for all my sins. For every unworthy woman before her who didn't meet my expectations or satisfy my unnatural craving. How could they serve me when Carina is the uniquely carved key unlocking my darkness?

The only woman to unearth bloodthirsty fantasies and

crack open the padlock I should never have found. With a turn of the key to the left, she could knock me from my throne, with a turn to the right she could be my salvation.

My hand lashes out like lightning to seize her nape. I slam her breasts into my chest so there's only her tiny gasp of shock and my throbbing dick between us. Dropping my lips to the shell of her ear, I feel the skin on my balls tighten and my pulse skyrocket.

"When I'm not with you, you'll behave. That's what I expect from you." Her palms settle on my shirt sleeves. "And when we're together…" I inhale the scent of her hair with a subtle fragrance of me. "You can be a bad girl all night long."

Her shiver is an aphrodisiac. Even without blood polluting my skin, I still want to fuck her. I notice the squall of goosebumps cover her neck and take my time to lick the length of her delicate throat. The warmth expelled from the sigh she can't contain tingles all over me.

Despite the ungovernable hardness behind my zipper, I'm too aware of how she's become a distraction. It's not easy to curb my appetite for the teenager in my bedroom —and that troubles me. I've had her more than once, and still, I'm hungry for more.

I quickly release her as if she's an unpinned grenade. Her hiss of frustration doesn't go unobserved. It pains my dick, so I swivel and continue to walk away.

"Get dressed," I say over my shoulder in an abrupt command. "Two of my men are guarding the front gates. You won't get past them and they aren't allowed inside the house. My housekeeper will get you whatever you need."

She nods with acceptance and then hugs her stomach. "I don't have anything to wear."

"By the time you've showered, new clothes will be waiting for you."

My arousal fades when I sink into the worn leather seats of a beat up dusty white Dodge Challenger with a thick black stripe up the hood. In this car, our enemies won't know it's me pulling up outside their front door. I own plenty of vintage classics, not rusty relics like this shit bucket. This hasn't seen a workshop since the seventies.

I retrain my thoughts to the task ahead and push Carina's long legs to the farthest crevasse in my mind. I've spent way too much time obsessing over the minor details I like about her. From lush pink lips with a pronounced Cupid's bow to how her pupils dilate when I touch her. Just one light stroke of her silky soft skin and she's overflowing with lust. It gets me off on repeat.

"Ready?" Shane asks, glancing over at me from the driver's seat. He twiddles with the knob on the old-style radio to find a music station and scowls when all we hear is white noise.

"I was born ready." I chuckle, even though my skin crawls under my shirt. Stale tobacco and exhaust fumes choke the sunbaked air inside the cramped space. It's unhygienic. "Where did you get this fucking thing from?"

The security gates open and the engine rattles to life. "Don't ask." He laughs darkly. "We'll give her one last adventure before she dies." And by that he means burned to its chassis.

I crank the grimy window open and relish the fresh breeze on my face as we pick up speed. Hours after Papá was murdered, we knew our rivals would attempt to undermine business. They all want a piece of our global trade worth billions.

It won't happen under my rule. No fucking way. I won't let the northern cartel leader, Carlos Blanco, who was my uncle's second in command, anywhere near my territory or tolerate threats from any of the others. I still need to prove the fucker is behind Papá's assassination, and when I do, his entire operation would be destroyed.

My mood nosedives further when Shane drops Carina into the conversation.

"What are your plans for the girl?" He lowers the volume on the radio.

I shrug. "A few nights of entertainment and then she's free."

"And you're certain she won't run to law enforcement?"

Instincts tells me she'll stay loyal after we part ways. I want to trust her—liars take on many guises and beautiful young women are no exception. But this time, every nucleus controlling every cell in my body wants to give her a chance and believe she'll stay faithful to our agreement. Angelo had always told me to listen to my gut. Trusting Carina is the biggest test of my instincts to date.

"Her family is collateral damage if she opens her mouth. She knows that."

"Right…" he says slowly. "And you don't think it's unusual how you've attached yourself to her?"

"Attached?" I laugh. "What do you think this is, a fucking romance, *cabrón*? It's sex, Shane. A good old-fashioned fuck."

"I'm just saying. You're marrying the Mexican girl in a few weeks and your focus is on Carina, not plans for your new fiancé. Have you even met Bianca Morales? I've heard she's got a rockin' body." He takes his hand off the gear shift and mimics a set of huge tits.

I turn to him when he chuckles, low and dirty. The horny son of a bitch.

"It's a marriage of convenience. Nothing more. I'll find out if she has a sister to suck the desperation from your balls." My lips quirk into a half smile even though my gut churns.

"Cabrón." He poorly mocks my accent with his Irish lilt, playfully calling me a dumbass in return.

I can take it from him, because we're like brothers. Anyone else and I'd punch their teeth out.

Maybe it was a knee jerk decision to accept the deal with Morales. I could call the whole thing off, start a war and damage our business, or marry the woman and get on with it. I'll never fall in love. The wall I stand behind is too high to let anyone climb, so this arrangement will suit me perfectly.

"You still going ahead with it?" Shane's eyes say everything. He's weighing up my options and wondering if I'll send a sicario after Morales instead.

I twist the family ring on my finger. "Why not? It would reinforce our position in Mexico and keep Blanco out in the cold. Plus, we'd be able to distribute more product. The alliance would be good for business." My shoulders bounce.

Some days I wish I'd grown up with a normal family, where guns weren't stashed in every home and the threat of death didn't shroud the future. Then again, I wouldn't be filthy fucking rich and hold so much power that people actually worship me. This is who I am and it's all I've ever known.

After an hour or so of uncomfortable captivity, the Challenger rolls along a tree lined dirt track toward an isolated wooden dwelling handed down from generations of ranchers and taken over by a mediocre cartel who clearly doesn't know how to repair or maintain a property.

The shithole is falling apart. Its flapping shutters are semi-closed, and the front deck needs to be ripped off and replaced. I'll give the assholes who hide out here credit to anyone who would stumble onto this land. They'd never suspect it is a stash house containing an arsenal of weapons.

We pull up adjacent to the front door. "We'll find out if these fuckers know who wanted Papá dead."

Shane reaches for his gun and checks the magazine. "There's a long list, Tommy. You know that. Elias pissed off a lot of people."

"I don't care. The Souza's deserve justice," I mutter, relieved to exit the vehicle. "My mother is a widow now."

"Teresa has bigger balls than any man." He's right. My mother knows the business inside out. She's not afraid of ruthless decisions or the threat of a rival. Teresa

Souza is a natural leader and the only woman I trust implicitly.

"We'll get the fuckers who killed him. Even if it takes months to close in on them." Shane confirms when I round the hood and head straight for the front door. "You want these guys taken out immediately?" he says under his breath.

I sigh, feeling an odd pang of humanity in my otherwise empty heart. Papá would give the order to hack off their heads, parcel them up, and send them to their cartel leader as a warning. Me, I'm after information first. Something of value to bring home to my family. Knowledge is power and I'll get it by any means necessary.

29

CARINA

He wasn't kidding.

I'm swaddled in the softest waffle robe after a long shower, staring at a plethora of gift boxes and bags set out neatly on the floor of his master suite. My heart thumps harder with a bewildered tempo. This is beyond extravagant.

Each one varies in size and designer branding, all immaculately presented. I recognize the packaging stacked against the wall in pillars—my favorite Dr. Martens. From what I can see at first glance, he's bought every conceivable color and style of boots and shoes in my size.

This is what obscene wealth and bribery looks like. A carpet of high priced presents for a woman he barely knows. There are enough items in this room to dress a small village of girls. Too many outfits for one woman—for four days.

Snaking through aisles of boxes, I peek inside a pearly bag tied with ribbon. Nestled amidst reams of metallic tissue is a black lace garment, so delicate and feminine. My hand trembles when I reach inside to lightly pinch flimsy straps and hold up a balconette bra in the sunshine spilling in from outside.

It's exquisite, sexy––and grown up. Quite the U-turn from my basic cotton panties. It's not that I didn't dare to buy beautiful lingerie for myself. I just never felt the virginal teenager had a reason to wear it. Besides, I'm not exactly sexual, or elegant, for that matter. Nor have I enjoyed the company of a man until Tomás.

Nausea bites my courage as reality vaporizes my zealous curiosity. I'm a naïve

young woman, a captive in the possession of a man with ungodly urges. What was I thinking? This isn't the movie where a gallant king rescues a damsel in distress—he *is* the distress. Tomás is mayhem itself.

I didn't ask the universe for a ticket into the underworld of Colombia or for an older man to steal me from a life unlived. No, I was perfectly content learning who the real Carina should be, who the girl deserving of a fresh start would turn into.

When I was younger, I indulged in heartwarming movies alone, read hundreds of romance novels to escape rejection, and prayed for a happy ending of my own––until I realized the common denominator was a thing called fiction—they were glorified fantasies.

And I wasn't a pretty princess living in a make-believe story. I was just a kid blighted by a facial catastrophe and ostracized from social interaction. Untrusting of every single person besides my family.

Happy endings with passionate kisses and promises of

eternal love were the pathetic dreams of a child who desperately wished for a life that wasn't her own.

My grim reality was endless days of self-loathing and torment, filled with cruel tongues and unjust inner loneliness. As fate would have it, I've grown into a distorted woman who fancies a narco king and his cruel whims. I shouldn't like his poison, but I do. I'm ashamed for surrendering to him and humiliated by the lustful ache I can't get rid of.

These feelings can't be ordinary.

I drag a hand down my face, blowing out a muddled sigh. I've no one to ask if my urges are toxic. All I can do is believe the connection we have is a temporary madness.

I slowly move to an adjacent package and shake off the lid, meeting snowy crepe paper and a pale blue ditsy dress skillfully folded. Tomás has replicated the style of clothes I wore the night he cut them from me in the shower. I'm guessing he had purchased disposable dresses that would end up in tatters after he rips them from me again.

When I think about him doing just that, I get all flustered and antsy with the thrill of it. My morals really are off-kilter. In the depths of my soul, I'm enthralled by his blood-tingling danger and bulletproof composure. I crave the beast's charred aura and his masculine dominance. So what does that make me—certifiably moonstruck?

My hands fly to my temples as the room spins. A shadow creeps over the gifts bought with felonious currency when sparse clouds cover the sun beyond the windows.

I've made a reckless error and now I'm at his mercy. None of these items were given freely. Everything before me is a payoff. A show of his ubiquitous influence and a way to ensure loyalty. Tomás thinks he can buy my silence and threaten violence against my family as an extra measure.

My limbs tremble as I sink to the rug and clutch my stomach, unsure of what to do next. Should I try on every expensive outfit or weep for my stupidity? Perhaps I should have fought harder to escape, or defended my honor with fists and clawing nails. I didn't, and now I'm tangled in his invisible ropes as a voluntary prisoner.

I'm such a fool.

"*Niña?*" Marta's motherly voice splices through the finely woven net of gullibility sprawling from every corner of the room. "Did you get everything you need?"

I draw in my lips to stop a sob and finger the lavish lace I always dreamed I'd wear one day. "Uh-huh," I hum out, keeping my lashes lowered and my turmoil low key.

Marta lets out a long sigh and crosses over the threshold. "Niña. It's time to get dressed," she scolds. "Get up."

"I shouldn't be here." I blink up at her impassive expression and wipe away a solitary tear of liquid regret.

She hunkers, her breath heavy as she gingerly lowers. "Don't question it. You've survived against the odds." Her words are hushed in a bid to keep them between us.

"Are you trapped here too?" I ask, turning into her.

"No, niña." Her head gently shakes from side to side. "I serve Tomás, because he's family to me."

"But these people are monsters." I pull my knees into my chest for comfort. "He's a monster... and I..."

Even though she chuckles, her expression remains ambiguous. "Everybody has a degree of evil inside of them. Some use it to survive, some to seek revenge, some to protect loved ones, and some to rule hostile kingdoms. Nobody is truly pure of heart." Her voice softens. "Even monsters are capable of kindness."

The weight of her statement crushes my lungs. I've only ever known unconditional love and agonizing hate. I'm attuned to the monsters lurking in my soul and blessed to know my family's shelter of love. It appears I've fallen within the vast spectrum of emotions and now I'm balancing on a thin line.

As much as I want to ask her if I'm mentally damaged for wanting Tomás like I do, I can't trust the woman. The last thing I need from her is ridicule or even pity for the path of destruction I'm crawling along under a starless sky.

"Come on." She pats my cheek gently, keeping the deformed hand curled on her lap. "There's cake downstairs. I heard you like sugar." Her knees crack with the effort of standing. "I'm sure there's something in these boxes that will make you smile."

"Aren't you afraid of him?" I unhook my limbs and force myself to elevate, feeling lightheaded when I straighten.

She closes her eyes briefly and when her eyelids drift open again, there's a glaze of something unreadable. It haunts me. "Get dressed, niña."

It would be easier squeezing blood out of a piece of his furniture. Her lips are sealed and her loyalty remains intact. She angles away from me and walks to the door. "Come down when you're dressed," she says over her shoulder, then disappears.

I'm left alone in Tomás' suite with the scent of his masculinity ingrained in the walls and my memory. Who wouldn't be impressed by this display of fortune? Me, that's who. I'm worried I'll get a taste for the forbidden. That the nineteen-year-old girl surrounded by affluence will never be the same after a collision course with a fireball.

Rather than open every box and look inside another bag, I try on the flirty bra. It's gorgeous. I'm in awe of how something so minimal and risqué in appearance can boost my confidence—and my libido.

I find the matching panties with string-like ties at the hips and step into them. Curious to know how they look on me, I prance into the expansive closet and sashay in front of the mirror.

The pale skinned girl staring back at me has flushed cheeks and faint bruises. She wears feminine lingerie and silvery scars that will forever remind her of the dark days. Yet here I am—still standing and fighting. Except for one thing—I've felt the power of sex like a thunderstroke. A bolt of lust so immense it casts light on the shadows clinging to my soul and gives me wings to fly.

I've kissed a man with the very lips I've been self-conscious of all my life.

I've orgasmed at the mercy of a stunning villain and claimed his wild releases as mine.

I've made bad choices. And now I'll suck up my decision to stay for a few days and embrace the madness inside of me.

Turning away from my unique metamorphosis, I silently give Tomás permission to stain every shred of innocence I have left. Instead of being afraid, I'll become the awakened version of myself—feminine and dauntless. I'm not a young girl on the cusp of womanhood—I *am* that woman now.

Stepping into the knee length dress I had first come across; I pull up the fine zipper and smooth my palms over the blossomy pattern. Without checking how it looks on me, I towel dry my hair, rake the damp lengths through with my fingers and leave the bedroom behind.

I have so many questions to ask Marta. Whether she will indulge my interrogation is another thing. It won't be an easy task, but I'll do my best to tease something out of her.

The pale marble is cool underfoot as I drop off the bottom step and pad to the kitchen. It's eerily quiet. I wonder if it's just the two of us, if Tomás had sent all of his soldiers away. Given he shot one of them dead, I imagine they've left his compound for their own safety.

A tip tap of doggy nails patter from behind. Brutus trots a lap around my legs, the fluffy stump where his tail should be wags and his black nose sniffs. He's such a big furball. By the way he nuzzles into my hand, no one would ever suspect his lethal jaws were clamped around my enemy's ankle in the middle of the night.

I lower to my knees, aware of every throbbing ache. When we're nose to nose, he sits and bows his head. I rub his ears and kiss the top of his silky head as a thank you for being my canine hero. Tomás had shot the asshole, but Brutus defended me—against all of them.

"You're the best guard dog ever," I whisper, close to his pricked ear. He smells freshly groomed and clean. Even

Tomás' pets are treated with first class care and attention. "I wish I could take you with me when I leave. We'd be a good team."

I hear Marta hum to herself from the kitchen, perfectly content in the devil's den. Brutus follows me, his noisy entry alerting the housekeeper to our arrival.

As expected, a yellow cake dusted in powdered sugar sits on the island, trapped beneath a glass dome.

"I see you've made a friend." Marta opens a cupboard and selects a side plate. "He's not usually comfortable with strangers. Then again, neither was Elias." I check out her black uniform as she raises the see-through bubble to reveal a scent of sweetness. The loose material is basic, with a frilly white collar and thin belt around her waistline. "Would you like to eat this on the patio? I'll bring it out to you."

I skirt the island, slide out a stool and sit, not wanting to be alone. "Won't you join me?" I nod to the neighboring stool, suddenly aware of a pang of homesickness chasing my energized mood.

Her forehead wrinkles as she thinks. "I have plenty of work to do, niña. There's a lot to be done while he's out."

"Let me help you." I raise my brows. "I've nothing else to do. Before I..." I stop a second and consider how to word my next sentence. "Before I bumped into Tomás, I worked in a bar, and I've helped out at a medical facility, too. I'm great at cleaning if you'd like an extra set of hands."

Marta picks up a long knife, her aged fingers curling around the handle. With her expression bland, she punctures the dusty top layer, cutting a wedge of cake and teasing it onto a plate.

"You're a guest," she replies like a grandmother chastising her grandchild. "It's not expected of you to work alongside the staff here." She slides the plate toward me and sets a tiny fork beside it. "Enjoy the sunshine before he returns."

The way she says the last sentence makes me wonder if she's seen his darkness, too.

"How long have you worked for him?" I ask when she turns away and carries on about her business.

She glances over her shoulder and sighs softly. "Many years."

"How did you meet him?" I persist.

Marta angles her hips back to me. "My husband. He was a loyal soldier to Elias." The lines on her face harden like grooves of worn out resentment. "He dedicated the best part of his life to serving that man..." Her voice fades and fine lashes lower to the uneaten cake on my plate.

She's debating telling me the story, which undoubtedly ends with her husband's death. I can sense the sadness ooze from her pores and bleed from her heart.

"What was your husband's name?" I ask softly, trying to keep the conversation alive.

"Pepe." Her throat bobs heavily, so she coughs. "The day he was diagnosed with cancer, Elias replaced him," she hisses under her breath, the waspish sound stinging with venom. "He cut him off without a second thought. The so-called financial payoff Elias gave him wasn't enough to pay the growing medical bills." The tone she uses turns caustic, her expression stern with bitterness.

"Elias wasn't human. Pepe watched him change over the years. Power does that to a man. It contorts the ego."

I take the blade and slice a triangle, cutting a large portion for Marta. "Here... sit with me. Please, tell me what happened."

She pivots on the thick sole of her flat shoes, slowly retracing her steps to the cupboard and collects a second plate. "That night, Tomás came to our home and took Pepe away." The hairs on my neck lift. "He personally drove him to a private medical facility for treatment. Tomás took care of the bills. He paid for everything. Everything..." she repeats in a whisper.

Hitching her dress at the hips, Marta grumbles a little as she tries to sit comfortably on the stool. "Even Pepe's funeral. The day after I buried my husband, Tomás told me he had an opening for a housekeeper, and asked if I'd like the position. He knew I'd never get a job because of this..." She nods to her frail hand. "Tomás welcomed me into his home and gave me independence."

Every word retold unlocks more secrets to the mystery of a man I've come to know. It makes me think she's right—we all have monsters inside of us, some more obvious than others. But that doesn't mean every one of us is bad to the bone. Perhaps there's some redeemable qualities in Tomás to work with.

Turning my attention to my plate, I stab the cake's jammy middle and hum out my approval as I chew. "Did you make this?" I cover my mouth so she doesn't see me eat. "It's so good."

"Tomás had me order it from the city. I picked it up earlier." Marta pinches a piece of cake between her fingers and thumb, then pops it into her mouth. "It's his mother's favorite. He thought you'd enjoy it too." Once she swallows, our gazes connect. "Be careful, sweet niña. Even an assassin will smile. People won't like you having his attention."

My spine stiffens. By the deadpan expression she wears, I can't quite tell if she means herself or someone else. But when she reaches forward and gently rests her palm over the top of my hand, warming affection seeps from her skin to mine.

"Never underestimate the cartel. They'll kill you, wrap your body in a sheet, and douse it in gasoline before you know what you've done wrong."

The mass of crumbly cake making its way down my esophagus feels like an indigestible mistake. "He didn't give me a choice. I had to stay with him." On a frustrated swallow, I drop the fork, feeling as though I need to defend my reasons for being here.

"I know." She holds me in place with a sincere stare. "And whether you want to believe it or not, Tomás Souza has good in him. This is the only life he knows. Elias bullied those boys..." A breath escapes her in a gust and she automatically swivels to check we're alone, afraid she's said too much. "Look... you have the advantage. Tomás sees something in you like he did with that stray dog over there." Her chocolatey eyes cut to Brutus, who sits by the French doors looking out, always on guard. "All I'm saying is, keep your wits about you and don't do anything silly. Now..." She drops off the stool and carries her plate away. "I'm meeting with the cleaning staff. Make yourself at home. I'll be around if you need anything."

How about more information? "Okay," I reply, feeling unsettled by our cryptic conversation. "Thanks for this." I nod to the plate and smile sweetly.

What should have been a fact-finding mission led to something more revealing. What exactly is it that he sees in me? Other than a woman he can control for a short period of time. I'm not a doting puppy or a pet he can train.

When she's left the kitchen, I eat a few forkfuls of cake and sit in silence, contemplating this lavish lifestyle. How Tomás has everything he could wish for, yet I get the distinct impression there's something missing. Shadows chase his every step with a smoky aura.

Brutus flinches when he hears the stool creak and leaves his post when my feet hit the floor. Together, we walk into the sunny living room. There's so much empty space without the enormous sofa he bled over last night. It feels oversized for just one man.

I head toward a bar area near the floor to ceiling glass doors, casually counting the collection of liquor bottles sitting on top of a mirrored cabinet. After thirty, with more labels to add to my tally, I get bored and select an unopened bottle. Alcohol doesn't interest me. I've never tried the stuff before or had the desire to find out what it tastes like. Until now.

Unscrewing the cap from a fancy bottle of caramel colored tequila, I fill a small glass to the brim. After the count of three, I hold my breath, open my mouth, tip the glass, and down it in one gulp.

Holy shit, it burns. The fiery heat in my throat is not what I expected, nor is the buzz it gives me. A shudder rattles my skeleton while my belly does a reckless somersault. I clear my throat and cough a few times.

With a few hours at least to kill, I snatch the bottle by the neck and wander over to the sliding glass doors with Brutus by my side. Intense sun rays settle on my face when we exit the indoors and pad onto the paved patio. I curl my palm to shade my eyes, squinting until I find the cream parasol offering shelter.

In the distance a streak of passing gray clouds threatens to kidnap the sun for the afternoon, slashing the moderate temperature with its creeping arrival.

A hillside breeze carries a blossomy bouquet and towering palms sway like giants watching over their territory. Banana, lemon, and avocado trees fringe the immaculate lawn beyond the infinity pool. It's serene and calm. A deceptive paradise nestled in the mountains where no one would suspect I'm held here under duress.

I recline on a padded lounger and check Brutus is comfortable in a shady spot. Taking a sip of tequila, I close my eyes and enjoy the smooth burn descending into my belly. Light footsteps from indoors don't bother my new friend. He's used to the flurry of organized cleaners moving from room to room.

With nothing else to do, I survey the staff who carry out their duties beyond the reflective glass until I no longer care. I'm restless and pumped with so many emotions. I can't help feeling alone, even though Brutus pricks his ears every time I move.

This idleness is alien to me. I've no books to read, Netflix shows to binge, or music to sing along to. It's just me, the dog, and a bottle of booze.

The shadows shift position on the terrace, telling me it's after midday. I should be hungry, but my stomach aches from the uncertainty of what will happen when I meet his family. I'm not his girlfriend, so undoubtedly, they'll treat me with little respect. What if his brothers are carbon copies of their father and I'm thrown to the wildlife after all?

I'm fed up waiting around like a naughty schoolgirl whose daddy confiscated her phone and irritated by the whole situation I'm in. I left Manaus for independence, to work, and to learn while I consider my future. Not stay locked up like a bird in a gilded cage.

Frustration escapes me in a grumpy growl. I climb off the lounger, unzip the new dress, and toss it behind me for when I'm done. Standing in only lingerie, I bring the tequila to my lips and take another glug. I could get used to the buzz it charges my veins with. It's nowhere near the addiction I have to Tomás' sexual control, but it's exhilarating nonetheless.

Walking the length of the pool, I stop at the far end and stare at the breathtaking view. Tomás is out there somewhere, plotting a war, and planning countless deaths. In my mind, I replay memories of the men who kidnapped, terrorized, and shoved me under the cartels' radar. For those men, I could easily cause havoc with a machine gun. Does that make me like them—hollow hearted and evil?

I chuckle at my alcohol induced bravado and then sigh. My mentor, el Fantasma, would be proud of my murderous fantasy even if he did warn me to stay away from guns.

Lowering to the water's edge, I sink my ankles into the heated pool and perch there like a bored ornament. There's probably a string bikini or a skimpy bathing suit in one of the gift bags upstairs.

Except I'm not in the mood to wander indoors and indulge myself in clothes I'd never have the opportunity to wear. I'd rather hang out here in the fresh air where the limitless sky doesn't close in on me like the bars of a gilded cage.

My gaze drifts to the fluffy patches of clouds decorating a bright blue sky like mist. Various puffy shapes take on different forms. From deformed dragons to abstract castles where unicorns probably live.

Latent thoughts of Salvador have manifested into the vision I now see. My brother's face looms above the compound, reminding me of his presence in my life—his importance.

The temperature drops when the illusion crosses the sun's path. Steam rises from the tropical blue water that seems to blend into the skyline at the far end. Thin rings ripple outwards with every gentle kick I make.

A shiver runs over me with the sickness consuming me. It's not the alcohol in my veins or the toxic desire I harbor for a criminal—it's palpitating anxiety.

Tomás could decide at any time it's my time to die. He has the power to make the light fade from my eyes and I'd never see my big brother again. My pulse races with blind panic, forcing me to double over with dizziness.

I bury my face in my palms to steady every erratic breath I'm gasping for and count from ten to zero. As if sensing the electrified disquiet within me, Brutus appears by my hip and nudges my elbow with his nose. I turn into him and carefully glide my shaky fingers through his textured coat, concentrating on the softness and his tenderness.

When my heart rate begins to settle and tears stop blurring my eyes, I kiss the top of his head, angle away, and push off the ledge into the pool. Languid heat surrounds my tense muscles like a comforting hug I desperately need, but would never ask for. I swim over to the glass boundary where the water meets the sky in a flawless mirage.

"I wish you could join me," I call out to Brutus, without taking my eyes off the horizon.

It's a silly wish from a lonely girl caught up in the wrong crowd with only a four-legged friend to keep her from going insane.

"Be careful what you wish for."

I suck in sharply, startled by the sonorous texture of a voice I'll never become immune to. Tomás' husky timbre chases me like a cyclone threatening to snatch me in its rotations. Uncontrollable chills swamp me as if a blizzard is nearby.

After a beat of grappling with self-composure, I paddle in a circle to find him standing at the poolside, shirtless, with his trusted guard dogs sitting upright, one at either side of his casual stance. A single beam of sunlight catches in the tequila bottle he's drinking from, lighting it up like fire. After that one comment, he takes another swig as if he needs it.

There's a moment of peace between us. No demands. No orders. Just his fascinating dark eyes pinning me to a picturesque panorama. He waits there, surrounded by the circumference of his enormous bachelor pad, so effortlessly superior.

A burst of energized vibrations surge over my scalp like I've witnessed an apocalypse and only survived because of his decree.

There's no denying it. He brings out the worst in me. The side of me that wonders what else he can do other than fuck my throat until my stomach convulses and stretch my insides with his thick, magnificent dick.

It's not easy for me to understand why a girl who's struggled with bullies now craves the man who overpowers her. A beast who takes and gives in equal measure. A captor who dominates and controls—a knight who protects me from bullets and his own men.

Truth be told, I'm infatuated by the older man before me, with or without his terms of employment and sexual requests. He wants my tortured body, and the lost girl inside of me wants him to claim it. She's not scared of the monster lurking before her. She wants him to devour her.

My nipples harden under his brooding observation. Beneath the water, my skin flames like I'm trapped in a liquid that's reached its boiling point. Some part of me enjoys the idea of a dominant man feasting on a girl like me, in an attempt of this being the best I'd ever have.

Little does he know, the position he holds is solid. There's not a chance in hell another man can brand his fingerprints on my soul like Tomás already has.

I breathe in a lungful of oxygen, sink until I no longer hear the chatty birds, and push off the infinity panel with my toes. My streamlined figure sails through the water to reach him. When my head emerges, I sweep drenched lengths of hair back from my face, swipe my eyes free of droplets and exhale slowly. He bends to set the bottle down and hunkers so our gazes are that much closer.

"I need something from you," he declares.

"I need something from you too," I counter.

"Get out of the pool and we'll negotiate." He offers me his hand.

Rather than accept help, I kick my ankles and swim backward until I reach the hodgepodge gray mosaic tiles covering the shallow steps rising out of the steamy depths. Taking my time, I find my footing and slowly tread each one in turn, aware my body is now prickled from a cool eastern breeze.

The flutters in my chest turn chaotic. I'm pretending his presence doesn't affect me, putting up a facade of alcohol fueled confidence, even if I'm crumbling with nerves on the inside. When I finally dare myself to catch his eye, my breath hitches.

I blink away the remaining beads of water caught in my lashes and stroll over to him. The obscure look he returns makes my knees wobble.

Before I lose courage, I snap back my shoulders for strength, unintentionally projecting my chest where lacey cages cover my breasts. It's not meant as a flirty pose, given sexual expression is not my forte.

However, the closer I get to him, the easier it is to see the bulge behind his zipper. Even though it's cooler now, the temperature soars. His muscular chest rises as if he's trying to conquer his reaction to me. I shouldn't love the reaction I illicit from him—but I do.

"Tell me what you want," I demand, stopping short of touching distance.

Inky pupils flare amidst eyes so dark they're almost warning me to run. When he clicks his fingers, the dogs' ears prick and they stand on all fours awaiting an instruction. "Inside."

Obediently, the duo trots off. Not before Brutus sniffs my dripping fingertips and then backtracks, happily leaving me with his master. The faithful dog senses something far more lethal than danger, something he has no desire to protect me from. I can barely breathe from my cruel libido blistering over me like a rotten infection.

Alone, Tomás reaches for the tequila. "Tell me what you want first, Carina Ferreira," he says, with a tone so hoarse it stirs up a heat wave.

He stands there with ragged patience and savors a mouthful of liquor. The liquid seems to heighten whatever changeable mood he's in.

I open my mouth to speak until his hot gaze creates a team of uncontrollable flutters behind my ribs. They burst into my throat, so only a whimper escapes me. I'm aroused by the sight of his sculpted abdomen, his stare fixed to my face, and how he should appear threatening to me. Yet his self-assured countenance appears wolfish —carnal.

"What do you want from me, Carina," he repeats gently, his tone marginally relaxed, as if he knows I'm struggling to find myself.

"My phone," I whisper as my fingertips mindlessly pad my scarred lip. "What do you want?"

Tomás steps into me, the glass bottle a buffer for his

advance. "I want to know if you've been a good girl." His eyes flash with the request. I curse the treacherous whimper that rushes past my fingers. "Well... have you?" He cocks an immaculate inky eyebrow at me.

"I'm here, aren't I?" I say with a childish eye roll to help regain a fraction of resilience in this confusing situation. "I was bored stiff and spoke to an animal for most of the morning."

His mouth curls at the corners to welcome a rare smile. My heart leaps when his cheek dimples behind the smattering of scruff he wears so well. I'm almost certain the energetic twinge in my chest is a broken rib from the fast pumping organ's unruly attempt to reach him.

"While wearing this..." He pinches the strap close to my collar bone and runs his fingers down the elastic until it stops over the lace covering my proud nipple. We both recognize the shiver it gives me. "Forever the rebel."

"I didn't plan to go for a swim," I say breathlessly. "It was a last minute decision."

I notice how his nostrils flare and his featherlight touch turns more aggressive around my breast. "Tell me..." He squeezes and I turn molten against his touch. "What do you really want, Carina?"

"I told you..." I protest weakly, scared he'll find out the truth I'm rapidly failing to hide. "I have to speak with my brother."

His head shakes from side to side. "We both know that already. What you haven't told me is what you really want from me... right now."

A long sigh shelters the soft moan I don't want him to seek satisfaction from. A blind man could tell his groping hand made my pulse react. The vein throbbing in my neck gives away my excitement. It's simply physical, nothing more than the curiosity of a girl finally having the attention of a man.

"Kiss me." His unexpected order snaps out like a horse bolting from its stable.

I sway, unsteady and shocked that he'd demand it from me when he's the one always in control. He snares my arm, his tight grip locking me in place before him.

"Show me how you can be a good girl and kiss me with those tequila laced lips of yours."

Despite the chill prickling every inch of bare flesh, my muscles' resistance weakens. "Whether you'll admit it to yourself or not, I suspect that's what you really want. You've been waiting for my dick all morning. My good little girl wants her king's dick inside her tight cunt. Am I right?"

We both know he's right.

"You're not my king," I smirk. "And I'm not your obedient subject."

A shadow passes over his features. For a split second, I fear he's about to lash out with his own brutal attack of lips and hands.

"Instinct tells me differently," he says, his tone rusty with limited control. I should know by now how he senses the lies spilling from my mouth like he's a human lie detector. "Do it. Kiss me. Show me how much you've missed your king."

I freeze when he releases my arm, leans sideways, and sets the liquor at the poolside. As he straightens, his presence looming over me again, my sight goes woozy with nerves. I habitually finger my scar to ground me and take a steadying breath.

In a daze of lust and fear, I inch into him and set my palms on smooth, taut muscle, instantly loving the glorious heat blazing from his skin to mine. This simple connection alone is erotic.

He's waiting for me to make a move, restrained and disciplined. Perhaps it's a test for us both. Either way, he demands obedience with this fake sense of control he's giving me, or maybe he needs the kiss of life after a morning dispatching inglorious death.

He reads my thoughtful hesitation and growls, "Do not keep me waiting. Let your instincts kick in and show me what you want... now."

Unconsciously, I tilt into him, his magnetism tugging me with an invisible strand. A shard of sunshine cracks the clouds, its beam splashing Tomás' eyes so they glitter with sunny specks. The unusual new hue gives them a supernatural appearance, claiming a universe lives within him. I swallow and quickly look at my fingers before I lose myself in his fixed gaze.

His spine stiffens when my short nails trace the curvature of his pectoral muscle, leading to his pointed nipple. A wave of goosebumps crash over his tanned skin and I swear he shivers. I've never had the opportunity to explore a man's physique before and now that I'm allowed to freely skim his torso, I'm not disappointed.

I take my time to examine every curve and dip belonging to this man's naked flesh before lifting my lashes to meet his white teeth trapping the plump expanse of his lower lip. He doesn't shift position, the demon inside him contained for this fleeting moment in time.

The persistent throbbing in my sex becomes uncomfortably needy. I'm a victim to the thrill of a woman meeting a man, to an inflamed desire driving me wild, and seemingly affecting him, too.

Rising to tiptoes, I press my achy nipples into his solid chest and pause before him. He immediately dips his chin to align our lips, but holds firm, waiting for me to take the lead. And that's exactly what I do.

For the first time in my life, I make a move, lightly pressing my lips to his and skating my tongue along the underside of his top lip with a bold stroke. The silken landscape feels out of this world. His distinctive flavor is sweetened with alcohol, peppermint, and sin. It's a poison that would undoubtedly be the death of my virtue for ever more.

When the tips of our tongues collide, his guttural groan excites me more than any adrenaline rush I've ever known. Yet he still doesn't overpower me with authority or demands. Tomás allows my casual exploration to tease his abstention, permitting my tentative licks and roaming hands.

I'm tingling all over, deepening the kiss to hunt for more of a reaction from him, but something feels off. It's unsettling how he's portraying calmness rather than matching the hunger burning within me like an inferno. As much as I love this new sense of womanly power I've unleashed, it's not the same. My hands drop to his belt buckle and my heels sink to the paving and our hungry kiss abruptly ends.

"What sort of game is this?" As I subconsciously reach for my lip, he seizes my wrist like a viper strike.

"It's not a game." His grip tightens, becoming uncomfortable. I squirm in protest, not because I want him to let go. Instead, I'm afraid of the uncertain dynamics—that he's not really attracted to me and this cruel situation is simply the show of a sovereign's boundless power.

"What do you want, Carina?" he grits out. His face dips into mine, casting his handsome features in shade, so he appears unholy. "Tell me." The unusual hiss from the back of his throat makes me think it pains him that I've stopped clawing at his trousers.

"I want you... inside me," I whisper before my nerves get the better of me. "I need you to fuck me like you do, Tomás." The urgency to my voice shocks me more than the indecent request itself. I'm too eager for this man—for his cruelty.

His mouth brushes the curve of my jaw until it settles at my ear. "That's all I needed to hear. As you wish." His tone drops to a feral growl.

A large hand finds my chlorine water and essence drenched panties, cups me possessively, and then Tomás kisses me this time, on his terms, with a passion so intense I fear he'll rip me apart with his teeth. He drags his mouth away, locking his serious eyes with my daze. "Now get on your knees."

There's no romantic gesture or assistance offered, only an expectation of obedience and watchful eyes. My heart slams, the rush of blood louder than the squawking birds in the trees and the sound of every quick breath I gulp.

Lowering before him, I shake with anticipation, fully accepting my fate at this man's mercy.

Without any help, he kicks off his shoes, tugs off his belt, unzips his jeans, and drags them past his hips with his boxer briefs following. He leisurely steps out of the shackles around his ankles, painting a picture of complete stoicism. However, from down here, on my knees, I witness the vein pulsating in his throat and find an unmistakable pearl of pre-cum nestled on the satiny head of his angry looking dick.

"Pass up the tequila," he orders, before swiping a palm down his face.

The small knife tucked against his leg catches my eye, but doesn't set alarm bells off. Not as it should. I grab the bottle and raise it in tandem with my gaze. Outlined by lush vegetation and serene blue, he takes it from me with one hand while the other fists his rigid length. My pussy clenches, needy for fulfillment. It's a wicked sensation to crave something with this much desire, even when I know it's not good for me and in the end it will be my ruin.

His stance widens. "Move closer," he orders. "You like tequila?"

I shuffle closer so my knees rest in the space between his ankles, my hair swings to the base of my spine. "It's the first time I've tried it," I admit.

"Another first." He chuckles darkly. "Well, here's a little secret for you," his turbulent gaze swallows me whole. "What I'm about to do next is a first for me too."

30

TOMÁS

"You're such a beautiful little thing, aren't you," I praise, admiring the dusting of freckles kissing her high cheekbones.

The way I'm feeling right now, so horny and hungry for her, I could blow my load all over her face. That wouldn't be enough of a release and I fucking know it.

Dainty fingertips skim my inner thighs. I can't help the low grunt my throat makes. The hedonistic touch catapults trillions of chills all over me. Every shiver is magnified by the vision of this stunning girl, practically begging me to destroy her.

It's not like I haven't had obedient women before. I have, many times. But this insatiable obsession I'm fighting is like fine grains of gold dust dredged from a stormy ocean—a valuable, rare reward after a dangerous mission.

"Wanna have fun destroying all your firsts?" I smirk, trying to conceal the man she'll never meet. The reckless side of me helplessly disintegrating behind the mask I wear.

Her eyes sparkle up at me, more desirable than gold bullion.

"And do I get to destroy any of yours in return," she baits, her soft feminine voice a breeze of seduction.

Adrenaline pumps into every organ until I'm over energized with the stamina of a lion. "Having you in my home is a first." I drag my thumb over her plush bottom lip and watch it plop back into place. "Not killing you when my father ordered it, that was a first. And fucking a gorgeous teenage virgin in my shower was also a first." A shudder rattles my bones, alerting her to my feverish arousal. "So I think we're even."

I scoff inwardly at my foolishness. Angelo would beat this distraction out of my skull and order me to send her away until I'd found my father's killers. However, the vice-like grip she has on my needs equals that of unruly street gangs hooked on cocaine.

The whole time Shane and I interrogated our enemies, I tried to forget the taste of her salty skin and to ignore the crackle of chemistry bonding Carina to me in unnatural ways. When traitorous blood spilled, my veins scorched. Not for the thirst of death—for the erotic memory of her falling apart on my dick with *my* blood tarnishing her hands.

I'm a fucking psychopath.

When I returned home and pinned her to the infinity scape of my territory, barely dressed in wisps of black lace and bruises, the evil within me tamed for a beat. Those purplish welts decorating her ribs are vivid reminders of the world I was born into. How unlawful motherfuckers walk beside us, even if I am one of them.

I could have snipped the lingerie right off her graceful body. Stolen her mouth to feed this bone-deep attraction, except in that moment, when she emerged from the water like a tortured goddess, unworthiness struck me stupid. Regret hit me hard, and I cursed the miserable bastard who attacked her in my home.

Intense admiration turns sickly in my belly, momentarily sabotaging my seat on the throne. Almost crushing the burdensome crown on top of my head and fooling me into believing Carina could be in my future.

Her unbending inner strength is both admirable and priceless. I've seen her confidence slip, uncertainty turn her eyes to smoke, but equally I've witnessed her unnerving courage and bold curiosity.

Blood seeped dollar bills wouldn't be enough of a ransom to keep this woman safely by my side. A war between allies would single her out as my only weakness.

Love is death.

Anger coils in my stomach, like a pit of unfed serpents ready to strangle anything that gets in the way. I'm not a weak-assed fool in love. I'd never permit that. Not even when I marry the Mexican girl for a pivotal move in an arduous game of chess.

It doesn't matter that a dark and twisted part of me finds it excruciatingly difficult to resist Carina. She's like a bolt of lightning trapped in a box. Bright and energetic with enough volts to electrocute my heart into action. If I set her free, she'd hold the charge to ruin me.

I stare into her big eyes, aware of every vibration this

exquisite mistake creates. My jaw twitches from a quelled temper. Amber irises loop jet black pupils in a ring of fire, widened by shivery desire. She's intoxicating.

"Open your mouth." My fingers wrap harder around my painful dick.

She obeys, her mouth yawning beneath my swollen balls. The wind carries flyaway sable strands across her freckled complexion, making her appear angelic. We both know that's one thing she's not now. Virtuous—perhaps. But angelic—not anymore.

My knees bend a little to bring myself closer to her flushed face. I wince when her tongue flutters over the underside of my balls, softer than a dragonfly's wings. A trickle of sweat runs the length of my spine—the need to fuck her throat becoming intolerable.

Inhaling hard, I pour the liquor, watching it flow steadily from the head of my dick to the base of my shaft. A glossy stream twirls around the puckered skin on my balls and siphons into her waiting mouth. The sound of her throat working catapults violent shivers through me, harsher than volts from an electric chair.

For a moment, I believe this could be Heaven until hungry fingers seize me. The Queen kneeling before her King engulfs my tequila flavored dick and stuffs her throat until she gags.

Fuck! It's better than Heaven. It's nirvana.

"Good girl," I manage to hiss out, my blood ablaze and my eyes drilling into hers as she takes all of me. What a sexy sight.

Everything I believe to be true is wrong. Drugs aren't the most lethal addiction we can die from. It's the salacious drug of sex that devastates a human's ability to operate at full capacity. My defenses have lowered and she's breached every boundary I've ever built.

Short nails dig into my thighs, the bite only making my pulse thrum harder and my desires more aggressive.

"Is this what you want?" I wait for her to hum around me, not expecting the reverberation to whip up a monsoon of longing inside me.

A cocktail of saliva and liquor leaks from the corners of her mouth and dribbles down her chin. The vision before me awakens an animalistic side of me that I don't wish to bat away. She'll never forget me. This. Us. And neither will I.

The driving force raging inside of me takes over. I toss the bottle away, hearing glass smash into pieces similar to my threadbare decorum. Startled birds take flight and the gentle hum of distant wildlife ceases. She flinches, her uncertainty propelling her backward, so she's no longer sucking me off.

I grab her wrists and wrench her body upward. The scrape of lace on my dick makes me shudder. It's all I can focus on. She doesn't have to beg me. I'm too far gone for games. I tug down the flimsy straps to reveal her tits and squeeze them so the nipples pop.

Dropping my face, I suck one pebbled nipple into my mouth, then the other. When she moans, I nip them between my teeth in quick succession. She gasps as soon as the sharp pain attacks, her eyes glowing like flickering lanterns lighting the pathway to destruction.

My hand dives between her thighs, rips her panties to tatters and two fingers plunge inside her. The heat offers me a second of reprieve from the darkness clouding my intentions. Her relieved moan is the sound of sweet purity kissed with sin.

"Fuck me," she demands, her lips hunting mine. "Do it, Tomás." Carina writhes, her hips shifting into my wrist as her high escalates.

The rhythm of my probing fingers and the energized buzz it brings stirs something uncharted within me. I snake my free hand to her nape and capture a fistful of sable hair. As if working against my wishes, the greedy fingers soaked in her essence jump to her chin where I secure her against me. Locked in place with nowhere to go, I hollow her cheeks until her pretty mouth takes an oval shape.

Finally, giving into the extraordinary compulsion, I smother her wet lips with mine and kiss her like she's the priceless cure to my terminal disease. It's a demanding kiss with clashing teeth and rushed sweeps. Her mouth tastes even sweeter with the kick of alcohol and eagerness. Fuck, I need this and I don't know why.

She whimpers and moans, so defenseless in my custody and thirsty for more. The fingers squishing her cheeks skate to her proud throat, stretched long to reach my height even though I've overpowered her.

Anchoring her with hands that had carried out vicious deeds hours earlier, it would be easy to snap her neck, to end this once and for all. Her pulse beats against my skin like earthquake tremors, the taste of her saltiness amplifying my instincts.

I crave this. I crave *her*.

Instinct urges me to fuck this woman; my *little liar*

who has never lied to me once. Beyond the haze, I'm immune to the tide of death and havoc from armed thrones and powdered crowns. At this moment, all I seek is pleasure in its purest form—with Carina.

My feet move without conscious thought, my body guiding her toward a circular woven daybed in the corner of the terrace. Our lips dual in this battle of wills, of rights and wrongs. Harshness and passion.

She lets me bulldoze her blindly until her calves butt the rattan patio furniture. I release her completely, press the heel of my hand to her solar plexus, and push her onto the slate-colored cushion. Looming over her nakedness, my back arched and my hunger insatiable, I rub my fingers over her sex.

"Do you want me to worship your cunt and fill it so full of my cum that you'll feel every drip spill out?"

Carina strokes her belly, the tips of her fingers floating from her navel to stiff nipples poking out above wrinkled lace. "Yes," she purrs, low and sexy.

"You want me to fuck your tight little hole without mercy?" I snatch her hand and shove it to my groin. "Is that what you want?" My question cracks through clenched teeth, the words turning to dust when she licks her lips and sets them alight.

"Yes," she repeats, her fingers caressing the wet head of my dick.

I muster a thread of fraying strength to slap her touch away and manhandle her by the hips until she flips over. She clambers onto all fours, naturally presenting glistening folds by separating her thighs. Predatory desire sears my veins. I run my hands over the roundness of her ass, over black-and-blue blemishes, and savor the erotic shiver she can't control.

"You've been a very good girl. After this, you can have your phone. You can have anything you want for the duration of our time together, and I only want one thing in return."

My sanity has all but left me when I smack her hot opening with my solid shaft. I bite my lower lip, watching how I drag the tip along her pink crevasse to coat myself in her wetness. The muscles in her back brace, pausing for the extra stimulation.

"I want to claim every single hole you have." Aligning my shaft at her entrance, a shudder rattles my bones. "I *will* own all of you, Carina. And you can't do anything to change it. No matter what happens after you leave, I will have owned you without question."

The second I finish announcing my claim, I ruthlessly thrust into her gloriously snug pussy, deep and uncivilized. Her gasp chills me with depraved prickles of excitement, the savagery of this lust being the reward she deserves.

Impaled from behind, she rears backward, throwing her spine into my chest. Wet strands whip my chest, the scent of her hair intoxicating. The closer position gives my groping hands easy access to her plump tits and my teeth sink into her neck. We grunt together, working hard to stay connected, to satisfy the darkest parts of ourselves that others would never accept.

My hand swathes her throat, the other snakes her pelvis to help angle myself better. "This cunt is mine," I pant into the side of her face before squeezing her neck to imprison her against me. "Understand?" She tries to nod, but I don't soften the constraints. "Say it," I snarl.

"You own it," she chokes out on a raspy breath.

"And all the rest of your holes," I confirm. "I own all of them, too."

Certain she's got the message; I graze her cheek with my lips and release my ruthless grip. Instantly, she sucks in a breath of air, and at that moment I take the opportunity to ram upward until she cries out. Drawing her elbows behind her back, I cross her wrists and shove her face downwards. Sparks ricochet through me, haywire volts so chaotic I almost enter her womb from tunneling in deeper.

The vision of her flushed skin abolishes the savage events of last night and replaces them with something I've never known before—unworldly possessiveness. For most of my life, I've lived beneath an oppressive dark cloud, and now, being with her under the vast Brazilian sky, I feel rays of sunlight like never before.

The world is bolder, brighter—powered by this goddess chasing an orgasm on the end of my dick. Without her, the light has no passage to reach me.

I slam inside her, at the end of self-control. My heart rate soars and my hips piston with punishing velocity. All the chaos inside me pours into Carina, both of us skirting around an almighty, satisfying release. My sweat laden spine tingles with the slap of my flesh connecting to her peachy ass. The brutal sting turns me on like a fatal switch and I shoot my load, hard and fast.

It's enough to trigger her own bone shattering orgasm. I love the sound of her muffled screams when I cover her mouth with my palm, so my dogs don't think I'm hurting her out of malice.

Once her clamped inner walls release me, I withdraw, move her around to face me and flip her onto her ass.

"You want to suck my dick?" I don't wait for a reply, straddling her face and pressing the weeping tip against her lips. She willingly opens her mouth, welcoming the crazed movements of a man hungry for more.

With my toes planted to the pavement, I dip my pelvis in a plank posture, fix my hands at either side of her hips and ram my dick into her throat. "Suck that dick," I hiss, achingly hard again. "Fucking suck it and taste more of me. Of us."

As she gags on the length, I cum again. Not as much as before, but enough to slay me. My eyes shut, my pulse gallops, and a tattered breath expels my burning lungs until I'm utterly depleted—mentally, physically, and emotionally. The way she responds to me is beyond submissive. It's gloriously potent and addictive.

Her hands twitch by my thighs, gently stroking. The attentive massage is magically intimate in an affectionate way. I want everything she has to offer, except for meaningfulness.

We can never indulge in that. I can't keep her. It would be selfish of me to drag her into the cartel world and stick a target on her back. My original plan is solid. She's a temporary fix, with no future in my life. I'll marry the Mexican woman as agreed and avoid emotional ties.

I move off her body and stand, preparing to burst free of her sexual spell. After that mind-blowing fuck, I'm dog tired and the bandage on my bicep needs to be redressed.

The thought of a grimy dressing next to my wound makes my stomach churn.

"And that's it?" The bitterness in her tone stops me mid-stride. "You own my *holes?*" I turn to face her, raising an eyebrow. Her eyes flash with a crown of fire. "I'm more than that, you know. More than just holes to stick your dick into," she challenges, folding her arms over her midriff.

In one stride, I'm opposite her naked body where visible chills rain over her silky skin. My hands ball, something unidentified bubbling behind my deadened exterior. I take a beat to drink her in, wondering what the fuck is happening to me. Fluttery lashes lift, so her eyes lock with mine.

I lower to my haunches and gently swipe the fine scar lining her lip with the pad of my thumb. "I own this too." A dark chuckle disguises my unhinged temperament.

This isn't any normal response searing my veins—it's beyond reasonable logic. There isn't a justifiable explanation for the possessiveness polluting my brain. She shivers when my knuckles skim her jawline.

"Your old scar is barely visible. Not everyone sees it, but I do. I see all of you." Her face tilts into my hand. "But you don't know me, Carina. You wouldn't want a man like me to keep you." Her fiery gaze clashes with my black stare. "Now go upstairs, clean yourself up, pack some clothes for our trip... and when you're ready, I'll give you the phone to contact your brother."

Carina's forehead furrows when my hand leaves her face. "No!" she blurts out.

When I pull away and straighten, she bounces to her

feet. My towering height forces her to lift to her dainty tiptoes. Yet the extra inch she creates doesn't match my looming posture.

"That's not how this works. I want my phone. Now." She prods my chest with a vigorous forefinger, completely slaughtering me with the unintentional lick of her lips that follows. "I did what you asked. We had a deal, Tomás. Or is your word not worth shit?"

Her warlike suggestion riles up my temper. Above all else, I'm true to my word. If I say I'm going to destroy someone, I'll fucking do it. I asked her to behave while I was out and she did. I'll honor my end, but only when it suits me. Handing over the one thing that tethers her to her old life, amplifies this temporary status and makes me uncertain I can trust her not to scream for help.

She glowers at me, her attitude brazen and unacceptable for a man of my authority. Luckily, there's no one around to witness her risky show of disrespect, or how I snatch her forearm, slam her close so our bodies collide, and cage her torso in my merciless arms.

"Be careful how you speak to me," I growl, low and menacing into the shell of her ear. "Talk to me like that in front of my family, or my men, and I won't hesitate to punish you... without pleasure." I add with a snap of annoyance.

Feathery hot puffs settle on my chest as she returns my gaze with her own anger fueled scowl. She grits her teeth, projecting a festering rage that stabs between my ribs with a knife-like ache.

"You know how much it means to me to contact

Salvador. He's *familia*. He's my big brother. Surely you understand that."

"Fine," I say bluntly. She breathes hard when I release her, the breeze dancing through the cavernous space now separating us. "One phone call. That's it."

I rotate away from her and march indoors, knowing perfectly well she's struggling to keep up with my long strides. The fact she's full of my cum and still bare-ass naked does freakish things to my heart rate. It stirs a primitive desire I've never known before, aside from the unnatural high of taking a man's life with my bare hands.

Men born into the cartel never change. I'll never be the law-abiding character she deserves, but I sure as fuck enjoy the high that comes from corrupting her. Of becoming the one man she'll never forget. As that notion plagues me, a strange sense of dread dulls the thrill. I recoil under the knowledge of her being a first for me, too.

Something I've never experienced before.

She's scorching red when I'm frozen blue. No matter how hard I try, I can't refuse the temptation, even briefly wishing I could keep her. The cruel inevitability of loss rages through the pathetic daydream in a deluge of gunshots.

Reaching my office, I move behind the desk and open the top drawer. "Here." I offer her the cell phone; aware I've relented to her demand. "Make the call on loudspeaker."

She snatches the phone. Her movements are sharp like a spirited kitten with eyes smoldering, almost afraid that

I'm baiting her with it. Quick fingers curl around the glittery casing.

Her forehead furrows before she does a one-eighty and scrolls the unanswered messages. I watch her closely, drinking in the sleek curve of her feminine hips, glorious firm buttocks slapped red, and long slender legs.

Fuck!

"Hey…" Her voice hitches a decibel higher, pretending to be chirpy. She holds the phone before her face and sits on the buttery leather couch, thighs held tight together, and spine arched so her elbows rest on her knees. "What's happening, Sal?"

"Where the hell are you, Cari?" Her lashes lower at the sound of her brother's crossness. "I told you to keep in touch. That was the deal."

I rise up from the chair behind my desk and prowl to the couch across from her, sitting slowly with my semi-solid dick shamelessly on display. Her eyes cut to the movement of my ankle flipping to rest on my opposite knee. Her lungs rise in bursts, her nostrils flaring as she breathes.

"Cari?" Salvador persists. "Where the hell are you?"

Her gaze travels from my legs to my face, snaring me with an indecipherable look. "I've met someone." She straightens, grabs a cushion, and hugs it close to her abdomen. The line goes quiet. "It's nothing serious, so don't get all big brother weird about it."

"What's his name?"

She swallows, locking her ardent eyes with mine. "Tommy. His name is Tommy. A random nobody I met at the jazz bar." She concludes, dropping her gaze to the top of the glossy coffee table separating us.

"Tommy who?" Sal's voice snarls through the airwaves.

"Sal," she scolds. "Stop it. I've already told you it's not serious. I'll be twenty soon, you know? Not some silly teen you need to protect from the wind. Every girl needs to kiss a few mean toads."

The corners of her mouth droop to a sorrowful grimace as her eyes close to block out the sight of my raised eyebrows.

A mean toad? Mean perhaps, but a rough-assed amphibian? I see myself as a hawk, soaring above the earth, surveying the vermin below me, and swooping down to catch a few toads when I'm hungry.

"Toads? What the fuck are you talking about?" Sal sounds just as unsure about her description of me as I am.

Sadness creeps over her posture, right down to the soft sigh escaping her parted lips and the alcohol matted tips of sable hair draping well-sucked nipples. I grit my teeth when an unusual twinge takes hold of me. She's the hottest woman I've ever bedded and I've been around the world too many times to count.

A sudden urge to choke the truth from her elegant throat rages through my veins as liquid fury. I want her to admit I'm not simply a one off man—I'm the one she'll never forget.

Her plump bottom lip slips between her teeth and she finally peers over at me. My dick stands to attention. Fucking rigid, like a soldier waiting for an order to destroy. I stare into her wide amber eyes and watch my pitiful wish to keep her catch fire.

"Let me run a background check on him." Her brother demands. "You don't know who you're getting involved with in Bogotá. He could be…"

"Sal!" Carina jumps up, the cushion diving to the rug under her dainty feet. "I'm not getting involved with anyone. He's just a random guy I'm using for sex. That's all." Her cheeks blaze from the admission. "Surely you can understand that. It's about time I grew up and faced the real world without hiding behind my big brother. And you need to let me figure out who I am, because I sure as hell don't know yet."

There's a moment of contemplative silence and then her brother finally speaks. "If he hurts you, Cari, I'll shoot him in the fucking face and bury him in the jungle."

I like this fucker. He's ballsy and protective of my woman. My eyes snap shut. The warning flare of her never being mine whips the venom from my temper, rendering me silent. When her long lashes flick upward, she quietly hunts for my reaction to her brother's outburst. I glower at her, my mood unstable.

"I know you don't mean that, Sal." Our eyes stay locked in a prism of daylight and unspoken impulses.

"You know I fucking mean it," he replies with so much conviction that I feel like recruiting him as a valuable soldier. "Cari…"

"What?"

"I know you're lying to me."

"Don't be stupid, Sal. I've nothing to lie about."

"He's not some random guy, is he?" The hairs on my neck lift as she turns away from me. "You don't trust people. You've never had a physical relationship with a guy. There is no way you'd hook up with a random man unless you..."

"You're reading too much into it, Sal," she interrupts abruptly. "We both know I'm damaged goods. I will never have a conventional relationship with anyone. I'm incapable of being normal. So let me find my own way."

What the fuck?

I flinch against the audacity of her statement. At the preposterous misconception of a woman like her needing to be normal. There's nothing normal about either of us. She doesn't need to conform or change a single hair on her pretty little head.

"Sal, I'll call you in a few days. Okay? I know you're only looking out for me, but this is the reason I decided to stay in Bogotá. To figure out who I am and find where the hell I fit in." Her hand skates over her heart. "Come to the city in a few weeks and we'll hang out together. I'll even buy you a *brownie con helado* and a chocolate milkshake from that gourmet ice-cream shop we found near my apartment. I love you."

My ribs jar. The pain quickly turning numb. That used to be my thing with Angelo. He'd buy me a milkshake and then we'd talk about cocaine production and distribution. I used to think it was the milkshakes I adored when it was simply his attention.

"Fine." He sighs. "I love you too. Be careful. I'm always here for you, Cari."

Once the call ends, she stares blankly at the phone. "I suppose you want this back now?"

"Damaged goods?" I'm standing in front of her in a flash. My pulse thrumming like she's sliced my jugular, so the main artery bleeds out before her. She's far from damaged. In fact, I'd go as far as saying she's impossibly exquisite.

She shakes her head and takes a step sideways, as if trying to erase every word she'd said to her brother. "Take it." The phone soars through the air and skids across the couch beside us. "Can I go upstairs? If we're done here, I'd like to take a shower."

We stand in a hushed impasse. Me, unsure of why the hell I'm so torn up and her naturally dabbing her flawed lip.

"You'll need a black dress for the funeral." I scowl at her for making the floor beneath my feet so unsteady. "There's plenty to choose from in the gift boxes upstairs. Pack a bag."

"Am I dismissed, *sir*?" she quips with a mocking bow.

"Unless you want to be restrained, bent over my lap, and spanked until your attitude changes, then I suggest you turn around now. However, calling me sir, that I like."

Her tongue slips between her pouty lips, almost unraveling my inflexible countenance. The vein in her neck pulsates with remarkable energy. She's thinking about it.

"For the record, Tomás. What I said to my brother about you being a nobody—I meant it. I've accepted this charade between us for his sake."

"Liar." I trap her wrists and thrive off the struggle she puts up. "I think you're fascinated with what I can teach you."

"I think you're too high up on that throne of yours to see clearly," she counters. Her anger is a thing of beauty, red-hot beneath my fingers where her silky skin is held. "I can't wait until this is over so I can find a normal man, a guy who has a normal job and makes me feel... normal things." Her eyes spark with scorching sincerity.

I let out a frostbitten laugh to curb my temper. "Normal is overrated, *Cari*." The use of her shortened name makes her freeze like a sculpted ice statue. "Neither of us are normal. I understand the perversion inside of you and you know exactly what gets me off. Now, be a good girl and run along. We don't have time for your pointless denial. My family is expecting me at the plantation in the countryside this evening. Be ready to leave in an hour."

31

CARINA

I'm sitting in the passenger seat of a sporty car with tinted windows. It's unlike anything I've ever been in before.

The matte black exterior and red detail trimming the wheels gives the sporty Bentley a futuristic look, and with Tomás in the driver's seat, it's the personification of sex in a vehicle.

He's been at the wheel for over an hour now while I've hummed along to his Spotify playlist. I'm slightly surprised, given the ten-year age gap, that we have the same taste in music. While his tunes fill the lull of muted thoughts, I take the opportunity to mull things over.

Once our time together runs its course, I'd return to the city and continue searching for the vices that make me tick. Perhaps it would be the kiss of a different devil who offers unsanctified ecstasy. I'm nervous I'll never replace the unusual passion I have with Tomás, that the simple sex I've only read about won't cut it for a broken girl like me.

It's just him and I traveling together in a very fast car.

Before we left the hillside compound, Shane hopped into a waiting chopper with my filled weekend bag and a troop of armed men. They'll arrive ahead of us to ensure everything is in order for Tomás' arrival. I pray Shane doesn't go through the contents of my bag, or he would find Elias' ring wedged in the inside zippered compartment.

I fidget with the hem of my dress and stare out of the passenger window, unsure why the old man's ring holds so much meaning to me. We've left the city of Bogotá behind and now I've no clue where we are. It's both daunting and exhilarating.

I'm going on an adventure with a handsome stranger, who made sure I'd eaten a chicken salad sandwich before we left and packed a crate of spring water to keep me hydrated after he poured tequila over his dick and into my throat.

Tomás lowers the volume. "Do you want to stop off somewhere to get a coffee?" he asks out of the blue.

"No thanks."

He keeps his eyes trained on the road and continues to make conversation. "Your brother sounds like a decent guy. I could use a loyal soldier like him."

I side eye him. "My brother is *not* on your radar. It's me you're fucking with. Not my brother. Pretend he doesn't exist. I never want to see you anywhere near him. Ever."

Tomás shakes his head and grunts in a half laugh. "I respect the guy for looking out for his little sister. Loyalty and honor are priceless. I'm not interested in fucking him, Carina. Only you."

"Well... he's my hero. No man will ever compare to

Sal." I smooth out the pink buds blooming on another new dress and skip to the next track on his playlist.

Closer by Kings of Leon haunts the limited space between his solid body and mine, the intro making my skin prickle and my heartbeat flutter.

"He tries to understand how messed up I am." I continue, gazing out of the side window. "He wants to help me figure it out... I guess no one can." I bite my tongue to stop myself from saying more.

The Bentley's speed goes from breaking the speed limit to a snail's pace. Tomás takes his foot off the gas and steers the car over to the side of the road. With one hand on the wheel and the engine purring, he angles his torso and stares right at me. "Messed up?"

"Messed up," I repeat, intentionally diverting my gaze to lessen the intensity of his unsettled mood.

"Eyes up," he snaps as quick as a bullet. When I look at him, I find his serious, dark gaze. It lingers a beat before dropping to my wrist. "What happened to make you try something so final?"

Soft strokes brush over my self-mutilated skin, visibly chilling me. I watch his fingers navigate the silvery ridges and embrace the odd show of tenderness he offers. I'm suddenly filled with so much emotion that my mouth dries.

"It's personal," I whisper.

His hand leaves the old scars and pinches my chin, guiding it upward until our gazes meet once more. "If I'm to trust you, I need to know all your secrets, Carina."

"Trust works both ways." I counter.

I can't escape his patient silence or how his eyes glitter

from the electric blue lights on the dashboard. My lashes drift lower, unsure if I should explain honestly, or lie. Should I trust him not to make fun of me for being so disturbed? Then again, he's the one who cut the anchor to my carnal side and left me floating in an ocean of desire.

What he serves up, I enjoy. Before I met this man, I looked at the world through the eyes of a child and now I see things very differently. My heart skips a beat. The two of us alone in a confined space with his attention entirely focused on me. Even if I try to stand my ground, my vulnerability is in his hands.

As if sensing the whirling disquiet within me, he traces the curve of my jaw and hooks a lock of hair behind my ear. I relish the tingles rushing over me and breathe hard.

"Why did you cut yourself? To die or to feel something other than numbness?"

I swallow the doubt in my throat and inhale slowly to stall my response. Shame and distrust whisper through my subconscious, always present and reminding me of the bullies who'd forced me into hiding. Hesitant to answer his probing question, I fire one at him instead. "Why do you live like this... in a life with so much violence and death?"

His throat works as he swallows. For a second, I think he'll throttle me for daring to question him. However, he stares at me for a beat, sits back in his seat, and scrubs his jaw.

"I was born into it." He shrugs. "This life is all I know. Papá taught us to be killers, businessmen, and, above all else, the creators of a product so pure we control the global market. Competitors come for our blood simply because we're Souzas. This way I get to decide who lives or dies before they do." The stormy expression on his face passes like the clouds, his stiff posture relaxing a fraction. "Who wouldn't want to own hotels, yachts, islands, jet planes... judges... federal agents?" I watch the subtle dent in his cheek deepen as he offers a smile as rare as gold dust. That small wink of a dimple does wicked things to my radioactive libido. "Your turn. What made you do it?"

I've encountered more men over the past few months than I have in my nineteen years in Manaus, and none of them have affected me like this. Every time he looks at me with that wolfish inquisitiveness, I'm a slave to my inner demons, to the sizzling lust in my veins.

I bite my lip, feeling my pulse thrum faster. "I was born with a weird growth directly above my upper lip. Over time, it grew bigger and completely ruined my life." His jaw twitches as he listens. "When I slit my wrist, I was a sad little girl who wanted to escape the life she was trapped in. Salvador found me on the bathroom floor..." I'm lightheaded from my confession, panting softly against the quick beat of my heart. "He figured out a way to pay for corrective surgery. And now I'm trying to find who I am. Even if that person is…"

"Even if you're what?" He angles into me and sinks his fingers into my hair. I gasp at the control he takes, how his fingers knead the base of my skull, and his beautifully shaped mouth looms so close I could kiss him.

All I can focus on is him. His musky cologne, the warmth of his breath caressing my skin, and the forbidden adrenaline sparking from his wandering touch.

And those smoky eyes, fixed on mine like I'm the only woman in the world.

Instantly, his power ignites my skin with gasoline to match the heat between my thighs.

"Disturbed," I whisper, barely loud enough to hear.

But he hears it loud and clear. "What makes you more disturbed than any other human being out there?"

My entire body trembles, his intoxicating closeness making me dizzy. "I want…" Twisted knots in my stomach tighten. It's not easy to open up. My fingers find their way to his designer t-shirt. "I enjoy…" I fist the fabric, eyelashes fluttering as a wave of need aches in my core.

His nose nuzzles my hair, the warmth of an exhale sinfully erotic. "Say it," he breathes the words. I fight hard not to moan at the seductive low rumble of his voice. "Say you enjoy fucking me even when you know you shouldn't. That you love how I've found your sweet spots."

An uncontrollable quake betrays me. His large hand floats to my bare knee, slowly tracing a shivery path beneath the floaty fabric of my dress. "I want to hear you say it, Carina."

He leans back to catch my eye, the tips of his fingers traveling upward to the new lacy panties he'd bought me, now shamelessly wet. I bite my bottom lip to stave a groan and stare into his haunted gaze. Carefully, he tugs the damp fabric sideways and tilts to my ear, his stubble grazing my cheek. "Is this what you enjoy?"

Tomás bites my earlobe, his hot words whispering over my scalp. I whimper at the sharpness, inexplicably craving more.

"Yes," I pant. "I want you... even when I know it's wrong."

Masterful fingers move over my sex, cupping me possessively and squeezing hard. I unwittingly part my legs for more.

"How does it feel when I touch you here?" His hold on my neck tightens. The husky tone of his voice combined with his teeth grazing the shell of my ear, liquifies my bones.

I'm reluctant to admit my insides are a syrupy fire. How he's the trigger to a reaction so extreme that I'm melting from his close proximity alone.

"It's good..." He clutches my pussy harder, making me groan into his cheek. The sinful roughness drives me wild. "So good," I say breathlessly.

"And what's your gut reaction when I'm doing this to you?" His speech turns coarse like a whirlwind of grit, the tone urgent and alluring.

I forget all about the cartel funeral we're attending tomorrow, and the fact I'll be in a house full of trained killers. There is no question. No sliver of doubt. No denial. I *need* this man.

"I like it. I want more... of this... of you..." I sigh, defeated and unbearably needy.

The hand around my nape jumps upward, securing my hair in a fist. Our foreheads butt together, and the tips of our noses collide. Face to face, we inhale together, mingling the same torrid air.

Two of his fingers leisurely dip inside my wanton heat. They aren't forceful or stabbing, just disciplined and teasing. When his thumb sweeps my bundle of swollen nerves, I suck in, unintentionally brushing my lips against his. They cling lightly, almost claiming a kiss.

Without fully connecting, he continues to take his time, seemingly enjoying this unusually gentle finger fuck with every powerful rise and fall of his lungs.

"You're not messed up. You're alive," he murmurs before angling his wrist, so wicked fingers penetrate deeper.

"It's only taken me nineteen years to feel alive." I confess against his chest.

Sunless eyes smolder from a fire neither of us can extinguish. And then it happens. The forbidden energy between us electrocutes me from the inside out. It absolutely terrifies me, but most of all, it excites me. With a rush of hormones, my core shudders and I breathe all of him into my soul. His taste, his scent, his power—combined, he's my weakness.

When his hands release me, he slots his wet fingers into his mouth and sucks them clean. Placing both hands back on the wheel, he glances over at my flushed face, his own twisted into a thoughtful scowl. His nostrils flare as if he's falling from the heights of humanity.

"It's not wrong if your instincts tell you it's right. That's the one thing my Uncle Angelo taught me. It's what I live by. Always listen to your gut. If it feels good, enjoy it... because *nothing* lasts forever."

I'm still panting, sitting on a wet patch of my dress when he slams his foot on the gas again. In his own way, he showed me I'm not deranged for wanting dominant sexual thrills—but what I really learned is that I don't always need roughness—I just need him.

"He sounds like a wise man." I cross my arms over my chest in a self-hug.

"He was *my* hero."

"Was?"

Tomás swallows, his spirit slipping into obscurity. "He's dead."

"Oh... I'm sorry."

The cars gather speed. "Don't be. I killed him."

I freeze. "Why... why would you do that?"

"Because I loved him." Pensive eyes drill into the windshield. "My baby brother Matheus was sick. Papá told Angelo to collect me from school. He took me with him to a business meeting in the city. Something felt off when we got there. By the time I listened to my gut, the building exploded." My fingers dance over my mouth as he speaks —a nervous reaction to his terrifying tale. "His leg was blown off. He had a fatal injury to his head... so..." Suddenly his heavy scowl cuts to me. "No one knows what I did for him."

"You... shot him?"

He nods slowly. "In a matter of minutes, my uncle had transformed from a respected god of great wealth and authority to a gravely weak, powerless mortal who was suffering... like pitiful roadkill. As his dying wish, he ordered me to end his life—as my duty. I was only a kid." His voice slips into the shadows. "I've never told a living soul what he made me do. Until now."

I'm dumbstruck. Shocked at the trauma he'd endured as a child. And even more surprised that he opened up to me about it.

"You've kept that secret all these years?" I stare at his

beautiful profile—chiseled features kissed by a halo of the setting sun. He nods, not saying another word. "I won't repeat it. I promise."

For a second, his eyes leave the road and his lungs rise as he inhales deeply, like the weight of his confession has exonerated his blemished soul. "If you do, I'll kill you the same way I killed him." Then he swallows hard, like he just told a fib. "The moral of the story is—had I trusted my gut sooner, he'd be alive."

I swallow the flutters trying to escape my chest. "What do your instincts say about me?"

32

TOMÁS

I usher Carina through the quiet foyer of my late father's sanctuary, up the ostentatious staircase, and straight into my suite without meeting another Souza.

This is the home where Papá had sought refuge from his enemies and spent hours muttering about imaginary plots against him and the Souzas.

She flinches when I lock the door, twirling the ends of her soft hair, quietly reminiscing the last time she was in this suite. I leave her side and stroll to the walk-in closet. The two of us alone in a small space fucks up my head. I need distance, violence, or a hard fuck.

The latter being the more urgent and the one thing I don't have time for when my impatient brothers have assembled under the same roof.

I brought her here as a temporary fix to a permanent glitch. But for some reason, the withdrawal symptoms I get from not touching her puts me on edge.

Fate had been the reason she turned up at the plantation to begin with, and now the tables have turned. She's by my side as a guest, or if I think about it with a clear head—an employee.

How can any man admit to the woman he's captivated by that his gut tells him she's his secret weapon? That she's unlike any woman he's ever met.

Our agreement was sex and obedience, not emotional warfare. My gruff response to her question earlier didn't seem to annoy her. She *is* trouble.

The hot skin beneath my clothes itches. Not fucking her in the Bentley was an insufferable strain. A mist of sweat prickled my spine and my painfully swollen dick complained for the rest of the journey. When I use her body, it won't be a quick experience. I'll take my time, do it right and ensure she's well and truly spent. Now I'm fired up, antsy and in need of a clean t-shirt.

Changing into brand new track pants and a fresh white top marginally releases the tension in my muscles. I hate how I'd rather throw her onto the bed and bury myself inside her, especially when I haven't seen my brothers for ages. I pinch the bridge of my nose, take a deep breath, and then check my hair is sitting as it should.

Focus, cabrón.

Carina idles up from behind, her steps barely making a sound. There's some irritating voodoo shit harmonizing her presence with my bloodstream. I sense her closeness simply by the vibrations we share.

"When will I meet your family?"

Silence thickens between us while I study the perfect arch to her raised eyebrows. "Tomorrow. At the funeral." I drag a hand over my face and dodge her body on my way past. "Don't leave this room." My teeth grit at the command. "I'll be back later."

Ignoring the burning ache in my dick, I put more distance between us. She doesn't rush after me or ask any more questions, and I don't look back before leaving the room.

Knots in my belly snarl and squeeze. Getting close to her was a mistake. And listening to the tragedy that formed the woman she is today was a massive error. I shouldn't care how she lived in a darkness so bleak it almost stole her life. Nor should I feel the insurmountable rage that implores vengeance for every cruel motherfucker involved in crushing her confidence.

I jog down the stairs, pumped for a fight and ready to face my family. Moving through the corridors, I hear my brothers' rowdy voices—family banter that hasn't graced these walls for a long time.

We each have duties to perform and our own lives to live. These days, all four of us are seldom together in the same room and it's even more rare we'd be together in this place.

"Wow, we're honored you could make it, Tommy." The eldest of the twins by five minutes tips his glass at me and smirks. "What time do you call this? *Mama* went to bed already."

André slouches on an oversized couch, his knee jiggling up and down. He wears his usual biker jacket and lazy grin. Ringed fingers tap a crystal cut glass, excess energy buzzing from his seated position.

I stalk further into the informal room where they all sit, skirting the table crammed with dishes prepared by the new chef. Hot food makes my stomach growl, and my thoughts cut back to Carina. I'll take a plate upstairs later. She hasn't eaten since we've left Bogotá.

"Dré." I nod at him. "I drove from the city to clear my head. Shane and I had business to sort out before I left. There's still no evidence pointing to Blanco as Papá's killer."

A brief silence settles among us. It's a beat of remembrance—good and bad.

My kid brother, Matheus, bounces to his feet and barrels into my personal space, diving in for a hug. "Well, if it isn't the king himself. You okay, Tommy?"

"I'm good," I say half-heartedly, unsure of how the hell I'm feeling.

I'm hit with a rush of cologne up my nose and brotherly brawn. He might be a few years younger than me, but he still matches me in height and strength.

Matheus is the over-educated Souza with kick ass brain cells. The twins had teased him for years, telling him our mother injected his fetus with a genius serum bought off the black market. Once he's a practicing lawyer, he'll head the Souza legal team. Then we'll truly be unstoppable.

"How're those college girls working out for you?" I wink.

He's a good-looking, horny son of a bitch. With André's influence, the guy parties just as hard as he studies.

"Who has time for college girls?" He jabs my shoulder and laughs. "I'm too busy with finals."

"Right." I cock a skeptical brow at his bullshit. "So you weren't in Vegas with Dré a few weeks ago?"

"That was a one off weekend," he muses, eyes sparkling with mischief. His private jet is always in the air. "You should have joined us."

"Maybe next time."

It's not that easy for the next in line to step away from business. He'll never understand the responsibility I've inherited. Not that it stops me from letting loose. That's what Carina is for.

I'm crossing the room to reach the second twin, Giovanni, when André saunters over and hands us both a shot glass of tequila. "*Salud*!"

"Salud." We clink glasses and throw back the liquor together. "I'm glad you're here, Gio."

I grab his outstretched hand and pull the lean fucker into my chest. He goes rigid at my unusual show of affection. Having him here, in this house, with hard memories, is a miracle. Since Papá died, I've realized these guys are all I have. *Familia*. My loyal three brothers and the backbone of our unit—mama.

Gio's green eyes tip to meet mine, the shade so pale I'd swear he's supernatural if I hadn't grown up beside him. He's the only one of us who has our mother's eyes. With his jet black hair and secretive jade gaze, he's every bit an Irish mafia grandson.

"Tommy." The corners of his mouth curl into a friendly smile. "It's been a while."

"Yeah. That's because you're a fucking recluse."

"I enjoy privacy like Dré enjoys *cocáina*." He shrugs.

"And I'm always on standby for when you need me. So quit complaining."

He's right. If I need a sniper, he's my go-to guy. Giovanni is our trusted personal sicario—the best I've ever known. With his extraordinary skills and lack of emotion, he's in and out, job done, and then disappears again. It's not what Papá trained him for, but it's what he ended up becoming.

"All I'm saying is, you're welcome to visit whenever you want. I'd come to your place, but I'd need your address first." I chuckle, knowing he'd never let me in. "What are you hiding in that beach house of yours, anyway?"

"Plenty of explosives to wipe out uninvited guests," he replies, straight faced, his expression dark and stormy. "Now you're officially *el jefe,* I'm sure you'll get an invitation at some point."

As much as I'm their boss, I get his desire to hide away. Giovanni is a strategic killer who understands exactly what our enemies are capable of—and what Papá had the power to do, too.

"How about we head outside?" I reach for my gun and pat my brother on the back. "Let's see if you still have the best aim, cabrón."

33

CARINA

I'm back in Hell.

I'm inside the monstrous residence I'd barely escaped from with my life once upon a time. The winding driveway leading to the plantation was longer than I remember.

A deceitful radiance of lamplight glittering from within gave the mansion an illusion of welcoming wealth. Only I know better than to expect warmth from this family.

The not so discreet soldiers with big machine guns and earpieces watched Tomás escort me into the reception hall. He didn't bat an eye as if it's a normal occurrence to have armed men guarding the outside of his mansion. I guess it's a safety measure following Elias' murder, and with the whole family in one place, they can't be too careful.

His palm pressed snugly to the curve of my spine as we climbed the sweeping staircase and strolled through empty corridors clad in weird artwork. Yet, the second we crossed over the threshold of his familiar suite, all contact ceased.

It reminded me of the fateful night when Tomás led me from the stables, soaked from torrential rain, and scared his father would shoot me. As it turned out, his father didn't pull the trigger, Tomás did, and I have a new scar to prove it.

This time, he locked the door behind us again and stalked away from me, hacking off any grain of chivalry he thought was necessary. His lofty shoulders gathered a skiff of frost from his sub zero mood he'd slipped into.

Now, I'm perched on the edge of his kingly bed, wearing a pearly silk nightdress that creeps up to mid-thigh and wondering if he expects me to wait up. My belly rumbles, nerves dancing their way through my tense muscles.

I notice a television remote control on his bedside table and turn on the flat screen TV stuck to the wall for a measure of comfort. There are hundreds of channels to pick from, but none of them grab my attention. I prop myself up on the bed and continue to flick from movie to movie. Bored of the search, I switch it off and lie there, deep in thought.

I wonder if Sal will snoop around the jazz bar to figure out the identity of my fake fling. Then I inwardly pray that he'll leave it alone like I asked. He has to trust me to make my own decisions, even if this particular one is off-the-wall dangerous.

In the stillness, gunfire blasts in quick succession from

outside. My scalp prickles with a ghastly shiver. I scamper off the bed and dart to the sliding doors, shunting them open and slipping onto the rose scented terrace.

Humidity licks my skin; the sub-tropical atmosphere is close to the Amazon climate I've grown accustomed to over the years. There's a brief amnesty of discord and then intermittent bullets ping, destroying it all over again.

The Souza family is under attack and I'm a sitting duck. I hurry back indoors and head for the closet, rummaging through fitted cabinets, wishfully searching for weapons. I've been in this position before and only found car fobs back then.

Once again, there's nothing remotely dangerous, only high price tag clothes and designer shoes. And I've never heard of anyone dying from a loose shoe thrown from across a room.

I give up looking for a hidden wall of loaded guns, grab a hooded top to cover myself and backtrack to the bedroom door, pressing my ear to the wood. Nothing. No thunderous steps from dutiful armed guards or shoot to kill orders.

Unlike the other times I'd spent in this suite, the main door is unlocked. My hand trembles as my fingers curl around the handle. Another explosion of gunfire shatters my nerves. Who knows what I'd face on the opposite side?

Sucking in a lungful of air, I cautiously peer through a sliver of space, searching for signs of life. Content that the hallway is empty, I leave the bedroom behind, my bare feet gliding over plush carpet. My pulse thuds in my skull with every hurried stride.

Before I descend the staircase, I freeze on the top step, my mind wild. Are they being shot at or are they the ones doing the shooting?

From up here I can't hear a thing, only a ticking clock and the hush it echoes in. It doesn't take long for my toes to meet chilly marble tiles and I pick a corridor to jog along.

I pass an unoccupied formal sitting room and a windowless nook with a sculpted male bust, his eyes pouring with solidified golden tears and a series of closed doors. The farthest set of doors on this wing takes me to an orangery where huge leafy plants thrive.

Cylindrical pillars guard the entrance and an impressive see-through dome stretches overhead. I scamper further inside, skirting the comfy looking couches, each one dissecting a heated porcelain floor. The mouthwatering scent of chicken and rice fires up my hunger. Though I'm too wound up to eat and plunder the oval buffet table.

More shots are fired from outside. I take cover behind a potted tree and catch my breath. When a new ceasefire casts deafening silence, I snatch an ornament from the side table to my right. It's heavier than I expected, the yellow sheen making me think the fierce lion donning a crown could be real gold. It could be a decent weapon to bludgeon a killer over the head in self-defense.

Symmetrical arches house thin French doors, all of them acting as a shield to keep the velvety night sky out of reach, except for one set. They're wide open, inviting cool air indoors and my gaze outwards to the terrace where the shadows begin to move.

Boots scuffing snaps my attention to the man dressed in a leather jacket and skinny black jeans. Disheveled hair is as dark as the night to match a layer of messy scruff and the hand wrapping a revolver is decorated in ink and silver rings.

My knees go soft. Not because he's roguishly handsome, because his dark eyes projecting murderous impulses are all over me, and the hefty object I'm gripping like a courageous knight with a needle sized sword. Immediately he takes aim, stalks past a pillow stuffed couch, and dips his hip next to the liquor cabinet.

"Who the fuck are you?" His voice is smokier than the cigarette he plucks from a pack with his teeth.

I try to speak, but the air has dried my parted lips and fright has turned my words to powder. Instead, I shuffle back, my ass butting into an ivory column.

His eyes narrow and then, as if assessing the entire room and its potential for danger, he sets the gun down. A solitary flame blazes until puffs of smoke escape his mouth.

"I'll give you three seconds to tell me why you're in my home with that fucking ugly ass lion in your thieving hands?" He tosses the zippo onto the counter, traps the butt between his teeth and unscrews the lid from a bottle of tequila. "Are you a new maid?"

His home. He's Tomás' brother.

My inhale is small but enough to help me breathe. "I'm with Tomás. We arrived this evening."

"Bullshit," he rasps, before taking a swig of tequila straight from the bottle. "There's no way you're here with Tommy." As he finishes a deep-throated laugh, he collects the gun and points it at my heaving chest. "Strip. Let's see what weapons you've got hidden under there."

"I swear…" I raise my hands, lifting the lion into the air. "This is all I have…"

"Do it."

"Tomás drove me here from Bogotá. Ask him. He'll confirm it." I barter with him.

The good-looking guy takes one large step closer, the threat of his aim unwavering. Impatience tightens his mouth, so he speaks with a sinister snarl. "You clearly don't know my brother, do you? Now take off your clothes before I shoot you in the head."

It's clear to me Elias' paranoia runs in the family. Then again, I can't blame him for being suspicious when Tomás hid me away in his suite the second we arrived.

I swivel slowly and let the statue tumble onto the soft fabric of the neighboring couch. Gradually, I drag the hooded top up and over my face. The negligee is still beneath, its silky satin skimming my chilled skin.

"And the rest," he mutters. Something dark lurks in the depths of his coal-colored eyes, a wickedness that tells me he's getting off on this control. "Once I'm certain you're not carrying a knife, we'll talk."

The nightdress puddles at my ankles, my bruises and scars visible under the lamplight.

His brow scrunches, those inky irises of his assessing my naked figure. "You in some sort of trouble?" He pinches the cigarette between his finger and thumb. "Who did that to you?"

When my mouth opens to speak, the words drown

under Tomás' sonorous voice, a thunderous downpour of icy hail and broken stone. "André!" he growls like the lion has come to life and taken over his soul. "What the fuck are you doing?"

André's head rotates the instant his brother storms indoors, with the rush of a hurricane and the bitterness of a blizzard. "You know this pretty little thing?" He cocks his brow, a look of confusion on his face.

Caught between lamplight and dimness, a trail of shade splices Tomás' contorted expression, making him the glorious monster I suspect him to truly be. His presence seems to swell in the half light, a nefarious temper mimicking the tones from the navy sky haloing his braced form.

My stomach flutters when our gazes clash, his slowly descending to my tattered dignity. The muscles in his jaw work in tandem with clenching fists, the kiss of shadows deepening the hollow of his corded throat. The blood-red stone trapped in a bed of gold deepens in color when he swipes a hand over well-kept stubble.

"I know her." His tone slides out with precise annunciation, controlled like the boss he's rightfully become. "She's with me."

"What the fuck, Tommy," André mutters under his breath, shaking his head. "You brought a fucking puta with you?"

The transformation from contained ruler to aggressive warrior happens instantaneously. He no longer possesses the godly aura of a king when his fists hammer his brother's chest, knocking him off balance and removing me from the firing line. His nostrils flare, the rings around his pupils morph to a shade more obscure than evil itself.

André staggers a few short steps, the back of his calves clipping a chunky coffee table. Fixing his boots to a solid stance, he points the gun in my direction again.

"Is there something you need to explain to me, brother?" he hisses. "Why did you risk bringing a whore to our family home? Is this what power does to you, cabrón?"

Tomás stands stoic, almost statuesque. His entire body vibrates, his hands ball, and his vicious glare burns into the man threatening me with a bullet. In a heartbeat, he charges, throws himself on top of André, and pushes him onto the cushion filled sofa. The handgun skids out of their reach and settles under the buffet table.

"I don't owe you an explanation. I'm the head of this family now," Tomás bites out between punches. "My word is final. She's mine, which makes her off-fucking-limits."

I swallow the dry lump in my throat, snatching a strewn pillow, to cover myself with and tapping my sternum helplessly as the two men continue to wrestle.

She's mine.

Two simple, short words with a variety of meanings. It's either a colossal admission or an offhand update. My feet merge with the heat blushed tiles underfoot, solidifying them to the spot where I stand. From my ankles to my thighs, my legs lock as though they too have turned from blood vessels and bone marrow to carved alabaster.

In a fair fight, I watch them crash into furniture and strike each other with bare knuckles. Neither of them make an effort to retrieve the weapon, both of them caught up in brotherly combat.

It only takes one direct blow to connect with André's nose for blood to trickle from his nostrils. He curses and shoves himself to his feet, pinching his nose. As he blinks through the throbbing agony, he puts a noticeable measure of distance between himself and Tomás.

A ripple of worry passes behind his eyes and he angles away to grab the nearest thing he can to contain the crimson downpour.

"Look…Tommy, it's only a little bit... here... quickly... use this." He pivots back with a napkin, hiding his bloodied nostrils and waves a clean one in the air.

Tomás glares at the negligible blood streaking his fist, his eyes frozen. Shaky fingers stretch and curl, his teeth bared to an ungodly snarl. Then he slips under a blanket of smog and goes deathly still. A shiver jangles my skeleton, a warning that Tomás could snap into a thousand shards of merciless regret. He's lost.

Without thought, I dash forward and slip my arms around the middle of his tense form and press my bare chest into his. "Tomás," I say his name softly, searching his possessed gaze. "Can you take me back to your suite now? I'm tired."

From the thick fog circling his mind, his eyes soften a little and the warmth of his torso catches fire. Dropping his chin to snare my concern, he lashes out, captures my cheeks in his palms and smashes his lips over mine.

He's no longer trapped in an invisible prison where demons taunt his humanity with flames of fury to expose his vulnerability. His body vibrates with ferocity, claiming my mouth like I'm his last breath before he drowns in an unforgiving ocean. He pours everything into our wild kiss—power, heat, gratitude.

When it ends, our eyes lock and he just stares at me in silence. It doesn't take long for the daze to evaporate when a new voice signals the entry of a woman into the room.

"I'm sure it looks worse than it is, my love. Thankfully, it doesn't appear to be broken." Tomás' gaze flicks up, settling behind me. "Tommy, why are you fighting with your brother?" the woman asks with a distinct Irish lilt.

His lungs visibly decompress as the tension and stress of his trauma evaporates. "Mama." He nods, swallowing back the dark lust he'd plugged into as a method to control his temporary malfunction.

I sense a burning need within him, a desire to reveal his stony dick to me and use it for equal gratification. It's there, digging into my belly, straining to reach me.

"I'm sorry if we disturbed you," he says, a little breathless. "André and I had a misunderstanding. It won't happen again." Firm fingertips dig into the small of my back, holding me tighter against his pelvis to either shelter me or use my presence as an anchor.

A womanly laugh meanders through the tension. "Of course it will happen again. You boys are hot headed like your Papá."

Tomás bristles. The softest silk skims my shoulders. A floral scented robe cloaks my nakedness with a flimsy layer of discretion. I turn my head in the direction of a uniquely striking woman with subtle creases at the corners of glacial green eyes.

Tendrils the color of molasses curl over black satin pajamas, now on show having given me her robe. She stands before us, her spine regally straight.

"Escort your friend back to her room, son. Then join me for a nightcap." She smiles at me for a split second and then cuts her unreadable gaze to Tomás.

"I'll show her the way, Tommy," André offers. I glance over at André, mopping his upper lip and nose with the soiled napkin. "You should have told us you were bringing a guest. It would have saved all this…"

"André, take the girl upstairs, won't you?" their mother suggests in a low purr, her raspy tone placating.

Tomás seizes my wrist, choking the bones as if he's throttling a traitor. "I'll take her myself," he replies, his stiff posture signaling malignant displeasure.

"Don't worry, Tommy. I'll be on my best behavior." The corner of André's mouth hitches to a grin, his straight teeth whiter than snowflakes.

"Keep your hands to yourself, Dré or lose them," Tomás grits out.

"Have a seat, Tomás." His mother squeezes his flexed bicep. "You've had a rough few days. Let me pour you a Scotch."

After a long sigh, he releases me. "My brother will take you upstairs, Carina."

He steps away from me and scrubs his face. The excruciating chill I feel from the absence of his body makes me shudder. Another round of bullets explodes from outside, yet no one bats an eyelid. When I flinch, his eyes narrow and hold me in a spell where it's just the two of us.

"Why are you down here?" he asks, his forehead scrunched as if he's resurfaced from a coma or a lucid nightmare.

"I heard the shots." My heart hammers as I answer, aware of the new set of eyes sizing me up like prey.

He pinches the bridge of his nose. "My brothers and I are competitive when it comes to target practice." Wicked lashes lower as he takes a balancing breath. "You best get into bed and stay there."

Tomás nods to his roguish sibling, a silent gesture of approval for him to usher me out of the room. I swallow the temptation to hug Tomás close and seek sanctuary by his side. Instead, I obediently traipse behind André. Glancing over my shoulder, I witness his nostrils flare and his eyes follow my departure.

"So your name is Carina," André saunters ahead, grabs an unopened bottle of booze and swaggers between a set of twin pillars. "Where are you from?" he says over his shoulder. "You must be... what... eighteen?"

"I'm nearly twenty and I live in Bogotá," I offer a reply without fully answering his question. He doesn't need to know where I was born or anything else about me, for that matter. The less he knows, the better. Once I've served Tomás, I'd disappear.

"Right. And how did you meet each other?"

"It's complicated."

"Complicated?" He swivels and stops by the sculpted bust with golden tears and waits for me to catch up.

I pad closer to him, the scent of lavender emanating

from the robe I've now tied at the waist. "I'm sure Tomás will answer your questions if you ask him."

André chuckles, wipes the back of his hand beneath his nostrils, checks it's clean of blood, and pulls out a pack of Marlboro cigarettes from his jeans pocket. "I can see why he might trust you." He exhales a swell of smoke. "I'm just confused, that's all. It's out of character for him…" His shoulders bounce. "To bring a stranger here, or even a woman."

We climb the stairs side by side, him in the center and me trapped against the handrail.

"You didn't bring anyone?" I ask, the sensation of my self-hug offering little comfort in this unusual set up.

"None of us did, except for him." His eyes drill into my side profile. "You can understand why I was suspicious." He hesitates for a beat to unscrew the bottle cap and takes a swig. "And what happened back there wasn't normal."

"Normal?"

"How he heard your voice when he was blipping out. The Tommy I know has been a slave to that fucking mind mess forever. And along comes a pretty little thing like you…" He sucks in a lungful of smoke and mouths out a few rings, each one floating into the atmosphere as vaporous lifebuoys as he sizes me up. "I wouldn't have believed it had I not seen it with my own eyes." My fingers skim the handrail to steady me, my feet tingling beneath me. André reaches the landing before me, swivels in his boots to greet me and offers a large, tattooed hand for the last step. "How much is he paying you? I only ask, because that whole show was priceless… and sexy as fuck."

Whether it's intentional or not, the implied undertone

crawls over me like he just dumped a nest of spiders onto my scalp. My unorthodox relationship with Tomás is purely contractual, no matter the unlawful feelings sprouting within me. He's using my services to heal himself, and once he's done, I'd be paid, banished, and watched over by his goons.

I choose silence rather than implicate myself in any financial or sexual wrongdoing. When my hand settles into his, there's no sexual appetite or surge of adrenaline. Although his husky voice is masculine and gritty, dozens of thick lashes frame mischievous earthy brown eyes and his muscular build is attractive, the deep ache I feel in my core for Tomás is absent. I'm uncomfortably numb.

Once the soles of my bare feet find their place next to his boots, I tug my hand away, slide my fingertips across my upper lip, and contemplate the desire in my belly for this man's older brother. I hoped it was simply the age-old fable.

How a man's forbidden urges can awaken an untouched girl, but when I look back on the men I've encountered to date, none of them have captured my curiosity for sex. Not the way Tomás does.

"Tomorrow is a big day for our family. He'll be preoccupied with the funeral arrangements." André's casual strides continue to eat up the carpet. "If you need anything, I'll be around."

"I'll be fine," I reply, my pace slower than his by a purposeful few steps.

He chuckles, the aroma of liquor and tobacco heavy on his breath when he turns into me and sets his hand on my shoulder. "It's okay, Carina. You're his medicine, not mine. I have a thing for busty blondes with deep throats." His cheek dimples as a roguish grin dances over his lips. "I love my brother with all of my fucking heart. Stealing his mistress isn't on my agenda. To be honest, I'll be relieved when this shit show is over. I've been planning Papá's funeral since I was your age."

34

TOMÁS

Throughout my entire life, Teresa Souza has been my one true constant.

The woman who tried her best to be a stable parent when my father was busy proving to the outside world that *he* was the best. Although my parents were married, my mother had a degree of independence, a life she led outside of this illusion—beyond the grand dwelling he referred to as the family home. We didn't.

It was meant to be the one place where we would all come together and celebrate the extravagant Souza lifestyle. In reality, it was my father's asylum and his mental penitentiary. A safehouse for his unstable mind and the only fitting place on earth where he would eventually be entombed.

I visited him here in person when there were important business discussions to talk over. Whereas my brothers reluctantly arrived as and when they were summoned. Aside from that, throughout the years, it was filled with more armed soldiers than family members.

With Carina out of the room, my mother puts her hands over the sickly blood dirtying my skin. The gentle act stops my hands from wringing in the absence of washing them. Where Papá saw a weakness that threatened his organization, mother recognized the weight of my distorted mind. She'd sought out professionals from every spectrum of the mental health discipline. Yet none of them could fix me.

She leads me onto the terrace, to a statue of a freakish bronze warrior in his natural born state, embroiled in a fight with a grisly beast. The ugly fountain spews water from the splayed throat of the wild animal, sprinkling the expansive pond lit up by a sheen of moonlight.

At the age of thirty-two, I still get comfort from her motherly compassion, from a woman who'd endured more than she should over the years. What my father offered to us as tyrannical lessons in discord and brutality; my mother replenished with affection.

We were raised by a devil and nurtured by an angel. My wily mother is silently shrewd, with the heart of an untamed lioness. Tonight, she's the widow of a madman who karma caught up with no matter how many precautions he took.

The two of us sit on the fountain ledge, her washing my hands with gentle strokes, and me observing the waterlilies so my focus is elsewhere. Only when the blood vanishes does she speak again.

"Who is she, Tommy?"

"No one to worry about," I reply curtly, flicking droplets off my hands and rising. We both know I need to dry them and drink a Scotch to take the edge off my viperish mood. "I'm using her. She'll be out of my life in a few days."

"Oh, I'm not worried." She gracefully glides beside me as we return indoors to the warm orangery. "I'm shocked. That little display of affection was rather... heart-melting." I step over a fallen potted plant, hunt out a napkin, and guide her through the carnage my brother and I created.

She stops beside the antique, hand carved liquor table with ugly claw feet, instinctively knowing I'll reach for the Waterford Irish Lace design tumblers that my grandfather, Don Hennessy, last sipped from when he visited a few years ago. He didn't feel the need to show up at the isolated plantation often when my mother rarely graced the hallways.

"That young girl did something none of us could ever do. Not even the highest paid psychiatrist. Perhaps it's you who should be worried, son."

I tug at the neck of my t-shirt, feeling claustrophobic by her inference, and irritated by the disorder around us. Either way, I need a large shot of Scotch and a tidy room to relax in. Nausea burns in my stomach and frustration stings in the form of regret.

Out of all my brothers, André and I are the closest. His twin, Giovanni, keeps to himself and Matheus will always be the younger brother I feel responsible for, like the father he never really had.

"I'll admit the girl has the ability to reach parts of me no one has ever found." I fill the duo of glasses halfway and serve her first. "But she's temporary."

"Oh?" She accepts the liquor with diamond-clad

fingers and waits for me to raise my glass to hers. "Salud, my dear boy."

"Salud, mama." I nod, tip my head, and swallow the whole measure.

"Temporary you say?" Her fluffy brow hitches as she sips with feminine decorum.

Filling my glass for the second time, I feel my chest tighten like an odd sensation of anger woven with sorrow.

"After we leave here, I'll pay the woman and drop her in the city where I found her. We have an agreement. I know her weaknesses and I'll use them against her if she snitches."

"So you're still going ahead with the wedding to the Mexican girl?" she asks, blinking up at me, her tone impossible to decipher.

"I guess so," I agree vaguely. "This way, we prevent an unnecessary war with our allies. Plus, I'd gain a better hold on the Morales cartel."

She hums to herself and walks away, her heeled slippers clipping the tiled floor. "Bianca Morales was raised with cartel beliefs and standards. She understands the importance of our family dynamics. That dainty little bird upstairs would find herself in a gilded cage for the rest of her days with a price on her head." Looking back at me, she narrows her eyes. "If anyone sees the effect she has on the heir to the Souza organization, to the new leader, she'd be an instant target. She'd become your real weakness, Tommy. Collateral damage." Her voice lowers with the accusation as if it pains her to point out the truth. "Bianca is the right choice for *you* in the long term."

I don't respond. Not out of disrespect for her observation. I just don't have the mental clarity to agree.

"What age is Carina?" she asks, her brow creased in thought.

"Nineteen."

"She's still a child." Mother sighs wistfully and toes a broken lamp out of her path. "A good-looking girl like her will land on her feet. She'll find herself a reliable man with a normal life."

My hackles rise. I think of Carina and how she considers being normal as the magic key to fit into society. How she feels like the deformed jigsaw piece to a beautiful puzzle. She's endured the world at its cruelest and still puts up a fight to survive.

The woman has been to Hell and wears the scars to prove it. Those big amber eyes of hers see right into my troubled mind and render me unworthy, no matter the status I hold.

Fuck normal.

And fuck the boring asshole who tries to tame her wild side.

As if reading my inner dialogue, mother's reasoning returns. "Or you could take her as a mistress? To the world, Bianca Morales would be your cartel worthy wife, and Carina would be your dirty little secret that no one could ever find out about."

I shoot her an unamused glare. "She deserves better than that."

She chuckles, her shiny black nails filed like talons press over her Irish heart. "I know, my love. I'm playing devil's advocate. She's not afraid of you. Either she's dangerously naïve

or she feels something... for you."

A shiver of dread freezes each vertebra in my spine. Maybe I feel something unnatural for her too. I get carried away in the moment when she's naked, on her knees, and spitting saliva from her mouth around my dick. My urges respond to her neediness with electric volts and hungry bites.

I understand why she's not scared of me, because she sees my flaws and I see hers. The darkness in me greets the darkness in her. Together, we become an eclipse.

When Carina's hungry for me, her fiery eyes flame with lust and curiosity uniquely combined. Her wild pulse always accelerates as her arousal switches up a notch when I'm controlling and uncivilized, balls deep in her tight pussy.

That fluttery, quick thrum of her life source transfuses an incredible power into me. I fucking love it more than the feel of any other woman on my dick.

My veins pump faster at the mental vision of bruised skin and a peachy ass ripe for feasting on. I turn my back to my mother to consume another drink and hide my dangerously hard dick. She doesn't need to see the perversion within me, nor does she need to know how I seek satisfaction from the woman she's trying to steer me away from.

"She's duty bound to obey me. Full stop." I add, hoping to end this pointless conversation. "Nothing more and nothing less."

"Forever the Souza." Mother pouts unstained lips, her usual muddy brown lipstick long removed before bedtime. "If that's the case, my darling boy, then make sure your little bird flies away before she's shot out of the sky." And there's the killer shot right there. The bullet of unconditional love and the pain of inevitable death. "Sometimes, Tommy, the path we're meant to walk isn't the one we lay for ourselves." She folds her arms and watches her words settle over me.

I don't do intimacy, and my mother knows that. Which is why I don't need to find sanctuary next to a woman at every opportunity.

Rather than join Carina in my bed tonight, I'll prepare for the funeral and take refuge in the guest wing. Laying with her, body to body, in a game of togetherness, isn't an option. She's employed to serve my whims, not tempt me at every turn.

I'm a dangerous man. Life with me would be apocalyptic for a good girl like her.

Blurred lines are now crystal clear. Her employment has begun.

35

TOMÁS

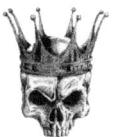

I spent the morning outdoors, jogging in the tangerine mist of a spectacular sunrise. afterward, I sat on the terrace by the gurgling water fountain and sipped a strong coffee.

I'm delaying the inevitable—facing Carina in the wake of my mother's warning.

My head knows this is a temporary situation between us. Yet I'm torn. For the first time, my gut is divided. Split right down the middle with an uncomfortable gap separating one outcome with the other. Make her mine or set her free. Get blood on my hands or settle in paralyzed peace.

When I finally enter my suite, it's a few minutes before midday. I don't see her straight away, which makes my stomach flip. I follow my feet past the ruffled sheets that tell me she'd slept in my bed. Lucky her. I had a shit night's sleep, even after I jerked off—twice. It was either that, or stalk back to this bed and suffocate her with my hungry dick. I drag a hand down my face and bite my finger at the vision that fantasy offers.

Near the walk-in wardrobe, she's huddled up on the corner couch, thighs tucked to her chest, and chin on her knees. Her gaze instantly finds my tired appearance. Rather than speak, she just stares at me with those big eyes the size of copper peso coins.

Her position exposes the curve of her ass where one of my t-shirts is caught up in wrinkles. Long, lean legs and soft flesh grip my attention for a beat too long.

"I thought you were staying here with me?" Her brow furrows ever so slightly. Waiting for my response, she bunches her hair in a fist and drags the sable lengths over her shoulder.

"You thought wrong," I say matter-of-factly, instantly feeling like an asshole.

"What changed?"

"Nothing." I shrug. "I didn't need your services." My ribs compress like they're trying to punish my thawing heart for being so frosty.

She nods once, as if understanding the arrangement. I ignore the strange look flash behind her eyes and stroll to the bathroom, rubbing the dull ache in my bare chest. With guests arriving soon and my father's pending burial, I'm tense and unsettled. I move to the toilet, take off my boxer briefs and start to piss before my shower.

Tingles sprinkle my scalp as if a force of nature is warning me of a torrential downpour. When I angle around, she's standing by the door, her gaze lingering on the dick in my hand, her sneaky tongue skating between rosy lips.

I'm screwed.

I take my time to finish, casually releasing my dick, and strolling to the faucet to wash my hands. Her tiny gasp lights a match and detonates trillions of ferocious chills. We both know I'm sporting another hard-on because of her.

Her exhale whispers through our electrified silence, the vibration of combined lust bouncing off the walls. She wants to fuck and so do I.

"I take it you're happy with the black dresses I picked out for you?" I ask, turning away from the vanity and sauntering into the open concept shower. Water gushes down on the mosaic tiles underfoot, hot and energetic like my volatile libido.

"They're fine," she says over the heavy waterfall noise.

"Fine?" I ask, looking back at her from the swirling steam. "You don't like the designers?"

"Were they influenced by the style of ninety-year-old nuns?" She keeps a straight face, arms folded over her chest like she means business.

For the first time in forever, I'm amused and horny at the same time. "I picked ones that would cover up your bruises." I trap my lower lip with my teeth when she crosses her thighs. "I'll speak with my mother. She'll have other options for you to wear tomorrow."

"What's happening tomorrow?" she fires back.

"A few important allies are flying in." No doubt Papá is cursing me from his brimstone throne. Outsiders aren't welcome here. Doing this is a show of faith to the men who've shown us loyalty. Once Papá is laid to rest, the plantation would be vacated. The rooms would echo, the floors would gather dust, and the manicured lawns would turn wild. Over time, this so-called family home would turn into a glorified mausoleum. "I'm officially taking charge and want to discuss my plans for the future. It's not really a party, more of a get together."

"Right…" Her gaze lingers on my stony dick.

I run my hand over the length of it. Aware I'm not only tormenting myself, but I'm playing with her too. My dick physically throbs, painfully straining to be inside her. "Now, if you don't mind, I'm going to finish my shower."

She inhales at the same time as I do, then brushes her fingertips through the lengths of her hair. I brought this woman here to serve me, yet right now all I can think of is worshiping her. Filling her so full of my cum that it trickles free while she watches Papá's funeral. The idea shouldn't turn me on as much as it does, but fuck, I'm seconds away from choking her with the stuff.

When she backs away, I move my head under the jets' welcoming warm water to sluice over my tired limbs. It feels good, but not half as revitalizing as her body plastered next to mine would be.

"Carina," I call after her. "Be a good girl today. If anyone asks who you are, tell them you're my personal assistant."

"Personal assistant?" The old guy with a smooth vulture-like head and thick wrinkles, chuckle-wheezes. "Is that what you call them these days?" My father's friend of twenty-odd years winks at Carina. It makes my skin crawl.

He keeps pace with us as we stroll over the sheltered walkway leading away from the main house. "Elias had many things, but never a peachy-assed *secretary*," Roberto scoffs, as if it's unheard of not to follow in my father's footsteps.

When we reach the outdoor location set up for Papá's send off, he taps the bronze tip of his walking stick on the dry boards underfoot to steady himself, unpockets a gold tin, pings it open, and picks out a fat, rolled Cuban cigar.

The way he's sizing her up has me close to stuffing the bound leaves down his throat, followed by his stick, and then my fist.

He secures the tip between his front teeth and sucks in a few times to help the end of his cigar catch fire from the Zippo.

"Very nice," he purrs like the dirty old bastard he is, puffing smoke around us.

His reptilian eyes roam the curve of her breasts hidden in the flouncy black material I know she hates. I sense her revulsion at his inspection, even when her naturally colored lips curl politely, playing the role perfectly.

It's not the slight shiver prickling her skin from being outdoors, it's the way she unintentionally moves closer into me. There's a secret undercurrent of chemistry between us, controlling my senses and tuning them to the same frequency as hers. It's a visceral bond that's proving difficult to ruin.

"I'm sure she enjoys being worked hard?" Roberto smiles darkly, his suggestion cutting too close to my bones.

My temper snarls beneath the three-piece charcoal suit I'm wearing. I imagine how he'd react to having his eyeballs torched, one followed by the other, and subconsciously slide my hand to the small of her back so she's nestled snugly to my hip.

"I'm not my father, Roberto." I pat his shoulder with the other hand, firm and assertive. "Don't forget, we own legitimate businesses too. Those require full time management while I focus on finding Papá's killer." Roberto swipes a glass of whiskey from the silver tray a waiter presents to him. "It means I can bring in more money to fund your special projects."

The greedy fucker hums out his approval. "Perhaps, if you're smart enough to find and slaughter the men responsible, you'll do me the courtesy of loaning out your assistant for a few weeks?" His gaze drinks her in as he swills the alcohol. "She's exquisitely intriguing."

I hate how he's baiting me. That beneath my usual cold exterior, I'm reacting to it. My guts are twisted to painful knots and my veins boil with rage. It would be easy to reach for my gun and systematically shoot each of his vital organs.

However, he never crosses a threshold without his own security detail. He's like family, an annoying old cunt who only shows up at weddings and funerals, and has his nose in everyone's business. Plus, I can't be bothered with a messy shootout moments before the ceremony.

Nor can I keep killing people in my circle all because this woman is under my skin. It won't be long before the charade is over.

This wrinkly bastard doesn't need to point out how gorgeous she is. Her youth alone is a desirable quality, and the celestial way her body moves when she's under my control is extraordinary. I know she's an expensive commodity, because I own her. Me. Not this old fuck.

Her sweet voice penetrates the murder I've just committed in broad daylight, in my mind.

"Unfortunately not." She returns with refinement. "I'm extremely busy with Tomás' projects. He's quite the slave driver," she quips.

Roberto laughs from deep in his belly and tips his tumbler in appreciation. "Let me know if he ever releases your shackles, my dear."

My jaw ticks as my teeth clench. "Take a seat, Roberto. The ceremony is about to start," I say with forced control. "It's time to say goodbye to the old and make way for the new."

The low-lying mist topping undulating lush hills has long receded. An earthy breeze carries murmurs from the few seated guests we invited. They congregate in rows before the gold-plated casket on a wheeled trolley, protected from drizzle under a cream marquee adorned with garlands of vermillion roses.

Roberto shakes my hand. "It's a sad day. You've big shoes to fill. Don't let him down." His lewd gaze slides to Carina for the last time before he shuffles to the seating area.

When he's out of earshot, I deliberately let go of her. "Stay away from him. He's bad news."

Her head whips around, bringing soft hair close to my nostrils. The subtle floral scent of the body wash I'd arranged for her wafts with the ticklish strands. That feminine smell lacing her skin has my engine growling to life.

We're surrounded by dense rainforest and abundant coffee fields. If I wasn't up first with the speeches, I'd drag her into the undergrowth and cut the dress right off her. I know she's wearing a black lace bra underneath, because I watched her dress while I forced my hands to stay pocketed. So far, my plan to show her who's in control is slowly falling apart.

"Really?" she snips, her tone dripping with sarcasm. "I hadn't noticed. I was hoping you'd loan me to him for a whole afternoon. What fun that would be! I'm sure he has plenty of expertise, given his old age." She fingers the tips of her hair while looking to the sky.

I'm livid, seething with a powerful force of jealousy. How dare she even joke about being with that fucker for even a second? I know she doesn't mean it. What woman in their right mind would go near a decrepit cunt like him? It doesn't matter, possessiveness slithers through me with minuscule grappling hooks that burrow into my organs, muscles, and bone.

Her lips pull in, guilt for her outburst painting her cheeks pink. "However, I agreed to your terms. So, I'm yours for now."

I cock my head. "Mine?"

"Your employee." She corrects.

"Exactly." Cuffing her wrist, I drag her off the walkway, where we slip behind the thick trunk of an ancient Colombian oak tree with wavy-edged leaves.

She gasps when I yank her into my chest so we're suffocatingly close and secretly stuff her hand against the erection straining behind my zipper. I hear her swallow as my lips descend to the shell of her ear.

"Don't joke about being with another man," I hiss, for her ears only. "I jerked myself off thinking about you last night." My voice is thick with frustration. "Stroke after stroke, I throttled my dick, while I imagined your bouncy tits and your tight little hole sucking me in."

I've often played out fantasies in my mind and then turned them into reality, however nothing could have prepared me for the horny thoughts I had of Carina. They made me come so hard that my muscles ached afterward.

"Want to know why I didn't sleep in the same bed as you?" Her chest lifts as her fingertips graze my lapels for support. "Because your mouth has become a dangerous addiction. It sickens me to want to fuck it so much." The small gasp of air she sips steals a piece of my self-control. "I think about it every second of the day, in ways I shouldn't. Not to mention how striking you looked with my blood on your skin and how it didn't faze you to ride my dick while you were covered in it." I repress a groan when my voice lowers to a seething growl. "Even now, minutes before I say goodbye to my father, I'm thinking of fucking you in the wild."

Sucking in a shallow breath, she leans backward, her gaze snaring mine. "Well, I had a wonderful sleep last night. I stretched out like a starfish. The mattress was comfy, the sheets were so soft, and the pillows were just right." Even though she smiles sweetly, I watch the vein in her neck pump faster. "The sooner you bury him, the faster this nightmare is all over for the both of us."

I release her like I've snipped the anchor to my prized speedboat. In a whirlwind of sable hair and angry footsteps, she hurries back onto the sheltered planks, weaves through the last guests still standing and sits in the back row. I could order her to move to the front beside my allocated seat next to my mother, and risk highlighting to the fake friends and long distance family members in attendance that she's significant, or I can let her stew.

Slowly repositioning my painful dick, I thumb my cufflinks and check the knot in my tie is neatly displayed. When I'm content, my suit is immaculately presented, I signal to a nearby guard to watch her.

I skirt the rows to join my brothers by the casket, kiss my mother on the cheek, and take my position as the head of the family.

After each of us vocalizes our sentiments, my brothers and I collect the machine guns waiting upright on stands. We line up along the length of his coffin, keeping our backs to the crowd. After the count of three, we take aim at the clouds and fire. Bullets spew out at the sprawling horizon, pummeling the peacefulness to signify the finality of our father's reign.

Souzas live by the bullet and we die by the bullet. That's who we are.

We're the men mothers warn their virginal daughters about. Criminals who rule the underworld. Crooked billionaires who walk with legal professionals and federal agents. Killers who terminate when necessary.

Emptying every last cartridge, we drape the guns over our shoulders, and each take a corner of the wheeled trolley. Together, we maneuver the gemstone encrusted coffin to the yawning mouth of a man-made path. Flaming tiki torches fringe both sides like a runway, illuminating the darkness where bushy foliage and low-hanging branches create a natural arched tunnel.

"Finally." André smirks when we leave the mourners behind. "Did Papá arrange for crates of booze in his tomb? You know, to sit beside the arsenal of weapons he'll never use."

I shrug, doing my best to steer the fucking thing while André removes his hands to light a cigarette. "Hurry the fuck up, Dré, or he'll end up rolling off the boards."

"Fuck him," Gio pipes up from the rear. "He was always rolling off the boards. Doing his own crazy shit."

"Christ, Gio. Not today. At least wheel him into the tomb first." Matheus groans. "He wasn't the stereotypical father, but look at the lives we have. We at least owe the guy an honorable send off."

"I owe him fuck all," Gio bites back.

André glances over his shoulder, his face dancing with flickering shadows. "You need to get fucked up today, brother. That'll help with all that pent up tension." He chuckles. "The guy's dead. You're free of him. We all are. Now you have to take orders from this asshole, right here." He winks at me, ash tumbling when he jabs his two fingers in my direction. "I have a feeling things will be different from now on."

"Hey... Tommy." Matheus prods my shoulder blade. "Who's the woman who cracked your glitch? I heard you were going to fuck her in front of Dré until mama interrupted the show."

Fuck...

36

CARINA

I pick an ivory covered seat at the farthest corner of the marquee, next to yo-yoing ferns and an older lady who stinks of flowery perfume. It stings my eyes and sticks in my throat.

Rainbow kissed parrots take position in the towering treetops. A sweetened breeze carrying an earthiness of the nearby jungle and a far off rumble of hungry predators reminds me of the danger I'm in.

For the short space of time I've been with Tomás, I'm almost certain he wouldn't kill me, and if he did, then my instincts would be the real traitors. As for the sea of heads that bob before me, any of them could turn a gun on me. That, I fully understand.

Tomás faces the assembled crowd, standing next to a jumbo portrait of his father, surrounded by a landscape of never-ending hills, and far-reaching gray sky. My stomach flips at the sight of him. He is the epitome of dark and dangerous, his soul dripping in sin.

Standing straight with broad shoulders drawn back,

his posture depicts the stature of a man who knows no boundaries. I stare at him without shame. How could I not?

The guy lures me into his cocoon, wraps me in silk, and gives me colorful wings to fly. Just thinking about his teeth latching onto my nipples is enough to make me squirm in a puddle of desire.

Behind the expensive three-piece suit, a flawless body waits to be worshiped. Tanned skin and hard muscles, curves and dips where my tongue freely explored.

He tortured me with his restraint and gave me a glimpse into his disturbing fantasies. Oddly, now I know what makes his pulse skip and it doesn't repel me, not when his husky commands whisper through me with out of control shivers.

I sit here, not feeling any emotion for the dearly departed other than utter relief. Apparently, I'm not the only savage with a heart carved from ice. When I scan the unknown guests, not a single tear is counted.

Tomás kisses his mother below her oversized sunglasses and opens the ceremony with a speech about Elias' passion and drive to succeed. No heartfelt, fond stories about the father who raised him, or cherished memories of a doting parent who quite literally gave him the world.

When he finishes, three similar looking men take the stage in turn. Men who I now know to be his brothers.

I recognize André with his rebellious hairstyle and unshaven face. Where his brothers fill well-cut suits, he wears slim slacks and a tight black shirt; the sleeves rolled to the elbows to reveal inked skin and black leather bracelets. He speaks of a father who demanded the best from his sons, followed by a casually raised tumbler filled with amber liquid and a simple toast stating Elias would finally rest in peace.

The following guy to his right is introduced as Giovanni. He's neater in appearance, his cultured baritone smooth with the right amount of grit. Remarkable green eyes stand out, a contrast to the darkness I've seen in his brother's gaze. Giovanni is more lean than muscular, yet he fills out his charcoal suit as if it was sewn by a goddess for her secret lover.

Out of all the brothers, Giovanni and André look almost identical, from their sharp noses to the shape of their mouths. But their personalities seem to be miles apart.

The final brother, Matheus, doesn't say too much either. His accent is refined and the flash of a cheeky dimple incredibly sexy. I get the feeling he's the youngest, even though he matches them in height and dominant stature. That his life had been more sheltered than the others. And maybe he's not a cold-blooded murderer —yet.

Had I gone to college and met Matheus Souza on campus, perhaps I'd be lured by his well-groomed charm —until he would introduce me to his eldest brother. Then, without falter, I'd drop everything for Tomás.

There's no denying it. Fate created Tomás Souza from the darkest vault in my mind, molding his entity from glorious flesh and strong bone, giving him veins of liquid nitrogen, and a heart of stone. He speaks of violence and carries a gun wherever he goes. Yet those large hands offer me sexual nirvana. His voice guides the way and his lips—they offer an escape.

This sickly sensation isn't just a girl craving her first forbidden crush. It's a molecular fascination. None of those other men spark wild flutters within me like Tomás does. Especially when his serious gaze spears me in place from across the marquee.

Long ebony lashes frame laser focused eyes. They purposefully hold me hostage during every word spoken, and when he stands in silence, his jaw clenches as if he's fighting unruly urges, too.

After Elias' sons rip up the serenity of his abundant estate with a barrage of bullets, Tomás and his brothers wheel the grossly ornate casket into a creepy natural tunnel shrouded by shape shifting shadows, hedged by thick foliage, and lit by flaming torches.

Once they disappear from sight, we're ushered inside the main house. Now I'm standing in a grand room where a full roasted pig sits in pride of place on a garnished platter. Trays teeming with petite caviar canapes are carried by well-presented serving staff.

The decor is cream and gold with four glitzy pendant chandeliers sprinkling rainbow shards over mingling guests, each of them oblivious to my predicament. How my silly heart beats faster for the monster they would soon crown king of their underworld.

Leafy plants sprout from tall planters, and champagne flutes are continuously refilled. An undercurrent of laughter echoes around the room where sadness should live.

When I walk to find the decadent Italian styled washroom, a man wearing an electronic earpiece is waiting outside the door when I reappear. I would find it daunting if there weren't smartly dressed clones, just like him, dotted throughout the mansion.

"Hey, kid," a familiar Irish accent skims over the haunting melody of a solo pianist, each note drifting to the high ceiling. "Glad to see you're staying out of trouble." Shane strolls to my side, his whiskey glass filled with a healthy measure.

"Trouble." I side eye him. "I'm bored stiff."

"I hate these fucking things too." He sips from his glass, gulps, and sucks air in through clenched teeth. "The sooner I get Tommy back to the city, the sooner we can put that bastard behind us."

I cock a brow at his statement. "You didn't like Elias?"

Shane's shoulders bounce in a noncommittal shrug. "You can't pick your relatives, right?" His voice rumbles under the music. "There's a long line of people who'd want him dead. Most of these fuckers in here are celebrating, not mourning. But the asshole was still family and whoever pulled the trigger will die a slow, painful, gruesome, nasty—" A pretty servant catches his eye, abruptly stopping his detailed description mid-flow. When he winks, her face heats hotter than the sun. "That, right there, is the only good thing about these gatherings." He chuckles to himself.

"Don't you have a girlfriend waiting for you back in the city?" Aside from his facial scarring, the guy has good looks in a roguish, masculine way. Like a bare-knuckled, no rules in the ring fighter or a motorcycle gang member. "No special someone?"

He narrows his eyes at me and then his head shakes side to side. "Guys like me don't hold on to the idea of forever, kid. In this job, women are a threat and a distraction. We don't get close for a reason."

The second I go to speak, a flurry of semi-quivers dwindle, animated chatter quickly fades, and all eyes turn to the doorway. My heart skips too many beats. Tomás leads his three brothers into the lavish room, his complexion cast in shadow, his shoes clipping the solid floor.

With a ragged sigh, I fumble the loose sable strands hanging over my breasts and slide an arm across my midriff. It's pathetic how I react to the sight of him. To the man who thinks he owns me.

Teresa appears from the parted crowd wearing a simple form fitting dress the color of midnight. She struts toward the four men and stops before Tomás. Her arm curls around his elbow, she tilts in her high heels, and pecks his peppered jaw.

"It's done." He nods.

"Thank you. And his ring? Did you ever find it?" The second she references the ring I stole, my belly flips like it's thrown from a jet plane without a parachute.

Tomás shakes his head. "It's gone, Mama."

'Very well." Teresa unhooks her arm and moves to Giovanni, hugging him close.

As she offers her sons condolences for the loss of their father, Tomás' eyes scan the room until the hunter finds his prey. Our eyes lock—solemn ebony to awestruck amber.

My knees wobble when his mouth twitches to a faint

smile. Somehow that barely noticeable quirk reaches inside me, its unintentional warmth heating me through like sun-drenched sand beneath my feet on a secret island.

The blacks of his calculating eyes mimic the depths of his suit, his diamond ear studs glinting as they bathe in fragments of light from above his head. I cross my arms and flex my toes into the expensive shiny kitten heel shoes he'd bought me.

He looks me up and down before tearing his striking gaze away to locate Shane and the security guy close by. Shane tips the crystal tumbler in his direction and takes a respectful sip.

Tomás, the man who has everyone's attention, turns away, his demeanor self-assured and his emotionless expression discharging undeniable power. There's no hint of weakness. No exposed soft flesh for the enemy to sink a blade into.

Guests move out of his way without question, the slickness of his tarnished aura warning them of his new authority.

I don't want to crave this man.

I shouldn't.

A wiser woman would take the opportunity to hide as a stowaway in a waiting helicopter. She wouldn't replay the pleasure found in the arms of a cartel king. She'd spend her time thinking how he'd make her future hell. Then she'd try to get past the subtle guards who pop up everywhere only to earn a bullet to the back of the head for daring to abscond.

My eyes slip over his movements. How he gathers a plate and selects a wedge of blush watermelon, speared chunks of pineapple, dainty *empanadas,* and a large spoonful of golden rice. He gathers a napkin and a fork, spins on his heels and makes a beeline straight for me.

He ignores the busty woman with false lashes and a plunging neckline, vying for his attention. His determined gait eats up the space separating us until he stops within touching distance. Toe to toe.

"Have you eaten?" he asks, eyeing the almost empty glass in my hand.

"Not yet," I confess. "I'll get something when I'm hungry."

He scowls down at me. "You'll eat now."

My stomach coils with hunger for nourishment and this man's masculinity. Nonetheless, he doesn't get to tell me what to do.

"I'll have something later," I say quietly, aware of his mother's eyes burning holes in our unusual pairing.

He doesn't look away from me, the plate held in place by my belly. "This is for you." His eyes narrow. "Please, eat."

My heart races at the thought of how he's considerate enough to think of me first, before feeding himself. And how it makes my skin tingle. What I hate most of all is that I want to accept it—to obey him.

Ignoring the growl in my gut, I lift the glass to my lips. "Maybe later." My shoulders bounce as I sip, feigning nonchalance.

He lets a heavy sigh free from his lungs, the sweet scent of alcohol lacing his breath. "I'm not in the mood to argue. Eat now or I'll take you upstairs and insert this pineapple inside your tight little cunt instead." His lips tug into a sinister smile.

I almost choke on the liquid bubbling down my throat when he plucks the skewer and snares a cube of pineapple between his polished teeth. He chews slowly, dropping his gaze to my chest where he deliberately peels off my dress with his eyes.

"It's missing something," he hums, pretending to think. "A certain unforgettable female essence."

I try to hide my shiver. "That's disgusting."

Tomás laughs, low and deep, the rich sound like a hooking melody. "I disagree. Have you tasted yourself? You're fucking delicious." Behind us, the pianist strikes a few keys and a soft murmur turns rowdy when a cork pops. "I know I thoroughly enjoy it."

My heart skitters. His gaze lingers on my face, the rare hitch to his lips playful. The shadow hungry girl inside of me hits a thousand shades of shyness whereas the attention seeking woman I've become pretends to fight the attraction.

Dipping into the side of my face, his nose brushes the shell of my ear, his voice siphoning into me, intoxicating with a powerful potion. "Remember the terms you agreed to. I'm only asking you to eat, Carina. It's going to be a long day and I want you energized for later. So please... do yourself a favor and eat something."

His manly cologne wafts up my nostrils and pollutes my mouth. The aroma, it's unjustly sexual. So clean and crisp, like the suit he wears. This guy just buried his father and on this unusual day, he's more concerned with fueling my energy levels for his dirty fantasies rather than mourn.

"Fine." I roll my eyes to stir up an illusion of indifference. He doesn't deserve to know how my insides are jittery and my clit is throbbing.

Quickly pinching a watermelon chunk, I sink my teeth into the watery flesh and start to chew. "There…" I slurp the juice it makes. "I'm eating."

A trickle rolls down my chin as I mumble. Before I get the chance to mop it up, his thumb is there, catching it with a slow sweep. I freeze when he sucks it into his mouth. The halo of darkness around his pupils blends into one everlasting whirlpool of chaos. "Good girl," his voice slips from regal to predatory. "I like watching your mouth work."

"Ummm, it's so good," I mock delight with a long drawn out hum and slip my finger between my lips. "So juicy."

He looks me up and down while he dents his bottom lip between his teeth. "Are you teasing me?"

"Teasing you? With watermelon? I'm far too innocent to think that would work." I grin up at him and bat my lashes.

He chuckles. It's a horny sort of rumble woven with a promise of punishment. I nibble the tip of my finger and hold his stare. Looking into eyes that drip with sex like a hive bursting with honey. And that right there is the toxicity to ruin my sweetness. It's the purest form of fuck me harder in one sinful glance.

I'm practically sweating when the creepy guy from earlier loudly taps his walking stick on the floorboards beside us, announcing his presence.

Tomás bristles, his mood switching to fire and brimstone

"Where's Hennessy?" Roberto's voice slithers into the atmosphere like a dying snake. He taps his bronze tipped cane again as if it's a habit. Tomás sighs heavily when Roberto continues to speak. "I expected to see your grandfather today. Surely the Boston mafia should attend a family funeral or send a man to represent them."

My eyebrows fly up. *I'd forgotten about his mafia bloodline.* I swallow the watermelon pulp with a noisy gulp. Tomás' eyes leave mine like a lightning strike. "They're in Ireland," he bites out, clearly unamused by this man's topic of conversation, or his untimely interruption. "Mama represents the Hennessy side of the family."

Tomás runs a hand over his mouth, returning his gaze to me. "Please finish your food, Carina." He orders coolly, grabs my hand, and sets the plate in my open palm. His tight expression falters, hinting a layer of kindness beneath his rigid composure. "Stay here. I'll be back in a minute." With a curt nod, he pivots and ushers the old man into the crowd with a sweeping gesture that herds the wolf away from me.

I stare at the tiny grains of rice and then look to my left where Shane had last stood. I'm all alone. Even the guard has wandered off.

Watching the guests respectfully part for Tomás' exit, my knees lock to stop myself from swaying. The way he confidently strolls out of the room has my heart rate soaring. They all study his impeccable persona and self-assured gait, just like I do. Each of them wondering what his next move would be. Except they aren't second guessing what he'll do with his dick later.

When he disappears, intrigue gets the better of me.

There's more to this family. More to Tomás Souza. So, I set the plate on a side table and race out of the room to follow him.

37

CARINA

I mosey along the same corridor Tomás just walked, finding myself at the main entrance hall. The hairs on my arms spike, because the first time Tomás led me over these polished marble tiles, I hated him.

Taking shelter behind a monolithic pillar, I wait until two suited men saunter past. The last thing I need is two assholes thinking I'm sneaking around. Technically, I am, but not with intent to cause harm. I want to figure out who the man I'm fascinated with really is.

There's a selection of corridors leading off the airy foyer like octopus tentacles. Looking up the impressive staircase with a snaking gold leaf railing, I check there's no one about. I'm not sure which way to go, so I choose the closest route, noticing the clip of my heels dull when I move onto an oversized floor covering.

A pitiful female whimper catches my attention. The throaty growl that precedes it lures me to a wood door, slightly ajar. That deep sexy tone sounds too familiar. My heart rate accelerates, stupidly scared I'd find Tomás with another woman.

I hold my breath and nudge the door handle to peek inside. Lacquered high rise bookcases line every wall, dominating the central couches of an unexpected library.

By the window, sprawled on an antique desk, lies a beautiful naked blonde. Long legs drape around a man's shirtless shoulders, his scruff buried between her thighs. Lost in the sensation of his mouth on her clit, she squeezes her plentiful breasts, that are considerably bigger than mine, and arches her spine. On the floor by the desk are her strewn clothes. Garments matching the servant's uniform.

Stunned by the insanely hot scene, I press my hand over my heart with stupid relief. Those inked muscles don't belong to Tomás. It's his brother, André.

My veins catch fire with voyeuristic intrigue. I shouldn't spy on them, yet something wickedly naughty reaches my bones and locks me in place. The woman mewls and gyrates with an air of experience and greed.

She's everything I'm not. Flawless and fair skinned, with golden hair and a face full of makeup. If I watch how she responds to him, perhaps I could learn a thing or two.

With wood shielding my vantage point, one eye stays hidden and the other drinks in the roughness he dishes out. There are quick slaps to each breast. A choking hand to her delicate throat. Assertive control of forcefully alternating positions. It's devilishly debauched and mind-blowing. I'm bewitched by it all. Every spank and grunt, it tingles in a rush from my scalp to my swollen clit.

I swallow hard and gasp for a lungful of oxygen in the

hope it will snuff out the bubbling fascination pulling me in like a riptide.

I'm entranced by André's aura of confidence. That similar show of dominance his elder brother exudes in abundance. Rather than feed off their arousal, I'm feasting off my own imagination and my own fantasies.

There's an elastic cord attached to my innermost desires. It tugs me back to Tomás every time I try to get away. He's my terrifying obsession. The man I should despise, but can't get enough of.

My fingers curl around the edge of the door for support. André's exquisite, tattooed form comes to life under the half-light as his prey writhes under his control. It's visually stimulating and deeply erotic to know they're oblivious to me creeping in the shadows.

I'm aching to touch myself as he lifts his face and unbuckles his belt. When he leisurely lowers his trousers to his knees, my belly swoops.

Something scandalous has awoken inside me. Tomás has unleashed a hidden element within me that I never knew existed. And now that festering black lust is out of control.

André plunges his dick into the hungry woman. She cries out. My lungs expand and contract in quick succession. I'm lost in the moment when a familiar voice growls close to my ear from behind, the seriousness to his tone chilling. "You want my brother to fuck you like that?"

My mouth dries. I instantly spin on my heels to meet a wall of solid muscle, unbelievably tense behind Tomás' immaculately pressed shirt. He stares at the crimson sweep of wanton coloring my neck.

"No." It's not a lie.

He cocks an eyebrow. "Then why are you watching him fuck?"

I narrow my eyes at him, furious at myself for being so turned on. "I—I was... I thought it was you... with someone else."

His eyes flash with a barrage of unspoken words. My skin catches fire. "Interesting." He takes a beat before speaking again. "Dré and I look nothing alike when we're naked. Yet, you continued to watch."

Slowly, with perfect control, he thumbs his mouth so the bottom lip lowers as those coal colored eyes of his drill into my face. My knees go weak. This is bad. I sense his demonic mood slither over my scalp like a grass snake following the tune of the piper. There's something about the slow drag of his gaze, how it flows with both danger and heat. It's terrifying and a turn on.

Unfurling sweaty fists, I roll back my shoulders and smooth my palms over my hips to wipe away the slight moisture. "There's no harm in watching them. You can't control everything I do."

His pupils darken, a starless vortex with a magnetic pull. "It seems to me like we've created a pretty little monster with a hunger for dicks."

Before I can argue, he twirls me around and kicks the door open. In a flash, he snares my jaw and forces my attention to the intimate show. An arm circles my waist and traps both of my arms by my hips. Once he's content I'm secured tightly against his chest, I'm frog-marched into the room, aware of his hard-on prodding the base of my spine.

I'm imprisoned in his merciless embrace, my neck straining against my forced gaze. The fixed palm squeezing my jaw is unshakable.

"The only dick you need to satisfy you is mine." His sexy, hot breath warms my ear.

André is now aware of our intrusion, clearly unaffected as he continues to screw without shame or care.

For a split second, he strips his eyes away from the woman, and rather than complain, he laughs. A dark villainous rumble that raises the temperature. His lips curl into a savage grin and his large hand cracks her bare flesh.

The willing young victim stabs her long nails into his shoulders, mingling streaks of red with inked flesh. She loves his violence. It's not just me who craves the dark side of the moon. We're all damned.

Tomás' mouth pauses at my ear, his breathing heavy. "I can feel your heart racing, *little liar*. I give you permission to watch, to enjoy, to learn... but do not get yourself off."

André pulls his sheathed dick out and manhandles the blonde so she's spread out, breasts down. He hooks his forearm under her pelvis to tilt her hips upward.

Once he's inside her again, he arches over her spine, sinks his ringed fingers into her platinum hair and yanks her into his taut chest. I hear her quick intake of air at the same time as Tomás' lips graze the shell of my ear. I almost convulse at the sensation of his hot breath.

"Watch them, *little liar*. Watch my brother fuck her while I touch you."

My core clenches and each limb liquifies. I crave this man's rough touch, that masterful authority he's shown me multiple times. The hand on my belly glides to the hem of my dress. With the back of my head firm against his shoulder, I've nowhere to look other than at his roguish brother. Controlling fingers slip beneath the black fabric, quickly finding me wet. Teeth nip my earlobe and I tremble.

My pulse jumps so violently that my vision blurs temporarily. With his fingers discreetly hidden under the dress he bought me, Tomás rubs my sensitive nub of nerves. I stifle a whimper by drawing my lips in. But when he dips a finger inside of me, I maneuver my pelvis to deepen the delicious plunder.

This scenario shouldn't turn me on so much, but it does. I'm riddled with hazardous goosebumps, aching to roll into him and hunt his mouth with mine. I could stay with him from dusk to dawn, days to weeks, and still I'd crave his touch. That's how desperately I've toppled off course.

"You're so fucking wet," he growls.

André glances over at us, his rebellious smile so seductive, so raw—so deadly. In that second, my insides prepare to convulse. Just as I rise, the wicked pressure coaxing me to the fiery pit of Hell abruptly leaves. Tomás turns me into him, our chests colliding.

"Your orgasms are mine. Every single one of them. When you fall apart, it will be my face you see. Only mine. Understand?"

I nod. The gravity of this entanglement suddenly hits me. Since I was a young girl hiding in my bedroom and suffocating in the safety of isolation, I wished for a different life. For adventure. For acceptance.

What I didn't realize was how I'd find it in darkness,

danger, and lustful thrills—in *him*. That tortured little girl never expected a ruthless cartel king could stitch her broken soul together, piece by piece, or that he'd activate a sexual woman with untamed urges.

But this isn't real. It's only a temporary arrangement void of forever. For the next couple of days, I belong to him and then he'll cast me adrift in a world that's shown me no kindness.

I stare up at him, my cheeks ablaze and a fast pulse thrumming in my neck. There's only one way this would go tonight. Pleasure threaded with pain.

Midnight colored pupils flare as his hand swathes my throat to angle my mouth higher.

"It's time to go," he commands, low and sexy. "I'll give you exactly what you need in private."

My stomach roils with anticipation when he roughly cuffs my wrist and trails me behind him as we exit the room.

Neither of us speaks. Adrenaline courses through me, matching him step for step. His serious expression meets mine when he glances over his shoulder at the top of the staircase. The right corner of his mouth hitches ever so slightly, just enough to dent his cheek. There's something in that one look he offers that holds so many secrets. His determined, confident strides give me chills.

Tomás hurries me into his suite and slams the door shut. A swirl of flutters crash against my ribs when he rakes his fingers through the hair on top of his head and licks his lips. This man's looks are lethal.

"You can watch my brothers fuck all the women in Colombia if that gets you off, but when you orgasm, it's my eyes you'll look into and my dick..." He seizes my hands, forcing them to the zipper of his expensive slacks and bites his bottom lip.

Beneath the funeral attire, he's rock hard. Tomás Souza's physique is equally as intimidating as his persona. "This is the only dick that will own your senses while we're together."

"Tomás..." I say his name on a telltale whisper, my mind flitting with thoughts of survival and sexual corruption.

His face is impassive when he pushes me past the bed toward the walk-in closet. He lets go of me, draws open the double doors and storms aside.

"In." The order snaps out like the crack of a whip. "No one will hear you scream in here." There's an edge to his tone that makes me obey. A sweet vibration of lust and supremacy.

When we're both inside the long room flanked with meticulously hung clothes and mirrors, he shuts the doors and turns into me.

Slowly, purposefully, he shrugs off his suit jacket and drapes it over a pintuck footstool the size of a single bed. Those dark eyes of his arrest me as he unfastens his diamond cufflinks and removes his shirt. I watch him undress, aware of how his naked torso makes my breathing irregular.

Silky smooth skin is carved into firm muscles earned from strict self-discipline. Impossibly glorious and god-like. I've seen it before, but not like this, not knowing I belong to him. That my sole purpose for the next number of hours is to satisfy whatever sordid demands he asks of me.

A shiver runs through me, fierce and terrifying. I've always been fucked up, but surrendering to this hysteria reveals how far I'm willing to drop into the lion's den.

He stands before me, lit only by the glow of strip lighting beneath the cabinets. Shadows dance over his face when he moves, eating up the space between us as I quickly back away. "There's nowhere to run to, *little liar*."

My ass hits the surface of a floor to ceiling mirror spanning a quarter of the wall. I've nowhere to go, other than a parallel world where our reflections exist beyond this room. A world where he doesn't see me as dispensable.

"Turn around."

Flutters rampage in my chest as I do a one-eighty and face myself. Neatly tamed locks pour over my shoulders, framing the face of an innocent young woman who's landed in the underworld with a demon.

Tomás moves behind me, studying the vision of us, the reflection of me and him in his domain. He lowers to his haunches and unclips the small knife hidden beneath his pant leg. I gasp, unsure of what he plans to do with it. The silver blade glints as it glides through the air and drops to the seam by my ribs. One at a time, he cuts through the thread without effort.

A tremor whispers over me like clouds passing overhead on a sunny day, briefly blocking the sun. For a moment, he pauses, watching me quietly. A heavy palm settles on my opposite hip as he tugs at the stitches like he's gutting a fresh carcass.

The sound of thread snapping matches the snap of my quick pulse. Once there's enough of a tear to satisfy him, his teeth clamp down on the handle of his pocketknife and he yanks my dress with so much energy it disintegrates into a puddle of torn fabric at our feet.

I watch his eyes flash in the reflective surface. He releases the knife handle and tosses it to the floor with the same detachment that he'd offer me when our extraordinary arrangement is over.

In a blur, he fists my hair at the nape and shoves the side of my face against the mirror, crowding me from behind. "You like watching people fuck?" His voice is thick, almost tattered with the growl biting at my ear.

My hands fly up to support myself, slamming on cold tempered glass. I don't respond, shaking from within when he laughs darkly.

"You'll watch yourself getting fucked by me now." He controls my head by tilting it, so my lips meet their own reflection. "Lick your reflection. Let me see you enjoy it." Tentatively, the tip of my tongue peeks out of my mouth. He angles me a fraction more to allow a little space. "Lick," he murmurs. I flatten my tongue and drag it over the mirror, connecting reality with a vision. "Do you see how pretty your mouth is? How perfect it is for me."

My skin chills with his words of praise. The recognition of my damaged mouth being something of value to him sets alight a tempest of emotions.

His face dips into mine. Our tongues mingle with flirtatious licks. It's not a kiss, far from it. Our lips don't meet and the second I try to go deeper, he breaks away.

His hand snakes under my pelvis and hitches my ass

into his groin. At the same time, he steps back, bringing my hips with him. I fold over, face forward, eyes to my naked reflection. With my palms pressed shoulder distance apart, he keeps his fingers woven in the lengths of my hair and secures me before the mirror that will reveal everything.

"Do you want my cock?" he hisses. I suck in sharply when his other hand skates over my buttocks and slips lower. "Were you hoping André would fuck you, too?"

When I try to twist around to answer him, the grip in my hair becomes unshakeable. "No," I snap with frustration.

"You're not fooling anyone, *little liar*." The echoes of his baritone quiver to my core, welcoming a savage thirst to kiss him like he's the only drop of water in a ruthless desert.

He doesn't permit me to budge from this position. Instead, he hunches over me and glides his tongue between my shoulder blades. There's a moment of silence, like we're underwater and lost in the ocean's quietness.

"I'm going to punish you for wanting another man while I own this body."

"No!" The word rushes out like a burst dam. "That's not what I was thinking at all."

"Liar," he grits out.

"You know I don't want André."

"Who do you want?"

"You."

All contact wanes. "Then be a good girl and don't move, or I'll spank you so hard you'll wish my brother was here to save you."

My legs start to shake when he unbuckles his belt. I study his stern expression projected before me, with a glimmer of something unknown flickering in his eyes. It's not malice or cruelty, more like excitement tainted with jealousy.

"Wait…" I pant, my knees wobbling when the leather is freed from his waist.

"Fight against me and I'll deny you pleasure."

He quickly unzips his trousers and drags them to ankles with his boxer briefs in hot pursuit. Looping the belt, he holds it one hand and saunters closer, his destructive cock nudging my bottom.

The fierce crack lands before I have time to prepare for its arrival. A swift strike cuts across my buttocks with searing pain, sharper than the edge of a flaming sword fresh from a blacksmith's forge fire. I cry out, my forehead butting the mirror when I jolt.

"Whose dick owns your pussy?" Tomás bites out.

Belts and force may harm my skin. Bruises may haunt me for weeks. But the thrill of an inflicted sting with the promise of pleasure to come—it's depraved and wrong—unbalancing and a major turn on.

"Yours…" I manage to whimper.

My sweaty fingertips slip down the hard surface, squeaking against the glass when another lashing is administered.

"Good girl." A third follows, weaker in its collision. A scream rips from my throat on impact. "Is this what it takes to get your obedience?"

I shake my head wildly, my entire body braced for more. My skin tingles with anticipation, uncontrollably prickling when feathery hot breaths warm the skin at the opening of my buttocks. The mounting awareness of his ownership seeps into my bones with a perversion so dark it's dangerous.

"Spread your legs for me. Wide." He instructs, rising tall and stepping to the side of me. "Eyes up."

I swallow hard, another scream embedded in my throat, ready for the unbearable sensation of pain I know he wants to unleash. Our eyes lock, spearing each other with unspoken deeds to come. "Watch me spank your perfect ass. These marks left on your skin are a reminder of me. The man who demands all of you. And this…" Smack. "This is how disobedience feels."

It happens without my approval. The deluge of hot tears plummet from my chin and the tingling of my sensitive nipples. They're so tight and hard. Absurdly pointed, as if the scalding pain still blazing within me is enjoyable.

He tosses the belt away, weaves his fingers into the messy strands hanging about my face and jerks my entire body into his.

"And this is how obedience feels." His mouth covers mine so our teeth clash.

Strength. Power. Dominance. It all wraps around me with the unusual sensation of safety—belonging. For once in my life, I fit into a misshapen world rather than believe it's me who's abnormal. This man empowers me to be the sexual woman I prayed to become one day.

My muscles relax, almost molten from the ache of his brutal lips. The fiery welts on my ass feel red hot and my hunger for him turns feral.

Breaking away with a snarl, he mutters, "If crazy is a

place, I'll buy it for the two of us, because I'm going to fuck you so hard. I might lose control, but I know you'll enjoy every second of it."

A moan rumbles through me, so terribly needy and desperate that I suddenly wonder how I'll ever replace this intoxicating euphoria. He's somehow cracked my thick veneer of self-protection. And now I'm tumbling into his black abyss without a safety harness, exposed by his darkness. This is bad, very bad, and one hell of a turn on.

"Tell me what you need." He manhandles me around to face our reflections again. Him and I, the captor and his willing prisoner.

I stare at his handsome face, feeling the burn of my spanked buttocks against his hard dick and the flames of desire ruining me forevermore. "I want you to own me."

When his hand roams over the stinging flesh, he hums into the side of my face. I stiffen, unsure if he intends more punishment. "I want that too." His nose nuzzles into my hair. "Believe me, I've been looking forward to this all day."

He stands behind me, hitches my hips, positions his dick at my slick entrance, and without warning, enters me. Fully. Deeply. I cry out, the sound becoming a guttural groan.

"I couldn't think of anything else, but this…" His violent thrust shoves me headfirst into the mirror, my planted hands just stopping my face from smashing the surface.

Being with him is wickedly forbidden, but this… this is unadulterated, addictive pleasure. It's an explosion of wrongs kissed with layers of rights. Our eyes settle on one another. The ferocity of his gaze so sexual, so primitive.

I inhale through the extraordinary feeling of him moving inside my body. I could never get used to this. It's remarkable how he fits so perfectly. How incredibly well we move together. His piston furious hips still for a moment as he widens my buttocks and spits into the crevasse.

My scalp prickles when something warm, like his thumb, pushes past the tight ring of muscles at my back entrance. And then he hisses, "Every fucking hole is mine.'

His pelvis rocks so his dick rams in deeper. I don't wait for permission. I'm struck by his energy, buzzing from the two of us fucking in this way. It initiates a climax, so intense I almost go blind.

"Fuck, yeah." A strong hand grips onto my waist while the digit on his other hand works to stuff me in a way I never imagined would be so erotic. "It feels good to have me inside you, doesn't it?"

"Uh-huh," I moan, incapable of forming proper words.

"I'll put my dick in that sweet ass of yours next time."

While I'm shaking in the aftermath of shooting stars, he scoops me up in his arms and carries me to the bed, where he lays me down gently. Tomás arches over me, hands pinning my arms to the mattress and his angry looking dick at my mouth.

"Open up. Give me your all, and I promise I'll give you everything you need, Carina."

As soon as my lips part, he fucks my throat.

"That's it. Take it all," he groans. "Your pretty little mouth has become a huge fucking problem for me."

I convulse at the length and squirm beneath the weight holding me prisoner. He pulls out to let me suck in a gust of air. My hard breathing is greeted with a slap to one breast and then the other. And just as I think he's going back in; he flips me over and roughly positions me in the middle of the bed.

Fingertips glide over the curve of my spine. Firm hands separate my buttocks and he buries his face. I pant wildly, barely able to keep control of myself. After he worships me from behind, he rears back, hungrily hitches my hips higher to align his dick with my swollen entrance, and then he gives me exactly what he promised. More of him. United in a way that's all encompassing and consuming.

The instant fulfillment is euphoric. There on the bed, he fucks me, violently, while mourners sip champagne downstairs. He must be out of his mind to think of sex on a day like today. But while his teeth sink into my shoulder and he angles in deeper to nudge my cervix, I understand his need to hide from the pain with a distraction.

Tomás doesn't care when I scream his name. He knows no one will hear how he's secretly dominating my demons with his body.

Once he's emptied his everything inside of me, he slumps onto the bed. A sheen of sweat kisses his torso and his arm flops over his face to hide his eyes while he recovers.

I lie there for a few minutes and catch my breath. It's this moment of vulnerability when we're both lingering in the wake of something earth shattering that he's simply a man, and I'm the woman who knows she's disposable, even if I'd likely stay a while longer if he asked me to. Emotion sticks in my throat. How could I be so stupid?

I didn't choose to enjoy his storm, but I've come to accept it. To want and long for it. It's staggering to feel this way about the man drifting into a deeply relaxed state beside me on the bed. He trusts me to be this close to him.

Except none of this is normal. Being with him isn't normal. Craving his brutality isn't normal. And kindling feelings for him definitely isn't normal either.

The fantasy leaves me and reality slams into my chest. I fight for a breath, sick to my stomach. Propelling off the bed, I hurry to the adjoining bathroom and close the door behind me. My ribs ache and my lungs argue for air. I sit on the edge of the bathtub and bury my teary cheeks into my palms.

I shouldn't enjoy the pain he unleashes as punishment or his demands for more orgasms that make me shake me from the inside out.

"Carina."

I swallow back a muted sob and quickly wipe my eyes, pretending I'm not unraveling. "Go away," I mutter, while angling away from his troubled frown to grab a rolled-up towel from the rack.

"Look at me," he orders, notably keeping his distance.

"No..."

I hear his sigh and sense his stealthy approach. My heart hammers behind my ribs. This time, he doesn't abuse his power. Instead, he sets his large hands on my shoulders and slowly maneuvers my torso until we're face to face. I draw in my lower lip to hide the quiver.

"Why are you crying?" His voice is hoarse with

exhaustion. I finally meet his gaze. Mine watery, and his filled with speckles of light like a starry cosmos of genuine concern. "Are you suffering? Do you need painkillers?"

He thumbs my cheek, his touch gently manipulating my skin. Automatically, my face leans into the affectionate sentiment he offers, seeking some sort of comfort in this unusual situation. It's wrong to assume he cares, but right now, I'd happily hide in a pretense of affection. I need it. As much as I crave his roughness, I desire gentleness too.

"I... I enjoyed it." I breathe him in, the rich scent of his cologne still haunting his smoky aura. "More than I should." My confession spins threads of desire between us, met with silence.

Rather than push me away, a hand splays my nape. Firm fingers cage my flushed face before him and snag tangles of messy hair. The power of his entrapment solidifies me. I'm a slave to his touch, now and forever.

His face drops, connecting our foreheads, so the tips of our noses brush against each other. I exhale into him; aware the potency of our bond has skyrocketed with my pulse.

"You're a hot little thing, you know that?" he says thickly. When I swallow, his lashes blink against my skin. "Fucking you is my favorite thing to do." And then, without waiting for my shock to settle, he covers my mouth with his.

Soft lips cling there for a few mind-melting moments, the gentle pressure curious as if he's figuring out how tenderness works for him. There's no clashing teeth or warring tongues. It's simply an indulgent, soul searching kiss without force or attack. In reality, it's not simple at all. It's unbelievably complex and every bit as addictive as the violence he offers.

If I allowed myself to admit it, this softer side of him is everything I've ever dreamed of.

But it won't last. We both know it.

"I have something that belongs to you," I whisper, sharing the same oxygen as him. "Before I give it back, you need to know that I found it. I didn't steal it."

His spine goes rigid and his hands fall away like his trust in me is being tested all over again. "What is it?"

38

TOMÁS

She gave me everything and didn't even know it.

I kissed her without barriers or sky-high walls.

With the euphoria it brought me, a tsunami of guilt crushes my stomach like sharp stones hurled from a tornado. I've always been fucked up, ever since the day I shot my uncle in the head, but now I'm beyond fucked up.

I stupidly crept over the threshold, poured gasoline all over the terms, and struck a match to engulf the agreement with flames. I've surpassed fucked up and landed in unknown territory without any defenses.

If I let this woman under my skin, it would jeopardize everything, including my family's legacy. Letting her live under my skin would make marrying another woman impossible. I can't choose a bloodthirsty war over an emotion I swore I'd never wallow in.

Love is death. And accepting her into this world would ensure her life expectancy significantly reduces. One day, she'd earn a fatal bullet on account of me, because that's how all this will end.

I'm *Tomás Souza*, the ruler of a mighty kingdom with the power at my fingertips to burn it all to shit—for her, if I choose. Except my stomach roils with the vision of that outcome. How my brothers would be targets and my mother vulnerable to every fucker out there. I can face my own inevitable end, but I couldn't live with myself knowing I'd sacrificed their lives for my happiness—or hers.

What happened after that kiss nearly ripped my heart out as an offering to the goddess I'm in awe of. She'd rummaged in the cupboards under the vanity and held out her small palm, handing me the blood red signet ring my father wore every day of my life.

The ring that signifies death by the hand of a Souza. A symbol we wear after the first life we've taken. I should have received mine at the age of eight, but no one knew I'd ended my uncle's suffering that day.

I thought I'd lost Papá's ring the night history repeated itself. I remember removing it and everything after that is lost to the savage black wrath that took over. Everything, until the moment I had seen her again. The woman who makes my world stop spinning, dulls the constant noise, and makes my numbness come alive.

Handing it over is a risk she didn't need to take, but a decision she made on the day I buried him. She did that for me when other women would have sold it for cash on the black market.

"Morning, mate." Shane joins me on the sunny terrace, his sunglasses reflecting my exhausted face back at me. "Are you sure about this?"

I nod, sipping my coffee slowly. "We'll show them

we're not afraid. Papá hid behind these gates for too many years. Now they'll see I'm not hiding. I'll be fucking everywhere." My voice turns hoarse, the result of a night spent with Carina cuddled up next to me.

I laid awake as she slept, drinking in the sight of my rare little butterfly so close to my flames. Her colorful wings were scorched and her wholesomeness jaded. She understands this is a short-term arrangement, but what she'll never comprehend is how she's unlocked a side of me that no one has ever known. Not even me. It's her privilege and our curse.

Shane drags a cushioned seat out and sits at the table beside me. "The second they land; our guys will remove their weapons. I've no doubt they'll disagree with the order to visit the Souza residence unarmed."

The fountain bubbles calmly in the background, doing nothing to soothe my vexed mood. "If they don't hand over their weapons, then treat them as a potential threat. They have no need to protect themselves against me unless they intend to strike first."

I've invited a few of the top leaders within our organization to meet with me later this afternoon. Loyal men from Miami, Rio, California, and Europe are flying into Bogotá. From there, my men would transport them individually to the plantation to make sure they aren't followed. The plan is to send the right message from the start of my reign. I'm in control—full fucking stop.

"You look tired." He points out, lifting the coffee pot and filling a cup to the brim. "That girl of yours keeping you up all night?" His chuckle turns into a hum when he puts the steamy coffee to his lips.

"I slept well," I lie, the image of Carina's marked buttocks at the forefront of my mind.

I checked them this morning while she was sleeping and then left my suite for my usual routine. It gave me a primal buzz to see how I'd punished her and then fucked away the pain. Knowing it's after midday, she'd have eaten the breakfast I sent to her room and used the jacuzzi to ease her aches. "Keep an eye on her when they arrive. Don't leave her alone with anyone if I'm preoccupied."

I ignore the cryptic look he gives me, riled by the silent assessment he's clearly considering. "You can still marry the Morales girl and have Carina as your mistress," Shane adds thoughtfully.

"Have you been speaking with my mother? She suggested the very same thing." I look away from him and gaze out at the swaying trees in the distance.

It would mean locking her up and starving her of a life filled with experiences and adventures. She'd become the most protected creature in the world, worshiped like the goddess she is to me and resentful of her invisible bars and clipped wings.

I'd rather she bloomed freely rather than to cut her off from the world and watch her die slowly. Even if it means I never get to touch her again.

"You have options. That's all I'm saying." Shane reaches for the sugar cubes and plops two in before he stirs. "She likes you. I can tell," he adds.

I laugh under my breath and flick my gaze to his. "Right, Shane. Since when do you know what women think? I've more or less forced her to stay with me. It's the big windfall she'll earn that has her heart racing, not the way I make her scream."

Shane stares at me with his reflective lenses hiding his eyes. "Money can't buy the look on her face when you enter the room, or when you're standing right next to her. It's like she's in lo—"

"Don't finish that sentence. She doesn't know me." I snap, at the end of my tether with whole fucking scenario.

"She might not, but I do. I know you pretty well, cabrón. And it's not just her who has that same look. You're obsessed with the kid and, from what I can see, she means something to you."

The man who's killed more men than he's screwed women, and that's a lot, is sitting here telling me Carina is my happy ever after, even when our hearts are corrupted beyond repair.

"We don't get happy endings, Shane. It's a bullet or a bomb blast. You, of all people, should know that." I rub the sudden sharp pain in my chest. "I don't want that for her." My hiss could poison wildflowers with the acrimony my words drip with. "I want you to personally escort her to Bogotá in the chopper tomorrow. I've already arranged for her cash to be packed up into bags. It's ready to go when she is."

He nods, understanding how cruelty and violence are second nature to me—to us. Letting her leave before I do shouldn't be a problem, especially when she finally gets her hands on the money. That should sweeten the deal she's been tied to.

But as I continue to drink my tepid coffee, I recall the intense emotion that snowballed inside my stone cold heart when I saw her beautiful face—tragic and glittering with tears. It's with that memory I suspect letting her go would be the hardest decision I'd ever make.

"No problem." Shane confirms. "When you tell her about your wedding, I'm sure she'll take the money and run as far away as possible."

39

CARINA

When I hear a knock on the door for the third time this morning, I pull the cord on my nightgown tighter and brace myself for whatever else Tomás has planned for me.

I've already eaten alone on the sprawling balcony after the maid wheeled in a trolley laden with exotic fruit, fresh pomegranate juice, and a pot of the richest coffee I've ever tasted.

An hour or so after, another rap on the door brought a second maid who'd moved quietly and made a beeline for the outdoor jacuzzi. She'd popped open a bottle of champagne, poured a gold leaf flute half full and switched on violent bubbles inside the tub big enough for four adults.

I'd sat in the soothing warmth, submerged to my chin until my fingers wrinkled. The powerful underwater jets massaged my stiff limbs and soothed the fiery red welts on my ass. It had given me headspace to think about last night and how he took control with commands and sadism, only to kiss me the way he did—with delicate compassion.

A distorted illusion to suggest he cared how torn up and confused I was, that he felt it too.

I open the door on the third rap. "Miss. Can you follow me, please?" A willowy male dressed in a black suit takes a step back, beckoning me with his eyebrows. "The lady of the house wishes to speak with you."

What could Teresa Souza possibly want to speak to me about? "I'm not dressed. Can you give me a second to change?" I ask, ruffling my hair in an attempt to unstick the damp tips.

"That won't be necessary. Please, come this way." He moves with long strides, expecting me to follow, which I do.

It's just the two of us strolling along a carpeted landing, moving far away from the safety of Tomás' suite. There's a change in atmosphere when we turn right at the end of the long corridor and enter a different wing. It's warmer and scented with a familiar lavender essence. Draping potted plants sit on ornate stands lining the artistically papered walls at intervals and twinkly glass lanterns dangle overhead.

The man servant knocks once and pushes a set of double doors inwards, revealing dark green walls, an emerald green velvet couch, and billowing gold curtains caught between the wild outdoors and the sumptuous indoors.

"Come in, child," Teresa calls to me, but I don't see her anywhere.

The doors close behind me and I'm left by the entrance, barefoot and curious.

"Oh good, you're not dressed yet." She walks out from

behind a freestanding screen at the far end of the room, its wooden panels stenciled with prancing tigers. "Tomás said you'd like to wear something different for the reception this evening. He'll talk business for a few hours this afternoon, and then he expects you to attend."

Her flowy, floor-length gown catches in the breeze as she glides toward a quirky mirrored drinks' cabinet woven with floral buds, stacked with crystal tumblers and bottles of golden liquor. She's every bit a Souza queen in her own right, down to her elegant gestures and expressionless poise. I'm in awe of her finesse and how she appears completely unfazed by my presence in her private quarters.

"Tequila?" She looks over at me, a defined brow cocked. "To celebrate this unforgettable day."

I know she's referring to her son taking her husband's throne, so I graciously accept. "Yes, thank you."

She lines up two short glasses and pours. "Tomás brought my husband's ring to me this morning. Apparently, I have you to thank for that." Her tinted lashes bat slowly, taking in my natural appearance in leisurely sweeps. "My gift to you is a vintage designer dress from my personal collection. It's one I've never worn before." A gust of air shoots down her nose. "A woman can never have too many dresses. The one I have in mind will suit your complexion perfectly."

Lifting the drinks, she catches my eye and offers me one. I move closer to accept it, cautiously meeting her toe to toe. "Salud." I smile, taking the tequila from her diamond encrusted fingers where black polished fingernails uncurl like talons.

"Salud, sweet child." Teresa sips, her gaze fixed on my face. "My son appears to like you." She adds over the rim of her glass.

I almost spill the liquor when my hand shakes. "Did he tell you that himself?" My brow furrows and my instincts sharpen.

She bends closer, so I can see the circle of viridian green fluctuate as her pupils dilate. "A mother can sense these things. I'm very close with my boys. It's clear to me you've made yourself indispensable."

The way her head leans sideways to assess me sends a shiver of childlike apprehension right through me. I've been judged on my appearance too many times. Mentally abused and bullied for being a misfit. If this woman claims I'm not good enough for her beloved son, I'd likely smash the glass and leave. And something tells me she brought me here to let me know that very detail.

In her silent speculation, I muster the courage to comment. "He's paying me to accompany him. That's all. There's no emotion involved in our arrangement. Or underhanded tactics." I confirm. "*He* brought me here. I would have happily gone home to my family."

Her low chuckle isn't forced, but it isn't natural either. "Oh child, that man has never paid for a woman in his life, nor has he brought one home to meet his family." She finishes her tequila, puts the glass down, and saunters across the room to her walk-in wardrobe, where she disappears.

He didn't invite me here as a guest. Nor was it his intention to introduce me to the Souzas. I'm simply an outlet for his demons, that is all.

In the minutes of hush, I tip the liquor into my mouth and swallow, fully embracing the sordid memory of it trickling from the crown of his dick down my throat. Somehow it tasted better then. Smoother. Sharper. Sinful.

Teresa's singsong voice snaps my mind back into the room. "This is definitely the right one for you." She holds up a stunning sequined dress, the texture fluid, like it's made from liquid gold, and carries it to the four-poster bed where she hooks the hanger on the nearest post.

A sweetened breeze cools the blazing heat of my skin and agitates my air-drying hair. I cover the silk floor covering and halt before the most exquisite dress I've ever seen. Its dreamlike material hangs with a precise hourglass structure. Gliding my fingertips from the low-cut neckline to the narrow waist, I find a risqué thigh slit that wouldn't leave much to the imagination.

His mother stares at me, her arms folded, the tips of her sable hair skimming fixed shoulders. "Do you like him too, Carina?"

If she's anything like Tomás, she'd sniff out a lie and punish me for it. So I opt for diplomacy. "He's generous." I smile at her. "As are you. This dress is stunning. Are you sure you don't mind lending it to me for the evening?"

Something dark powders her expression, instantly putting me on high alert. "My son has had numerous therapists and psychologists over the years. All of them were paid very well... yet none of them could fix him. And then you appear out of nowhere with the ability to reach right inside his mind. Tell me the truth, child. Do you like my son enough to kill for him?"

I freeze. My brows snap together. "Kill who?"

"Anyone."

I blink at her. "I don't understand?"

"The woman who deserves to stand beside my son knows the sacrifices she has to make. If you're not born into this lifestyle, you'll never understand. From where I'm standing, you're the singular weak link in his armor. So when I ask if you like him, I'm simply trying to establish if it's the power you enjoy or the man himself, because if he chooses you, we'll all be at risk."

I'm caught off-balance by her straight talking inquisition. She studies me with the eyes of a concerned mother and a stance of regal arrogance.

My heart trips up in my chest. "I've already told you; it was his decision to bring me here. He ordered, and I obeyed. I'm nothing more than a pawn in his real life game of chess." I turn into her, my shoulders drawn back and my temper on a short leash. "Our situation is crystal clear. He won't *choose* me, whatever that means. It doesn't matter how I feel about Tomás. Once we return to the city, I'm going back to my old life. Then we'll never see each other again."

Her eyes flare, green to black, as her appraisal of me comes to an end. "So you do have feelings for Tomás."

I shrug lightly. "I'm grateful to him for the compassion he's shown me, given the circumstances."

She laughs darkly. "Compassion? That's one word strangers would never associate with my eldest son."

It's on the tip of my tongue to tell her she's wrong, that I'm not a stranger to him. That he's had parts of me on his lips, so intimately it makes me blush to think about it. Despite that, arguing with his mother would be futile. I'm still a stranger to her. "Nonetheless, we'll go our separate ways. Rest assured; I have no ulterior motive."

"Oh child, you've misunderstood me. I want my son to finally find happiness. To have something I never had. But I can't let him make a mistake when it jeopardizes our entire world." She walks around me and moves to the tequila bottle, pouring a second measure just for her. "How would that little heart of yours react if he married another woman?"

I trace the old scar on my lip, inadvertently hiding a sudden twinge in my chest. "I... expect him to carry on with his life, as will I," I reply vaguely. My mouth dries. "It's inevitable. If he marries another woman... I... I'd be fine with it." The lie slips out easily, disguising the whirlwind in my head.

I'm lost in a vision of Tomás with another woman, doing the wicked things we do together—fucking, touching, kissing. The hallucination replaying in my mind sickens me, without any justification for feeling that way. He claimed my virginity, not a future with him.

Of course, I'm attracted to him. Even his mother can see it. One touch from the man has my pulse thrumming and my insides all jittery and jelly-like. But on the surface, with his handgun and superior status, he's not a good man. Besides, I don't want to die young.

"Interesting." Putty colored lips purse as her hand shelves above her hip bone. Peridot eyes narrow, her brow hitched with skepticism. "My Tomás is a strategist. He leads with his brain, not his heart. For you to be in our home means he sees value in you." She wanders closer, reaches out, and lightly trails her nails through my hair, sending a shiver over my scalp. "You're very attractive, with that same look in your eyes as him." Her hand falls away as she sighs. "But you should know, sweet little girl... the man you think you know won't put his heart on the line for you. He's too damaged to accept love. He'll always consider the tactical move as the right decision. He was raised with mafia finesse and cartel chaos. It's that simple…" I wither inside, her truth crawling over me like dying spiders caught in a downpour. "Wear the dress this evening. You'll look sensational in it." Her lips half curl into a smile that almost portrays sadness. "One of the maids will apply your makeup. She'll be here any minute."

On cue, there's a gentle tap on the door. "Come in, Natalia," Teresa calls out, squeezing my wrist as if it should comfort me. She nods toward the velveteen stool in front of a tri-fold mirror with lights. "Take a seat, Carina."

I shoot her an uncertain look, feeling helpless, like an insect caught in a Venus flytrap. "I don't usually wear makeup."

"You have youth on your side. A little mascara and eyeliner will suffice."

When I'm seated, she disappears onto the terrace with a third shot of liquor and stays out there while Natalia works her magic. Coated in jet black, my lashes appear longer and thicker than before, and the winged eyeliner creates a feline illusion.

I barely recognize myself with the dusting of a shimmery bronzer on my cheekbones and hot barrel curls twisting over my shoulders in segments. But when I put on the dress, even the maid gasps.

The person staring back at me isn't the tortured creature hiding in the shadows of a tragic past. She's a woman who's fallen for a dark knight in a lawless nightmare.

40

TOMÁS

"I expect your loyalty, without question." I finish my speech and watch the suited men around the oval dining table nod. "My father might have fallen, but the Souzas are still on top."

Matheus raises his glass. "To my brother, our leader, Tomás."

The men echo his toast, each of them accepting my rightful place. It's been a long day made even harder by the distance I've put between myself and my medicine, my glitch elixir. The woman I should set free before she rips out my thawing heart and takes it with her. I shudder, sensing her presence in my family home where deadly orders replaced kind conversations.

Shane grunts, his glass clinking with mine from the left. "Congratulations, cousin. You're officially the king."

His praise should give me a buzz, a thrill of success. Though it doesn't. I haven't been able to replicate the high I get when I'm balls deep inside Carina. Not even this charge of power can resuscitate my soul like she can. "Thanks." I smile tightly and throw back the Scotch.

Gio strolls across the dining room from where he'd stood in the corner, watching the guests like a hawk with his revolver discreetly hidden from sight. We expected the guests to step over the threshold of our domain unarmed, but I'm still not that trusting.

A few of the men around this table plotted against our father, and some of them are still under investigation for his assassination. In this game, we keep our allies close, and our sights directly on our enemies until the time comes to wipe out the motherfuckers.

Tonight, however, isn't that occasion. They'll leave in peace and I'll pick them off one by one in the future if needed.

Our liquor emptied glasses tinkle with melting ice cubes. "I'm flying out to Rio tomorrow," Giovanni says quietly. "For business."

We've had a small-time cartel in Rio under surveillance since Carina was transported to my father as a gift from his estranged daughter, Maria Rebello. He'd sworn blatantly she wasn't my half-sister. Except we still don't know the truth, given she was poisoned and her spineless minions fled the scene.

Some of them were easily tracked, and others disappeared. I want to know if Maria was working alongside Carlos Blanco. If she was trying to infiltrate our family with lies and gifts for a bigger cause, to help Blanco take over our kingdom.

"Do what you have to do, Gio. I trust you, brother." He swallows, his pale green eyes flashing with a faint glint of appreciation. The sound of trust and praise is a rare commodity in this house. We shake hands, his golden ring digging into my fingers and mine into his. "We'll talk before you go."

André claps his hands to get everyone's attention. "Let the party begin." He leads the guests out of the formal room to reunite with their partners. *"Mi casa es tu casa,"* he laughs. On the way out the door, he flips open the lid from a carved box and displays an obscene amount of cocaine. "Who's up first?"

I fix my cufflinks and follow behind Shane. I've no need to get fucked up on chemicals tonight. There's only one thing on my mind—Carina.

The second we stroll into the entrance hall, my brain malfunctions. This time, it's not the sensation of blood on my skin that triggers me. It's the ethereal queen standing at the top of the staircase.

"Jesus…" Shane mutters under his breath. "The kid's all grown up."

I stop dead in my tracks. Gold fabric clings to her feminine figure like it was poured straight from a melting cup by the gods. Sable curls tumble over breasts that are visibly pushed together, a sight that energizes my veins with untrained adrenaline. But it's the slit leading to her bare thigh, finishing just shy of her pussy, that steals the breath from my lungs.

Christ.

Fucking… wow.

My pulse goes berserk and my guard slips. Putting all the bullshit around me aside, I stare up at her as she descends, each step slowed by sky high strappy sandals adorned with tiny glittering gemstones. I'm well aware my unruly dick is rebelling against my zipper, but my cursed feet, they move without conscious thought, eating up the stairs two at a time until we're almost face to face, her a step higher.

Her dainty hand grips the banister and amber eyes sparkle under the gaudy Italian chandelier my father bought on a bipolar whim. Showy fragments of light crown the top of her head, highlighting the power that lives inside of her. The atmosphere surrounding us crackles, invisible sparks bouncing off her dignified posture, catapulting toward me as barbs of welcoming light.

At a standstill, she nods in acknowledgement of my predatory arrival, then pinches the fabric at the side of her hip to shift the flowing length out from under her heels before moving again. I offer my hand, a slave to the unfathomable spell she's cast.

Her distinct natural beauty is remarkable, but up close, the slight trace of makeup she wears this evening enhances her features to such an extent it leaves me speechless. I'd go as far as saying I'm stricken with a disease so deeply spread that no amount of radiation would eradicate it.

The second she sets her palm on top of mine, my reflexes take control, locking it in place. I struggle to breathe, fighting the urge to snare her throat and kiss her glossy lips until I'm drunk on the taste of her. There's not a hair on her head I'd change or a curve on her body I'd ignore.

She's perfection.

And for a man like me, with particular habits and

requirements, that's a fucking dangerous label for her to behold.

Her hand trembles within mine and every quick breath she takes elevates her chest, so the skin shimmers with whatever heavenly lotion she's rubbed into her cleavage.

"You're beautiful," I finally admit at the foot of the staircase, the words freely floating from my lips to my family's ears. "Naturally beautiful when you're naked and I've just cum inside you, but in this dress––you're stunning."

They're all present to witness this intoxicating witch robs my mind and renders me a damn fool. My obvious attraction to her isn't private anymore. It's a collective whisper carried on the tongues of every dangerous person I've invited here.

However, they didn't come alone. The invitation was extended to partners and seconds in command. That way, I would learn every detail about my people, including what makes them vulnerable. Turns out I'd fallen into my own trap and now they know my weakness.

If I hear one single threat made or insubordinate remark about Carina, I'd fill their throats with liquid gold like the entitled fucks they think they are.

"Thank you," she says softly, the heat of her body coaxing my tortured mind out of the haywire assumptions I've already made.

Matheus saunters into the imaginary bubble I want to hide her in and greets us with his charming grin. The fucker is a lady killer and he knows it. "That's one breathtaking dress." He smirks. "My eyes nearly fell out of my face."

Her nervous giggle dances over my scalp, coiling my guts with a sensation I'd thought I was immune to. Jealousy. I've never had a reason to envy anyone, let alone my kid brother. Tonight, I've gotten everything I ever wanted and something I never knew I needed.

Yet I'm turning into the man I swore I'd never become —my father. With Carina on my arm, paranoia kicks in. Her safety is the only thing I'm concerned about. My skin itches beneath my dress shirt. The incurable temptation to drag her out of the room and lock her away eats me from within.

My stomach aches. Everyone is staring at her and they see us together. Watchful eyes burn into my navy suit jacket, through my cold exterior and right into my chest where my heart beats out of time. Her fluttery pulse replaces the missing beat.

The stars in my eyes extinguish with every stride we take. Having her here, in front of these people, is a terrible mistake.

"Don't forget, if anyone asks, you're my personal assistant. Nothing else," I snarl, somewhat breathless by my irrational temper. "These men might pretend they're loyal to me, but any one of them could betray us. That makes you vulnerable if they think you mean something to me."

Intrigue sparks from her eyes, penetrating my chest where my wretched heart thumps for her.

"Why would they think that?" Her forehead creases with the daring question. The melody of her sweet voice will forever break through my demons. "Surely I'm just another woman on your arm like a shiny new toy."

My fists curl tight, the timing for such a question is completely wrong. Then again, when is the right time to address this insanity? It's not like we have a future.

I pivot, my torso bumping into her breasts. My dick grows even more painful. "Everyone in this house can see you're not a toy. I've no doubt my mother quizzed you on our unusual situation and warned you of a world you don't belong in."

Shane joins us, his interruption necessary before the floodgates burst and I reveal how she heightens my senses and shines a light into my darkness. I'm a fucking fool.

"She doesn't think I have what it takes to stand beside you." Carina raises her chin and strikes my unsettled mood with a simple bat of her long lashes.

"She's wrong," I say behind clenched teeth.

Her cheeks flush the perfect shade of pink. A color so pretty I could paint the world with it just to remind myself of her.

"Tommy," Shane offers me a drink. "Can I have a word?"

"About what?"

"Private."

I knock the hard liquor back, enjoy the burn as it slides down my throat and cock an eyebrow at him. "Fine."

Carina nods at Shane and turns away. My hand lashes out, cuffing her wrist like she's caught by a powerful magnet. "I won't be long. Get something to eat. You'll need a lot of energy for later."

She glances at my tight grip and then meets my gaze with hungry eyes that arrest me. "I'll mingle with these men, shall I?"

I snarl under my breath, keeping check of the mayhem running riot in my chest. As difficult as it is to stay calm in the wake of such a teasing threat, I catch Matheus' eye and signal over to him. He saunters through the crowd, rolling his shirt sleeves to the elbow and loosening his thin tie. "Everything okay?"

"Stay with Carina until I come back." I release her arm, the struggle to step away from her crippling. "And keep your hands to yourself," I add on a growl. "I know where they've been."

Matheus chuckles. "She belongs to you, brother. I wouldn't dream of it."

Carina stiffens, her fingers twitching to touch her lip. This is our last night together before the agreement goes up in flames. I'd rather spend that time wisely—like feasting on her sweet pussy and coming over her bruised ass. Accepting that it would have to wait until later, I nod to Shane. "Let's go."

I swipe an open bottle of tequila from the bar on my way past and hold it to my lips as we leave her behind. Suddenly my chest tightens, so I look back at her for another glimpse. Everything has changed. She's not the same girl my father had wanted dead. When I stare into a room full of people, she's the only one I see. Her eyes. Her skin. Her breasts. Her fragility.

I'm an asshole.

A confused fool.

Half of a man.

I want her so much, my brain short circuits and my swollen dick pleads to be touched by her. The only traitor in this house is me. I've betrayed my own wishes, burned my beliefs, and ripped my own goddamn heart out from a cage of ribs.

I grip the bottleneck hard, curbing the impulse to snatch her away and leave this place in the ashes of my bad decisions.

"Tommy?" Shane clears his throat.

My head aches, the whirlwind of thoughts fucking with my sanity. "What's so important?" I snap at him when we're further down the hallway, out of earshot.

He scrubs his face, exhaustion tugging at his eyelids. Shane isn't a fan of my plan to gather everyone at the plantation in the middle of nowhere. The guy has been on high alert since they arrived. It's his job to advise me and watch my back.

So it's not easy when I don't listen to reason and take calculated risks. They're all unarmed, stripped of mobile phones, and our location is unknown. The only threats I face are their eyes and ears, but that could easily be remedied at a later date.

"Morales wants a date set in stone for the wedding with Bianca." Shane lights a cigarette and pockets his zippo. "He's just on the phone, demanding to speak with you directly."

"What did you tell him?"

"That you were burying your father and to be fucking patient."

I laugh, walking the empty corridors with Shane a step behind me. "I haven't decided if I'm going ahead with it yet."

Why the hell would I agree to marry a woman who'd never capture my full attention like Carina just did on that staircase? I was spellbound, almost rendered speechless. She's worn girly dresses before, but nothing like the intoxicating, sexy as fuck layer of gold that spilled over her sexy curves and plump tits.

The woman is as rare as an expensive gold-plated Bugatti Veyron sports car. She's more powerful than Aphrodite ruling an Empire. Which also makes her priceless and irreplaceable——something of unspeakable value that could be snuffed from existence in a heartbeat.

"You're serious, aren't you?"

I shrug, ignoring the tight pain in my chest. "I've got some shit to sort out in my head first. There's no rush."

Approaching my father's office, a shudder jerks my bones. As a teen, I'd spent many a night prowling outside this door, hoping he'd invite me in. It was only after he put a Glock in my hand and told me to pull the trigger that I'd learned about my glitch.

That day, I should have blown a hole in a stranger's head. Papá ordered the assassination without telling me why the man's life had to end. Instincts told me not to do it, that maybe his crime didn't deserve death. In that flicker of hesitation, Papá shot the guy in the face instead.

Blood hit me like a slap, the coppery taste hurtling me back to the bomb blast and to Uncle Angelo—the first man I killed. After that, everything went black. Apparently, it took two men to restrain me and three months to find my way back to the edge of darkness.

Until Carina threw me a rope and pulled me to her

warm sandy shore where the sun shines on my face and forgiving waves lap at my feet. It's paradise.

The stench of stale cigar smoke still taints the air, his leather seat unoccupied, and the heavy curtains are respectfully drawn. I switch the desk lamp on and sink into the winged chair beside the bookcase. I might wear his crown, but this room belongs to him. This is the one place where his unsettled spirit still lives.

Shane props his shoulder against the ceiling high bookcase and stares at the Souza family portrait hung beside the framed photograph of Papá's pet tigers. "The girl... you're thinking of keeping her, aren't you?"

"It's not about that." I swallow the lie, finding Shane's incredulous glare. "I won't be held to ransom by anyone. I agreed to marry Bianca before I took over the organization. Things are different now." My ribs squeeze. "Anyway, Carina has a family of her own and a life she must return to. One that doesn't include me, or my world.

"Nothing's different, Tommy. You were running the show long before Elias entered that fancy ass tomb. From where I'm standing, you've fallen for an innocent and you're trying to figure out if she's worth starting a war for."

"She's worth it." I confess, the power of my words tingling all over me. "But this life isn't for Carina. It never will be. I'll end up falling in love with her and then…"

Shane sighs, expelling a lungful of smoke as the air leaves his nose. "Our enemies will try to kill her." He finishes my sentence.

"They *will* kill her," I gnash my teeth at him. "You saw them all eyeing her up in there and those guys are the loyal ones. Carina isn't safe with me. What good is all this wealth and power when I'm a curse for death?"

"I get the impression she can handle herself." Shane scrubs his bloodshot eyes. "She's got Tomás Souza by the balls and that's a fucking scary thing to deal with." His laugh echoes in the stillness of Souza history. "The question is, are you ready to put everything on the line... for her, including her neck."

I lose a few seconds as a black rage plows through my soul. "Stick to the plan. Get Carina out of here first thing in the morning. I'll call Morales about the wedding when she's gone."

41

CARINA

When I saw him at the foot of the grand staircase, my whole life flashed before me.

From the unthinkable mistake I made as a young girl under a shroud of depression, to the second chance I'd been given to find myself. To find the striking man who stared at me like the world was on fire and I was the only thing that mattered.

The pulsating darkness he exuded crept up the stairs with him, stealing my fear of criticism and replacing it with a deep-rooted want. The flaming desire unfurling in his gaze made me wet. Wetter than I could tolerate.

Then his sexy voice rumbled like thunder on a sunny afternoon, thrilling me with its energy and heating me with intense sunshine. He told me I was stunning. It didn't matter that his mother stood behind me or his brothers were watching with shock etched on their handsome faces.

Hunger seeped out from under his custom designed suit and covered me in a wild shiver. Our connection forged a new strand, where his need for control sprouted into a desire to nurture. He didn't manhandle me, or leave me to navigate the heights with my heels alone. No, he clasped my hand as a mannerly king and watched my every step until we reached the bottom tread and then the floor together.

I thrived on the sensation of his authority guiding me through the hallway where the crowd parted to allow their ruler passage. But what made me dizzy was the roughness of his trimmed stubble against my cheek when his lips settled by the shell of my ear.

"You're beautiful. Naturally beautiful when you're naked and I've just cum inside you, but that in this dress--you're stunning."

Tomás' praise was my undoing. The flint to my inner flame. The force of sexual immorality that makes a good girl like me want to be bad.

The instant Shane requested a word in private and Tomás' powerful hand left my lower back, all my strength drained to my caged toes. I swayed a little, having never worn spiky heels before, never mind enduring such marked attention from strangers.

"I'll get us a drink?" Matheus beckons to a pretty server with a bundle of auburn hair on top of her head. "Could you grab me a bottle of champagne?" He smiles and the poor girl almost buckles, her face awash with a shade more vibrant than beetroot.

"Of course." She does an awkward curtsy thing and scurries off on a mission to please.

Matheus runs long fingers through floppy jet black hair, leisurely unsettling the strands hooking his brow. It's then when I realize he's not wearing the same red ring I've seen on the rest of the brothers.

He stares at me with inquisitive eyes. As the corner of his mouth lifts, his cheek dents. "I never thought I'd see the day."

I blink up at him, unsure if he's talking about burying his father or his big brother becoming the boss.

"I knew it would take a special woman to finally get his attention. But what I want to know is how the fuck did you get inside his head to interrupt the glitch? It's mind-blowing."

Smartly dressed men and their glamorous women glare at me from all corners of the room. It makes my stomach knot and my skin scorch.

"I'm only his personal secretary," I point out with a pinch of sarcasm, instantly sensing his mood faltering with the lie. He knows Tomás only brought me here to indulge himself during his downtime.

"Bullshit." His golden watch glistens under the light when he folds his arms. "That's his narrative for you, so these people don't catch wind of your importance. The brother I know doesn't need a PA. He doesn't even *need* a woman by his side. Mama is the only woman he listens to. Yet, here you are. Abso-fucking-lutely gorgeous and right in the middle of our private affairs." As he speaks, he gradually lowers his voice. "The guy I was raised beside never looked at a woman like he looked at you at the top of those stairs. All I want for him is happiness…" His words trail off when the eager server bustles up beside him with an unopened black bottle and two wafer thin glasses on a tray. "I hope you can forgive him," he adds, accepting the bottle to uncork it himself.

"Forgive him?" I echo behind the robust pop.

"Matheus!" A man dressed in military attire joins us. "How's college?"

The older guy, twenty-odd years older, shakes Matheus' hand firmly. "General Herrera, how are your kids?"

I'm itching to find out what he meant. My heartbeat stutters under the choking blanket of suspicious murmurs. Matheus pours me a glass of bubbly. "Here you go, Carina."

The man who'd interrupted us offers me a sly smile; a smile so stitched with evil it makes the hairs on my arms lift.

"Thank you." I take the glass and keep my lashes lowered.

"*Carina*, it's a pleasure to meet you." The man juts out his hand, pretending courtesy comes naturally to him. I'm not convinced when he licks his lips, his eyes wandering lower than my face.

"You're with Tomás, is that right?" he continues. "You're his…"

My hackles rise, aware he's alluding to something more personal. When our palms connect, a shudder jars my bones like death has a shadow and this asshole owns it.

"I'm his personal assistant," I snip, glancing up at Matheus instead of meeting this man's stare.

"Oh really." He clears his throat to command my attention. "What sort of assistance do you offer him?"

Even though his suspicions are justifiable, I'm not a glorified whore whose sex life is open for comment.

While I tame my festering temper, Matheus answers on my behalf, "She deals with our legitimate businesses. Mostly pharmaceuticals and acquisitions. Tomás would be lost without her phenomenal acumen." He tips his glass at me and swiftly changes the subject. "Tell me, General, did you bring your wife with you on this trip, or did your mistress come along instead?"

The General nods respectfully, aware he's prying too far into Souza business. "Zara is here. My wife has a busy schedule." There's no shame or regret in his tone, like his indiscretions are perfectly acceptable.

The pompous aura he wears makes my veins thicken with anger. He's a smug gangster with an undercurrent of malevolence woven through the seams of his military status.

I'd rather not be in his company, so I take the opportunity to excuse myself. "While you two catch up, I'll nip to the ladies. It was nice to meet you." I offer a saccharine smile, surreptitiously playing the role of a professional businesswoman.

I need space from all the whispers and examining stares, none of which have eased since Tomás left the room. Matheus holds out his arm, expecting me to latch on. "I'll escort you."

General Herrera laughs darkly seconds before I obey. "The lady doesn't need assistance to use the bathroom. Unless she's a prisoner?" He jokes with a slight ceremonial bow, like he's mocking me, or he knows something.

Taking the bait, Matheus drops his elbow, simultaneously searching my blank expression. "I guess not." He concludes when I act unaffected. "There's a washroom down the hall. Come straight back. We have this bottle of Dom to finish."

I nod and turn away, managing to take one step before Matheus seizes my bicep and leans into the side of my face, so close I can taste his musky cologne as I suck in. "He's an asshole. I'll make sure he's gone by the time you get back."

I exhale, grateful for his honesty. "These people look at me like I'm for sale," my whisper stays out of hearing distance while the general's eyes burn into our close interaction.

"They're fascinated. That's all. Tomás is well-known for being shut off and now it appears he has a potential weakness. And that... is you."

My eyes narrow at him. "And what exactly do I need to forgive him for?"

His mouth opens as if he's about to unravel a tale and then he looks away. "For putting business first." His right cheek dimples and villainous lashes frame guarded eyes. "That's who he is."

I squeeze my arms tight to my sides for a little comfort and nod. "It's okay. I'm not under any illusion," I say with a mild smile. "Tomás looks at me with the eyes of a poacher who's claimed his first unauthorized kill. It's simply his satisfaction of being the best that everyone sees. Nothing more."

The brave woman within me knows that to be true. However, the foolish little girl wishing her captor would become her true master holds a beat of hope for a different truth.

The moment I leave the room, I finally breathe. I despise their scrutiny and judgment. Inquisitive gazes inspected my appearance, assessed my relationship with Tomás, and put a value on my head. But what's worse than their visual audit is how the Souzas underestimate me.

They think I've fallen for a man with no heart. I didn't fall, I tripped. And tomorrow afternoon I'd get back up on my own, dust myself off, and carry on without him.

I take my time in the restroom and check my winged eyeliner in an ornate framed mirror hung over a cream marble topped vanity. I've come a long way in such a short period of time. The transformation started the day I was kidnapped. Being beaten and overpowered would do that to an innocent young girl.

Yet I survived, because Tomás saved me. My tortured monster gave me a second chance and now our journey together is coming to an end. Even if it confuses and pains me, I'd say goodbye.

Reluctantly leaving the solace of a locked room, I step into the hallway, bracing myself for more questions.

"Carina?"

I spin around at the sound of my name, not recognizing the suited man stepping out of the shadows. Thick curly hair is scraped back as if it's captured in a ponytail and a clean-shaven face showcases swarthy skin and thin lips. He takes a step closer and sucks the tip of his lit cigarette.

As his fingers hover before his face, a black tattoo on

his hand sends a shiver right through me. There's something familiar about it, something I can't quite put my finger on. But when he speaks again, there's no animosity in his tone.

"It's Carina, right?" He props his shoulder against the wall. "They say you're Tomás' personal assistant?" His brow cocks.

"That's correct," I reply flatly, elevating my chin. "And you are?"

"Paco. I'm here with General Herrera. You met him earlier." He pauses for a moment, reading my look of disdain. "And we both know you're not his secretary."

I stare at him for a beat, then angle away, a niggling awareness chewing at my stomach. "Matheus is waiting for me."

"Carina..." he calls after me. "You're not safe. I can help you." I keep walking, pressing a shaky hand over my heart. "I know you were sent here as a sex slave. And I know the Souza men. You might think you're special, but the second you landed in their kingdom; your life ended. They'll never let you walk away alive." I stop dead. "And if they told you otherwise, and you believed them, then you really need to hear me out."

I spin on my heels, loose curls whipping like unruly serpents. "Who the hell are you?"

"That doesn't matter," he speaks with icy control. "What's important for you to understand is that Tomás *will* kill you. You don't know him like we do."

"You're wrong," I spit out, my veins pumping with anarchy. "He's had plenty of opportunities to do it. You don't know anything about me. And you clearly don't know a thing about Tomás. He'll kill you for cornering me alone."

Paco's brows drift higher. "I bet he promised you a sum of money that would change your life. An absurd amount to secure a future that will end with a bullet in your brain. That bastard has made you think he cares about you, hasn't he?"

I swallow, frustrated with how his questions are ripping up my common sense and replacing my private thoughts with pandemonium. "I have nothing to say to you. Please, leave me alone."

He drags his tattooed hand over his mouth and shakes his head. My skin chills as a foggy memory tries to replay, only to dissipate. "He really has fucked you up."

With my hand on the wall, I muster the strength to stand even taller and hold my ground. "Like I said, I work for him. It's as simple as that."

He nods slowly. "You're a decoy." I try to breathe slowly as he continues. "He's calculative and strategically astute. Everyone here has been duped this evening. They're now of the opinion you're his one true weakness. Not only does showing off a beautiful young woman serve to play down his mental vulnerability, but it hides the real truth…" I inch away, not wanting to hear what he has to say. Even as I wobble, he still speaks. "While those ruthless men in there watch you and make devious plans to either steal you for themselves or slaughter you, Tomás has plans to marry Bianca Morales. A Mexican beauty who'll make a powerful ally even stronger." Black blobs float across my vision and my hands tremble. "He's blindsided you, sweetheart. Your arrival here was a perfect disaster."

He's lying.

It's all a lie.

Every word.

I look over my shoulder where there's no one around to either confirm or deny the allegation. My pulse gallops, making me lightheaded. "Why are you telling me this?" I say breathlessly. "Why should I believe you?"

My mind sinks beneath a veil of violence, where I imagine killing this man for all the venom he's spreading.

"Because I can offer you a way out." The sincere look on his face is a beacon of light dragging me away from a rocky coastline where I'd surely smash into a trillion pieces if I'm not careful. "I can give you what Tomás Souza never will." Each word comes out like a swirl of sooty smoke. "If you kill him, I'll set you free. I'll personally make sure you have a seat on our helicopter. We've bribed one of the Souza pilots. He'll take us wherever we need to go."

I start to laugh, slowly at first and then more deranged as fear cracks my heart. "And you think I'm going to betray him simply because *you* asked me to? You're kidding me, right? What is this... a set up? Is Teresa hiding behind a door waiting for me to conspire against him?"

"This isn't a joke, Carina." Paco steps into me, bringing the reality of his accusations closer. "You're in danger. Save yourself before he betrays you." I fold my arms to protect my shrinking heart. "You don't have a future with him in it and the second you think you're free, he'll send a sicario to your door. He's meeting with his second in command to iron out the details for his wedding—to confirm a date. That's why he left you alone... dressed like a queen. So all those bastards could get a good look at you. You don't mean shit to him, sweetheart."

"Liar!" I hiss through gritted teeth.

"I know it's a lot to take in." Paco reaches for my arm. I flinch, shirking away from his touch. "Don't take my word for it. He's down the corridor right now, talking it over with Shane. Your best move is to prepare yourself with ammunition first. Then strike. If he realizes you're on to him, you won't see the next sunrise."

My teeth clench, almost biting my tongue in half with every insult I can think of because I'm already helplessly trotting in the direction he pointed to. I snarl inside, fighting the urge to cry and praying this isn't real. It has to be a trap and this guy thinks I'd fall for it. None of it rings true and yet all of it makes sense.

The closer I get, the more my body shakes. When I hear Tomás' godly voice rumble through a sliver of space between a solid door with locks and its frame, I press my forehead to the damask wallpaper to steady myself. To catch a breath and listen.

"Stick to the plan. Get Carina out of here first thing in the morning. I'll call Morales about the wedding when she's gone." His masculine tone is as inflexible as steel.

No!

I stumble backward with no one to catch me. My lashes bat a thousand times on repeat as the words I just heard slice my foolishness to shreds. He took advantage of my vulnerability, abused my body, and forged a fictitious bond of trust.

How dare he?

The black haze stealing my vision goes red. The blood in my veins turns thick like tar, and my entire body quakes from unforgivable shock.

I can barely stand upright, until Paco swaggers into my personal space, clamps my biceps and guides me along the corridor, pushing me into the shadowy mouth of an empty room. With the lights off, I can't see his face, only the whites of his eyes.

"For your own safety, do not say a word," he whispers, his voice husky and low, his breath smoky.

I lean away from him, my fists balling for war. "Get the hell away from me."

"Listen to me, little girl. You've fallen for a man who's using you to keep his fiancé safe."

"And why would you warn me?" I squirm free of his hands. "What could you possibly gain from telling me this?"

He angles into the light streaming in from the hallway, checking over his shoulder. "The Souzas have ruled for long enough." His face contorts to a sinister grimace. The flare of darkness widens his pupils, so the steely gray of his eyes switches to black. "They're out of control. You're the only one who can get close to him with a weapon."

The longer I stay in the shadows, the quicker my soul whispers to the darkness. I thought I recognized the damaged part of Tomás, that his trauma clicked with the twisted part of mine. This whole time, he had tricked me into believing I'd met the real man hidden in the depths of a monster.

But this deceit... this is a brutal jagged blade eviscerating my natural born instincts. It's a wound so fathomless that the vital organ in my chest fails to function.

I've personally felt the fingertips of death.

I've watched Tomás deliver despicable men to Hell's cast iron gates.

However, nothing could strip my body of life like the acidic wash of his deception. I understood our time was temporary, but I never expected him to use me as bait. To deceive me with so much conviction that I truly believed we had a connection.

Paco stands before me, patience belying his threatening presence.

"Either you kill him tonight, or I'll get the motherfucker another day. You and I have something in common—we've been wronged by these people. His soldiers slaughtered my men and their families in Rio. The General has agreed to help me take out the Souza brothers one at a time, then he'll step in to take their place. He'd be indebted to you."

Moving further into the room, I embrace the veil of blackness disguising my misfortunate heartache. My gut is screaming from within, yelling at me to run far away from here, far away from Tomás, but mostly, far from Paco.

"Do it yourself," I spit out behind mindless fingers, tapping my mouth. "Do your own dirty work. I'm not your puppet."

The grunt coming from the doorway prickles my spine with needles of fear. "While the Souzas rule, your family is in danger. One day they'll be sitting around the dinner table, laughing, and enjoying life. The next, they'll be mutilated by a bomb blast."

Liquid regret stings my eyes, the curse of my kidnapping coming back to haunt me. This whole time, I was under Tomás' radar.

Finally, I learned how to open my heart and mind, growing from a teenage girl into a woman. All the while, he was leading me along like a sacrificial animal.

In my broken silence, Paco strolls closer.

"It will be easy, Carina. Elias has weapons stashed in his tomb. The crazy fucker wanted them as a precaution, just in case he wasn't dead the first time. No one will ever expect a trusting young thing like you would have the scruples to seek justice."

He places his palms on my shoulders with a terrifying firm grip. "If you take out the king, your loved ones will be safe. These people are all laughing at you behind your back, Carina. Every single one of them."

To be continued…

Continue Tomás & Carina's duet with Hostile King, Book 2 in the Souza Cartel series.

ALSO BY AUTUMN ARCHER

Romantic Suspense

The Unforgettable Series
His to Steal
His to Keep
His Addiction

K. Bromberg's Everyday Heroes World Project
Call Out

Dark Romantic Suspense

Vow Duet
Vow of Revenge
Vow to Protect

Hostile Kingdom: Jungle Oasis
Vengeful Captor
Vengeful Obsession
Vengeful Lover

Hostile Kingdom: Souza Cartel
Hostile Heart (Prequel)
Hostile Heir
Hostile King

Contemporary Romance

ALSO BY AUTUMN ARCHER

Miles from Home (Standalone's)
The Chance
The Photo
Wild Heart

Sign up to Autumn Archer's Newsletter for more details on upcoming releases.

ABOUT THE AUTHOR

USA Today Bestseller Autumn Archer spends her days romancing the darkness to create delicious, tortured men who deserve to be loved. Not only does she bleed Dark Romance, she dabbles in the lighter side of love with Romantic Comedies written as A. Archer. With all of her books, you can expect high heat, passionate emotions and happy endings.

For more information on her work visit:
www.autumnarcher.com

"When there is darkness, the light will always find a crack to shine through."

Printed in Great Britain
by Amazon

20513060R00294